Outside the Saloon the Crowd
Suddenly Became Quiet,

and no one moved. But inside loud, furious voices and taunting laughs were evidence that they were still goading Haskel. Suddenly the giant Haskel came plunging out across the walk. His coat was missing; his shaggy bearded head was lowered, and he had a gun in each hand.

"Haskel! Better go back! . . ." called out Bradway from the sidewalk. His warning voice was cool and insistent. . . .

"Whar are you, cowboy?" roared the giant.

"Far enough, Haskel!" Bradway warned. His gun glinted in the light of a store window.

The giant gave no heed to Bradway's warning. He sighted his adversary, and lurched across the dusty street, both guns swinging to cover the motionless Nebraskan.

"Nothin' agin you cowboy, 'cept yore sharp tongue. But I'm aimin' to kill you . . ."

Books by Zane Grey

The Arizona Clan
Black Mesa
The Border Legion
Boulder Dam
The Call of the Canyon
Drift Fence
The Dude Ranger
Fighting Caravans
Forlorn River
The Fugitive Trail
Lone Star Ranger
Lost Pueblo
The Lost Wagon Train
Majesty's Rancho

The Maverick Queen
Raiders of the Spanish Peaks
The Rainbow Trail
Riders of the Purple Sage
Rogue River Feud
Stairs of Sand
Thunder Mountain
Under the Tonto Rim
The U.P. Trail
The Vanishing American
Western Union
Wilderness Trek
Wildfire
Wyoming

Published by POCKET BOOKS

THE MAVERICK QUEEN

ZANE GREY

Revised Edition
Foreword by Loren Grey

PUBLISHED BY POCKET BOOKS NEW YORK

Cover art by Murray Tinkelman

POCKET BOOKS, a Simon & Schuster division of
GULF & WESTERN CORPORATION
1230 Avenue of the Americas, New York, N.Y. 10020

ISBN: 0-671-83590-4

First Pocket Books printing May, 1982

10 9 8 7 6 5 4 3 2 1

POCKET and colophon are trademarks of Simon & Schuster.

Printed in the U.S.A.

Foreword

The true-to-life accounts of the early West that are best remembered are, of course, filled with the exploits of such legendary heroes of that day as Daniel Boone, Lew Wetzel, Kit Carson, Buffalo Bill Cody, Bat Masterson, and Sam Houston, to mention just a few. There were the anti-heroes as well, whose exploits aroused as much fascination as those of the heroes. Men like Billy the Kid, Doc Holliday, Wes Hardin, and the James Brothers have been the subject of countless tellings and retellings, both real and fictional. There were, of course, also the fictional heroes and their counterparts, perhaps the most famous of whom was Owen Wister's "Virginian."

However, many Zane Grey heroes and villains are as well-known among readers of the West as those in real life. Many of his fictional heroes are such popular characters as Lassiter from *Riders of the Purple Sage,* whose name alone inspired a whole series of Western novels by another author; Buck Duane of *The Lone Star Rangers;* Pecos Smith of *West of the Pecos;* and Laramie Nelson of *Raiders of Spanish Peaks.* The bigger-than-life villains include "Killer" Kells, "Hell Bent" Wade, Jim Lacy, and numerous others.

There were also the real-life Western heroines, although many fewer in number—women such as Betty

Zane, Calamity Jane, Annie Oakley, and Lily Langtry. My father also had his hand in creating a number of legendary fictional characters such as Majesty Hammond of *Light of Western Stars;* Molly Dunn of *The Drift Fence;* Lucinda Baker of *30,000 on the Hoof;* and Marian Warner, the golden-haired heroine of *The Vanishing American.*

It seems ironic that despite my father's immense popularity as a Western writer, and even though his conception of the cowboy-gunman is the one that has been and still is used by nearly every other Western author who ever wrote—and by countless motion picture and television script writers as well—his attempts to depict true historical characters in his books have been fraught with extraordinary difficulty. His first novel was about his pioneer ancestor Betty Zane, whose daring deed of carrying a sack of gunpowder in her apron from the blockhouse to the fort helped save what was then Fort Henry from being overrun by the British and Indians during the Revolution. Her bravery earned her a statue that still stands today in a suburb of Wheeling, West Virginia. This book was so poorly viewed by potential publishers that Dad had to buy the plates and have the first edition printed himself. However, in 1978, nearly seventy five years after the original publication, no less than three separate paperback editions of *Betty Zane* were issued—which does testify to the enduring popularity of this story.

Though the novel, *The Maverick Queen,* was initially published by Harper & Brothers only a little more than thirty years ago, it underwent as baffling an adulteration of history from its original version as can be imagined today. It was a fictionalized manuscript based on an actual historical character whose name was Cattle Kate and whose unique exploits brought her great notoriety—if not adulation—during her lifetime and after. When the editors of Harpers first read the manuscript of *The Maverick Queen,* they insisted that what Cattle Kate really did to earn the sobriquet of the "Maverick Queen" did not fit the Zane Grey "image" of a Western heroine—or even anti-heroine for that matter. They demanded that what was really the heart and soul of the story be cut out and changed to make it more palatable to what they felt was the "taste" of Zane Grey readers at the time. Perhaps a comparable act of foolishness occurred even as late as some twenty years ago when the District School Board of Downey, California, ordered that all copies of Zane Grey books be removed from the school libraries because the words "damn" and "hell" were frequently used in them. They also mandated that all the Tarzan books be taken from the school library shelves because Tarzan and Jane lived together without being married!

However, times do change—and perhaps for the better. I am pleased to announce that with the full co-operation of the editors of Harper & Row, Pocket Books is now presenting for the first time in book form the complete, unexpurgated story of *The Maverick Queen*. Though, as is true in most historical novels, there is fiction interwoven into the story of Kit Bandon, her historical link with Cattle Kate has been restored. It also serves to illustrate that in the hands of a master storyteller such as Zane Grey, history can be as fascinating and absorbing as the wildest imaginings of fiction writers.

Loren Grey, Ph.D.
Woodland Hills, California

Chapter I

～ ⁶ ～

It was almost dark, that day in early June, when the stage rolled down off the Wind River Mountains into the notorious mining town of South Pass, Wyoming. Lincoln Bradway, a cowboy more at home on a horse than in a vehicle, alighted stiff and cramped from his long ride, glad indeed to reach his destination. He had not liked either the curious male passengers or the hard-featured women. With his heavy bag he stepped down upon the board sidewalk, and asked a passer-by if there was a hotel in town.

"South Pass brags of twenty hotels, stranger, with a saloon to match each one of 'em. Take your choice," returned the man, with a laugh that derided Bradway's ignorance.

Bradway looked down a long wide street, lined by two straggling rows of dim yellow lights. He heard the tramp and shuffle of many boots, the murmur of voices, loud laughs, the clink of glasses and coins, the whirr of roulette wheels. The sidewalks were crowded. The visitor sensed an atmosphere similar to that of the Kansas border towns, to Abilene and Hays City. They had passed their wild prime, but South Pass was in its heyday. The newcomer went by a number of hotel signs garish on high board fronts, and finally found a lodginghouse away from the center of town. The proprietor was a pleasant-faced and hospitable woman who asked for her fee in advance. The clean little room, smelling of fresh-cut pine lumber, satisfied Lincoln, and he paid for a week's rent. The keen-eyed woman observed his roll of greenbacks and favored him with a more attentive look.

"Where you hail from, cowboy?" she asked.

"Nebraska. How're things here?"

"Humph! Lively enough without any more fire-eyed cowboys. You want work?"

"Not much."

"I reckoned that. Cowboys with a roll like you just flashed usually don't want work till the roll's gone, and in South Pass that'll not take long. I advise you to keep it hid."

"Thanks for the hunch, lady, but I can look out for myself."

"I didn't miss the way you pack that big gun of yours."

"Gosh! you have sharp eyes, lady, and handsome ones, too," he replied mildly. "I'm a starved hombre. Where'll I eat?"

The landlady looked pleased. "Try the Chink, half a block in town," she offered. "He can cook, and cowboys patronize him. China Bar, he calls his shack, but he doesn't sell any hard liquor."

"Many of my kind hereabouts, lady?" continued the tall Nebraskan, casually.

"Not of *your* kind, cowboy," she retorted, and both words and look appeared to be complimentary. "But there are a plenty of cowboys in western Wyoming. Outfits all down the Sweetwater River, a few big, and lots of little ones. It's the coming cattle country."

"So I was told. . . . Lady, did you ever hear of a cowboy named Jimmy Weston?"

"I should say so, stranger! Jimmy used to stay with me. A mighty nice boy. Pity he . . . say, who might you happen to be?"

"Well, I might happen to be anybody. But it's enough to say that Jimmy was my pard."

"Pard? . . . Could you be the pard he was always bragging about? Linc something?" she queried, without troubling to hide her keen interest.

"I am the pard, lady, Lincoln Bradway. And I've come out here to find out what happened to Jimmy."

"He's dead."

"Yes, I know that. Word came to us back in Nebraska. But I'm not satisfied with what I heard."

"If you're smart, stranger, you'll keep quiet about your curiosity," she rejoined, her tone and manner altering subtly.

"Thanks, lady. I don't aim to make any sudden noise. But when I do it'll be loud. . . . Were you a friend of Jimmy's? Can you tell me anything?"

"No."

"Well, I'm sorry. You spoke sort of kindly of him. I had a feeling . . ."

"Stranger, I liked Jimmy Weston. He was just about the salt of the earth, and it was hard for me to believe he was shot in a card game, for cheating."

Bradway made a swift, angry gesture that silenced the woman. He leaned toward her. "Lady, that is a damned lie. Jimmy Weston never turned a crooked card in his life. I know it. His friends back there would swear to it, and I'm out here to get at the bottom of this deal, whatever it is."

"Everybody in South Pass believes the—the talk," said the woman nervously.

"Did you?"

Her hurried nod did not deceive her lodger. He left her then, convinced that she knew more than she cared to divulge. It might be well to cultivate her and win her confidence. He was playing in luck. Here at his very arrival in South Pass he had hit upon something that concerned his old friend, in whose interest he had journeyed so far. Lincoln Bradway was not too surprised, however. In countless previous situations, where he had been deeply concerned, things had gravitated his way, right from the start. Many a time he and Jimmy Weston in the old days had played their hunches and pressed their luck together. Now Jimmy, wild young-ster that he had been, was gone. Bradway looked away from the silent woman, out of the window. Slowly his face hardened and a shadow seemed to darken his gray eyes. He had a job to do. Jim Weston's name had to be cleared. And someone had to answer for his death. Well, time was awasting.

Bradway found the Chinaman's place, a tiny res-taurant with a counter and a bench, and several tables covered with oilcloth. Three cowboys were emerging as the Nebraskan approached the door. Lincoln stepped aside into the shadow as they came out. They smelled of horses and dust and rum, mixed with an odor that it took a moment for him to recognize. It was the aroma of sage. The third and last cowboy was tall, lean and set of face, tawny-haired, a ragged, genuine gun-packing range rider, if Linc had ever seen one.

"Aw, Mel, you're a sorehaid," growled one of his companions, a short bow-legged youth, somewhat un-steady from an oversupply of liquor. "Lucy gave you a raw deal, and no wonder. But 'cause of that an' you bein' sore ain't no reason why Monty heah an' me cain't open our mouths."

"Hell, it ain't!" flashed the cowboy called Mel, fiercely. "Blab all you want, Smeade, but not about *that*. Not heah in town!"

"An' why'n the hell not? Jest among ourselves. You make me sick. Even if it's never been admitted among us where an' for why them mavericks went, we know, an' *you* know damn wal, Mel Thatcher, that they . . ."

"No! I never admitted it," interrupted Thatcher, "There's some things you can't talk about on this range. Go on, you fool, and you'll get what Jimmy Weston got!"

They passed on down the sidewalk, leaving Lincoln standing there in the shadow, transfixed at the mention of Jimmy's name. He would recognize Mel Thatcher when he met him again.

Profoundly thoughtful, the Nebraskan went into the restaurant. While waiting for his meal he tried to separate into detail the things he had heard. The name Lucy? That name had occurred more than once in Jimmy's infrequent letters. Whoever that girl was, his old pard had been sweet on her. And somehow she had given this cowboy Thatcher a raw deal. Perhaps she had given Jimmy the same. Why? Maybe she was no good. That was one of the things he would have to investigate. Then there was the implied peril of speaking out loud concerning a certain something on that range?—Something to do with mavericks!—It so happened that an unbranded calf had been one of Jimmy's weaknesses. Like most open range riders he had been convinced that a maverick was any man's property. As a matter of fact that was true according to range custom everywhere; but it was a law that only cowmen and cowboys who owned cattle could burn their brand on a maverick. If they did not own any stock the appropriation of mavericks made them cattle thieves. Lincoln had heard that the ranchers of western Wyoming, hoping to induce rustlers to give their ranges a wide berth, had adopted the ruthless practice of hanging a cattle thief without formality.

Bradway concluded that it was possible, though improbable, that Weston might have had something to do with mavericks. In such case, however, it was hardly conceivable that he would have been shot while sitting at a card table. The report had been spread, he surmised, to cover murder. Thatcher's warning to his companion, Smeade, that he would get what Jimmy Weston got!—There was something ominous about that warning. To the man from Nebraska that warning was the clue to the mystery he had come to South Pass to solve.

After having appeased his hunger and made a fruitless effort to be friendly with the far from loquacious Chinaman, Bradway got up, paid for his meal and went out into the street. It was quite dark and the air was thin and cold, with a tang of mountain snow. Lincoln remembered how Jimmy had raved about the Wind River Mountains, and how he himself had watched from the stage to see them appear as if by magic out of the haze of distance, and grow and grow during two days of travel until the jagged white peaks, magnificent and aloof, pierced the blue sky. Little as he had seen of this western Wyoming country, he could easily have been captivated by it but for the grim mission which had brought him from his home.

He walked up through and beyond the center of the wide-open town. Then, crossing the street, he started back on the other side. This time he heard the babbling of a brook which evidently passed behind and paralleled the row of unpainted houses on that side. Lincoln peered into every open door. He scrutinized every passer-by that he encountered. Miners in red shirts, black-frocked and wide-hatted gamblers, flashily dressed women, cowboys and ranchers, teamsters and sheepmen, well-dressed travelers and ragged tramps, all made up that passing throng. A few Indians lolled in the shadows, smoking the white man's cigarettes. Stores and hotels appeared busy with customers, and the saloons were thronged with noisy crowds. Once a gunshot penetrated the din, but nobody in that milling crowd seemed to pay any attention to it.

Bradway's careful observation confirmed his earlier opinion that South Pass was indeed a wide-open mining town at the height of its prosperity and youth, as raw and violent as Hays City, as flush as Benton, the mushroom town that flourished during the building of the Union Pacific. He had seen both of these border towns in all their frontier turbulences and color. He did not need to be told that law and order had not yet come to South Pass, that gold was to be had for the digging, or stealing, or gambling for, that vice was rampant and life held cheap.

After his survey of the town Bradway began methodically to enter each public place, from the canvas dens at the foot of the street, to the stores and saloons and gambling halls that bordered the sidewalk. He spent an hour of most diligent search before he again came upon Mel Thatcher and his two pals. Thatcher was standing beside a table where his two friends were playing cards with two other cowboys. There was more liquor on the table than money. Smeade appeared the worse for drink and his luck clearly was bad.

Thatcher's lean visage wore a worried look, but it showed none of the heat of dissipation that was reflected in the faces of the others. Lincoln watched them a while. He knew cowboys. He had known a thousand in his time. They were all more or less alike, yet there were exceptions. Thatcher seemed to be one of these. The Nebraskan liked his looks. Thatcher was too young to have had experience that matched his own, but it was evident that he was no novice at anything pertaining to cowboy life. He packed a gun, but did not wear it below his hip, as was the practice of most gun-throwers.

When Lincoln approached this cowboy he was yielding to an instinct, deep and inevitable, for something had told him that here was a hombre who might supply the answers to some of his questions.

"Howdy, Thatcher," he said, coolly, as the other wheeled at his touch. "I've been looking for you particular hard."

"Hell you say?" returned Thatcher, with angry insolence. "And for why, mister smart-aleck?"

"I reckon you better return the compliment before you go shooting off your chin."

"Yeah?" The cowboy straightened up, turned squarely to face the stranger beside him. Then he said: "Never saw you in my life. I'd have remembered. So you must be looking up the wrong man."

"Maybe so. I hope not. Come aside for a minute," replied Lincoln, and he led the curious cowboy away from the players who did not seem to be aware of the interruption. "No offense, Thatcher," continued the Nebraskan, in a low and earnest voice. "I'm from over Nebraska way. Name is Linc Bradway. Ever hear it?"

"Not that I can recall."

"Do you remember coming out of the Chinaman's restaurant an hour or more ago?"

"Yes," said Thatcher, with a visible start. "But what

the hell business is that of yours?" he wanted to know.

"I was just about to go in the Chink's when two of your tipsy pals busted out. I stepped back in the shadow. . . . I heard every word you and Smeade said."

Thatcher's red face seemed to pale a bit in the lamplight. "Ahuh . . . and what if you did?"

"One crack you made I'm calling on you to explain."

"Say, I don't explain nothing to nobody, especially to strangers," retorted Thatcher.

"I heard you tell your loud-mouthed pard that if he didn't stop gabbing . . . *he would get what Jimmy Weston got!*"

Thatcher gulped. "Cowboy, I never said no such thing," he declared, defiantly. But he looked as if he had suddenly been hit in the midriff with the hind foot of a mule.

"Don't make me call you a liar," retorted Bradway. "I heard you. I couldn't be mistaken, because I was Jimmy Weston's pard for years. We rode trail together and bunked with a dozen outfits. I loved that boy. . . . He got in trouble back in Nebraska—lit out for Wyoming. He wrote me some queer things about a girl named *Lucy,* for instance, and another man. . . ."

"Judas!" muttered Thatcher, grabbing Linc Bradway's arm. "If you know what's good for you you'll shut up altogether."

"Thatcher, I can't be shut up. Of course, I've no way to make you talk, but if you're honest—if you were no enemy of Jimmy Weston's . . ."

"I swear I wasn't his enemy," replied Thatcher, hoarsely, "He was as likable a feller as I ever met. But that's all I can tell you."

"Do you believe what they say that my pard was shot in a gambling den for cheating?"

"Man, you can't hold me responsible for what's claimed in South Pass," protested the cowboy. His tenseness, his apparent concern amazed the Nebraskan, and confirmed his growing impression that there was something menacing as well as mysterious in connection with the death of Jimmy Weston.

"I'm not holding you responsible," argued Bradway. "I can't shoot a man for believing loose talk. But I've a hunch that you know damn well Jimmy wasn't shot for cheating at cards."

"A hunch is nothing. Naturally you take your pard's part. You can't prove he wasn't."

"The hell's fire I can't. That's what I'm here for."

"Then my hunch to you is, beat it hell for leather off this range while the getting's good!"

"Thatcher, you're advising me to do what you wouldn't do yourself," asserted Lincoln. "Isn't that the truth?"

"I'm not saying what I'd do."

"Well, are you coming clean with what you know—or are you lining up with the dirty coward who shot my pardner?"

"I can't tell you—I don't know any more," returned Thatcher, his eyes on the sawdust on the floor.

"You're feeling pretty lowdown to have to lie like that," said Bradway. "Thatcher, I'm on the trail of something rotten. Your warning to Smeade proves it. All right. Make a friend or enemy of me, as you choose. But I'm a bad hombre to enemies, as you're going to damn soon find out."

Thatcher, apparently torn between a powerful and resistless inhibition, and what might have been an effort to give an honest answer to an appeal to his true self, met Bradway's level gray eyes for a fleeting instant, then turned back to his gambling comrades. Smeade was glowering at him, and not too drunk not to be suspicious.

Lincoln turned on his heel, burning within, cold without, and stalked from the noisy saloon into the street. The sensible thing to do was to go back to his room and calmly to think through the information he had gathered during the past few hours. But he could not bring himself to do it—not quite yet. He might fall afoul of something more that would dovetail with what he already had learned. He never failed to yield to such an urge as compelled him now. Besides, the driving passion that had brought him to Wyoming, demanded action rather than contemplation.

In a little shop down the street he bought a cigar from a young man who seemed to be of a friendly sort. "Been in this hole long?" asked Lincoln in a conversational tone, as he lighted the cigar.

"Most a year. Too long. South Pass is gettin' too rough for an honest businessman. I was held up an' robbed twice in one night not long ago," replied the young store proprietor.

"Huh. I rolled in only today and gathered that very idea myself. Don't you keep a gun handy?"

"Shore. But I was lookin' into one when it happened."

"I reckon that gunplay here is pretty common."

"There wasn't so much when I first came. But lately you're lucky to dodge bullets."

"Did you happen to know a cowboy by the name of Jimmy Weston?"

"Shore did. Liked Jimmy a lot. Did you know him?"

"Yes, back Nebraska way. I asked for him here, and heard he'd been shot."

"Too bad, if you were friends."

"Where was Jimmy killed?" queried Bradway, from behind a cloud of smoke.

"Emery's place. Biggest gamblin' hell in town. Used to be named *Take It or Leave It*. Mean' gold, of course. Someone painted out the first three words. Now it's called the *Leave It*. Shore's appropriate. Rumor had it that Jimmy Weston rode his horse under that big sign, stood up on his saddle, an' climbed up to do that paintin'! Anyway he was shot in a card game, for palmin' aces in a big jackpot—or so they said. No one except the gamblers saw the fight, or know who shot Jimmy. Sort of a queer deal all around, I thought. But that was the talk."

"Ahuh. Big poker games at this Emery's joint, I reckon?"

"You bet. Sky limit. No game for a cowboy, stranger."

"Thanks for the hunch. All the same before I leave town I'll take a fly at Emery's *Leave It*."

"That's just like Jimmy. No two-bit game for him! But if you do, you're not as smart as you look. Emery is a cardsharp. An' his right-hand man McKeever is a gambler to steer clear of. He'll shoot at the drop of a card. Jerks a little gun from inside his vest."

"Gosh, must be interesting people! Any women hang around Emery's?"

"There's one, an' she shore is plumb interestin'. Kit Bandon, the Maverick Queen, they call her. Handsome as hell, an' when she cocks her eye at a man he's a goner. Better not let her see you, stranger, 'cause you're shore the finest-lookin' cowboy who ever struck South Pass."

"You are flattering, my friend. I reckon you filled poor Jimmy with such guff. He was a vain gazabo. . . . But this Kit Bandon—what is she?"

"Runs a big cattle ranch down on the Sweetwater. Leans to mavericks. Her brand is K I T."

"Mavericks—well, you don't say! Reckon she runs a two-bit outfit?"

"*You* might call it that—comin' from Nebraska. Kit hires cowboys for short spells, to round up and drive. Last fall she sent a thousand head of two-year olds to Rock Springs. . . . Excuse me. What'll you have, gentlemen?"

A couple of new customers diverted the garrulous cigar salesman from Bradway. He yawned and left the store. Once more he mingled with the sidewalk throngs, his mind active, his eyes scanning the lettered signs on the buildings. Presently across the street he espied a white two-story frame structure. It had an ornate balcony along the second story. Over the wide doorway below shone the brightest lights on the street. Above on a high board front stood out garishly a crude splotch of red, where words had been obliterated, and to the right he saw what remained of the name: *Leave It* in large black letters in relief against the white!

"By thunder!" muttered the Nebraskan. "I bet that clerk was right! That's the very stunt Jimmy would have pulled when he was feeling sort of reckless—and ornery."

Lincoln crossed the street and entered, to find himself in the largest hall he had ever seen. The room was deep and wide, with a low ceiling. A bar ran its entire length, and it accommodated two rows of drinkers. Lincoln stepped back to get a better perspective of the crowd.

After all, there seemed little here of raw frontier life that he had not already seen in Benton and the Kansas cattle towns. It might have a newer note. Sweat and smoke and sawdust and rum and leather and sage gave the noisy room an atmosphere characteristic of all boom towns of the West. There were a dozen or more games of chance all crowded with players, among whom he noticed several women. Could one of them possibly be the woman he was so curious to see? He had heard of cattle queens, but had never had the good or bad fortune to meet one of them. He shared the rather general opinion of cattlemen that women should not stick their noses into the cattle business.

Then in an alcove under the stairs he espied a circle of eagerly watching men who were undoubtedly intent upon a big game. Bradway made his way through the arch and gradually, without being obtrusive, he penetrated the circle until he could see over a man's shoulder to a card table, covered with gold and greenbacks, in front of six gamblers. Instantly he realized that this was the establishment's big game and that these were the individuals he wanted to watch. One was a handsome, dark young woman of perhaps twenty-five years. She wore a diamond as big as a gooseberry, and she was dressed in some black material becomingly relieved at the yoke and the waist by touches of red. A couple of newcomers probed their way in behind Lincoln. "That's her," whispered one of the men excitedly. "Ther's Kit Bandon, Queen of the Mavericks. She's ahaid of the game, too, as usual." The other of the two exclaimed under his breath, "Glory in the mornin', look at that stack of yellows! An' ain't she a pippin for looks?"

The Nebraskan found himself staring at the lovely, reckless, excited face of the Maverick Queen. Even though she did not glance in his direction Lincoln Bradway felt the impelling lure she seemed to exercise over every man in that excited group. Suddenly, one of the players directly in front of him threw down his cards.

"I'm cleaned. You're all too good for me," he said, shaking his head dolefully.

"What do you mean by 'good'?" asked the russet-bearded gamester sitting next to the woman. He had thin blue lips and piercing gray eyes, cold as ice. Lincoln's critical eye flashed from the gambler's soft white hands to his open flowered vest. Could the little bulge on the left side possibly represent a gun?

"Sorry, you can take that 'good' any way you like," bitterly replied the loser, getting up from his chair.

The gambler snarled and made a sudden movement, only to be restrained by the strikingly dressed woman beside him. "Emery, let him alone," she commanded in a voice that was low-pitched but clear as a bell. "He's got a right to feel sore. He dropped two thousand dollars, didn't he?"

"No man can hint like that to me—"

"Let's go on with the game," interrupted another player, evidently a rancher judging from his garb and deeply bronzed face. He had a direct clear gaze, and a strong chin under his drooping mustache. The remaining two players, one of them obviously another gambler and the last a burly miner, seconded that motion. Then the disgruntled loser pushed by Lincoln and was lost in the crowd. Almost simultaneously the watchers about the table exhaled a breath that expressed their relief.

Without a word the Nebraskan slipped into the vacated seat, and leaning back he put a slow hand inside his coat. His heavy gun sheath had bumped the table, upsetting some of the stacks of yellow coin.

"Folks, I'm setting in," he announced coolly. His look, his manner, his quick action turned every eye in that group upon him. He was suddenly conscious that the Maverick Queen's dark, smoldering eyes were fixed upon his face.

"This is no game for two-bit cowboys," spoke up Emery, sharply. It was plain that he did not care for contact with range riders of Lincoln's type.

"Money talks, doesn't it, in this shack, same as in the gambling halls of Dodge and Abilene?" drawled Lincoln, and pulling out a tight roll of bills he dropped it on the table, exposing a one-hundred-dollar bill on the outside.

"Yes, money talks here, but not for everybody," snapped Emery.

"Is there anything offensive about me, lady?" asked Bradway, courteously, as he turned an intent and smiling gaze upon her.

"There certainly isn't. You're welcome to play," replied the woman, turning her back upon Emery and half nodding and smiling in Lincoln's direction. With difficulty, the cowboy turned his glance away from the strangely disturbing eyes of the Maverick Queen.

"Thank you. . . . Mister Emery, I'll take up your insult later. . . . Is it a table-stakes or limit game?"

"Five dollar limit," said the rancher, "except in jackpots. Make your own limit then. . . . My name's Lee."

"Glad to meet you, Colonel. Mine's Bradway."

The next man, McKeever, sneered, exposing yellow teeth like those of a wolf, but for a gambler his gaze was furtive. Bradway felt an instinctive distrust of him that was even sharper than his feeling for Emery. The red-shirted miner nodded his approval and the game began.

Bradway was gambling with more than cards, for something even more important than gold. He felt capable of matching these men, unless he had a run of poor cards, for like most cowboys he was keen and shrewd at poker, and when luck was with him he was well-nigh unbeatable. But he had to watch Emery and

the wolf-toothed man especially closely. They might be
in cahoots. He studied his opponents with unobtrusive
scrutiny, well aware of the fact that they were studying
him in turn. But the rancher Lee, the miner, and Kit
Bandon were not cold or insolent—nor calculating
about it. The woman was interested in the newcomer
and clearly showed it. Bradway could see right away
that her actions were displeasing to Emery.

The first hand of note was a jackpot which the
dealer took for fifty dollars. Lincoln's eyes watched the
swift, dexterous hands of the gambler. Everybody
present was aware of his scrutiny. He made no effort to
disguise his watchfulness. The onlookers wondered if
the cowboy would catch the gambler in a crooked deal,
and what would happen if he did.

The hands were dealt, and Kit Bandon promptly
opened for the size of the ante. Lee stayed, likewise the
miner. Lincoln had four hearts, a hand to raise on, but
he merely stayed, wanting to see what McKeever and
Emery would do. The former raised it to one hundred
dollars. Emery studied his hand a while, then stayed,
and the Maverick Queen followed suit. Lee dropped
out, and the miner put in his hundred dollars. Without
hesitation, Bradway doubled that sum in his raise.
Gamblers never reveal their feelings, yet Lincoln divined that this raise roused conjecture, to say the least.
They all stayed, and cards were drawn. Kit Bandon's
opening bet was a hundred, which the miner saw. The
cowboy also called, but both McKeever and Emery
raised and she raised them in turn. Lee manifested a
curious hard expression in his eyes as he watched the
tall stranger. Probably he was thinking what Lincoln
was certain of—that Kit Bandon and her gambler
friends were tilting the bets with the old purpose of
driving an odd player out. But the Nebraskan kept
calling until finally he forced them to quit raising. There
was over a thousand dollars in the pot.

"Opened on three queens," said Kit, with a dazzling
smile.

"Well, counting you that makes four queens," replied

the cowboy, smiling back at her. "Almost unbeatable, but the hand is no good."

McKeever dropped his cards upon the deck.

"I called you. Show your cards," demanded Lincoln, curtly. Then as the gambler made no move Lincoln overturned the hand to expose a pair of tens.

"More than I figured you for," said Lincoln, sarcastically. "Emery, what you got?"

The chief of the *Leave It* laid down a pair of aces, and Lincoln showed them a flush. As he raked in the gold and bills he drawled: "This isn't bad for a small-town gambling joint!"

Emery rasped. "Feller, I don't like your talk."

"Gambler, I don't like your tone either. If you address me again try to be civil."

It was evident then to the gamblers of the *Leave It* that they had caught a tartar. Kit Bandon seemed amused and intrigued by this steel-nerved stranger. Lee did not hide his admiration, and even the miner's bleak visage expanded in a broad smile. McKeever's face was sullen and dark; his smoldering gaze was downcast. Emery's cold gray eyes rested without expression upon the fingernails of his left hand.

"My deal," announced Kit, cheerfully. "Your ante, Lee. . . . Cowboy, thanks for showing us some real poker."

And real poker it turned out to be, for Bradway. The cards ran in his direction with phenomenal good luck. He drew in nearly every hand, and almost always filled when he raised before the draw. Kit Bandon and the two gamblers pitted their united skill, and as much trickery as they could get away with against Bradway, only to be beaten at every turn. The miner went broke, and declined the money Lincoln offered him as a stake. Lee seesawed between breaking even and a little money ahead. He was enjoying this game. The crowd that had been augmented to twice its original size watched with bated breath. There was a charged atmosphere around that table. Everyone of the watchers could see it in the woman player. Kit Bandon was a sport, a good loser, a fascinating creature who thrived on excitement and danger. Her color was high, her eyes sparkled, under her breath she hummed a little tune. And the glances she shot in the direction of the stranger conveyed more and more interest in his person than in his poker game.

Linc had met and played against greater gamblers than Emery and McKeever in his time, but none in whom he had encountered as much open hostility. Evidently they were determined to break the newcomer's luck who so blandly and coolly matched every bet and won nearly every pot. When their stake was gone they borrowed from Kit, who kept a goodly sum in front of her. Finally Emery lost all his money, including what he had borrowed from his woman companion.

"Lady, you sure are a banker," drawled Bradway. "I hope when I get broke here in South Pass that you'll stake me to a few bits the way you have these local gents."

"You can bet on that," she countered sweetly.

"With your luck—and peculiar style of play you can't ever go broke," snarled Emery, with emphasis on the "peculiar."

"Sure, I'm lucky at cards," drawled the stranger, "but all-fired unlucky at love," and he smiled at Kit as he spoke.

"Cowboy, I just can't believe that last," she returned. Perhaps her arch look and warm tone accounted for the ill-concealed glint of hatred in Emery's gaze.

"Gentlemen, and Miss Bandon, the game has slowed up," continued Bradway, exasperatingly. "Too much talk. And talk appears cheap in this town—I reckon almost as cheap as life."

"If that's one of your smart cracks, it just happens to be true," snapped Emery.

"In case there's anything personal in that remark, Mister Gambler, I reckon you-all haven't figured that the outfit who makes mine cheap will be biting sawdust ahead of me," drawled Linc.

"Who in hell are you?" demanded Emery, in an effort to be sarcastic. But there was curiosity in his voice.

"Linc Bradway. Hail from Missouri, more recently from Nebraska—nephew of Cole Younger, if that means anything to you."

"Suppose we play one more jack," suggested Lee, manifestly nervous over the turn the conversation had taken. He sensed the direction events were taking and wanted to get out of the game before things got too tense.

"What a lot of cheap fourflushers!" exclaimed Kit. "But all right, one more jack. Only Mr. Cole Younger's nephew, I'll want satisfaction."

"That'll be a pleasure, ma'am. I'm sorry, but this will have to be the last game I'll sit in with your gambler partners," drawled Linc, deliberately. Apparently these worthies wanted a peg to hang suspicion or accusation upon, and Lincoln was willing to let them have it. It was plain to see that Emery was a snake in the grass. The silent McKeever might be the more dangerous one of the two, after all. Neither, however, made any reply to Linc Bradway's deliberate insult. The hands were dealt, the pot opened, raised, and cards called for. Linc stayed on a pair of deuces and for once failed to add to the strength of his hand. Betting was light. They were afraid of the stranger's luck. When he raised the limit of the money in front of Emery that individual followed the lead of the others and threw his cards down in disgust. Then Lincoln, with a queer little smile, laid down his pair of deuces.

"Jess, he stole it!" Kit cried, and it almost appeared as if she were pleased with the gamblers' discomfiture. "You and Mac took this cowboy for a tenderfoot, and he has cleaned you."

Lee laughed. "He cleaned us all, and if I know poker he pulled as straight a game as I'll gamble he can shoot."

"Thanks, Colonel, that's Texas talk if I know folks

from the South," returned Linc. "And now, Mister Emery, you can eat that hint about my peculiar play."

The circle of spectators shifted uneasily and there was a perceptible sway toward the alcove portal. But there was too much uncertainty, too great an undercurrent of excitement for the crowd to bolt yet. Emery, however, no longer labored under his misapprehension.

"Bradway, no insult intended," he said.

"So you are willing to crawl? . . . Emery, every look and word of yours to me has been insulting. . . . I'm calling you."

"Cowboy, you must be looking for trouble."

"Yes, and I've found it. But not much trouble for a hombre like me. Come on!"

Kit Bandon suddenly interposed in the tense situation. "Bradway, these friends of mine often forget there's a lady present. But you're a gentleman."

"Thanks, I haven't overlooked the fact that you're a thoroughbred in bad company."

"I reckon I can stick it out," she returned flatly. She did not show the least fear of Bradway or concern for her friends. "Jess, it looks as though you and Mac have riled the wrong cowboy."

"Kit, you forget what happened to the last cowboy you took a shine to," flashed the gambler, angrily. If these two, the gambler and the girl, despite the obvious close relationship between them, did not hate each other, then Bradway was a poor judge of character.

"Hell no, I haven't," she returned, just as angrily.

Linc, after pocketing his winnings, pounded the table with his left hand. His right was significantly not in sight. "Cut it, Miss Bandon, begging your pardon. Let Emery talk to me."

At this juncture Lee and the miner quietly vacated their chairs. "Lemme out," demanded the red-shirted giant. "If I know this stripe of feller there'll be hell poppin' here pronto." His remark started an exodus. Still the morbid remained.

"Bradway, you're unreasonable," shouted Emery,

shrilly. "I can't crawfish for something I may have said unintentionally."

"Crawfish—hell! Your liver is as white as your face. . . . Lady, kindly get up and out of this."

Kit Bandon neither flinched nor moved. She appeared fascinated by this drama in which a young and personable stranger was forcing the issue against her friends.

"Emery, you're a cheap gambler—a poor loser—a damned liar. . . . Stop! Keep your hand out of that vest!"

The remaining watchers broke pell-mell to get out and for a moment there was a mingling of whistling breaths, and the trampling scuffles of hurried feet.

Emery's white hand sank twitching back to the table. Out of the corner of one eye Bradway caught McKeever's hand slipping inside his vest. Then the cowboy gave the table a tremendous shove and sprang erect, his gun leaping out.

Chapter II

Kit Bandon, who had half risen just as the heavy table caught her, fell and rolled clear out of the alcove. The gamblers both went down, with Emery under the overturned table. But McKeever slid free and as he sat up, propped on his left hand, he reached for the gun in his vest. It gleamed brightly. Lincoln's shot broke that draw, and evidently the gambler's arm, for it flopped down, and the gun went spinning across the floor. McKeever let out a hoarse cry of fury and agony.

Linc, smoking gun in hand, swung the table off Emery, who then slowly labored erect, his features livid and contorted. Kit joined him, her face red with rage, and stood brushing the sawdust off her black dress.

"Damned fools! I told you," she burst out, furiously. "Did he—kill Mac?"

"Looks that way," muttered Emery, hoarsely.

"No, I just winged him," spoke up Bradway. "Miss Bandon, I'm sorry I had to mess up your party, but it could have been a lot worse. You'll please excuse my rough manner."

"I excuse you, Mr. Bradway," she said, in a low voice, her dark eyes meeting his gaze. Whatever she felt, it hardly seemed to be anger for the cowboy from Nebraska.

"Emery, you made a crack to this lady a minute ago about what happened to the last cowboy she took a shine to," flashed Lincoln to the gambler. "Wasn't that cowboy Jimmy Weston?"

Amazement and fear held the gambler mute, and Kit Bandon stared at Lincoln, startled, her red lips parted, the rich color fading out of her cheeks.

"Weston was my pard," went on Bradway. "I've letters of his that give me a hunch as to what happened to him, and I came here to prove it. . . . Get out, Emery." Lincoln made a move with the still smoking gun that sent the gambler hurrying out into the crowd which was edging back again toward the alcove.

"Mac, are you bad hurt?" asked the woman, kneeling beside him.

"Arm busted. High up," rejoined McKeever, weakly. "I'm bleeding bad."

"Don't move. I'll get someone to look after you."

Linc picked up the little gun and examined it. The weapon was a derringer and it had a large bore for such a small gun. He put it in his pocket.

"Mac, you better pack a real gun next time you meet me," said Bradway, and started to go out. By this time Kit Bandon had arisen. She stood before him, visibly agitated, and was about to speak when he asked her: "How come such a fine girl as you could be hooked up with hombres as lowdown as these?"

"Mac is Emery's friend, not mine," she whispered hurriedly. "Jess and I . . . we have cattle deals. I own part of this place. It goes back to a long time ago . . . Bradway, I must see you—talk with you. . . ."

As he stood there close to this girl whom they called the Maverick Queen, Bradway felt himself drawn by her beauty and personality, just as she was clearly moved by the courage of this stranger. Linc saw the unmasked emotion in her dark eyes. She must have had a deep cue for passion, and he divined that it had its origin in his reference to Jimmy Weston. Remembrance of his friend and the part which this woman may have played in Jimmy's death brought Linc back to his senses.

"Well, this is not the time nor place," he replied coldly, and left her. The crowd opened to let him pass through and out into the street, where he sheathed his gun, and joined the stream of pedestrians on the wooden sidewalk of South Pass's main street.

Linc kept looking back to see if he was being followed. He could not be positive until he had cleared the center of town. He passed the last pedestrians on his side, and then crossed the street. He caught sight of two men whose actions were kind of suspicious. Quickly he squared around, gun in hand. They made a quick retreat down a dark alleyway. This enabled him to gain his lodginghouse before his pursuers could tell where he had gone. The cowboy found his room, barred the door and lighted a kerosene lamp. Then for the first time in an hour he drew a breath of profound relief, and threw off his coat, its pockets heavy with gold coins and bulging with rolls of bills. The room had a window, but it was too high up for anyone on the outside to see in. Walls and doors were strongly built. For the time being he felt safe. But just how permanent his safety was depended upon how strong and bold the gamblers were in South Pass. He had made two treacherous men his bitter enemies. Moreover he had now in his possession between five and six thousand dollars, a fortune to Bradway, whatever it might be to them. As for Kit Bandon, the way she flashed money and bet it and lent it augured that it must come to her as easily as it went.

As he thought over the events of the evening he exclaimed under his breath. "But maybe it's bad luck. That outfit will do for me if they can. As for Kit Bandon—either I'm loco or she cottoned to me pronto. Did she turn white when I came out with Jimmy Weston's name? My hunch must have been right. Whatever happened to Jimmy, the Maverick Queen had something to do with it. And whatever it was I've got to find out!"

He turned out all the rolls and wads of bills, and the many gold coins upon the bed. That pile of money amounted to more than Lincoln had ever seen in his life, let alone owned. He had won it fairly. And he was going to hang on to it! No more gambling. He would not need to ride trail or drive cattle while he was solving the riddle of Jimmy Weston's death. He had not a doubt, however, that his problem would have been far easier and less perilous if he had not gambled and shot one of the players, thus bringing himself into prominence in South Pass. And yet, as a result of his forcing things tonight, he had learned some facts that might save him some time—if his luck still held.

Lincoln kept an old money belt in his bag. He took it out, stowing away in it all the bills of large denomination. The others and the coin he would exchange tomorrow. After that was done he thought of Jimmy's letters, and taking them out he reread them with mingled emotions. Poor Jim had had no conception when he wrote these lines of the tragedy stalking him. There were several mentions of a girl named Lucy, and evidently she was someone of whom he thought a great deal. The fifth letter bore signs of labored writing. Jimmy was not himself. It was written in lead pencil, and some of it was hard to decipher. But so much was poignantly plain: "This dam black-eyed female I lost my haid over has queered me with Lucy. Honest, pard Linc, I didn't mean to be that yellow. But you know what likker does to me an' this woman made me forget all the decency I ever knew. I'll get even with her. I'll be as yellow to her as she made me be to the kid. . . ." No doubt the kid referred to was the girl, Lucy.

Evidently the girl lived in or near South Pass, because Thatcher had mentioned her. And she was the one person Lincoln wanted to see next, before Kit Bandon, or anyone else.

Linc undressed and, turning out the light, he went to bed. But he was far from sleep. Over and over again he tried to piece all these details into a logical sequence. Each time he found that Kit Bandon seemed to be the nucleus of the plot. There could be no doubt that she was the "black-eyed female" Jimmy had referred to in his letter. Linc had a premonition, as he sat there in his pine-boarded room, that the "black-eyed female," whom he had heard called the Maverick Queen, was going to play an important part in his own life during the coming weeks in South Pass.

He lay there in the dark thinking, and before he went to sleep he came to the conclusion that he must not let his feelings run away with his intelligence. He must imagine less and learn more. As for the menace to himself—that was certain. In the morning, when he was clear-headed again, he would give some thought to plans for his own self-preservation. Afterward, he would have patience and wait, and be as cunning as a fox. The incentive was great. Yet there was more to it than his love for his old friend and the firm resolve to avenge his death. There were some facets to this problem that intrigued him and whetted his curiosity. Who was this Lucy? And the dazzling, seductive Kit Bandon? Lincoln suddenly realized that he must be on his guard against succumbing as easily to her wiles as had Jimmy. There was passion and temptation in those sultry dark eyes. As sleep began to overpower him, his last conscious thoughts were of the Maverick Queen—the color and vividness—the fragrance that emanated from her—the symmetry of her form, and the provocation in her black eyes.

Linc Bradway was awakened by a yellow ray of sunshine that streaked through his little window. He was cold and glad to get up and dress. With daylight his mind again worked clearly. The possibility that he would have to fight for his life bothered him not at all. All these mushrooming gold towns were noted for bloodshed; it was hardly to be expected that he would meet an even break at gunplay in South Pass. His risk, he thought, lay in being shot from ambush. It would be known that he carried a large sum of money. Robbers and bandits would be as eager for that as Emery and his partner. Night would be the time for extreme caution, although he realized that he would have to move with care even during the day.

Lincoln went out on the street to have his first glimpse of South Pass in the light of day. He was most agreeably surprised. It spread along the bed of a narrow valley, and despite its new raw atmosphere of pine-board buildings and canvas tents, it seemed the most picturesque mining town he had ever seen. Early though the hour, there was already color and bustle in the streets. Heavy-booted miners, packing tools, were passing along the wooden sidewalks; stores were open; the saloons were being swept out; and Linc heard the rattling whirr of roulette wheels that never stopped. Over the hill east of the town hung clouds of yellow and black smoke from the gold mills. The western hillside was dotted with prospectors' tunnels, where they had dug for traces of the precious metal. Beyond the hill that rose to the north, white peaks of snow glistened in the sunlight. Cold and white, they noti-fied the watcher where the nipping air came from. They marked the southern end of the Wind River Range, where it opened out into the Pass that Jim Bridger had discovered in the early days, and through which ran the famed Oregon Trail.

Entering the restaurant Lincoln found a few early birds, too hungry to pay any particular attention to him. The Chinese proprietor did not appear. A serving girl waited upon Lincoln. He ordered a good meal of ham and eggs that would last him the whole day and longer if necessary. Then, with a hitch to his belt, Lincoln went out upon the street again, his gaze as restless as a compass needle.

South Pass, by this time, had definitely awakened for the day. Miners and other workmen had increased in numbers; ranch vehicles and horsemen were in evi-dence; a chuck wagon was being loaded with supplies in front of the big store at the intersection of the two main streets. Cowboys' saddled horses stood bridles down before the saloons. Lincoln crossed to the op-posite corner, where he encountered Thatcher coming out of the store. The cowboy jerked up his head and stared.

"Ahuh. You must be more'n one feller," he said.

"Good morning, Mel. I saw you first," replied Linc, cheerfully.

"Yes, I'll bet that's your way."

"Look here, Thatcher, you got me wrong. I'm not such a bad hombre, if I like you."

"Mebbe you're not at that. . . . I was in the *Leave It* last night when you called them gamblers. I'm bound to admit it looked pretty good to me, and others."

"Mel, now you're being more friendly. I won a little coin. Is there a bank in this place?"

"Up this side street. That low stone building . . . only stone building in town. So you won a little coin? Lordy, what would you call a lot? But, cowboy, you don't need a bank. You need a morgue of which we have none here."

"You reckon they'll lay me out?"

"Sure do. You bucked the wrong tiger last night. I think I'm giving you a good hunch when I advise you to take the eight o'clock stage and vamoose with your little coin."

"Thanks. You're right kind, or else you want to see the last of me around here."

"So do we all," replied Thatcher, with a smile that disarmed his words.

"But for what reason?"

"One reason is you're sure a handsome stranger. And we only have a few women in these diggings that a feller can be serious about."

"Can't you be sport enough to introduce me?"

"Well, you didn't need no one last night."

"Is Kit Bandon one of these few women you're bragging about?"

"Nope. She's not in the class I mean. She's in one all by herself."

"Struck me deep, that lady did. Does she specialize in cowboys same as mavericks?"

"You'll have to find out for yourself," returned Thatcher, significantly.

"Where you bound for? I see you're packing out supplies."

At this moment Thatcher's comrades of the preceding night showed up, clean-shaven and bright of eye. They responded to the cowboy's civil greeting.

"Boys, when I go broke I'd like to ride on your outfit," he said.

"You could get on, all right," said Thatcher. "I'm foreman for Lee. You met him last night. Any cowboy who calls him Colonel is riding high right then."

"Mr. Lee, eh? Nice man. No fool at cards, either. But that outfit seesawed him broke. . . . So long, boys. I'll be riding out to see you some day."

"Doggone it! I reckon I'd be glad to see you. . . . Bradway, you won't listen to no good advice from us cowboys?"

"Not if you're advising me to move on," concluded Lincoln, and turned up the cross street. Those boys were not half-bad fellows. They just had some secret or were in some fix that they preferred a stranger not to know about. Linc began to think that perhaps he had been too precipitous in mentioning his connection with Jimmy Weston.

The street ended at the bank, a low, squat building made of irregular-sized bareheads. Entering, Lincoln presented himself at the counter and asked if he could exchange some gold and small currency for large bills. It was evident that word of his little to-do at the *Leave It* the preceding night had not reached the bank official, who proved to be most agreeable and business-like. Perhaps such a gambling flare-up was no rarity in South Pass. He was not invited to open an account. Other customers stamped in, some of them rough miners with sacks of gold dust. There was a scale on the counter. Linc lingered long enough to observe that gold, too, was far from rare in this camp.

A path led along the hillside back of the buildings on the main street. Linc followed this path around the slope from which vantage point he could view the northern side of the town. The narrow valley widened here, and from it a rocky gully led up to the noisy, smoking mill. The street crossed below the mouth of the gully, and followed it up to where the big rusty structure stood dark against the sky. Houses spread all over this area; and back of them, on the slope, clung rough little shacks and huts; their crude chimneys or stovepipes told of permanency, and that the winters were severe. The brook brawled down from the mountains, and all along it for a mile, until it disappeared in a green-timbered gorge where huge banks of sand and gravel indicated an extensive placer mining operation on each side of the rushing stream.

South Pass was the only town near the center of the Sweetwater Valley, already alive with cattle. Some traveler had told Bradway that there already were several hundred thousand head of cattle between Independence Rock and the end of the valley where the Sweetwater flowed from its source in the mountains.

Lincoln walked up to the mill, conversing with any miner he met who would talk. The mill turned out to be a huge structure filled with noise and smoke. He was not permitted to enter. The guard pointed to a small building on one side of the works, and here the Nebraskan found an office with busy clerks. He hung around until he was able to see the superintendent, a robust, bluff man of thirty.

"They threw me out down there," complained Linc. "I didn't have any idea of holding up the place."

"What did you want? A job?" inquired the man, quizzically, directing a sharp gaze of recognition upon his visitor.

"I might buy your gold mill," drawled Linc, in reply to the mill man's look.

"Didn't I see you in Emery's saloon last night?"

"You must of, if you were in there early," replied the cowboy. "Hope you're not a friend of Emery's."

"No, indeed. As far as I'm concerned personally, I think you let them off too easily. . . . Excuse me for being inquisitive, but are you any person in particular, or just a wandering cowboy, quick of temper and trigger?"

"Well, I reckon I'm just a wandering cowboy, and I'm not offended. Now let me ask one. Who in hell in this mining dump will talk?"

"Talk!—What about?"

"Oh, everything in general, and in particular that outfit I bucked last night, especially the Bandon woman."

"I doubt if there is anyone here who will talk about Kit Bandon," rejoined the superintendent, coldly.

"Ahuh. All stuck on her or scared to talk," said Linc, with heavy sarcasm.

"Hardly that. Couldn't you see for yourself that she is a good sport, a thoroughbred gambler, square as they come on this frontier, and friendly with everybody?"

"Sure, I saw all that, and a heap more. But that isn't enough."

"Sorry I can't oblige you, cowboy," returned the mill boss, curtly.

Linc stalked out, a little nettled until he reflected that suspicion, even hostility, here in this town were all he had any right to expect. He must curb his impatience and proceed more slowly. On the way back to town he saw a livery stable and made for it with quicker step. Anyone who earned his living with horses was a potential friend of Linc Bradway. He found in charge of the stable a cheerful red-bearded man of the miner type, who limped as he came out to meet Lincoln.

"Howdy, cowboy," was his laconic greeting.

"Howdy, miner. How come you're dealing with horses?"

"Wal, son, when I had this laig broke I bought out Jeff Smith, an' hyar I am, not doin' so bad either for a miner."

"Say, anything to do with horses is good. I'm from back Nebraska way. Name is Bradway."

"Mine is Bill Headly. Glad to make yore acquaintance."

"Same to you. Bill, I want to buy a horse, and have someone to take care of him while I'm in town. Only he's got to be the best horse in these hills. 'Cause I might be chased!"

"No! Not really? Son, I'd never took you for that kind of a cowboy."

"Well, Bill, I'm not crooked, and if I *am* chased it'll be by men who *are*. Savvy that?"

"Don't savvy exactly, but you sound convincin'. . . . In any case, howsomever, I have not only one, but two horses hyar that can't be beat in the Sweetwater Valley. Just happened I got them. Yestiddy, a cowboy down on his luck—fired off his range—come to town. Red likker an' cyards. You know. An' he sold his horses to me. He's due hyar at ten o'clock to get his money."

"How much?"

"Wal, I shore hate to tell you. Shows me up. But he done it. I'm no horse buyer. I had to borrow the hundred dollars."

"Only one hundred for two good horses? Bill, you are a swindler. . . . But here, take two hundred. I'm buying that cowboy's ponies."

"Without seein' them?" queried Headly, dazzled at the sight of the two greenbacks thrust into his hands.

"I take your word."

"Wal, I took the cowboy's. Let's see—his name? . . . Vince somethin'. But he'll be hyar in a minnit. Set down, Bradway. I'll fetch them out."

Presently the man led out a sorrel, and a white-faced bay. Both were superb, the sorrel having a shade the better of it. But that glossy bay, deep-chested, strong-limbed, would have thrilled any cowboy, even one more critical than Bradway. He decided not to put a hand on either animal until an idea of his had a chance to work out.

"Hyar comes Vince now," spoke up Headly. "Comin' to his funeral! . . . Bradway, wouldn't thet wring yore heart?"

A sturdy, bow-legged cowboy appeared shuffling slowly toward the livery stable, his sombrero in his hand, his towhead bowed.

"Headly, don't mention the sale right off," suggested Linc. How many times had he seen cowboys come or go like this! Grief, shame, despair could not have been better exemplified, not to Linc Bradway's keen eyes. Inexplicably he liked this down-on-his-luck cowboy without ever having seen his face. A moment later, when the young man arrived and showed his face, Linc saw a homely, suntanned young countenance, darkly shadowed by two days' growth of beard.

"Mawnin', Bill. Heah I am, an' I hope to die." . . . Then the speaker espied Linc, who stepped out from behind the horses.

"Howdy, Vince," spoke up Headly. "Meet this young feller who jest called on me. Linc Bradway—Vince— I didn't get yore other handle."

"Vince is enough, I reckon. . . . How do, cowboy. . . . What you lookin' over my horses for?" asked Vince. He was sober, but a little surly.

"Glad to meet you, Vince. I'm a cowboy on the loose. Asked for a horse and Bill here showed me yours. That sorrel is mighty nice. And the bay, well, he'd suit me. . . . Which one do you fancy most?"

"Fancy?—Hell, I raised 'em both from colts. Brick is the best horse on the Sweetwater, bar none. An' Bay is all horse too. Only I could stand to lose him."

"Vince, I just bought both your horses," said Lincoln, quietly.

"Aw! . . . Then it's too late? Bill, I was goin' back on sellin' Brick. I jest couldn't. I'm sober this mawnin'."

"Sorry, Vince. I been paid for them, an' hyar's yore hundred dollars," interposed Headly, regretfully.

Vince's reception of the disaster and the money thrust upon him brought about one of Linc's quick reactions. At that moment he thought he saw through the cowboy. He remembered that Jimmy had been weak, too, and prone to make mistakes and regret them afterward.

"Vince, I happen to have a weakness for good horses, too," he said. "I bought Brick, but I'm giving him back to you."

"What the hell! . . . Givin' him back? . . ." The cowboy burst out incredulously, and though disbelief leaped to his face, so did a dazzling light of hope.

"Straight goods. Just a little present from a flush cowboy to one down on his luck."

"Flush! . . . By thunder! Then you could be the feller who cleaned out Emery's joint last night an' shot thet hatchet-faced McKeever?"

"Yes, Vince, I'm that hombre. Did you happen to be there?"

"No, wuss luck. My Gawd, I'd like to have seen thet mixup. . . . But, what's up yore sleeve? Shore you're flush. You must be a millionaire. An' I savvy what a cowboy can do. I was damn near thet big myself once."

"Vince, there's nothing up my sleeve, as far as you're concerned," replied Lincoln, earnestly. "I felt sorry you had to sell your horses. That you had been fired. And I like your looks."

"Bradway, I shore like yore's. But ain't you got no other reason at all?"

"None, except I'm a lonesome cowboy in a strange country, a long way from home, and I've made enemies."

"Wal, you've made a friend, too. One who'll stick to you till hell freezes over, if you want him." The cowboy's voice shook and there was fire in his blue eyes. "Things happen powerful strange, don't they? I was jest thinkin' downtown, when I heerd about you, how I'd like to meet you. An' it shore was worth-while! . . . But, Bradway, you an' Bill please excuse me for ten minutes. . . . I sold my horses to get money I'd borrowed from a woman. An' I could kill myself runnin' to pay it back!"

Vince hurriedly made off. His earnestness was manifest in his effort, but one could see he had not been used to foot races.

When he disappeared Bill turned to Linc with a

queer expression, which Linc could not quite solve, though he read in it approbation of his conduct over the horse deal, and something that might have been a better understanding of Vince. He did not care to inquire how the ex-miner felt. Again he had stumbled upon an incident, if not fateful, certainly one that was pregnant with possibilities important to him.

"Bill, I wonder who was the woman Vince rushed off to pay so quick?" queried Linc, thoughtfully.

"Wal, it couldn't be no one else but Kit Bandon," returned the livery man. "She stakes cowboys an' shore holds them to strict account. Howsomever, I reckon no cowboy would want to cheat Kit. She's as square as Calamity Jane. Why, any lone rider, or cowboy on a grub line, or tramp, is always welcome at her ranch."

"Stands ace-high with the cowboys?" asked Lincoln, his question an assertion.

"You bet. But Kit an' the cattlemen don't seem to hit it thet way. I reckon because most of them have tried to marry her one time or another."

"Does that cardsharp Emery have the inside track with Miss Bandon?"

"Wal, when she's in town weekends. But out on the range it's another story, so they say. Emery never goes there."

"Just life. Like any other cattle country. Same old things underneath the surface. . . ."

The talk became desultory after that, until they saw Vince returning. The cowboy who approached now might have been someone else, so changed was he. This boy had recaptured his self-respect. He beamed upon Headly, and in his attitude toward Bradway there seemed the birth of something big.

"Pard, if I may call you thet, you'll never know how I feel," he said.

"Gosh, Vince, how come paying some dame fifty bucks can brighten you up so?" asked Linc, casually.

"It wasn't just payin' thet debt. It was endin' somethin', by Gawd, forever!" He spoke with finality and his dignity at the moment permitted of no inquisitiveness. Linc registered that subtle expression in his mind as one to ponder over later.

"Where's your gun, cowboy?" he asked. "Or don't you pack one?"

"Yes, I pack hardware, an' I can use it, too, as I'll bet you discover," Vince replied, spiritedly. "But mine's in hock. I'll get it out somehow."

"You can't trail around with me without being heeled," said Bradway, quietly.

"Am I goin' to trail with you?" the cowboy asked, eagerly.

"Didn't you make an exaggerated statement a little while back about sticking to me?"

"Shore, but thet was more hintin' than sayin'. If you want it straight, no feller I ever met hit me so deep an' hard as you. It was the time, I reckon. Someday, mebbe, I can tell you."

"Vince, you hit me plumb center, too. Part 'cause you were in trouble, but most because you're like an old pard I lost."

"Daid?"

"Yes," returned Linc, looking down. To think of anyone taking Jimmy's place was strange, almost unbelievable. Yet life had to go on and he needed a friend.

"Aw, thet's hell. I'm sorry."

"Before we shake hands let me warn you that trouble and gunplay and blood seem to trail me everywhere."

"All in the day's ride for me! Let me tell you thet I'm a ruined cowboy on this range."

"Ruined? You mean there's no outfit you can ride with any more?"

"I reckon not—thet is, not in the valley. I cain't tell you, pard. . . . Mebbe, some day—"

"Tell me nothing. I don't want to know. I've pulled crazy deals myself. I take you for what you are to me. . . . Let's mosey down the street and reclaim your gun. And you're a pretty ragged cowboy, I notice.

Just about walking on your bare feet. I've done that, too. . . . Bill, take better care of Brick and Bay from now on."

They walked down the street wrapped in an eloquent silence. Linc had an idea this chance meeting might prove to be even more fortunate for him than for Vince. Just before they reached the main thoroughfare, he passed some greenbacks to Vince. "Get your gun out and strap it on. Then meet me in front of that big outfitting store on the corner."

"Would you kick me one in the pants jest to prove this ain't no dream?" asked Vince.

"Cowboy, it'll be a nightmare pronto. Rustle now."

Bradway strolled along, close to the buildings on his side, watching everything that went on in the street with hawk eyes. He halted every little while to back up to a wall and lean there just as though he were in no hurry at all, the better to appraise what was going on. It was a busy street, and it bore evidence that South Pass was the supply center for a wide area. Freighters were unloading. One big wagon was full of kegs which spoke eloquently of the favorite beverage South Pass consumed. The cowboys and chuck wagon he had seen in the early morning were gone. An overland stage was just rolling in from the West, down the dusty hill road, its four leathered horses breathing hard. Several canvas-covered prairie schooners were laboring up the same slope, headed westward on the Oregon Trail. The tall Nebraskan ambled on down to the store. It was a lively corner. Some boys were playing dangerously close to the busy street, and a spirited team hitched to a buckboard came within a few inches of running them down. The youngsters were scrambling on the board sidewalk, and one of them, the oldest evidently, had bent over to pick up something.

"Hey, kid, you're too big to be sprawling in front of horses," said Linc, severely. He made a grab at the youngster, but he dodged and piled headfirst into the three smaller ones and down they went in a heap.

The lad Linc had tried to seize leaped up with amazing agility and whirled as quickly. The cowboy looked into the scarlet face and blazing eyes of a girl dressed in boy's clothes. As if by magic the youngster in gray blouse and blue jeans was transformed into a slim feminine creature, burning with fury.

"What do you mean?" she blazed, swinging a gauntleted hand which just grazed Linc's cheek.

He drew back thunderstruck, staring incredulously, his hand going to his face.

"Oh! a girl—excuse me—miss," faltered the tall cowboy. "I—I thought you were a boy old enough to set these little tykes a better example—" He stopped in confusion as he saw the girl's pretty face with its eyes of blue fire.

"You did—like hob!" she retorted, and her scornful glance raked him up and down. "I'm used to fresh hombres tryin to introduce themselves in this town but I'll thank you, Mr. Cowboy, to keep your hands off me!"

Clinking spurs and quick footsteps announced the presence of Vince, who stepped between the fiery girl and the stammering Nebraskan.

"Whoa girl, what you doin'?" he burst out, in alarm, as he held her.

"Oh, Vince!—Shoot this cowboy for me," she cried.

"Aw!—There's some mistake," exclaimed Vince.

"Mistake, nothing. This—this hombre insulted me. He tried to grab me—" The younger children were standing by, speechless, watching the action. Linc was looking for a hole to fall through.

"Aw, no! Not *this* cowboy."

"Yes, *this* cowboy. You punch him, Vince, if you haven't nerve to shoot him, or I'll get someone else."

"Insulted—*you!* I jest cain't believe that, Lucy. This cowboy is my pardner."

"I told you, didn't I? . . . He—he attacked me—when I was just—just—trying to stop the boys fighting—"

"Attacked you? . . . My Gawd! You must—why, Lordy, he jest ain't—why—"

Suddenly Linc came out of his trance. "Yes, she's right, I did, Vince. It's unforgivable—but I took him—her—for a boy—too close to the street. But what he—I mean she—says about attacking her was only—I just tried to hold her—I mean restrain her. Vince, you'll have to believe me, I don't strike girls even when I think they're—She won't listen to me, Vince. You seem to know the young lady. Tell her I'm sorry for what she says I did."

"He apologizes, Lucy," interposed Vince, most earnestly. "He's my friend, he's not drunk—or one of these—you know—kind of cowboys. . . . Lucy, this is Linc Bradway, from Nebraska. Speak up, Linc, square yoreself."

But Linc had been struck dumb by that name, Lucy—by the remarkable change he noted in the girl's expression.

"Oh, . Vince—did you—did you say—Linc Bradway?" she faltered, her face paling, her eyes growing large and dark.

"Shore I said Linc Bradway," declared Vince, puzzled. "Cain't you folks heah?"

Suddenly the girl's two gauntleted hands seized Linc's arm and she leaned impulsively toward him, gazing pleadingly into his eyes. Lincoln caught his breath. He actually thought she meant to kiss him.

"Linc Bradway? . . ." she breathed. "Oh, what a way for us to meet! . . . Indeed I know you very well. . . . I was Jimmy Weston's girl—Lucy Bandon!"

driving two black horses, climbing the winding
that led to the west. He watched her until she
out of sight. The Nebraskan was deep in thought.
ng along between the brook and the high placer-
d bank Linc looked for a ford. When he found
he crossed the stream and rode along the other
among the willows until he gained the open. The
e was gradual, here and there, indented by gullies
ked with brush and dwarf pine trees. Lincoln took
gzag route up to the road, and from there soon
hed the summit of the Pass. The Pass was a fairly
l saddle, probably four miles wide, stretched from
th to south. Beyond this, outcroppings of rock
ges, strips and thickets of pine, and increasing areas
gray sage led to the low spreading foothills, which
dually reached higher and higher to black-belted
untains that in turn rose to form the base of the
w-clad peaks, glittering in the sun, towering into the
e sky. Southward Lincoln could not see where the
s ended in that direction. But far beyond the un-
lating gray prairie, dark foothills heaved up in the
stance, and tips of white appeared remote and un-
bstantial.

"Big country beyond this Pass," he soliloquized, and
lized that he was eager to get his first glimpse of the
ned Sweetwater Valley. "Well, here I am, forking
horse on the old Oregon Trail. And if I can believe
y eyes, there roll some prairie schooners westward
und! But what's become of Lucy's buckboard?"

He already was half through the Pass without having
ught sight of Lucy Bandon's team of blacks. He lost
erest in the landscape as he wondered how he could
ve missed her. He put Bay from trot to pace to lope,
ding each gait easy, yet ground-gaining, and he
red a moment to delight in his new horse.

Suddenly he swung round a rocky outcropping and
saw Lucy. She had slowed down. Even at a distance
saw her looking back. He raised his hand. Again he
the mounting wave of excitement and emotion that
held him tongue-tied an hour ago. As he gained

Chapter III

Just then one of the ragged boys, a freckled-face imp,
tugged at Linc's coat, and shrilled: "Hey, ya big cowpoke! You spoiled our holdup!"

The Nebraskan, without taking his eyes from the
girl's face, reached into his pocket and gave the lad a
silver dollar. With a whoop the three youthful bandits
ran off.

"Lucy Bandon! Jimmy Weston's girl!" stammered
Lincoln, dismay mingled with his bewilderment. "You
can't be. . . . Excuse me, miss, but I'm sure loco, I
reckon. Jim wrote me about you. I came as soon as
I heard that he—that I— Honest, Lucy, but I'm not
the dumbhead you must think I am."

They stared at each other, oblivious of the gaping
Vince. For Linc it was a profoundly moving moment.
Jimmy Weston's girl—the Lucy he had written about
so eloquently! A slender girl, scarcely eighteen, a pretty
tanned face, paled now, blue eyes set wide apart, dark
with excitement, red lips, sweet and tragic, a small bare
head covered with golden curls, a lithe form typically
western and capable in boy's garb, yet compellingly
feminine—a girl who was clinging to him as though he
were a brother. As Linc looked down at this sweet-
faced girl, he suddenly found himself wishing that she
would cling to him all his life. Mr. Lincoln Bradway

39

of Nebraska was finding it very difficult to keep his wits.

"Lucy! . . . You are the one person I wanted most to meet," he cried.

"Linc! I can say that, too. . . . Jimmy told me all about you. He worshiped you. I've heard a thousand tales about you."

"Poor Jim! . . . Oh, it's hard to hear that. . . . You were engaged to him?"

"No, it never went that far."

"But, you were in love with him?"

"Hardly that. I liked him very much. I—I guess he was in love with me—until— Perhaps I'd have fallen in love with him some day. But, it—it happened, and—"

"You mean he was shot?"

"No, I don't mean that. . . . But I can't talk to you—not here in the street."

Bradway came to his senses. "Forgive me. I could talk to you anywhere. . . . Lucy, I must see you. Please give me an opportunity."

"I want to see you, too. But it won't do here in town. . . . I'm driving out home at once. Alone. Aunt Kit is terribly upset. She is staying here. She sent me home. Please follow me on horseback. West on the trail. That's the road up there. Catch up with me on the hill."

Then she was gone, leaving Lincoln standing there as one in a trance. Vince nudged him. "Say, pard, you'd be easy meat for some gent with shootin' on his mind jest about now. Come out of it."

"Right, Vince. Thanks. I'm damned if I didn't clear forget where I am. But, Lordy! What is it that has happened?"

" 'Pears like a lot. So you are Jim Weston's pard? By golly, this is jest like a story. I knowed Jim, not close, but the same as other cowpokes you meet in town."

"You seem to know Lucy?"

"I should smile, we was always good friends."

"That girl couldn't be—what I almo[st] [ut]tered Linc, as if accusing himself. "W[hat a] suspicious hombre I am! Why Jim nev[er had] an idea what a wonderful person she is[.]"

"Pard, I've no idea what you almo[st but] I'll tell you that Lucy Bandon is as clea[n as] a desert flower—as different from her au[nt] as day is from night," declared Vince, f[eelingly.]

"So Kit Bandon is her aunt!"

"Yep . . . say! Linc, you an' Lucy jest [fell into] each other's arms."

"Nonsense. But it got me. Jim's girl—[his] niece!—she asked me to follow her. We'll [put] a move on. We'll go back to Bill's and sad[dle our] horses. Ride out of town up the brook, ar[ound the] road over the hill. But not together. You t[ake a] couple of miles back. . . . Come, let's rustle."

Vince was out of breath and panting hard whe[n they] reached the livery stable. "Wal—if you—ain't [a] walkin' cowboy!" he gasped. "I'll never—keep up [—] with you—on my feet."

"Fact is, I always could outwalk most any cowbo[y.] But my wind isn't so good—especially here in Sou[th] Pass. Every time I get it back, something happens [to] knock it out of me again."

In a few minutes Linc was mounted on the b[ay, with] saddle and stirrups that fit him. It felt good to hea[r the] creak of leather again. But it wasn't only b[ecause he] was in the saddle again that made him want [to sing] and holler. "Watch me, Vince, and when [I hit the] ridge ahead, you come on. And if you got [eyes keep] them peeled from this moment."

"All right, boss, I shore have eyes. Bu[t what am I] supposed to look for?"

"How do I know, you dumbhead. Look [for any-] thing."

With that none-too-explicit command L[inc rode off] and on across the flat between the slope of [the hill and] the edge of the town. Long before he got [any distance] beyond the last house he espied Lucy, seat[ed] on the buckboard he realized that he was not going to be able to remain calm and self-contained. His object had been to meet this girl simply to learn from her all he could about what had happened to Jim Weston. But that motive had taken second place now to his interest in the girl herself. A few moments later when he reined Bay in abreast of the girl, he still was far from being calm and collected.

"Oh, I thought something might have stopped you," cried the smiling girl on the seat of the buckboard. "And when I did see you at last, I thought you'd never catch me."

"Lucy, I can't tell you what I thought. But, all this seems too—too good to be true," he said as he dismounted and came over, hat in hand, and stood by the front wheel of the rig.

"Isn't it? But it is happening. . . . Oh, Linc, I'm so embarrassed over the way I treated you—down in the village—in front of Vince—"

"I deserve it, Lucy. But I want to see you again—often—there's so much I want to say. How far to your home?"

"Twelve miles from the hill. Half way across the valley."

"Only that far? I can never say all I want to say in twelve miles. And I hope you'll want to say something, too! Won't you stop a while?"

"I have all day to get home. Perhaps it'll take that long for me to—to . . ."

Linc interrupted her gently. "Lucy, I reckon you know why I came out here. I had to come when I heard about him—what they were saying about him. It was a job I have to do. I was going to find out what I could and pay a few visits. . . . I was going to pay a debt and maybe get killed in paying it. I was going to hunt you up and ask some questions. . . ." He paused. "But, Lucy, I never was prepared for anything like, like—"

"Like what?"

"Like you. Of course I knew from Jimmy's letters

that there was a Lucy—a sweet kid. But I hardly took him seriously. I'm afraid my impressions were not flattering to you."

"Jim made you his hero—and I'm afraid you became mine, too," she said simply, gazing straight ahead.

"I'm afraid that I did not appear very heroic in your eyes this morning," he replied.

"I'm terribly ashamed of the way I acted toward you, Linc," said Lucy looking down at the reins she was holding in her hands.

Bradway longed to place his hands over those little hands. He felt himself caught up by an almost irresistible tide. It did not seem to matter any longer that this girl there before him had been Jim's girl, that she was the niece of the Maverick Queen, that she might be connected in some way with his partner's mysterious death, that he knew almost nothing about her except the few references to a girl named Lucy that Jim had made in his letters. Nothing mattered except that, as he watched Lucy's hands twisting and untwisting the reins, he felt a great tenderness for her and a sureness that somehow, someway, their fates were bound together. After a long silence that was broken by the shrill nicker of one of the blacks, Linc spoke.

"Suppose I tell you some things about myself that Jimmy never knew?" said the cowboy softly. And at her smiling eagerness he proceeded. He was twenty-three, but much older than his years. He had been born in Missouri somewhere, and his father, whom he had never seen, had been a brother or cousin to the notorious Cole Younger, the elder, a guerrilla after the war, and later a notorious desperado. In fact, Linc had never known either of his parents. A kindly neighbor named Bradway had raised him, and sent him to school. He had taken Bradway for his name. At fourteen he had been thrown upon the world, which for him meant the cattle range. By the time he was sixteen he had landed in Nebraska. There he had become Jim Weston's partner and there he had ridden the ranges until the news filtered back of Jim's death and he had pulled up stakes and headed for Wyoming.

"It's been a hard life, Lucy. And I have had my share of hard knocks. I've stopped lead a few times, and there are not many bones in my body that haven't been broken by horses. I never was much on drinking, though I would get drunk with the cowpokes on occasions. It was my tough luck when I was eighteen to meet a bad hombre—a gun-slinging half-breed—and kill him on the main street of Abilene, in an even break. That wasn't good for me. It established my status as a killer. Well, I was pretty slick with guns. . . ." He sighed. "Did Jim ever tell you I—I had shot a lot of men?"

"Ten or a dozen, if I remember correctly," she returned, solemnly. "But don't look so blue, Linc. Your fights never bothered me, but your love affairs . . ."

"Lucy! . . . Jimmy must have exaggerated," expostulated Linc. "It wasn't ten or a dozen men I stopped. Not half that many, and I should remember. . . . Lucy, every time I ever drew on a man it was to save my own life. That I swear."

"I'm happy to get that straight. But your hundreds of love affairs!" she rejoined teasingly. "That's a little hard for me to overlook."

"That's even worse. I never had any— Oh, maybe one or two which might or might not have become serious. But there was so little time—so few of the right kind of girls. And I was never keen about the dance-hall women."

"You're very modest. Jimmy said that was one of your charms."

"Lucy, please take me seriously," he begged. "I give you my word. Jim had a fancy for telling tales. And he liked to hear 'em, too. I used to make up affairs just to feed his love of romance."

"Very well, I will take you seriously," she returned, but there was still a gleam of humor in her eyes. "We'll cut off the road here—over to that point where you see the rocks and trees. There's the finest view of Sweetwater Valley that I know of."

As they followed an unused road through the sage to some tall gray rocks and a clump of pines, Linc looked back over the road he had come. Even before they reached the spot Bradway could see that the land fell away sharply. Presently, however, the view was obstructed by the trees. Lucy drew up behind a thicket, where the horses and buckboard were not visible from the road. Lincoln dismounted to tie Bay to a sapling.

"Were you expecting someone?" the girl inquired. "I saw you looking back."

"I told Vince to follow me," he said.

"We'll watch for him. . . . Come. It makes me excited and happy to think of showing you *my* Wyoming."

"Wait a moment, please," said Linc, taking her hand and holding her back. She stared up at him, but did not withdraw her hand. "Now it's your turn to tell me about yourself. That's more important than all the scenery in the world."

"Is it? . . . My story is almost as filled with loneliness as yours. . . . I don't remember any mother, only my aunt. She took me when her sister died. That was in Kentucky. I went to school in Louisville for five years. I was twelve when we came west. In a prairie schooner. Oh, I loved it. . . . First we lived on a ranch near Cheyenne. . . . Then some man followed Kit. . . . She shot him! She's 'most as bad with a gun as you are! She's killed two other men since we came to South Pass several years ago. A gambler and a cattleman."

"Kit Bandon!" exclaimed Lincoln. "That handsome-looking girl a killer?"

"She looks twenty-five, but Aunt Kit is older. You'd better not mention her age to her face."

"Well! . . . I guess there are times when you just have to use a gun," he said. "But enough of Miss Bandon; I want to know more about you."

"There isn't much more. . . . Aunt Kit's a strange woman. But she was always good and loving to me until we came to South Pass. She suddenly got interested in gambling. She really owns the *Leave It,* you know. Then she bought a ranch out on the Sweetwater, and took to cattle raising. Naturally that brought cowboys. I was the only girl around. They seemed to like me. She would have none of that. . . . Then Jimmy came. I met him by accident, same as you, only he wasn't so rude! . . ." Lucy smiled mischievously. "After that we met often enough to get to like each other before Aunt Kit found out. She was terribly angry. She forbade me seeing Jimmy. But I couldn't keep him from waylaying me out on the ranch or there in town. In spite of his feeling for me, though, Jim became as infatuated with Aunt Kit as all the other cowboys were. We quarreled. He took to gambling and drinking. He grew strange and morose, no more the happy-go-lucky cowboy I had grown to like. We made up. I forgave him because he swore not . . . he swore to keep a promise to me. And he broke it. I never saw him again. Soon after that he—he was shot. . . . Sort of a pitiful little story, isn't it?"

"Pitiful and tragic," replied Lincoln, with constricted throat. "Poor Lucy! And poor Jim! If I had only come out here with him! But that's spilled milk now. . . . Thanks for confiding in me, Lucy. Now come. Show me your valley."

She led him between two rocks to the rim of a bluff that sloped precipitously down into a gray gulf.

Bradway, still thinking of Lucy's unhappy story, was not at all prepared for what he saw. The colorful valley seemed to leap up at him, confounding his senses. The girl was watching him, anxious that he share her enthusiasm for her Wyoming.

The scaly slope on which they stood fell away a thousand feet or more to a gray sage floor that spread for miles to the west. A winding green line of trees traced the course of the river which snaked the length of the valley. The stream which here and there glinted in the sunlight must be the Sweetwater. Lincoln followed its meandering course down the valley as far as eyes could see until it became lost in gray-purple obscurity. South of this dim line he knew spread a limitless red desert.

The cowboy brought his gaze back to the rim of the precipice. Beyond the rim stretched leagues and leagues of sage that rolled to the far side of the valley. The western rampart of the vast Sweetwater Valley rose blue-gray and mauve against the distant sky. As far as he could see to north and south the near wall of the valley was broken by rocky capes and bold palisades which cast their deep shadows on the valley floor. There were no trees to soften the stern majesty of the valley wall that stretched before his eyes for perhaps a hundred miles.

At first sight Lincoln had failed to notice several ranches dotting the valley along the Sweetwater directly in his line of vision. A white house stood out distinctly in the midst of a vast green patch; and beyond that, at long intervals, other dark spots and dots indicated other ranches down the valley. On this side of the river thousands of cattle speckled the sage.

The whole effect was magnificent in the extreme. Lincoln was at a loss for words as he stood there in the presence of the girl, who was quietly waiting for him to speak. Almost any locality in the West might have been as vivid and striking. But this valley appealed to him strongly beyond any point inspired by sentiment. Lincoln would have to live in this country for a good while before he could fully appreciate why it silenced and inspired him. But the great open range, bare under the blue sky and bright sun, the winding ribbon of green and silver, the endless carpet of sage, the mosaic of colors, the somber grandeur of the carved escarpments, and the snow-white peaks far beyond, rising like sky specters—all these combined to fill the man who was seeing them for the first time with a deep feeling of loneliness. Long and silently he gazed into that enchanting valley sculptured out of the rugged range. Almost reluctantly he turned away from it to face Lucy's wistful gaze.

"Do you like it?" she asked hesitatingly.

"I feel bewitched," he replied. "As I was looking across that valley I thought what a pity such a beautiful place with such a pretty name must harbor hate, greed, bloodshed!"

"I have thought that often. But it is men, not nature," said Lucy, bitterly.

"Don't blame it all on the men. Women are usually around too, where there's trouble."

"Linc, I should have said women *and* men. God knows, I've no reason to be proud of my sex."

"Lucy, I was just poking fun," protested the cowboy. He already had noted how swift were her changes of mood. She looked happy only when she smiled. And she had not laughed once. "Which ranch is yours?"

"Follow the road straight down. The white ranch house. It's pretty from here, but nothing to brag of down there. Logs and mud and whitewash."

"Have you comfortable quarters?"

"Oh, yes, except in winter, when I almost sit in my open fireplace. It's cold on this range. Fifty below zero sometimes. And colder up here on the Pass. Men have been found frozen to death."

"I'll bet a blizzard here would be hell. . . . Lucy, this sight does me good. It must be wonderful up where that river starts in the mountains."

"Glorious. I've been there twice, the last time in June, just about this time of the month. I didn't want to leave. I wanted to build a cabin and live there always."

"Why?"

"Oh, it had everything I love. Far away, lonesome, only a few Shoshone Indians—elk and deer, moose and antelope tame as cows. Birds and flowers. Meadows of sage and grass—little patches of forest—then the foothills, the belts of black timber, beyond them the great country of rocks and cliffs and canyons. And last, the wonderful peaks, always snow-white."

"Sounds just about ideal. But you didn't mention fish."

"Oh, you are a fisherman, too! I'll bet I can beat

you. The Sweetwater is full of trout up there. Long as your arm, some of them. And fight! . . ."

"Listen, child. The girl doesn't live in all this West who can beat me fishing."

"It's a challenge. Only I haven't much to bet."

"You have all that any man would want to ride a chariot race for."

"You are a new kind of cowboy to me. Pretty speeches. But I like them. . . . But—Oh! I forgot! I forgot!"

"What?" he asked, alarmed by her tone of distress.

"We won't be able to ride together—or go fishing—or anything."

"And why not?"

She was silent a moment, then turned to him, suddenly older, more constrained, with the sweet lips set sternly and her eyes veiled. Suddenly her tone was serious.

"Lincoln, you said this morning that you had come on a rather grim errand. How did you know where to come?"

"Jimmy's letters. I'll let you read them. News of his death. And the stigma left on his name. . . . Jimmy was weak, but he was honest. He couldn't cheat. Drunk or sober he never had a crooked thought. He *might* have been shot in a brawl at a card table. But never for cheating. I'm as sure as I stand here that he was murdered. And I've come out here to find out—to clear his name, at least."

"Jim said if anything happened to him you would come out here and kill everyone who . . ."

"Lucy, what would you think if I allowed Jim's murderer to go scot free?" he demanded.

"Revenge can't bring Jim back."

"No!—But I'd have no self-respect left if I didn't avenge my partner. I grew up in a hard school. I loved Jim. I'll always regret that I didn't come with him. He might be alive today if I had. All I can do now is get even."

"They will kill you," she cried, with a catch in her voice.

"Who are *they?*"

"Emery and his outfit. They'll do it while you sleep."

"Lucy, I don't sleep when someone's gunning for me," he said, quietly.

"But, you have to sleep," she protested. "I'm from the West. I understand. You might be another Wild Bill, as no doubt you really are another Cole Younger. I heard what you did last night. But these men will not meet you openly. They'll assassinate you, Lincoln. There are I don't know how many low-down dogs at Emery's beck and call. They would knife or shoot you for two bits."

Lincoln was amazed by her eloquence, by the dark fire in her eyes and the pallor of her cheeks. "Why do you feel so deeply?" he asked.

"You were Jim's friend and therefore you are mine. I—I don't want you to be killed."

"Well, that makes my life doubly precious," said Bradway. "And it was fairly precious before. . . . But *why* do you think Emery's outfit is on my trail? Because I cleaned him at cards?"

"Oh, it has happened before, with far less reason. . . . Lincoln, I must tell you all I da—all I can. . . . Last night at the hotel, I heard Aunt Kit cursing Emery. They were in her room, which was next to mine. Mc-Keever is being cared for there. He has a broken shoulder. . . . Well, my aunt and Emery had been talking too low for me to tell what they said, until they began to quarrel. Kit said: 'I won't let you shoot Bradway!' and Emery swore: 'You can go to hell, Kit. This cowboy is dangerous. He's got to be put out of the way. The letters he bragged about—from Weston. We can't afford to have him on this range with those letters in his possession. You ought to have sense enough to see that!' and my aunt swore back at him. '. . . I have. And I'll get those letters. You leave Bradway to me. . . .' 'By God!' burst out Emery, in a fury. 'You've cocked your eye at another cowboy. What the hell do you care for Weston or letters or *anything* when there's a handsome new cowboy to tickle your miserable vanity? I tell you we've got to kill Bradway!' "

Lincoln was more concerned with the girl's sweet voice, her earnestness, her beauty, the anxiety which her face betrayed, than with the foreboding conversation which she had overheard and just now repeated.

"So, that's why? . . . Lucy, it might barely have been possible for you to persuade me to run away. But not now."

"And why not now?" she wanted to know.

Linc looked out into the gray-blue void, without seeing any of the features that before had enthralled him. Suddenly he realized what it had cost this western girl to tell him what she had. She had cast her lot with him, a stranger, just as surely as he had already involved his life with hers.

"Lucy, suppose I fell in love with you at first sight?" he asked, simply.

She gave a little cry, and suddenly sat down, as if her limbs had grown weak. Linc expected protestation, even ridicule, anything but silence.

Probably this revelation of his was nothing new to her—a pretty girl in this world of men must be able to read a man's mind.

"Same old story, eh?" he asked.

"Yes, always the same—with cowboys. It seems so easy for a man to say—and do," she replied sadly. "With a girl—it's different."

"I'll admit that it couldn't be as easy for you to fall in love with me as it was for me to fall in love with you. Is it a crime to fall in love, Lucy?"

"I thought you were different," said the girl, looking down at her hands.

"I am a man."

"But you are—you came to kill a man. You—"

"After all, I am only human, Lucy. I have known you only a few hours except for Jim's letters. But is there any reason why I shouldn't fall in love with you?"

"Forgive me, Lincoln. I didn't mean to hurt you. Only it hurts *me* to think—to think you take love so—

so lightly—as lightly as you take a human life. . . .
Even if it *were* true—that—that you care—it will not
keep you from—"

"From what?" he interrupted, turning to lift her erect.
His hands gripped her arms; his sudden intensity
startled her.

"Why, from what a girl hates," she burst out, her
lovely face becoming suffused with red from neck to
temple.

"You don't mean gambling, drinking, or even throwing a gun in self-defense or in a good cause? You
have something else in mind. Tell me! What have
I done or what am I doing that a girl like you hates,
Lucy?" He released her arms and caught the lapels of
her jacket, to draw her closer.

"It wouldn't keep you from her. It didn't keep Jim,"
she returned, with bitterness.

"From whom?" he demanded mercilessly.

"Oh, you know! From *her!*"

"Do you really hate her, Lucy, your aunt?" he
asked gently. "There must be a good reason for a
sweet girl like you to hate another woman."

"Oh, I do—I do! . . . I used to love her. She was
good and kind to me until we came to this wild country.
She can be so lovely. She is so fascinating. No one can
help loving her. . . . But when she took Jimmy—
ruined him—I—I just had to hate her."

"All right. Granted Kit Bandon is an irresistible
woman. *You* can keep me from her. Do you want to?"

She swayed for a moment into his arms then and
her head found his shoulder. But she resisted her weakness and stood back to gaze up at him, tears giving her
eyes a soft and tender light. "Yes, I want to, Linc, more
than anything ever in my life, before. Even more than
I wanted to save Jimmy! . . . But a girl can't give her
trust or her love the way she'd give her glove— Oh,
I feel how it'd be with me. And if you failed me, too,
as he did—that would kill me. . . . Lincoln, I'm so
weak, and she's so strong. She just has to crook her

finger. And the men—she'll want to use you the same way." She had her hands up to her face, crying bitterly.

"You've had a rotten deal, Lucy. But I'm going to try to make up for it. Here you are, my dear. Wipe your tears on this handkerchief, the only white handkerchief I could find in the store this morning. I'm pretty disgusted with myself for upsetting you the way I have. I'm not very clever with girls." To marshal his confused senses he said quickly, "Here, wait, while I go look for Vince."

Lincoln strode away, his thoughts in a whirl. Jimmy must indeed have made this girl believe in him, and her disappointment over the cowboy's dereliction had left her at once defenseless and disillusioned in regard to men. He must not take advantage of her willingness to trust him, at least until he was sure of himself, sure he could do something worthy of her admiration, even—of her love.

Outside the zone of rocks and trees Lincoln scanned the gray expanse back toward South Pass. There was no horseman in sight. Vince probably was loitering along below the crest of the ridge. Hurrying back to Lucy he found her sitting on a low rock ledge staring down into the valley.

"Lucy, have I upset you? Please tell me." Linc was on tenterhooks.

"I'm afraid you have," she said. "You disturb me so I can't think."

"So I'm a disturbing person?"

"You are, indeed."

"Gosh, I didn't know I was as disagreeable as that," he replied ruefully.

"Did I say—disagreeable?" She averted her face and stood up, drawing on her worn gauntlets.

"Lucy, you've been seeing only the dark, hard side of everything," he said, earnestly. "Really there is a brighter one. This is a tough time for you—and for me. Probably things'll grow worse before they can get better. But you're a spunky girl—as you very plainly showed me down in South Pass this morning. You don't have to stay with your aunt if it's hard for you—"

"Oh, Lincoln, somehow you give me hope . . . even if I haven't told you everything—"

"Sure. I savvied that. You have a sense of duty and honor if some other people haven't. Vince is in the same fix. He couldn't tell me much either. Well, you needn't tell me anything you think oughtn't be told. I'll find out what I can for myself. . . . You're no tender-foot. You're a real game western girl. If I had come out here before Jim—before it was too late, I'd have fought his battle and yours. Now I have only yours."

"I—I think I'll go now, Linc—before I make a baby of myself."

"You'll see me again?" he asked, almost pleadingly.

"Yes. Any time and any place. *She* can't stop me this time."

"Of course you ride often?"

"Half the time. We have no cowboys right now. I ride around a good deal, trying to keep track of stock. But it drifts all over the valley."

"Well! A cowgirl! I'll bet you're the real thing. . . . You can meet me without trouble, then. Could you see smoke signals from this point?"

"Yes, easily on clear days."

"Say on the third morning from this. That will be Wednesday. Look for smoke after breakfast. But don't take any risks. . . . I might not be able to come. There's much for me to do."

"I drive Aunt Kit to town every Saturday morning. Usually she sends me back home, like today. Then she comes back on the stage, or with someone, on Monday. So really I lead a free and lonesome life."

"No cowboys waylaying you?" he demanded.

"Oh, that happens. But I have sharp eyes. And the only horse in the valley that can catch me is Vince's Brick."

"Golly, I should have kept him instead of Bay. . . . Well, I'll see you on Wednesday, or if not, then in town next Saturday. It's a long time for me to wait.

I hope you'll know by then whether you—like me or not. But don't worry, I can wait and I can take care of myself. And I've a thousand times more to live for now than ever."

Lucy played with the fringe on one of her gauntlets. The color slowly mounted, leaving her face pink under her tan. "I'll be looking for smoke on Wednesday," she said.

They returned to the buckboard. Lincoln untied the horses while Lucy climbed over the high wheel to take up the reins. Then the Nebraskan's roving eye caught sight of Vince loping his horse along the road. Linc let out a shrill yip, and as he strode from behind a clump of mesquite the cowboy espied him, and turned off the road.

"Wait up a minute, Lucy," called Lincoln, as he watched the cowboy ride swiftly toward them across the sage. "That sorrel is a real horse."

"Brick is a beauty. I've ridden him, Linc," said Lucy. "You know what I'll bet? Vince borrowed money on his horses and you bought them back."

At that moment Vince reined the sorrel before him. Linc greeted him, "Howdy, Vince. Anything on your mind?"

"Wagon just turned off the main road onto this one," replied Vince. Then he doffed his sombrero to Lucy. "Wal, who's got rosy cheeks an' shy eyes? Lucy, I never seen you look so pretty."

"You look sort of pert yourself," she retorted. "Must be the company we keep."

"Lucy, hadn't you better rustle ahead and get out of sight over the hill before someone comes along the road. . . . Good-by. Don't forget!"

"Don't you forget!" she returned, and with a flash of her blue eyes and a wave of her arm, she drove the team into the sage. In a few moments she had reached the road and turned to the left waving a gauntleted hand as the buckboard dipped below the crest of the hill.

The moment Lucy disappeared, Lincoln sat down on a rock and wiped the sweat from his face.

"Vince, my breastbone feels like it had taken a beating, especially on the left side," he said. "I put up a strong front before Lucy, but it was all nerve."

"Pard, down there in South Pass this mawnin' I reckoned you was in one hell of a mess, and I was about to advise you tò pass up this range while you had the mazuma an' a whole skin. But not now! Not after the way Lucy Bandon looked at you!"

"How'd she look at me?"

"Wal, you must be blind. . . . Linc, if Lucy had looked at *me* thet way, a year ago. I wouldn't be a done-for cowboy now."

"The way a girl looks don't mean anything," the Nebraskan protested.

"The hell it don't!"

"Lucy has seen a lot of men thet was no damn good at all. She's had to fight off the whole kit an' caboodle of them. But it sorta looks as though in you she sees one of another breed. An' if she falls turrible in love with you, for the Lord's sake, pard, don't let her down!"

"I won't . . . but you exaggerate—and how about you—you bow-legged little cowpoke! Are you going to help her by not failing *me?* I haven't the deal figured out yet. It's too big, there are too many things I don't know—and which no one seems to want to tell. Lucy knows a lot that she wouldn't tell me, too, but I'll have to find out in my own way. That gambling outfit is as crooked as hell. Kit Bandon seems to be mixed up in it. Lucy suspects it, of course, but *that* is not the big secret—the terrible deal I've got to tackle alone."

"Pard, it's shore turrible," replied Vince, hoarsely, swallowing hard. "But I can't tell you no more. There's somethin' a man owes to himself, though after all you done for me, I feel like a coyote for holdin' back what I know."

"I savvy, pard. Sorry I distressed you," said Bradway, contritely. He would have been blind indeed not to have noticed Vince's deep struggle with himself. "I'm a good judge of cowboys, and despite all you seem to be hinting about, I say you're a man to tie to."

"Much obliged, Linc. Thet'll be about all I need," returned Vince, in great relief. "I'll say you're on the right trail to find out about yore pard. But I wouldn't be surprised if his part in this mystery was little enough. As little as mine— Yet follerin' Jim Weston's trail may lead to somethin' big enough to expose the boss of some operations thet'll stun all Wyomin'."

"Operations? Can those gamblers be the head of a big rustler business?"

"I don't know, pard. Only there's nothin' but two-bit cattle stealin' in this country yet. Thet's all to come. I've a hunch the cattlemen reckon it's comin' an' want to stave it off. Anyway, Linc, I'm with you, an' when the deal busts wide open I'll be in there blastin' away."

"What more could a man ask of his pardner? . . . Let's ride back to town."

It developed that Vince was the kind of comrade who had an instinctive sense of when was the right time to keep silent. They walked their horses across the road, over the hill so as to avoid any oncoming wagons, over ridge and down draw for three miles without conversation. Vince smoked cigarettes and appeared to be doing some pondering himself. As they rode along Linc set his mind to work in earnest, trying to anticipate every possible event which he might be called upon to face. Soon they reached the placer diggings above town, and there Lincoln halted his horse and addressed his companion.

"Vince, listen," he began. "First we'll shut Bill Headly's mouth. Then maybe it'll be better for us not to be seen together too openly. Your job is to loaf around town, or ride out to the valley, just as a good-natured cowboy would do who's on the loose. But be as sharp as a whip—to see, to listen, to spy, to find out everything, especially what angle Emery's outfit will take toward me. Of course we have an idea. You're no fool, Vince, and I know that with none of the local gentry suspecting you, there will be plenty of information you can get for me. I'm counting on you, boy."

"Pard, I'll eat thet job up," replied Vince, grimly. "It's just my kind of a deal. Reckon I'd better not spruce up yet a while, so I'll hold off on buyin' new clothes. Meet you tonight jest after dark at Bill's. So long."

Chapter IV

Bradway dismounted to wait by the jack pines and the brawling brook. Bay, with loose bridle and free of his bit, grazed on the fresh green grass. Lincoln saw several big trout rise in a pool, and was reminded of Lucy's description of the headwaters of the Sweetwater. He supposed that the inhabitants of South Pass, almost to a man, were so greedily bent on earning or stealing some of the lush gold thereabouts that they never thought of fishing. But Linc could think of fishing, even with men seeking to kill him. He had been a woodsboy in Missouri, and it would take an Indian to surprise him.

"This job is going to take everything I've got—maybe more," he told himself, as he stood there by the stream. "I must discount everything, except Lucy. She's scared stiff of me. . . . Of what she might let herself betray. Yet she liked me! . . . If I didn't have such a stubborn streak I'd take her away from here while I have all this money. We could both make a fresh start. But I can't give Jimmy a deal like that, though he'd be the one to advise it. Besides I've never been so keyed up over anything in my life. So hell bent! But what's to be done first? . . . When I walk back into this rotten town, where they all have been bitten by the goldbug,

I've got to be the hardest hombre that ever winked into a gun barrel."

It was late in the afternoon when Linc Bradway rode into Headly's place. He was greeted by the ex-miner in a manner that indicated to him that Vince had said the right things about him. But Linc added his own two cents' worth. And Bill seemed to see things his way.

The street was so crowded at this hour that the Nebraskan felt reasonably safe. Near the Four Corners he ran into Lee.

"Howdy, Colonel," drawled Linc, at the southerner's cordial greeting, and he shook his proffered hand. Then, as Lee appeared anxious to hold him in conversation, the cowboy backed against a store window in order to be able to have a clear view up and down the street.

"I've been looking for you all day," began Lee.

"Well, I made myself kind of scarce," replied Lincoln.

"You showed your good sense. But you'd be wiser still to leave town. I can give you a job down in the valley, Bradway."

"Thanks, Colonel. But I'm through riding the range for a spell. I got a job to do here."

"Bradway, you're looking for someone. You have that restless eye that never stays quiet. I'm a Texan, you know."

"Well, you guessed it, and I'm sure glad you talk so friendly."

"I'd like to be your friend. You won my respect last night, not to say more. Come and have supper with me. We can talk."

"Colonel, that might be a risk to you. I'm expecting gunplay from any quarter any time now."

"Yes, and you'll get it, too, but hardly in the open. . . . Bradway, I'll hunt you up when next I come to town. The job I want you to take is to boss a bunch of range riders. I'm organizing a secret outfit, something like the California Vigilantes. You'd be just the man to lead them."

"Thanks, Colonel. That's mighty interesting. Vigilantes, eh!—What for? There don't appear to be any big rustlers working these parts yet."

"That's all you know, young man," returned Lee, harshly. "At least about western Wyoming. I'd like to give you a responsible position for several reasons. One in particular! Think it over, Bradway. I'll see you next week."

The newcomer remained standing there pondering Lee's information and offer. He might accept it later, when he had settled his deal, and gotten the lay of the land. Lee puzzled him. But there was no doubt about the Texan's forceful and forthright character. Something was rankling in him, you could see that! And he was no man to antagonize, let alone do him wrong. Try as the cowboy might, he could not figure out what particular reason prompted him to offer a stranger such an important job.

Presently Linc approached the little street stand where he had purchased the cigar and made the acquaintance of its engaging young proprietor. This time Lincoln bought two cigars and gave one to the dealer. They stood and chatted a moment.

"Just had a job offered me," said Lincoln. "Rancher named Lee. Know him?"

"Yes. Big cattle buyer from Texas. Stands well here. Like all the rest of the men here he had a go at Kit Bandon. Had a clash with Emery over her. It's my hunch Lee will have to shoot Emery one of these fine days."

"I want to be around," drawled Lincoln. "Bet I've seen a hundred Texans throw guns. . . . By the way, have you heard how McKeever is?"

"Not so well. Lost too much blood before they got old Doc Williamson waked up, and down to the *Leave It*."

"So you've a doctor here? Reckon I'll look him up. Where'll I find him?"

"Doc's shingle is around the corner there—over the store. Side stairway."

A few minutes later Linc located the doctor's hand-painted sign and climbed up to find the office. It appeared to be part of a loft, and not any too spacious for the heavy ponderous man who occupied it.

"Good day, sir. Are you Dr. Williamson?" asked Linc.

"I am that, worse luck. What can I do for you?" replied the doctor. He had a heavy countenance, lighted by cavernous eyes and equipped with a bulbous red nose. "Strikes me you appear a pretty healthy cowboy."

"Doc, how's that gambler gent I shot—Mac Somebody?" asked Lincoln.

"So, you're the possible accessory after the fact. . . . McKeever is not a very robust man. You gave him a compound fracture of the shoulder joint. Not a bad injury, but he won't provoke you or anyone else again for some time to come."

"Gosh! So I busted his shoulder? I must be losing my eyesight. I aimed to break his arm. . . . But, Doc, that wasn't what I called for. How'd you like to make a hundred dollars?"

"Young man, there's very little in this sorry town I wouldn't do for that much—inside or out of my profession."

"Do you remember when Jimmy Weston was shot here in South Pass?"

"Yes. I keep track of deaths. We don't have any births. Ha! Ha! . . . Weston was killed something over two months ago. I have the date."

"Do you know where he's buried?"

"I could find his grave for you. I know the fellow who buried him."

"Doc, get that fellow to—to dig Weston up—and you find out if he was shot with a gun like this," said Lincoln, and he produced the little derringer.

"It's a strange request, cowboy," returned the doctor, stroking his beard. "But I'll do it for the sum offered—in advance. You'll excuse me. Here in South Pass people seem to neglect a physician's bills—also the unimportant fact that he has to live as well as anybody else."

"Certainly, Doctor. Here you are. When can I call for your report?"

"By this time tomorrow I'll have the job done."

Lincoln left the office and made his way down to the street again, feeling a little sick. But he had to know! He couldn't afford to leave any possible clue untried.

The hour was sunset, when nature should be at her best, but the little heap of shacks and houses separated by their sprawling, tawdry street appeared an eyesore in a landscape of exceeding loveliness. The sage hills were gold, and the white peaks glowed with a rosy effulgence. In the west a purple mountain rose somberly against the golden rays of the sun. Bradway stood idly against the wooden wall of a building and turned his attention to the pedestrians. It amazed him, the number of men who passed before him, all intent on something. As he watched them the westbound stage rolled by with a full complement of passengers. Two eager-faced young women peered out of one of the small windows. What errand, he wondered, could be bringing them to South Pass! For all he could determine, not one passerby was paying any attention to him.

Presently Lincoln turned the corner of the street, and set out on a roundabout way to his lodgings. He reached his little room without meeting anyone; here he leisurely washed, shaved, and changed his shirt and scarf. He also buckled on a second gun. He disliked the weight of this extra weapon, but he might need it, and it might make some trigger-happy hombre think twice before starting anything. On the way out he encountered his landlady.

"Say, cowboy, you don't look very happy," she said, dryly. "Don't know as I blame you."

"Well, the fact is, I don't feel happy, though I reckon I ought to. . . . Hope you're not going to turn me out."

"Not me. I've kinda taken a fancy to you. It's all right with me if you shoot up the town, so long as you don't do it here. . . . Did you really win ten thousand dollars at Emery's last night like they say?"

"Nope. But I won some."

"You look mighty sharp-eyed and pert. Cowboys usually get drunk after makin' a lot of money. Easy come, easy go. I'm glad you're different."

"How'd you hear about my little party last night?" inquired Lincoln, curiously.

"At the store where I deal."

"Reckon I'm a pretty low-down cowboy, eh?"

"I didn't hear that, and I don't believe anyone thinks it."

"Thanks, lady, I kinda like you, too. Good night."

It was almost dark when Lincoln stepped into the street. He went first to the Chinese resturant for his supper. Vince was there eating at the little counter but he appeared not to notice Lincoln. Three other men sat singly at tables. Vince did not linger long after Lincoln entered, but as he passed by he gave the Nebraskan a glance of grim intelligence. It was enough to cause Linc to make haste with his own supper.

Linc started down the street, suddenly to be startled by Vince appearing apparently from behind a board fence.

"Hey, don't do that!" he said nervously, his arm relaxing. "I might have plugged you."

"Like Wild Bill, huh? He killed two of his friends thet way, comin' around corners. One was reachin' for a cigar an' the other pullin' out his handkerchief. . . . But you was lookin' for me, shore?"

"Yes, but not popping out of nowhere like that. . . . What's on your mind?"

"Pard, the opposition, whoever in the hell they are, have made the first move. They figure you're like all cowboys. You cain't stay from cyard games while you've got money. An' *if* you stay away Kit Bandon will lure you back. Reckon they want yore money first an' then yore life."

"Kit Bandon doesn't want me shot—not right away,

at least," murmured Lincoln, thoughtfully. "Lucy heard her quarreling with Emery about that very thing."

"Wal, mebbe the Queen has some particular reason to want you alive for a spell. Don't trust thet dame, pard, even if she gets stuck on you, which she shore will. Anyway, you're slated to buck the tiger again. An' a gun-slinger from Atlantic, the other minin' town, is heah to beat you to a gun."

"Vince, it strikes me that if this is true Emery isn't being very smart. That's a poor way to try to get rid of me."

"What the hell does he care? He'd try every chance 'cept that of meetin' you himself. South Pass isn't old enough yet to have its eyeteeth cut. There's never been a real gunman heah yet, onless you're him. An' I've a hunch you are. Thet gamblin' outfit could hire men to kill for two bits, let alone inflamin' them with the idee of big money."

"Reckon my deal is to see them first," muttered Lincoln.

"Wal, so long as you're hell bent in goin' ahead with yore deal, another crack at them will make you all the stronger. But I want to be there when it comes off. You can gamble on this, pard. There'll be one or more of thet outfit hanging' back somewhere, aimin' to plug you from where it's safe."

"How'd you get this information?"

"Bill tipped me off first. Thet hombre from Atlantic rode over hossback. Answers to the handle Gun Haskel. Funny, but they do call names appropriate. Wal, he was a big whiskered gent, double loaded with artillery, an' Bill said he was a loud-mouthed feller who made no bones of claimin' he was sent for to put some slick cowboy out of the way. Then I saw Haskel in the Gold Bar Hotel: I followed him in an' out of three other saloons. He wasn't drinkin' none or shootin' off his lip. I reckon he's the makin's of a hard customer. So I rustled to the Chink's place, hopin' to see you there. Now I figger thet Haskel had his orders even before he got heah."

"Wonder what his plan is?"

"Easy as pie to figger. Fust locate you—size you up—insult you or somethin' accordin' to the lay of the ground, an' then set across from you in thet cyard game at Emery's."

"Vince, you're not so slow. You'll be a mighty helpful pard, especially if you can handle that gun."

"Say, Brad, I'll bet you I can beat you shootin' at jack rabbits an' coyotes."

"I never shoot at them unless they're running. But we're talking about coyotes who'll be trying to beat you to a gun."

"Wal, I cain't beat *you* there. All the same I'll bet I give a good account of myself."

"We've got the cards. Let's play. Keep a ways ahead of me. Go in Emery's place and look around. If you locate Haskel, or any other suspicious hombre, be in sight when I step in. If you're not in sight, I won't look for action pronto."

"I savvy, pard. An' it'll be my particular job to bore any hombre who acts queer behind yore back."

Linc watched his friend trudge off in the direction of the *Leave It*. Then the Nebraskan, slowly following him down the center of the street—which he shared with many other pedestrians who had been crowded off the narrow board sidewalk—saw Vince saunter through the wide portal of Emery's brightly lighted emporium of cards and rum. He, himself, passed on down the street to where it turned up the hill, waited on the corner for a while, then crossed to the other side and faced back.

This deliberate hunting for trouble was a new experience for him. But his mood, usually cool, began to take on a feeling of excitement. As he stepped into the bright, garish hall, Vince stalked past him. Out of the corner of his mouth he whispered: "Rustle back!"

At the same instant he became aware of a white figure standing at the foot of a stairway just to the right of the entrance. Kit Bandon ran to catch his arm, her usually florid face as white as her dress.

"Linc Bradway—Wait! Don't go in there. Come with me!"

Steeled to draw a gun and kill an enemy, Bradway felt helpless before the compelling power of this beautiful woman. She drew her bare arm under his, and pulling him close to her fragrant and bewildering person, almost dragged him up the narrow stairway. Lincoln felt sure that an intense sincerity actuated Kit Bandon. She simply could not be leading him to slaughter.

The ceiling above the landing was so low that Lincoln had to bend his head. There was an open door leading into a little parlor where a lamp under a colored shade gave a subdued rosy light. Kit Bandon drew the bewildered cowboy into this room and closed the door behind her.

Then for the first time Linc turned to look at her. The white gown augmented her lush beauty. He caught a glint of diamonds. But the Nebraskan was only half conscious of these details; it was her face that transfixed him. He had never looked into such a passionate and alluring face as the Maverick Queen's. But in the dark, soft beauty of her eyes he could see both fear and courage reflected. As she stood before him in that little room, Linc became aware that a red mark marred the whiteness of her forehead.

The cowboy pointed toward the ugly welt. Then he asked: "Who did that?"

"Emery. Just a few moments ago. He knocked me down—on your account." The woman paused to note the effect of this surprising announcement on Bradway.

"Why?"

"I had spoiled—his plans. . . . He accused me—of falling in love—with you. . . . I admitted it—laughed in his face."

"What plans of his?"

"He sent for Gun Haskel—to meet you. But his original plan—was to have you slugged—at the card table—robbed and murdered."

"Why are you telling me all of this, Miss Bandon?" the Nebraskan demanded.

"Because—because you are a man, Linc Bradway. I've met many men in my time, but none who had ever made me forget my own self-interests in favor of yours. Men are cheap out this way—but they'll have to kill me first before they get at you."

Lincoln had no doubt of the truth of her statements. She radiated it. There was something damnably false about her, yet he knew that this time she was telling the truth.

"But you can't stop it for long."

"I could—if you'll go out to my ranch with me. The gamblers swear you can't keep away from cards. They bank on that. But even if they're wrong, Haskel will force a meeting."

"Lady, he won't have to force it."

"Don't call me that," she cried.

"Very well, *Miss* Bandon," he replied with a smile.

"That's better, but I'd prefer Kit."

"Was your motive in dragging me up here wholly unselfish?"

"I'll say not. It was one for you and two for me."

"All right. What are the two?"

"You're the only—decent man I've met out here since I came. . . . And I—I like you. . . . The other thing concerns those letters you said you got from Jimmy Weston."

Lincoln studied her, through eyes that were expressionless. Her eyes, wide and dark, seemed to search his very soul. Whatever the varied emotions were that moved her at this moment, the dominant one was terror. This fear seemed so all-engrossing that this once it prevented her infallible woman's intuition from reading his mind. He was thinking that once Jimmy Weston had learned her secret and his learning it had cost him his life. He was thinking, too, that some day he, also, would learn her secret and that her life, not his, would be forfeit.

"Yes, I have Jimmy's letters," admitted Lincoln,

warily, playing for time. He wanted to learn all that he possibly could before this keen woman divined that there was nothing in Jimmy's letters that might endanger her.

"What did he—he write about me?" she whispered. Her sultry smile could not conceal her intenseness as she leaned close to Linc and caught his sleeves between hands that trembled.

"Not so much—about you," replied the cowboy slowly. "He admired you, ma'am, but most he seemed to say in his letters was about a girl he liked."

"Was her name Lucy?"

"Yes."

"Did he tell you—I had wronged him?"

"Why, yes, ma'am. He said you had queered him with her—and he was going to get even—said he had to be yellow . . ."

"Weston told me that, but he didn't—live—long—enough," returned Kit, huskily. Suddenly, without warning, Kit Bandon threw her white arms about the cowboy's neck. It was at once a gesture of abandon and, as Linc felt, of relief. It was as though she had been released from a fearful strain. Was it possible that after all she had read his mind? Did she realize somehow that whatever she had feared now would never come to pass? That Weston had never betrayed her?

"Kit, I don't savvy. . . . Still, you can hardly have cause to—to—"

"Haven't I, though?" she interrupted, with a deep-throated laugh, and she raised a face, while wet with tears, that was almost radiant with relief and sudden freedom from anxiety. But she kept her arms about his neck. "Linc, it's all right now. I thought Weston had made you hate me. . . . You don't, do you?"

"A man would find it mighty difficult—hating you," he said haltingly. Any man would find it mighty difficult, as Linc, himself, had said, hanging on to his reason while this amazing creature was embracing him with such abandon.

"Then—kiss me," she whispered.

It was as if fire had taken the place of blood in his veins. His knees seemed to have turned to water. Still he released himself from her arms. Afterward he was never able to recall where he found the strength to resist those enticing lips, those hungry arms. But resist them he did.

"That'll be about all—Kit," he said, hoarsely.

"But it was a great deal, wasn't it?" she replied, softly. "Linc, will you come out to my ranch?"

"What for?" he parried.

"To get away from this deal to put you out of the way."

"I can't do that, Kit. I'm not the kind to run from anyone."

"Then meet this Haskel. Outside in the street. . . . You don't have any fear for yourself—do you?"

"Hardly."

"Haskel is a notoriety-seeking trigger-happy lout," she went on, with contempt in her tone. "He has been in shooting scrapes. But to meet you in an even break he knows would be suicide. . . . I dared Emery to meet you like a man."

"You did? . . . Kit Bandon, you're beyond me," exclaimed Lincoln, half-admiringly.

"I'm what you would call a fickle woman," she said, with her dazzling smile. "But I tell you I never before met a cowboy like you. Or such a really dangerous man . . . that I could love!"

"Listen, lady. Before you start winding me around your little finger, as you must have done with many a man, including Jimmy Weston, I can save you some time and trouble. I just don't rope easy, Kit."

"I'm not trying to. I'm in earnest. When I fall for a man I have the courage to say so. What's wrong about that? You don't believe me? I don't care. It's true. It's in me to move mountains for the man I love. I don't trust myself any more where you are concerned."

"What do you mean?" asked Lincoln.

"I've saved your life twice already. Oh, yes, I have!

Usually I don't go out of my way to save the lives of strangers. . . . Bradway, if this thing is honest, if it's not just infatuation, such as I've felt for a hundred cowboys, then I'm a woman come into her own. And I'd destroy these black-hearted men to save you. I'd be like that ancient woman Semiramis, who burned down cities and fought battles for the man she loved."

"Kit, I'd be glad for you to turn your back on Emery and his kind. But leave out the Semiramis part of it."

"Cowboy, I'm spoiled. I've never had to plead for any man's favor!"

"Favor? That's an elastic term. If you mean love, which seems preposterous, then I'm sorry, but you're out of luck."

"Linc Bradway!" she cried, with a passion that amazed him. This woman was a tigress. Again she threw herself upon him, but this time Linc coolly took her arms from about his neck, and stepped back.

"Kit, please don't make a damn fool of yourself nor of me either. You've had your little scene, as you must have many a time before. You've only seen me twice—only been with me once. I'm one cowboy who don't tie easy, don't fool easy and don't kill easy. Don't make me think any worse of you, than you are."

"No man would dare say so if he did think it." Her voice, which a moment ago had been so warm, was now cold with the anger of the woman scorned.

"I'd tell you, if I believed that."

"Then I'd kill you."

"You couldn't."

She had suffered a repulse, obviously something wholly unprecedented in her experience. Yet she fought down the anger that possessed her, for the sake of her self-respect, perhaps even because she loved this man who had resisted all her blandishments.

"You will make me *love* you," she cried, almost desperately.

"Kit, I won't make you do anything but behave reasonably," he declared, soberly. "Let's get this over.

Thanks for keeping me from butting into more than I'd figured on."

"What are you going to do?"

"First look up this man Haskel."

"That suits me. I want to see you meet him, but not inside here. Let me go down with you. Even these dogs wouldn't shoot you while you're with me." She opened the door and went out on the landing. It struck Linc that Emery's place was unusually quiet. Kit looked down over the banisters, then she motioned Lincoln to come out.

The Nebraskan followed Kit Bandon as far as the landing. Letting go with a shrill cowboy yell, so harsh and earsplitting that it silenced the hum below, Lincoln vaulted the stair railing, to land on the floor of the flimsily-built house with a jar that shook the glasses off the shelves behind the bar.

As he stalked toward the alcove there was not a movement among the dozen or more men present, except the furtive glances of their eyes. There were five at Emery's table, including a burly-shouldered, heavy-whiskered individual, who sat across from a vacant chair. Emery's white hands dropped flat on his cards, no doubt to conceal their shaking. Two miners and a well-dressed man, evidently a traveler, completed the quintet.

Lincoln waved a greeting with a quick left hand. His right appeared tense at his hip. "You fellows are in bad company," he said curtly. "Don't you know it?"

Vince suddenly appeared staggering through the alcove, giving a realistic performance as a drunken cowboy.

"Whas goin' on in here?" he asked, and he lurched to a point behind Emery, where he backed against the wall.

The younger of the two miners, thick-browed and hard-featured, spoke up: "Cowboy, it's none of yore bizness unless you want to set in with us."

The traveler, paling, pocketed the little money before

him and rose hurriedly. "Gentlemen, I'm afraid this is no place for me."

He went out amid a tense silence. Linc broke it by pointing to the bewhiskered man and saying, "Emery, is this big clown your man Haskel?"

"Yes, that's Gun Haskel," replied Emery, in a low, uncomfortable tone.

"You looking for me, *Gun* Haskel, by any chance?" demanded Lincoln, looking squarely at the badman from Atlantic.

"Who're you?" snarled the other.

"I'm Linc Bradway. Does that mean anything to you?"

"Nothin' at all. Never heard of you till today."

"Ever been in Dodge or Hays City or Abiline?" queried the cowboy.

"Nope. I hail from Montana."

"Well, if you ever had seen one of those towns you'd have thought twice before riding over here to scare decent folks with your little peashooter."

That taunt stiffened Haskel. He fastened his dubious gaze upon Emery, and failing to get whatever assurance he might have expected from that worthy, he slammed down his cards. "Bradway, I was lookin' for you, but you don't 'pear to be the little runt of a hell-bent cowboy Emery here made you out to be."

"That's your tough luck! What did you want with me?"

"Wal, in particular I wanted some of yore game."

"Not with guns!"

"Fact is, I heerd you was a hot gambler who'd won a big stake. An' I was layin' to git my share of it."

"You're a liar! You bragged in every saloon in town of what you had ridden in here to do. Everybody in South Pass knows it. And now you're suddenly not so keen for gunplay as you thought you were. Could it be you're yellow, *Gun* Haskel?"

"Is thet so?" blustered Haskel. He did not like the situation. Probably the last thing he wanted was to be

bearded in this den and taunted by some cowboy who
had been misrepresented to him.

"Yes, it's so. I know your kind," flashed Bradway.
"You're one of these cheap fourflushers, Gun Haskel?—What a joke! Do you pack a gun? Or do you
carry a little toy pistol like your cheating cardsharp
Emery here?"

The giant let out a rather hollow laugh and looked
around to see how the crowd was taking it. He was
caught in a trap. Perhaps it was not so much cowardice
as anger that inhibited him.

"No, I ain't packin' any toy pistol," he muttered,
and his right hand edged slowly off the table.

"Pull it out if you're game!" the Nebraskan demanded, suddenly taut as a wire.

Haskel did not react to that demand. His hand came
away from his hip. Bradway waited a long moment,
then he relaxed.

"Haskel, you might be a cut above the low-down
dirty job they imposed upon you," said Linc. "But if
they fooled you, that's no excuse. I called you and you
crawled. You're smart enough to save your life. But
you're stupid to mix with this rattlesnake outfit here.
You'll be hooted out of every saloon in this town, and
given the laugh when you get home. But if that's the
way you want it, why that's the way you can have it."

Lincoln backed out through the alcove into the barroom which was now comparatively empty. As he
passed through the barroom, Haskel could be heard
pounding the table and bellowing at Emery. The
Atlantic gunman was being answered by the taunts of
the gamblers. Kit Bandon stood at the foot of the
stairs. She met Lincoln at the door with a smile and
look that almost any man but the Nebraskan would
have given all he owned to receive. It was plain to see
that she certainly had expected him to return through
the alcove alive.

"Linc, it was as good as a show. Only why didn't
you bore him? You'll have to eventually. They'll nag

and egg him on to a draw or fill him with rum until he goes after you. Come with me."

"No. I've got to walk the street."

"All right. I'll walk with you."

"My God, what manner of woman are you anyway?" cried Bradway in amazement. "Can't you lock yourself in your room and go to bed?"

"Me go to bed! . . . Linc Bradway, that's funny. I wouldn't miss seeing you shoot that fool's white liver out for anything. And wild horses couldn't keep me from being here when you call Emery."

Lincoln stalked out into the street, in a hurry to escape from the Maverick Queen's distracting person and speech. This woman was a revelation to him. It began to seem as if she had a man's nerve and courage in a woman's form.

The crowd in front of the *Leave It* opened to let the cowboy through. He felt aware of a multitude of eyes, as he began his stalk up and down the street. This was the custom of the West. And the public always favored the man who waited for his enemy.

In a quarter of an hour practically all of South Pass knew there was a fight imminent. The stream of pedestrians passing Emery's gaudy door thinned out and finally ceased; watchers lined up on each side of the street at a safe distance.

As soon as Bradway had passed by the *Leave It* he crossed to the opposite side of the wide street, where fewer lights permitted deeper patches of shadow. His alert eye had caught the opening of a door on the little balcony above the *Leave It* doorway. It remained open though no one appeared. From that moment Lincoln shortened his promenade so that he could keep his eyes on the second floor of Emery's saloon.

He was therefore prepared for the muffled bang of a gun and to see a man stagger out on the balcony. His hands were upraised. From one of them dropped a rifle that clanged to the street below, and after it hurtled the body of its late owner, landing like a sack of potatoes on the sidewalk.

Hoarse cries rose from the spectators on the other side of the street. No doubt they believed the motionless body to be that of Gun Haskel, but it was not. It was Bradway's calculation that one of Emery's henchmen had stolen aloft to the upper floor, where he had stood back in the dark with a rifle. Vince had accounted for him. The cowboy's boast had been justified.

Outside the saloon the crowd suddenly became quiet, and no one moved. But inside loud, furious voices and taunting laughs were evidence that they still were goading Haskel. They were driving him to fierce resentment, to rum, and therefore to his death.

Suddenly the white form of Kit Bandon emerged from the door. She stood in the bright glare of the light searching for someone in the shadows, presenting a striking picture, wholly out of keeping with the place and the hour. She waved a white handkerchief down the street. She might have seen Linc standing erect against the shadowy building. Could she be warning him?

Suddenly the Nebraskan saw her step aside from the lighted doorway just as the giant Haskel came plunging out across the walk. His coat was missing; his shaggy bearded head was lowered, and he had a gun in each hand.

"Haskel! Better go back! If you're raring to shoot someone make it that snake Emery!" called out Bradway from the sidewalk. His warning voice was cool but insistent. He had no stomach for shooting down this rum-crazed man who had been goaded to frenzy by Emery and his friends.

Haskel stumbled over the prostrate body on the walk and kicked the rifle into the street.

"Whar are you, cowboy?" roared the giant.

The swift clatter of boots on the wooden walk proved that not all of the watchers had the nerve to see the meeting through.

"Far enough, Haskel!" Lincoln warned. His gun glinted in the light of a store window.

The giant gave no heed to Linc's shout of warning. He sighted his adversary, and lurched across the dusty street, both guns swinging to cover the motionless Nebraskan.

"Nothin' agin' you, cowboy, 'cept yore sharp tongue. But I'm aimin' to kill you. . . ."

Two shots going off almost together, halted Haskel's stumbling advance. He uttered a loud yell of pain and dismay. His guns fell on each side of him, exploding as they struck the ground; clapping his hands to his big paunch he sank to his knees, swayed and slowly collapsed a few yards from the sidewalk.

Bradway ran quickly to where the bearded giant lay and bent over him.

"Come here, somebody," he shouted to the line of watchers. "Anybody who has the nerve!"

This taunt brought two bystanders running into the street. One was a young rider in boots and spurs, the other well-dressed traveler who had left the poker game at Lincoln's suggestion.

"Haskel . . . *Haskel!*" cried Linc, bending over the giant. But there was no answer. "You're bored clean through. No chance! . . . Did Emery put you up to this?"

The giant's ox eyes rolled, and his beard and chin wobbled from side to side as Linc tried to lift him to a sitting position.

"Sealover . . . came after—me . . . offered me—thousand . . . Emery's—hand—back . . ."

Haskel's mouth remained open, but he said no more. His clutching hands fell away from his big belly, allowing his insides to spill out upon the street.

"Men, you heard?" queried Lincoln, of the two beside him.

"Wal, we shore did," replied the cowboy. The other witness nodded his head, while he mopped his brow.

As Bradway straightened to face about, Kit Bandon came hurrying into the street. Behind her were some of the *Leave It* customers. Reaching the group, the Maverick Queen looked down upon the dying man. She held her white dress away from the blood-soaked dust. Haskel presented a horrible sight at which most women would have fainted but the face of this incredible woman was without expression. Linc lowered the body of the dead man to the street, arose and started striding across to the door of the *Leave It*. With a sudden cry Kit caught his arm, only to be shaken off. She had to run to keep up with him, holding on to his sleeve, then his pocket, while all the time she talked excitedly.

"Awful mess you made of him. Why'd you shoot him in the belly? Oh, I savvy! Wanted to ask him something. I saw you. What'd he say? . . . Linc, I had nothing to do with this dead man who was shot off the balcony. You have to believe me, Linc. *You* have a dark horse, Mr. Bradway! . . . You'll need him more and more! Emery will be worse than ever *unless you kill him!*"

This last she whispered, close at Lincoln's side. But the Nebraskan did not seem to hear. All of his faculties were intent on the next move in this brutal drama.

Emery, with half a dozen other men, one of them a white-aproned bartender, stood under the bright light, in a half-circle. The gambler's eyes burned out of a face that was ash white. As he saw Bradway advancing with Kit clinging to his arm he backed hurriedly toward the door, only to bump into one of the men, who promptly shoved him forward. Linc saw that the man behind Emery was Vince. Now it was too late for the gambler to get away. He probably realized he might be the next victim, but his jeaous rage had overcome his terror. His eyes, blazing into hatred, were upon the woman and not the man.

"Bandon, let go of that cowboy," he shouted, and his hard tone implied an accustomed mastery over her. As least, she obeyed him. "Anyone would think to see you hanging on to that stranger, that you were on his side."

"I am, but he'll never believe me," she retorted. "He's one cowboy against this whole cut-throat outfit. You see: I *told* you."

"Shut up, you man-crazy hellcat!" There was murder in his low voice. Then Bradway confronted him, gun still smoking, over the dead man on the sidewalk. The Nebraskan touched the prostrate figure with the toe of his boot; but he did not lower his eyes from those of the man before him.

"Is this man Sealover?" he asked.

"No. His name is Mike something or other. . . . Whatever he had in mind he was on his own."

"Yes, and you'll claim that Sealover rode over to Atlantic after Haskel on his own, too," sneered Linc, shaking himself free from the woman's clinging arm. "But no use to lie. Haskel told me *you* were behind this. I have two witnesses to his statement. An' they're right here."

With a sweep of his gun Lincoln indicated the cowboy and the traveler who had left the spot where Haskel had fallen and now stood on the sidewalk. It was the cowboy who spoke:

"Thet's true, Mr. Emery. I heard him."

The traveler, pale of face, and obviously reluctant to be drawn into the vortex of this fight, nevertheless corroborated the cowboy's testimony.

Emery met this proof of his implication with a gambler's nerve. He barely glanced in the direction of the two witnesses, then turned again toward the Maverick Queen, his voice charged with sarcastic politeness.

"*Miss* Bandon, if *you* step in line with these two witnesses I suppose Bradway will force me to meet him. In that case I'll ask for time to give him a little information he will be glad to know about *you*."

A blow in her face could hardly have had more effect upon Kit Bandon than the gambler's veiled threat. For an instant the smooth beauty of her white face seemed to shrivel. Suddenly she looked old. Then the spasm of sheer terror passed and she was herself again.

"Jess, I didn't hear what Haskel said," she said, sharply. "My interest in this cowboy was only in fair play. You know me."

"Ha! I should say I do!" snarled Emery—"where cowboys are concerned. . . ."

Bradway interrupted. "See here, Emery! Leave the woman out of this. She had absolutely nothing to do with it. . . . Threatening and browbeating a woman who seems to be in your power isn't going to save you from answering to me. Emery, you slimy, yellow snake, your hand is called. . . . But for one thing—just one thing— I'd bore you where you stand."

"Just one thing I suppose I'm to be grateful for?" snarled Emery sarcastically. "Could it be, by any chance—that one thing might be this frail and lovely creature who seems to have fallen for another cowboy?" In his slight gesture toward Kit Bandon he clearly intimated a contempt that matched his speech.

"No!" roared Bradway. "That one thing is *to see you hanged!"*

The gambler stared. His amazement overpowered all his other emotions. Hanging had not yet come as far west as South Pass. Emery tried to step back from the tall Nebraskan, but Vince pushed him forward again.

"Bradway—you must be crazy," he declared, uneasily.

"Yeah?—Stretching hemp may seem farfetched to you, but I've a hunch I'm going to live to see you do it."

"Who's going to do it?" blustered the gambler; yet for all his effort he seemed shaken by the cowboy's calm conviction.

"That's one you can ask yourself," replied Bradway, "and I'll be glad to help you find the answer." Wheeling abruptly Linc slipped into the shadow beyond the lighted doorway and strode swiftly away behind the crowd that had gathered. Knowing Vince would follow, he made straight for the livery stable. Headly was not in his little office, but the door was open and a rickety armchair stood on the veranda outside. Lincoln sank into it, meaning to wait a short while for Vince, then backtrack to his lodging.

It was too soon for the inevitable feeling of sickness and reaction that always followed the killing of a man. Excitement and anger still gripped him. He smoked a cigarette and sought some semblance of calmness.

"Let's see. What came off?" he soliloquized, and reviewed the swift moving events of that evening. "Got by lucky. Had to force the action—and it worked! These low-down hombres have been used to having their own way in making their own deals work out. . . . Still, I was lucky—in more ways than one. It wouldn't have come off so well without Vince there to back me up. . . ."

But was he any nearer a solution to his problem? It did not seem so. The plot to get rid of Emery by fair means or foul had failed so far. South Pass would be agog over this latest development. The gambler had more guts than Linc had given him credit for. And what was his sinister hold on Kit Bandon? She was unquestionably guilty also. But of what? Emery knew, but was he the only one who did? Lincoln could not kill him until he, too, knew the truth about her. The belief slowly established itself in his groping mind that both Emery and Kit Bandon were connected with Jimmy Weston's death. She evidently was a person of fiercely changing moods. It was easy to see that she hated Emery. But she might have loved him once, might still be allied with him in carrying out his shady deals. But that she loved him no longer, he was certain. Had she not suggested that Bradway kill him? Dead men could tell no tales of past events. Evidently she would feel more secure with the gambler out of the way.

A dark form appeared coming down the street! He could not mistake that awkward horseman's gait. Presently Vince arrived out of breath. It was too dark to see the expression on his face.

"Linc! Heah you are. . . . My Gawd, I had one stiff drink, but it ain't done me no good yet," he said huskily, and sat down, back to the wall.

"Swallow your gizzard," advised Bradway, "and fight the thing. It never is a pleasure to kill a man. It'll be worse the next time. . . . I reckon you saved my life."

"Ha! I know damn well I did, pard, an' I gotta think of thet."

"I'll never forget it. You made good the first move. . . . How come you bored that hombre Mike?"

"Jest as you left, I seen him sneakin' upstairs with thet rifle. I follered him. He didn't go in the parlor where Kit took you, but into the front room, an' he left the door open. I couldn't see till he opened the door out to the balcony. I watched—slipped up closer. When he raised the rifle—I—I bored him."

"Slick work, pard. And what else?"

"You was in all the rest, 'cept when you left Emery scared yellow. Thet hangin' idee got him where it hurt. He turned on Kit again like a bitin' rattlesnake. But what he said he whispered. They went upstairs. I had my drink at the bar. Pretty soon games started up again. But Emery an' his Queen failed to show up. Pard, my hunch is he'll kill her onless she beats him to it. An' I'll gamble the little lady has thet in her mind right this heah minnit."

"She has, Vince. She wanted me to bore him."

"Hell you say? Wal, thet's a sticker. But mebbe it ain't. I'm jest kinda thick-haided."

"Vince, she's afraid of him. Why?"

No answer came from the squatting figure beside his chair. Presently Vince went on: "When I come out some of the help was packin' Mike in. But Haskel lay where you left him in the middle of the street. Daid, an' shore an' appallin' sight, if I ever seen one. Not a damn man near! I reckon, though, everybody seen him."

"Have you spotted Sealover yet?"

"No. I'll get a line on him tomorrer. What'll we do to thet bird?"

"It will depend on him. If he'll talk, well and good. If not . . ."

"Pard, you got plenty of coin. Let's bribe Sealover to talk, if proddin' a cocked gun in his ribs won't do it. These low-down geezers have been doin' Emery's biddin' for a few bits. Let's try some real money on them."

"Another slick idea, Vince. We'll try it. Say, pard, I hired Doc Williamson to have Weston's body dug up and examined. I want to know what kind of a bullet killed him."

"I'll be damned! But, pard, you can't look at Jimmy?"

"Yes, I could, if it'd help me to find out who shot him, but let's cross that bridge when we come to it. Vince, it's been a long, long day. Let's turn in."

"Good. I'm dawg-tired. I'll hit the hay heah in Headly's barn."

"Do you know where to find me in case you want to?"

"Yep. I marked the house. Mrs. Dill's. I know her. . . . Good night, pard, an' go the back way. From now on you an' me must be Injuns."

Linc felt as exhausted as if he had been in the saddle since dawn, cutting and branding calves. South Pass social life, such as it was, was still going full blast, as he stole through town by the back way. A few minutes later, barred in his little room, he stretched out in the dark, feeling he would never move again.

But despite his weariness, he could not sleep. That terrible hour had come in which he had to fight the physical and mental effects of being driven to take a human life. This time what saved him from the mood of black mental sickness was the thought of Kit Bandon. He recalled every act and look and word of hers, since first he had met her. She had made no effort to conceal her feelings for him. Even his rebuff of all her advances had not seemed to destroy her self-confidence, possibly because she was one of those strange vain creatures who had never before failed to make men mad for her. Was a woman such as Kit Bandon really capable of unselfish love for a man—say, for instance, as a girl like Lucy would be? If he did not know that a girl such as Lucy existed, would he have been able to resist the lure and passion of the Maverick Queen? In all honesty, he couldn't be sure.

He had had very little opportunity since boyhood to learn the ways of women. He had never experienced a serious love affair with any girl, let alone with a fascinating willful, unscrupulous woman such as Kit Bandon. He could not help pitying her. As he remembered it now, her passionate kiss, calculated and demanding as it had seemed at the time, now in retrospect seemed warm and sweet. He realized that similar kisses had been given to other cowboys—to Jimmy Weston—setting their blood on fire and leading inevitably to their destruction. He had a feeling that were it not for the debt of vengeance he had come to pay and for a memory of the look of hurt in a pair of blue eyes that he, too, would have yielded to the strange enchantment of Kit Bandon.

As Linc Bradway lay there in his boxlike room he found his thoughts turning away from the Maverick Queen. He swore to himself that he would find the strength to resist her. And he thanked God that he had met Lucy Bandon—was it only that morning? So much had happened since she had waved good-by to him from her buckboard on the road to Sweetwater Valley. He recalled her lovely face, her boyish figure in the old blue jeans, her bitter outburst against her aunt who had killed her love for Jimmy Weston even before it was born, her gallant refusal to betray the secret of Sweetwater Valley.

How could he even think of the Maverick Queen when this lovely, brave, unhappy girl was waiting beyond the Pass? He realized now that he loved her, that he would save her from her unhappy situation if she would let him. He longed for the night to pass so that he could ride over the Pass to tell Lucy that he loved her, that if she would place her faith in him, he would never give her cause to regret it.

He wished desperately now that he had planned to meet Lucy tomorrow. He clung to the thought of his love for her as a drowning sailor clutches a spar; and at last when slumber came, Lucy's sweet wistful face hovered in the shadows of his darkening consciousness.

Chapter V

Awakening late, Bradway found the same somber mood of last night settling down upon him again. "Ahuh! I reckon I was hunting for trouble. And it's piled up on me," he muttered, as he went out. It was noon in South Pass, the quietest hour of the twenty-four. Passing the center of town he found an eating place where he had himself a late breakfast. From there he went on to Headly's stable. Vince had been gone for some time, the liveryman said. Lincoln holed up in the tiny office, watching the street and the queer variety of passers-by. A stage stopped for an exchange of horses.

"What's the news over Lander way?" asked Headly, of a cattleman who had stepped out of the stage.

"Wal, with summer here some of us are drivin' stock over into the Sweetwater range."

"You're all welcome. It's boom time around South Pass these days. Plenty room, plenty grass, plenty gold."

"Yes, an' plenty shootin', if all I hear is true."

"Shootin' frays are perkin' up, at thet," drawled Headly, with a touch of pride.

Some time after the stage had departed Vince limped up the street in his high heels to the livery stable, and was just asking for his partner when he espied him.

"Gosh, I didn't run into you nowhere," he complained. "Finally jest had to go to yore bunkhouse. Mrs. Dill said you went out about midday, black as a thundercloud. . . . Wal, I hoofed it some today, an' you can ask my pore feet."

"Vince, you're bursting with news," said Linc, impatiently. "Come out with it."

"Wal, I been everywhere I could get in, an' picked up some talk thet you can take for what it's worth. . . . There's news afoot thet ranchers in the valley air formin' a secret band of night riders. News from Rock Springs thet cattle are up two dollars a haid. Rustlers workin' down the valley near Red Desert. I heerd thet if Kit Bandon breaks with Emery he will get run out of South Pass. She left this mawnin' early for her ranch. By hossback, an' kinda in a hurry. I seen her ride off an' she looked like a mighty troubled woman. 'Pears she had rooms at Aldham's—thet's the best hotel. She has a room also at the *Leave It,* as you remember. Later I had a look at Emery. He was mad as a hornet. He was with a nervous dark-complected little feller who I took for Sealover. An' I found afterward thet my hunch was correct. An' last it 'pears thet Emery is thought damn pore of about town. O'course he always was, as I know, but this fracas with you an' the dirty bizness it brought to light, has hurt him with the decent town folks, of which there are quite some few. Altogether, pard, it ain't been a bad forty-eight hours for us."

"Right. If I can only lay low and go slow! . . . But that's almost impossible in this kind of a deal."

"Shore. The thing for you is to get away from heah often, an' relax from this watchin' game. Steady work as thet will get on yore nerves."

"Where'll I go? I promised to meet Lucy tomorrow. I wish it was today. After that—I don't know. . . . Right now, I've an appointment with Doc Williamson. Meet me at this first little restaurant down the street, just about dark."

"Okay, pard. Keep yore eyes peeled. There's some stink brewin', but I can't tell the turn yet."

Lincoln cut across the slope to the street which led down from the bank, and approached Williamson's office that way. He found the doctor in, and evidently awaiting him.

"Evening, Bradway. I see you are on time," was his greeting.

"Have you any—any word for me?" queried Lincoln, grimly.

"Yes," returned the doctor, a curious gleam in his eyes. "Bradway, your friend Weston was shot with a light caliber gun—a thirty-eight, and from the front."

A little later Bradway asked the doctor to take him to see McKeever.

"This little gun I showed you belongs to him," said Lincoln. "I had the notion that it or one similar had been used on Weston."

"Come along," replied Williamson. "I haven't had time to call on McKeever today."

They went out. The afternoon was waning, but it was still too early for lights to be burning. Williamson led Bradway upstairs in the Aldham hotel and, without the formality of knocking, pushed open the door to McKeever's room. Linc followed. It was a corner room with two windows; McKeever, his thin face pale and drawn, sat propped up by pillows. A dark-visaged little man arose hastily as the two men entered.

"Howdy, Mac," said Williamson, then testily to the little man: "Sealover, I told you to stay away from my patient. You upset him."

Linc stepped from behind the portly doctor. "Ahuh. So this is Mr. Sealover. I've a word with you, if you don't mind."

"Who're you?" demanded Sealover, warily, as if he suspected the identity of this visitor.

"You know damn well who I am."

"Sealover, thet's Bradway, the cowboy who shot me," spoke up McKeever, and it was evident that interest if not pleasure attended the introduction.

"Sealover, I've been looking for you," said Linc quietly.

"Well, you've found me," said the little man. "And what do you want with me?"

"I want an explanation of your part in the Haskel deal."

The beady-eyed little man had a bold front which did not deceive the Nebraskan. Here was evidently another accomplice of Emery's who did not strike Lincoln as one to respect.

"What do you mean by the Haskel deal?"

"Don't try to put me off. You got him over here to kill me, one way or another."

"I did no such thing. I told Haskel there was a wild gun-toting cowboy over here who had won a pile of money. Haskel said that was just his meat."

"But Haskel told me before he died that you came after him, and that Emery was behind it," said Lincoln.

"Well, he lied, that's all," returned Sealover, pale to his thin lips.

"Men like Haskel don't lie when they are dying, unless loyalty is involved. It seems he had no compunction about implicating you and Emery. . . . You're the one who's lying."

"Bradway, I'm not an armed man," protested Sealover. "A fact which you seem to take advantage of."

"Yeah? Listen, you shifty-eyed little skunk," said the cowboy contemptuously. "Make sure you pack a gun next time you run into me. Because I'm sure going for mine. Now get out pronto!"

Sealover, haggard and worried, hastily left the room, banging the door behind him.

"My word, Bradway, but you're an outspoken fellow!" said Williamson, admiringly.

"Bradway, you're no friend of mine," spoke up McKeever, wtih a red spot on each of his cheeks, "but I've got to thank you for scaring the liver out of Sealover. I enjoyed it."

"Humph! Then Sealover isn't a friend of yours, either?" returned Lincoln.

"I've never been so hard up for friends as to need him."

"Who is he, anyway?"

"Outside of being a four-flush gambler, that's another question."

"Oh, I see. . . . Here's your little gun, McKeever, that you were fool enough to draw on me the other night. It's not loaded, so don't make the mistake a second time," said Linc, and laid the little derringer on the table beside McKeever's bed.

"I'm not liable to," replied the gambler, constrainedly. "Did you expect to find Sealover here? Or what brought you?"

"No. Meeting him was just some of my luck. I brought your gun back, and I wanted to apologize."

"To me!—For what?" asked McKeever, in amazement.

"I thought you might have killed my friend Weston with that little gun. Found out you hadn't."

"Weston? Oh, I see! . . . No, I'm glad to say I didn't kill him."

"Do you know who did?"

"If I did I wouldn't tell you. But as a matter of fact I don't."

Bradway pondered a moment, then sat down near a window. "Doc, you attend to your patient, and then please leave me alone with him for a few minutes."

"Well, I reckon that'll be all right, considering," returned the doctor. "Mac, you seem to be doing fine. Let me look you over once more."

Bradway gazed out of the window at the street below. The sun had set. Above the town the hills were bathed in golden light and the peaks were rosy red. South Pass had ended the day's toil, and was ready for what the night might bring. Presently Dr. Williamson appeared ready to depart, but before he left he asked Lincoln not to excite his patient. When he was gone Lincoln stood up.

"McKeever, you tried to pull a gun on me and I shot you. I'm sure you won't try that again, because you know what another attempt would cost you. So we are quits—if you want to leave it so."

"Thank you, Bradway, I'd prefer it to be quits."

"Fine. Calling it quits means one less enemy for me, and it means a better chance of your dying a natural death. . . . Of course, I figure you belong to Emery's outfit here, whatever it is. I'd like to ask you a few questions, in spite of that."

"Go ahead. But you'll be wasting your breath," replied McKeever, apparently intrigued in spite of his resentment.

"Is there any particular reason for you to be loyal to this coyote Emery?"

"None whatever. Rather the contrary. But a gambler's honor, you know."

"Is there any particular reason for you to be loyal to Kit Bandon?"

"Hell no! She made a fool of me," rejoined the gambler, not without heat. "Same as she did of Lee, and other of his cattlemen friends, as she is doing to Emery, and will probably do to *you*. . . . Still and all . . ."

He made a slight gesture with his thin hand. His eyes were dark and unfathomable.

"You are forearming me, McKeever," went on Lincoln. "I take it Kit Bandon likes men, likes to gamble with them and their gold—and their lives. And she is a little on the fickle side."

"You said a heap, cowboy. I hope to enjoy seeing her face when I repeat that to her."

"I find her an interesting woman, McKeever. . . . Would you—for a price—tell me a few things about her?"

"No. Not for all the gold in South Pass."

"Why not? Are you afraid?"

"Men don't betray Kit Bandon—and live," returned the gambler, quietly.

"Which is equivalent to admitting there *is* something to betray," said Bradway, quickly. "Thanks for letting that slip. . . . But does your code of honor apply equally to Emery?"

"What do you want to know?" queried McKeever, curiously.

"His relation to Kit Bandon?"

"Ask *her*. . . . She's the only person who can tell what her relations are to anybody."

"I see. The observer might be all wrong. . . . But— do you know that Emery did *not* shoot Weston?"

"No!"

"Weston *was* shot by someone else!" flashed Lincoln.

"I can't say. All I know is that Weston was shot by somebody for cheating at cards."

"Somebody! I'm looking for that somebody. . . . That somebody hauled Weston to South Pass in a wagon—dead!"

It was a random shot, inspired by Bradway's suspicion that his friend might not have been killed in the *Leave It*. McKeever's astonishment was clear evidence that he knew Weston had not been murdered there.

"Who told you that?"

"That's my business. . . . McKeever, I see you know more than you care to divulge. I hold it against you."

"If you know so damn much why do you pester me with questions?"

"I'm determined to get to the bottom of this murder. The safest thing for you to do is come clean with what you know."

"Bradway. I swear to God I don't know who killed Weston—or how it was done," protested McKeever, weakly, and it was obvious that he was telling the truth.

"All right. I believe you that far," concluded Bradway. "But you know something which would give me a clue."

"Hell, man, what do you take me for? Suppose I do? I'm not beholden to you."

"No, but you're beholden to your life! Think that over, before I find some excuse to draw on you again."

Lincoln rose and left the room without bothering to say good-by. The corridor outside was quite dark.

He felt his way to the stairway, his gun out, peering into all corners as he crept cautiously down the bare wooden stairs. Reaching the street without incident, he crossed to the other side, making his way toward the rendezvous with Vince. It was early and the restaurant was empty. While Linc waited outside in the shadow for Vince he thought over the events of the afternoon. His visit to McKeever had been vastly worthwhile, yet it only magnified the mystery. The sole absolute fact he could deduce from this encounter was further substantiation of Kit Bandon's power to hold the loyalty of men. In view of her acknowledged treatment of them, this loyalty seemed extraordinary. Emery was the only one who had hinted at her double dealing, yet even he had withheld something that might have discredited her. A threat was one thing; but betrayal another. Kit Bandon cast an incredible spell over men; nevertheless Linc felt certain that someone of them would, sooner or later, betray whatever there was to reveal concerning her strange actions.

Vince came along to find Linc still turning matters over in his mind. "Kinda ponderin' myself, pard," he said soberly, after a look of understanding at his friend. "Let's go feed. Mebbe thet'll help."

"Lordy! I clean forgot I was hungry," laughed Lincoln. They repaired to the little restaurant up the street, ordered their supper and finished it almost in silence. Fifteen minutes later they were outside again.

"What's yores, pard?" queried Vince, gruffly.

"My what?"

"Wal, I'm no mind reader. But you shore seem to have aplenty to think about."

"Ha!—Let's mosey out of this parade. . . . A man can't think and watch a hundred gun hands at the same time."

A cold night wind whipped down from the mountains; the roar of the brook vied with the hum of the town; the throng thinned as they climbed to the outskirts.

As they left the town behind, Linc told Vince of Doc Williamson's disclosure.

Vince grunted, "By gun! . . . Pard, I reckon thet jest about settles it!"

"Then I went with Doc to see McKeever," continued Bradway, "and he told of the meeting with Sealover, and the subsequent talk with the gambler."

"Wal, it's one step more, but a step in the dark. This shore is the underhandedest deal I was ever in. . . . Pard, I picked up a speck of information while you were havin' yore seance with Sealover."

"Yeah?—Every little bit helps."

"I run into Bill Haynes," continued Vince, after taking a slow deep breath. "Bill is a big hombre, broad as a wagon end. Red-faced an' one-eyed. You'll know him when you see him. He hit it rich up at the diggin's, an' then bought cattle. His ranch is about twelve miles down this creek. I did Bill a good turn once an' he's a friend of mine. Wal, he gave me what he said was good advice to rustle out of this neck of the woods."

"Why?"

"He didn't say. But I reckon there's something afoot thet'd make it healthier for me to leave."

"Vince, have you made any enemies among the cattlemen?"

"Ahuh."

"You been cutting your eyeteeth as a rustler?"

"How'd you guess it, pard?" queried Vince, bitterly.

"What's more, you have been stealing mavericks," accused Linc.

Vince did not reply.

"I had that figured pretty pronto. . . . Could you *pay* for those mavericks and square yourself?"

"Lord no, not even if I wanted to! An' I'd go to hell first."

"Can they prove you rustled mavericks?"

"Ketched me red-handed, thet is, one rancher did."

"That's bad. In fact, it's mighty serious. Why did he let you off?"

"Wal, out heah in Wyomin' the cattlemen haven't

come to hangin' rustlers yet. But they're comin' to it pronto."

"Perhaps you'd better show this range your dust."

"Nope. I'm standin' by you, pard. Besides, I'm good an' sore."

"At whom?"

"Wal, I'll let you figger thet out yoreself, seein' how smart you are. . . . Bill give me some other news thet I reckon he went out of his way to tell. Lee fired his foreman Thatcher. You met Thatcher. . . . Bill didn't make anythin' much of this. Mebbe he reckoned I'd see through it. An' you bet I did. It shore hints of a hell of a mess thet's brewin' round South Pass."

"Thatcher?—Fine type of cowboy, I thought," declared Lincoln.

"They don't come any better. Lee knows thet."

"Could it be that Thatcher side-stepped a little over some mavericks?"

"Hell! It could be, only it ain't. Lee fired Thatcher for refusin' to belong to thet secret rider outfit he's organizin'."

"Are you sure of that?" cut in Bradway, snapping his fingers.

"I could swear to it. An' it proves jest what I was thinkin', pard. Lee jest cain't raise no band of night-ridin' cowboys on this range."

"Lee struck me as a strong and resourceful cattleman. He's a Texan. I'll bet he does raise that vigilante bunch."

"Umpumm, pard. Anywhere else in Wyomin' mebbe, but shore not heah."

"Vince, do you realize what a—a strange—what a hell of a statement that is?" demanded Linc.

"It's a hell of a country, pard," returned his comrade, evasively. "But neither it nor anyone in it can fool you very long. . . . Tomorrer you're gonna see Lucy. Wal, thet's fine. Give her my love. An' make hay while the sun shines! I'll set tight an' have more to tell you when you come back. Be orful careful, pard. Good night."

They parted, each going in a different direction. The June night was cold, and Linc almost wished he had brought his sheepskin-lined jacket. He reached his lodging room unobserved.

"This mess grows stickier and stickier," he muttered as he undressed. "But it'll be coming to a boil pronto, if I figure things right. . . . So Vince was a maverick rustler? Caught but not punished, except to go jobless in the future on this range. Queer as hell! But why should they be so hard on Vince? Every cowboy who ever forked a horse has stolen a calf or two. . . . By thunder! I've got it—or I'm close to it. Vince sold his stolen mavericks to Kit Bandon. . . and so have other cowboys!"

Linc was only thinking in the dark. But it made sense. Cowboys were a canny lot. They would stick together, and some who were not guilty would protect those who were. Thatcher cautioning Smeade that night was an example. Smeade, of course, had been doing the same as Vince.

"Only a two-bit rustling at that," muttered Bradway, as he crawled wearily into bed. "Only flea bites to cattlemen like these, running stock in the thousands. . . . But if all the cowboys on the range took to maverick stealing—Lordy, that would be something! . . . Still, couldn't that beautiful woman work a hundred cowboys as easily as a few?"

The Nebraskan resolved to go down into the valley in order to find out. It meant riding and keeping out at night, camping in secluded spots, scout work with which he had plenty of experience.

"But if this cowboy-maverick angle is what I figure it, could that be what's behind Lee's organization of vigilantes?" After a moment he answered his own question: "Hell no! Cattlemen would be crazy to organize a secret band of cowboys to spy on other cowboys. It'd mean a war. . . . No, that's something else. More cattle stealing has been going on than has been admitted or more is expected. Lee wants to clean up something pronto. I should think he'd get the other ranchers

in with him. Still, he's a Texan. . . . Tomorrow I'll ask
Lucy. . . . Maybe she has heard about it."

Thoughts of Lucy and their rendezvous tomorrow
drove everything else out of the cowboy's mind. As he
lay there in the dark, he determined not to waste any
time in courting Lucy. He would sweep her off her
feet. The very suddenness of it might be in his favor.
Lucy had indicated that she liked him; by her own
confession she had made a hero of him. Well and
good, he would not only let her continue to believe
that, but he would try to do something to warrant it.
He found himself dreading another meeting with Kit
Bandon as keenly as he longed for the next opportunity to be with Lucy. Lincoln did not doubt his
honesty as a man or his quckly-born love for this
lonely girl who had been loved by his best friend. What
he doubted was the power to continue to be steel and
flint to this seductive Bandon woman if she flung herself at him again. What if Kit Bandon actually had
fallen in love with him! It was possible, and might
actually be true because he was one cowboy who—apparently—had not been overwhelmed by her beauty
and charm. As he drifted off to sleep it was with the
realization that it would be very foolish to take Kit
Bandon's outspoken flattery to heart. And it was with
the determination that hereafter he would keep Kit
Bandon at a distance.

Early next morning Lincoln bolted a hurried but
hearty breakfast, then went over to the merchandise
store, where he purchased saddlebags, a rubber-lined
blanket, and a small stock of supplies. Any night now
he might be kept out in the open, and he wanted to
be prepared. At the livery stable he found his saddle,
bridle, and a bag of grain, thoughtfully placed within
easy reach by Vince. He led Bay from the stall and
fed him. After saddling, he adjusted the saddlebags and
packed them. It was still early morning when Bay and
his rider took the trail west out of South Pass.

The sun rose behind him as he topped the gray rise
of land. Once out of sight of town the silence and

austerity of the vast open sage country enveloped him. A band of antelope stood with twitching ears to watch him pass. He descried deer down in the brushy draws; coyotes skulked through the sage, and jack rabbits darted across the trail. The sunrise-flushed peaks of the Wind River Range rose, grandly aloof in their beauty and isolation. It was a glorious June morning. And it was good to be on the trail again.

In due course he arrived at the rocky point with its fringe of dwarf pines where he was to meet Lucy. As he paused a hawk sailed above in the clear blue sky peering down for its prey. Dismounting behind the cover of the trees, he tethered Bay and set about collecting wood for his signal fire. He kindled it a few feet from the rim, throwing on several armfuls of green brush to make a smoke. Then he went to the spot where Lucy had shown him the valley of the Sweetwater.

Weeks, even months, might have passed since he had been here with Lucy. In tense action, in ceaseless vigilance, in stern thought, and in the resistless emotion of love that grew with leaps and bounds it seemed to Linc that he had lived that much time.

"Lordy! I never felt this way before," mused the Nebraskan, falling into his old habit of talking to himself. "Trying to dodge Kit's advances and to court Lucy's love would just about make a man balmy if it wasn't that I've got the fight of my life on my hands."

Fight indeed, for his own life, for his friend's good name, for love that called with all the tenderness and insistence and fire-filmed enchantment of this valley. The surroundings seemed as boundless as his emotions. In the clear air of early morning, the mountains, range upon range, to the farthest snowy peak stood out sharp in the distance. The rose-tinted peaks two hundred miles away seemed to loom just beyond the valley rampart; the carpet of sage seemed to stretch on endlessly. The wavering line of the river bed and the dots that were ranch houses accentuated the valley's vastness. No veil of purple haze obscured the cowboy's sight at this early hour. He wished that the future might be spread as clearly before his gaze as that valley in the clear morning light.

Several times he replenished the fire. Column after column of gray smoke he sent aloft in the signal agreed upon with Lucy. He wondered whether the girl had seen his signal fire from her aunt's ranch house below. Was she having trouble in getting away? Had Kit Bandon unexpectedly come home?

As midmorning arrived he became aware of activity down below. His range eyes caught the telltale clouds of dust, the movement of countless black objects that meant that a roundup of cattle was in progress on the ranch belonging to Kit Bandon. There were herds of cattle on other ranches, as far as the eye could see. Linc wished he had brought his field glasses. He would like to have a closer view of the Bandon ranch.

Time passed. The noon-day hour was at hand. The sun stood straight overhead. Lincoln paced to and fro, growing definitely worried over the girl's delay. What could have detained Lucy? She had said positively that nothing could keep her from seeing him. Apparently something had, and he felt the beautiful spell that had been building up in his inner consciousness begin to fade away.

Suddenly Lincoln knew that she was not coming. His first reaction was one of bitter disappointment. Then he began to wonder whether Lucy really ever had intended to come. He remembered the scene on the sidewalk in South Pass. But he remembered, too, the honesty in her level gaze, the genuineness of her emotions when he had told her he must see her again. No, little as he knew of women, he would stake his life on that blue-eyed girl. Her failure to keep her tryst with him was not just a young girl's whimsy. There was something sinister behind her absence. Perhaps her aunt had found out. Perhaps it all had to do with the mystery of her strange tangled loyalties which had sealed her lips when she had so obviously wanted to confide in him. He shook his head hopelessly. Again he was up against that same blank wall that had confronted him ever since he had come to Wyoming.

Lincoln extinguished the fire, and mounting Bay turned back toward the road. Soon he was descending the bluff, around long zigzags and winding turns. He found, presently, that from the base of the bluff, the road led in a gradual descent out into the gray sage. Its tangy fragrance filled his nostrils, and the seemingly endless expanse of the gray-green floor of the valley stirred his senses. But Lincoln bore a troubled mind. His perplexity and anxiety grew as Bay's gentle pace covered distance and brought the belt of golden-green willows closer and closer. Cattle began to appear in increasing numbers on each side of the road, but none close enough for him to distinguish their brands. He rode on, conscious of an unaccountable foreboding pervading his heart. Had Kit Bandon bragged to Lucy of her conquest of Lincoln in South Pass? Once she had discovered his friendship with Lucy she would fight it with all the tremendous force and unscrupulous cunning of her dual nature. Lucy had experienced a cowboy's faithlessness with Jim Weston. It would not take too much persuasion on the part of Kit to make the girl believe that he, Jim's partner, was just another opportunist! But he would find a way to prove his love, no matter how completely Kit had prevailed upon the girl.

Nearing the willows and the river he decided to leave the road, and not go directly to the Bandon ranch until he had formed some definite plan of procedure. To this end he took a trail leading off to the left which approached the willows at an angle. Presently the trail leading toward the willow-bordered Sweetwater showed the tracks where antelopes had crossed it on their way to water. The presence of game in such profusion reminded Lincoln that he had not brought a rifle, almost a necessity if he expected to travel about the range, camping at night. Rabbits and other small furry animals fled before him. The river was evidently still some distance ahead. Many of the ancient willows were as large as cottonwoods. Following the well-worn trail, which wound in and out among the trees, the cowboy presently smelled smoke. Halting Bay, Lincoln slid out of the saddle and led the horse by the reins. It was soft loam and the shod hoofs gave forth no sound. Lincoln heard the gurgle of swift water some distance ahead of him. The smell of smoke grew stronger. There was a camp, or at least a smoldering fire, not far away. The trees thinned out and suddenly Lincoln found himself in a clearing that bordered a swift-running, amber-colored stream. Beyond shone the bright gray sage, but close to the stream the cowboy could see tarpaulin stretched on poles, some camp duffle and a burned-out fire with skillet and coffeepot upon it.

Suddenly Bay's long ears shot up. Lincoln's restraining hand prevented him from snorting. Then a rustle in a treetop to the right of him drew Lincoln's swift gaze. High up in a giant lone willow he espied a man with a leveled telescope pointed toward the sage in the direction of the Bandon ranch. Stepping aside from his horse Lincoln drew his gun and called out: "Hey you! up in the tree!—What the hell do you think you're doing?"

"Yes, his best friend. And I let him run away out ere to be murdered!"

"Jim was a great rider an' a likable boy. He rode or me once."

"Did you——let him go?"

"No. He quit. He wanted to be near Bandon's anch."

"Why?"

"Wal, he was sweet on Lucy, first off—an' then he went the way of most cowboys on this range."

"Kit Bandon's way, you mean?"

But the squat man turned away to his smoldering campfire, without replying.

"How long will you stay here?" asked Lincoln.

"Reckon I'll leave soon as thet roundup is over. Pretty pronto."

Burton's information, uncertain as it was, had rekindled Bradway's smoldering flame of vengeance. He swore he would see this thing through unless he found that by persisting in his search he would lose Lucy. She had been right—to kill Weston's murderers, even to clear his name, would not bring their friend back. Nevertheless, it would take a great deal to turn him aside from the task he had sworn to fulfill.

"Burton, tell your partner Hargrove, that I'll be calling on him before long," said Lincoln, as he kicked the stirrup around so that he could step up in it. He mounted. Burton was gazing up at him, evdently withholding speech with difficulty. There was a glint in his eye.

"Shore. I'll tell him. But I reckon my meetin' you heah won't please him none. I was to hide my movements."

"Well, on second thought, then, don't tell him I caught you in the act. That won't do any good. I can drop in to see him without sending word."

"Thanks, Bradway. Thet suits me plumb better," rejoined the other, considerably relieved. "But I won't be xpectin' you so positive."

"Yeah? I said I'd come, didn't I?"

Chapter VI

The man handling the spyglass was so startled by Lincoln's terse call that he all but lost his balance and fell out of the tree. He stared. He saw the gun. His jaw sagged and his eyes popped.

"Well, pile down out of there in a hurry! I might take you for a squirrel," ordered Lincoln, truculently. "I don't hold with spying on folks!"

The man came scrambling and sliding down the rough tree trunk, at the expense of his worn garments. Once upon the ground he appeared to be a squat middle-aged individual, mild of eye and homely of face. He approached Lincoln with hesitation, but after a moment with more confidence.

"Ain't you that cowboy, Bradway?" he queried.

"Never mind who I am. The thing is who are *you*?"

"My name's Bloom Burton. I have part interest in Jim Hargrove's cattle."

"Hargrove? Where's his ranch?"

"Twenty miles, I reckon, below Lee's."

"And where's Lee's?"

"His range joins Kit Bandon's, about ten miles down the river."

"How'd you come to take me for Bradway?"

"Wal, I've heerd about the look of you."

"And why aren't you so scared as you were, when you first saw me?"

"Hargrove told us you was *one* cowboy who'd be on our side."

"Our side! Who's your side?"

"Wal, we're the cattlemen of Sweetwater Valley."

"Ahuh. I begin to savvy. What were you doing up in that tree?"

"Did I look like I was pickin' flowers?" retorted Burton, coolly.

"You looked like a spy."

"I reckon thet's what I was."

"On your own account? Or under orders?"

"Wal, I reckon I'd better say my own."

"Suppose I walk you over to Kit Bandon's and tell her what I caught you doing?" demanded Lincoln.

"My Gawd—don't do thet, Bradway! . . . She's packin' a gun and she can throw it. She'd kill me as quick as you could say 'maverick.' "

"All the same, Burton, I think that's what I'll do."

"You got the advantage, Bradway. . . . I'm shore damn disappointed. I reckon Lee was right about you bein' taken with Kit Bandon. An' Hargrove was wrong."

"What did Hargrove think that was wrong?"

"He saw you meet Gun Haskel, an' then call Emery to his face, an' most damn plain, Hargrove swears, you turned yore back on thet woman, an' he took from thet you are *one* cowboy she won't bamboozle."

"Hargrove is right. I'm no friend of Kit Bandon's. And I'm dead set against Emery's outfit. All the same, it's to my interest to turn you over to Bandon."

"Yore interest!—How? I cain't see how gettin' me shot will benefit you."

"All right. If you'll consent to do some talking I won't give you away."

"Talk? Say, I've already shot my mouth plenty—thet is, about myself an' my pardners."

"What I want you to tell me is all you know about Jimmy Weston's death."

"An' thet's all?"

"Yes. You don't need to tell me why you in that willow spying upon Kit Bandon's You were taking a count of cattle—probab and yearlings that were mavericks a litt back. . . . But you spill all you know about death right now and quick—or I'll walk you the Maverick Queen's."

"I honestly don't know much, Bradway," the cattleman, plainly disturbed and turning pa

"Wasn't he murdered?"

"We ranchers reckon he was."

"Ranchers!—What do the cowboys think?"

"Nobody knows. They are close-mouthed about thet."

"Weston was killed out here on the range?" ventured Lincoln.

"Yes. He was drove to South Pass in the daid of night."

"From where?"

"Out heah in the valley someplace. A cowboy named Hank Miller was teamster for Hirsh, my neigh down the valley. He hadn't been long heah. But drove Hirsh's wagon to town thet night—an' nob never seen him again. The wagon was left in town, Weston's Stetson was found in it. Course thet do prove Weston was murdered, or drove from the v into town, or shot in a card game at Emery's late night. But the wagon part in it, an' Miller's disap ance, looked queer to us out heah."

"Hank Miller?—Did you ever see him? De him."

"Strappin' cowboy. Young. Nice face an' sleepy He was seen in Rock Springs two days ago Slocum, driver of the eastbound stage. Thet got today—from a visitor I had. . . . An' thet know positive about the Weston case."

"Thanks—Burton," returned Lincoln, almost "It's a good deal."

"You was Weston's pard, I heah?"

"Shore. You said so. But judgin' by thet spark in yore eye I'd say you was huntin' trouble. An' you'll get it over there, mebbe."

"Where?"

"At thet roundup."

"Thanks for tipping me off. Do you know any of the outfit I'll run into?"

"Not a damn one. But them riders jest don't belong to this Sweetwater range."

"Ahuh. Outsiders. Well, in that case I won't be so sensitive about stepping on their toes," drawled Lincoln.

"Bradway, you're a cool 'un!" declared the little cattleman. "Naturally I distrust your bizness out heah. You cain't be offended at thet. But doggone it, I like you, an' I'm goin' to tell the members of our—er, my neighbors so."

"That'll be fine. But wait a while."

"Shore, I'll do thet. . . . Are you ridin' right into Bandon an' her outfit?"

"Yes. I'm powerful interested in what's going on over there."

"Man, I cain't help but think you're . . ."

"I'm what?" interrupted Lincoln, tersely, as the other hesitated.

"Wal, ya don't seem to be a feller thet it'd be safe to tell yore mind to."

"I savvy, Burton. You figure I'm like all the other cowboys—loco about this Bandon woman?"

"Wal, thet's gone over the range—an' it wouldn't be no surprise to nobody."

"I see, and your personal angle is that you're damn sorry?" queried Lincoln, with a grin.

"Eggsactly," replied Burton, also with a grin.

"How do you feel in regard to the destroying angel in question?"

"Wal, the fact is I never knowed what to think," returned Burton, seriously. "I've seen Kit Bandon a lot of times—talked to her a few. When I was close to her I jest couldn't think at all!—But then I'm a lonely

man. I never had no woman. An' I reckon in Gawd's
sight thet ain't natural or good. So any woman affects
me queer. I jest ain't no jedge of woman. But as for
Kit—wal, it's my notion thet you called her proper.
She's a destroyin' angel."

"So long, Burton," concluded Lincoln, soberly, after
a long look at the earnest little man. "Hope to see you
soon. And if you're friendly, don't worry about me."

"Well, I'm friendly, Bradway. I cain't help it. Hell,
I oughta know men an' cowboys an' horses, even if I
don't know women. Else I've lived twenty years on
the range for nothin'. . . . So long. Good luck." He let
Lincoln turn away to leave the clearing, then called
after him: "Them riders are bad medicine if you rile
them. But they're Mormons an' chances are they'll
be straight."

Lincoln . . .
ing sally, for all the response he made . . .
surprised and startled him. Mormon riders were something absolutely new to him. After a moment's thought,
however, he believed he would have less to fear from
them than from the valley cowboys who were involved
in more or less degree with the mysterious doings of
this Maverick Queen.

The ride back through the willow brake to the sage
seemed very short, owing to his preoccupation of mind.
But once on the road he began to realize that he was
nearing the home of Lucy, and what was even more
disturbing, the presence of Kit Bandon. What if he
were to meet them together? How he would conduct
himself in such event he had no idea.

He saw the lane where the road bisected the willow
brake, at that point not nearly so wide. And at last he
came to the river and the ford. The amber water ran
clear and shallow over a gravel bottom. Bay could not
pass through it without drinking. Presently Lincoln
surmounted the high bank to find he was close to a
long white log cabin that stood out in the open. The
mental picture he had of Kit Bandon's home, given
him by Lucy, did not fit this pretty and picturesque

place. Boldly Lincoln rode into the grassy yard, and dismounting, he knocked on the door with his heart in his throat. But there was no response. He repeated the knock, louder. But if there were anyone in the house, there was no evidence of it. No doubt Kit and her niece would be out with the roundup. That would be better, Lincoln thought. Nevertheless, to face both of them, even before a bunch of curious cowboys, would be an ordeal Lincoln had to steel himself to undertake.

Mounting Bay he rode out to where he could see the clouds of dust marking the roundup. He located them beyond some corrals and sheds back of the house. Kit Bandon's home appeared to be more of a farm than a ranch: chickens overran the yard, which reminded Lincoln of the Missouri farmland of his boyhood. Fenced pasture ran all the way back to the river bank, within which some fine horses grazed. He sighted, too, some cows and calves far down near the willows. The barn was a substantial structure, constructed to provide for severe winters and to shelter at least a score of horses. Beyond that a long shed extended, open in the front, but with a long manger running along the sheltered side, evidently intended to house cattle in cold weather. Linc examined everything with keen interest as he rode past to turn into the sage.

The dust cloud hung over a roll in the sageland a mile or more from the corrals. Lincoln espied stray cattle all over the range, but did not catch sight of the main herd until he reached the ridge top. He was somewhat surprised to see perhaps two thousand head. As he approached, his sharp eye detected four riders. They were circling the herd, cutting a large bunch of yearlings and calves out to one side. The cattle seemed rather tame. Many cows and a few steers, all full grown, bore the brand K I T and as the roundup showed no indication of branding work he supposed the younger cattle had also been similarly marked. He was sighted by one of the riders the moment he topped the ridge.

By the time he was within five hundred yards, all

the riders were together, three of them dismounted. Lincoln felt it might prove ticklish business, this bold approach. But there was no help for it, and he knew that boldness was the only logical attitude he dared show. After sighting several hundred yearlings in a single bunch, he concentrated his attention upon the riders.

Lincoln hardly expected to be held up, although the fact that neither Kit Bandon nor her niece was in sight made the situation rather uncomfortable, especially if these riders were the kind to resent intrusion. They all packed guns; that he could see even at this distance. He caught the glint of a rifle on one saddle. They were lean, rangy, ragged riders like almost any other cowboys, but at closer view he saw that they were young and wore short, fuzzy beards. They had still, intent eyes, hard to look into under their worn sombreros.

Leisurely riding up to them, the Nebraskan reined in Bay and slipped out of his saddle. He did not want to risk gunplay mounted on a strange horse.

"Howdy," he drawled, dropping his bridle and stepping clear of Bay. Then he felt comparatively easy.

"Howdy yourself," replied the nearest cowpoke, gruffly.

In build and feature they appeared to be brothers. Their attitude was one of intense curiosity, but little if any friendliness.

"Miss Bandon offered me a job," said Linc, blandly. "I rode out to see whether I'd like it or not. But if she was home she didn't answer my knock."

"Which Miss Bandon?" queried the spokesman of the quartet.

"Is there more than one? It was Miss Kit Bandon."

"She's gone to Rock Springs with her niece, Lucy."

At this information Lincoln's heart skipped a few beats, and a strange feeling of relief flooded over him. This would account for Lucy's failure to meet him.

"When did they go?" he asked, in apparent disappointment.

"They left on the morning stage."

"And when will they get back?"

"Not very soon. It'll take us several days to drive to Rock Springs."

"Ahuh. Cutting out a big bunch, I see. All yearlings and calves. Nearly five hundred head, if I know my cowboy business."

"There will be six hundred, if it's any of *your business,*" returned the rider, curtly.

"Well, it's a hell of a lot of *my* business, if you want to know," flashed Lincoln, suddenly changing his approach. "Where did Kit Bandon get so many calves?"

To this blunt query the rider answered readily. "That's not *our* worry. We're hired to drive them to the railroad."

"You're all Mormons, I understand."

Their silence manifestly affirmed that assertion. Presently the Nebraskan spoke again: "Even if you are Mormons you've no call to act so suspicious of a Gentile."

"Aren't you the gunman Bradway?"

"Yes, I'm Bradway, but packing a gun and shooting up some low-down hombres doesn't make me a gunman."

"We don't make friends over here, even with cowboys," returned the spokesman, shortly.

"That's not hard to see. Is it because you are just naturally hostile—or are you taking orders from Kit Bandon?"

That query seemed a shrewd guess, and though it was answered briefly in the negative, Linc could see that falsehood was distasteful to this Mormon. He concluded that if there were anything shady in this deal the fault was the woman's responsibility.

"What's your name?" asked Lincoln.

"Luke Mathews."

"Well, Luke, you probably think me a low-down meddling cowhand. But if I look that way to you, you're mistaken. My best friend, Jim Weston, was murdered out here, and I'm on the trail of the hombre who did it. I'd be right friendly with you if you'd let me.

I liked your looks as soon as I saw you. I don't know what sort of a deal you cowpokes are in with the Bandon woman. But you're probably willing to take the risk."

"How so? It's legitimate work. We get paid and ask no questions."

"Hasn't it occurred to you to ask yourself *where* these calves and yearlings come from?"

"Yes, we've been curious, but it's none of our business."

"They were all mavericks and you burned that brand on them."

"No, we didn't. And we had no idea they were mavericks," declared Mathews, positively.

"Ahuh. Well, I'll be damned. I'm not so smart as I thought I was. . . . Somebody branded those calves and it's got the appearance of hurried bungling work, as you can see. . . . Luke, I'll ask one more question. Have you ever heard them call Kit Bandon the Maverick Queen on this range?"

"No. We never heard that."

"Well, that would seem to let you out. But take a hunch from a Nebraska cowman who knows tricks of the range you Mormons never heard of. Make this your last drive!"

With these words of advice Linc stepped astride his horse and turned back toward the ranch. A glance over his shoulder showed Mathews standing in profound thought, and the other riders still motionless and staring after the Nebraskan.

"If they tell Kit Bandon, she'll scalp me alive. But hell! What else could I do? I have to find out whether they were in this thing with the Maverick Queen." And he fell again into his old habit of self-examination. What would be the legal status of the case if Kit Bandon were really inducing cowboys to steal mavericks from the ranchers and selling them to her? There could not be any legal status on a new range where there was no law. It was a question that undoubtedly was keeping the ranchers awake at night, now that they

had begun to suspect what was going on. Linc was convinced they did suspect it and that it was the reason
behind Burton's actions and Lee's offer of a job leading the vigilantes. On a vast new range where hundreds
of thousands of cattle were grazing, and more arriving
every day, where more and more cowboys into whose
past history the ranchers had no time to inquire, were
an absolute necessity, it seemed to the Nebraskan that
the black-eyed Maverick Queen had selected a profit-
able deal. She could claim that she did not know nor
care where the mavericks came from. What a unique
and clever and almost foolproof way to amass a herd
of cattle! People could suspect, but proof was difficult
to obtain. Then there was the personal element. Kit
Bandon would have had the best of the cattlemen even
if she had been a homely unattractive woman, but
beautiful as she was, to whom conquest was a passion,
she could keep them all at her heels. You don't question too closely the moves and acts of the woman you
want to marry! Yet Linc knew, through his experience
with Texans like Lee, that if Kit Bandon kept on riding
this range in her ruthless and unscrupulous fashion,
if she continued to break the hearts of cowboys upon
whom she depended for the building up of her herd,
and to ride roughshod over the desires of matured and
lonely cattlemen, in the end she must come to grief.
But she was as cunning as she was bold. There was a
possiblility that before things went too far she would
marry one of them, or a cowboy, and leave the range
with her fortune, or settle down to honest cattle raising.

Reaching the corrals, the Nebraskan deliberately rode
around inspecting them. Presently, down a lane between two fences of peeled poles, and hidden behind
the long shed, he found what his inquisitive, suspicious
mind had hoped to find. A smaller corral had been
built against the back of the shed. It was empty, so
far as livestock was concerned. In a corner he found
a neatly stacked pile of wood, carefully split into small
pieces. With such wood a cowboy could kindle a hot

fire in a few minutes! Under the eaves of the shed was a shelf upon which lay branding tools. Lincoln's restless eye espied the remains of little fires scattered all over the ground in the little corral. He dismounted to examine the heaps of ashes. One of them had been built within the last forty-eight hours. Another was scarcely four days old. Many calves had been branded in this hidden corral, and probably all of them at night by the light of the little fires.

Here again, however, was nothing that constituted damning evidence against Kit Bandon. Many ranchers branded calves in corrals instead of on the open range. Yet in Linc's mind's eye he envisioned a cowboy riding into that corral in the dead of night, dragging or packing a maverick, quickly building a little fire and hurriedly heating an iron to burn a brand.

"But why the hurry?" pondered Lincoln. He knew cowboys. Many of the bold and callous type would do that work leisurely and effectively, smoking a cigarette during the process, perhaps with a sardonic grin on his lips. "Those brands I saw out there were botched. All done in a hurry! . . . Scared of being caught? Hell no!" Lincoln planned to spend a night or two hiding in the shed, watching until he caught one of these cowboys red-handed. There was a chance it might mean gunplay, but he had to know.

Having learned everything it was possible to discover for the time being, Linc headed Bay back on the road toward South Pass. The afternoon was far gone, with sunset not an hour away. The air already was getting cool. Snow clouds hung over the peaks and their dark veils streamed down to the foothills. The loneliness of the waste of gray sage fitted in with the mood of the cowboy as he started back to South Pass.

"Well, horse, let's see what you've got," he said to Bay. It developed, presently, that Bay owned a long, easy, swinging lope like that of an Indian mustang. It was a fine gait and a ground-gainer.

Lincoln's thoughts revolved around his plan to take the stage next day for Rock Springs and find Lucy

Bandon if he could not locate the man whom Burton had called Hank Miller. He scarcely noted the passing of time. At sunset he reached the bluff, and looked up to see the rim rock where he had stood with Lucy. He let Bay choose his own gait up the zigzag road. The deep-chested horse seemed tireless and never once halted of his own accord. Once on top Lincoln rested him while he turned to watch the sunset, a marvelous pageant of painted clouds in long stripes and streamers, red, yellow and mauve. Soon he rode on again deep in thought, pondering how he could achieve a meeting with Lucy Bandon, in spite of her aunt.

Soon after dark Lincoln arrived at Headly's livery stable, where he turned over his horse and inquired for Vince. That worthy had not been in evidence all day according to Bill. Lincoln hoped to find his partner at the Chinese restaurant, but again was disappointed. He began to feel a bit anxious. He had his supper and went outside to wait. But Vince did not show up. Finally Linc went to his lodging and to bed, worn out more from worry about Lucy and now Vince than from the day's activity.

In the morning he was up early. He gave unusual attention to his appearance, as he did not want to meet Lucy Bandon without looking his best. He had never found it so hard to choose a scarf. He decided to wear a coat with large pockets in which he deposited articles indispensable to himself on this particular trip. Vince failed to show up again either at the restaurant or the stable. Lincoln left a message with Bill to the effect that if he did not return from Rock Springs within a week Vince was to follow and hunt him up.

When the westbound stage rolled out of South Pass Lincoln was on the seat with the driver, an ex-teamster named Slocum. He was the kind of westerner that Lincoln regarded as the salt of the earth. Raw-boned, rugged of build, with a leathery visage and eyes like slits of gray fire, he showed his years of hard contacts with the frontier. There were eight passengers inside the coach, and a full complement of baggage and express. Before starting, Slocum had been loquacious with his passengers, especially two young women from the East. While waiting at the hotel he had given Bradway an appraising glance, and later, after someone no doubt had acquainted him with the cowboy's status there, he deliberately looked the Nebraskan over to make his own estimate. Linc knew he would not have to open a conversation. But they had surmounted the long grade out of South Pass and were bowling along through the sage before Slocum spoke.

"Bradway, whar you hail from—Deadwood or Abiline?" he drawled.

"Nebraska. I was born in Missouri. But I know both those towns," returned Lincoln, in an agreeable tone.

"Wal, you have the look of them range-ridin' fire-eaters I'm thinkin' of. Boy, you're out of your latitude hyar."

"How so?"

"Ain't it kinda slow fer you?"

"I haven't noticed it."

"From Missoury, eh?" So'm I. I was born in Westfork before they called it Kansas City. Never was a cowboy, but I been everythin' else. Scout, soldier, pony-express rider, teamster. Seen a sight of western life, in my time."

"Which is telling me you know western men," rejoined Lincoln.

"Wal, I ought to. The Dakotas, Montana, Wyomin' are open books to me, knowed all the desperados. Been friends with Wild Bill and Calamity Jane, an' all the gunmen of their day. . . . Anythin' you want to know about Wyomin', son?"

"What makes you think I might want to know something?" inquired Bradway.

"Wal, you rode with me on this stage from Lander. You had thet look. An' I've heerd what you done to them fourflushers in South Pass. . . . Son, you're lookin' for someone."

"Slocum, you hit it plumb center," admitted his

passenger. "Did you happen to know a cowpoke named Jimmy Weston?"

"Not personal. But he's daid."

"Yes. That's why I'm here."

"I see. Weston was yore pard, I reckon. You figger there's somethin' queer about his death?"

"I figured that before I came out here. Now I know it."

"Wal, it looked queer to me. That is to say—it didn't 'pear all open an' simple, like the run-o'-the-range deaths of cowboys, whether by violence or bein' piled off a hoss. But I don't know anythin'."

"Did you happen to see Hank Miller in Rock Springs?"

"I shore did. How'd you know he was there?" asked Slocum, in surprise.

"Heard it down in the valley yesterday."

"Yes, I seen Hank. He interest you?"

"Yes, he does, a little," returned Lincoln, with a short laugh.

"You lookin' for Hank?"

"Yes. Rather."

"Somethin' agin him?"

"I've never seen the man. I haven't a thing against him—that I can prove. All the same I'll kill him if he doesn't come clean with how and why he hauled my dead friend from somewhere in the valley to Emery's joint in South Pass."

Slocum slapped his long reins and urged his four horses to a somewhat brisker trot. His leathery visage betrayed nothing, but there was a thoughtful look in his bleak eyes. Linc saw where the main road turned away from the head of the Sweetwater Valley. Bold bare mountains heaved up in the west. A herd of antelope crossed the road and turned to gaze, long ears erect.

"Son, I reckon you know more'n I do about thet deal," spoke up Slocum. "Thet is, about whatever is gossip in South Pass. Yesterday I dropped mail back at the forks we jest passed. One of Hargrove's riders.

An' I told him I'd seen Hank Miller in Rock Springs. But I didn't tell him what I'm goin' to tell you. An' I'm tellin' you because I had a pard once, close as a brother."

"Go on!" urged the cowboy, as the driver paused and seemed to lapse into thought.

"Three days ago Hank Miller came to me in Rock Springs," continued Slocum. "He'd been soakin' up consid'able red likker. An' he looked mighty mean. He asked me if Kit Bandon had come on my stage. I told him no. An' he bit out: 'You tell her when you git back to the Pass thet by Gawd she'd better meet me hyar pronto, as she agreed!' "

"Well!" exclaimed the Nebraskan. "I wonder what Miller meant by that." Here was news of tremendous significance, if he could fit it in with what he already knew.

"I couldn't git thet message to Kit by word of mouth," went on Slocum. "She wasn't in town."

"Kit's Mormon riders told me yesterday that she had taken the stage for Rock Springs."

"Missed me by a coupla days, by Judas! Wal, mebbe it's jest as wal I didn't git thet message to her. She'd kill Miller."

"If she doesn't, I will—unless he talks."

"Wal, you can kill him, but thet won't make him talk. I'd go slow if I was you. The cowboys out hyar 'pear a queer breed. . . . Bradway, how you figger thet message of Miller's to the Bandon woman?"

"How do you?"

"Wal, since I spilled it to you . . . but no! you tell me, an' if I agree, I'll say so."

"Fair enough. . . . I figure that if Miller actually hauled Weston's dead body from somewhere in the valley to South Pass, then Kit Bandon had something to do with it."

"No doubt at all, son . . . an' I'll be damned!"

"Slocum, you're thinking that it's a long lane that has no turning."

"Nope. I was thinkin' how the pitcher thet keeps goin' to the well always gets broke in the end."

Lincoln snapped his fingers in the air with that peculiar characteristic of his when something that had puzzled him suddenly cleared itself up in his mind, or when one of his uncertain ideas was definitely falling into place.

"Slocum, you're the first man I've met in Wyoming who has had the courage to meet me even halfway in respect to my opinion of this Bandon woman."

The stagecoach driver coughed and replied, almost apologetically: "Wal, Bradway, mebbe I'm one man who doesn't feel inclined or obliged to knuckle down to Kit Bandon. An' again, mebbe it's because you're like my old pard of the Injun days."

"Plenty reason, and thanks," returned Lincoln, feeling depressed. He discovered that despite all the damning evidence against the woman he had come upon he yet did not want to find Kit Bandon to be guilty. He could not explain it. In his heart he knew that the Maverick Queen in some way was implicated in the death of his best friend. Yet, such was the magnetism of this beautiful outlaw woman that he wanted to think her guiltless. Was it because she had shown him so plainly that she loved him? It was something hard for a man to resist—even when he knows that she has revealed her passion to a dozen other men.

Slocum's seatmate lapsed into silence, brooding over this new angle to his problem. Fortunately, there was a chance of finding Miller, and he counted on the teamster in Rock Springs to supply him with the proof he needed to avenge Jimmy Weston's murder.

And while he brooded the stage rolled on over a good road through a lonely country of gray-green sage bounded on all horizons by gray escarpments and scalloped slopes above which the white and black ranges rose in their ageless majesty. In the distance he saw a browsing herd of elk. And the sage was dotted with white-rumped antelope. The hours passed, the passengers slept as the wheels revolved and the steady clip-clop of rhythmic hoofs ate up the distance. The rich sage and grassland gradually gave way to barrens and dry lake beds, and a rougher country generally. They forded several amber streams of swift flowing water. Lincoln saw many signs of beavers in the willow thickets.

The time came when Slocum roused himself from the silence that apparently he had thought his passenger preferred to keep. And he began to talk of interesting events that had taken place in the old days and more recently in the country they were passing through. Not until late in the day did they pass a ranch house, a lonely little cabin, bravely facing the vast range. But after that ranches appeared few and far between, until around about sunset when they arrived at a post where they were to spend the night. Linc avoided as best he could contacts with the well-meaning and affable passengers. After supper he paced a lonely windswept road and soon sought the bed provided, anxious over the events of tomorrow when the stage reached Rock Springs, and restless over the thought that tomorrow he would be seeing Lucy.

Rock Springs appeared to be much more of a town than South Pass. It was an important station on the Union Pacific Railroad, and the center of a soft-coal mining district. As such, it seemed to have the orderliness and stability of a permanent town. South Pass was like a mushroom. It had come up in a night and if the mines played out it could vanish almost as quickly.

Nevertheless as Linc walked down the main street, early in the afternoon, he saw that saloons and gambling halls were not conspicuous for their scarcity. While there was no rush of pedestrians as in South Pass, there were plenty of ranchers, farmers, and cowboys in town on business.

The Elk Hotel, to which Slocum had directed the Nebraskan, was a large and commodious frame building facing the railroad station. He went in to inquire if the Misses Bandon were registered there. The clerk replied in the affirmative, and the knowledge that Lucy was being sheltered in that same building set his nerves tingling. Not often had he written his name so illegibly. He had a room assigned to him and then asked where he could find the best clothing store in town. Upon being informed he hurried out, desiring to change his cowboy garb before he met the Bandons.

The suits available in the store did not greatly impress the suddenly hard-to-please Nebraskan. There were plenty of them made of fine material, but too plain to appeal to his present mood. An elaborate black broadcloth gambler's outfit, with flowered vest and ruffled white shirt, wide-brimmed sombrero and high-top boots, all of the richest quality, went a bit to the other extreme, but in the end Lincoln purchased a suit of rather extreme cut that fit him as though it had been tailored for him. He returned to the hotel and to his room on the second floor without meeting the two women he feared yet longed to see, and it was with great relief that he threw his new purchases on the bed. Beads of sweat dampened his brow.

"Lordy!" he muttered. "What would Jimmy have thought of me? Vince will think I've gone loco. . . . And so I have! . . . But I've got it pretty bad! I guess I'd wear an Indian war bonnet if I thought it would impress Lucy Bandon!"

Whenever Linc was not in action he was deep in thought. What on earth, he wondered, was he going to say when he met them? Fortunately he could go slowly. The Bandons would stay in Rock Springs until the herd of young cattle arrived. Kit Bandon would sell or ship by railroad before leaving town. Leisurely Lincoln bathed and shaved, and arrayed himself in his handsome new outfit. Then he surveyed himself with grim amusement. He discovered that he really was vain of his good looks—something he had always felt was a point where he differed from other cowboys. He scarcely recognized himself in his city garb, as he turned this way and that to observe himself in the wavy mirror. He would miss his guess if he did not give Lucy Bandon the surprise of her life. And he had to laugh when he remembered Kit Bandon. If she had liked him in his old range outfit, what would she think of him now?

The big guns belted on bulged the frock coat a little at the hips. Gravely he made sure that they could be drawn quickly in case of need. The mirror showed the butts plainly, glinting darkly against the black fabric of his clothes.

As Linc viewed the somber apparition in the mirror he could not restrain a queer feeling of satisfaction at the thought of Lucy Bandon. After all, this masquerade was for her. Suddenly he espied his spurs. He always wore them except when he slept, and often even then, when he was out on the range. At length he decided that he would not feel himself unless he wore at least these accouterments of his trade. Leisurely he buckled them on. Long, with huge rowels, worn bright from long use, the Spanish silver spurs looked most effective against the fine black leather of his boots. And as the cowboy stepped they jangled musically.

Then Bradway extracted a roll of greenbacks from his jeans, and with another glance at his stern image in the mirror, left the room to go downstairs.

It amazed him to find that his preoccupation had been so great that the day had passed and lights were bright in the hotel lobby. The lobby appeared to be noisy and active with people; loud voices and the clink of glasses came from a bar near at hand. He could look through the parlor into the dining room, where guests were entering.

The Nebraskan stood back at ease and watched for the two women he expected to see sooner or later. He was aware of the attention his presence created, and felt utterly indifferent to it. Outwardly cold, burning within, he awaited a meeting he divined would be a crucial one. Ready for he knew not what, he felt equal to any situation.

A handsome stripling of a cowboy slouched into the lobby. He answered the description given Lincoln by Bloom Burton, except that his actual presence bore a vitality and a cool demeanor that Lincoln had learned to associate with cowboys of the hard and reckless school. He packed a gun and wore it low. Lincoln did not get a full look at his face.

The cowboy was looking for someone with an impatience and boldness that kept him on the move. Linc had just about made up his mind to accost him when he disappeared into a corridor that evidently led to the bar. He had a pretty good hunch that it was Hank Miller, and that he was here to meet the Bandons. The Nebraskan kept his eye on the lobby where Kit Bandon and Lucy would have to enter from the floor above, and he had scarcely returned to his point of vantage when they appeared at the head of the broad stairway.

Lucy was holding her aunt's arm, evidently trying to detain her. But Kit descended, step by step, until Lincoln could see her great black eyes searching the lobby. The two women had dressed for dinner. The Nebraskan's gaze devoured the slim girl, attractively clad in blue. But she was only a pale shadow beside the colorful Kit. They reached the bottom of the stairway and paused under the bright cluster of oil lamps.

Linc watched them with intense curiosity, restraining his eagerness to approach. Lucy had not ceased her importunities. Her pretty face betrayed repressed agitation; her eyes shone darkly. Her aunt's beautiful face, too, wore a troubled look. Without her smile, the play of her features, and her customary animation, she appeared older. He muttered to himself: "You bet you're in trouble old girl—a hell of a lot deeper than you know!"

At that moment the handsome cowboy put in an appearance. Linc saw only his back as he entered the scene. He moved with grace and assurance. Bradway thought he could read in Kit Bandon's dark eyes as she glanced up at the cowboy a fleeting suspicion and fear, and at the same time a look of anger which she made no effort to conceal. If the cowboy were Miller he was evidently on her black list. But something the newcomer must have said seemed to mollify her. Then the cowboy turned to Lucy; his manner toward the girl was one of bold admiration and he held her hand so long that a fire of jealousy was kindled in Bradway. So this was the way the wind blew! Kit stood by laughing at them. Evidently she was enjoying the little byplay, but Linc did not share her enjoyment. He regained his cool equilibrium only when Lucy pulled her hand free. It was a deliberate move, expressive of annoyance if not disgust, as was the look she gave the smiling cowboy. The tight hot band around Lincoln's heart fell away.

He approached the trio. Kit's attention was on the cowboy, whose back was turned to Linc. But as the Nebraskan drew close Lucy recognized him. He bowed, but she only stared, her lips parted. Suddenly she gave a violent start and turned pale. Then the Nebraskan spoke to Kit.

"Miss Bandon, here I am, late, I'm sorry to say," he remarked, smiling coolly. Kit wheeled at the sound of a voice that was familiar. But for an instant she did not recognize him. With a magnificent flash of her eyes she swept him up and down, and back again! Lincoln removed his new Stetson to make her a gallant bow. As he straightened up he saw Lucy stiffen. The cowboy turned as on a pivot. Then Kit recognized Bradway. What followed was infinitely more than Linc had counted on. As if by magic the troubled face of the Maverick Queen was transformed. Amazement, incredulity, wonder—and something even more revealing, a lovely light flashing in her smile—flooded her expressive and lovely face, leaving him anything but sure of himself. She was obviously overjoyed, overcome at the sight of him. And as Linc looked into those melting, eager, dark eyes he seemed to forget all about the younger woman beside her.

"Linc Bradway!—You—you—" she cried, her voice rich and full, breaking with emotion. "You followed me? Dressed like a flash gambler! You fooled even *me!* . . . Oh, you dear boy!"

She caught his outstretched hand and shook it with

an unrestrained fever of delight. Her fervor seemed considerably greater than he had anticipated. His nerve and wit did not desert him, but he felt as if he suddenly had been enveloped by a burning wind. He suffered a moment of helpless inability to cope with the effusiveness and fire of her greeting. Then she was presenting him to the others.

"Lucy, this is the cowboy friend I told you about— Linc Bradway. It appears he is also a gambler and actor. Lord only knows what else!"

As Linc met the level blue eyes of the young girl he tried to send with his gaze a message expressing joy at their reunion and a plea for understanding. She acknowledged the introduction with a slight bow and averted glance.

"Linc, this is a cowboy friend of ours—Hank Miller," went on Kit, happily. "Hank, shake hands with Linc Bradway."

But Miller did not offer his hand. If he had done so Linc would have ignored it. He was concerned with the fact that he was meeting Miller face to face, and the moment was pregnant with many possibilities. Perhaps the instinct so powerful in Lincoln had communicated itself to Miller.

"How do, Mr. Bradway. Reckon I wouldn't take you for a cowboy," he drawled, insolently.

"Howdy, Hank Miller," retorted Lincoln, curtly. "Same for me. I'd take you for a teamster."

"Teamster?" echoed Miller, taken off his guard.

"Sure. *Teamster,* you know. A hombre who drives wagons!" As he spoke Lincoln disengaged his arm from Kit's, and stepped aside. This man was no unknown quantity to him. Miller was the rank poison type of cowboy. His handsome tanned face blazed scarlet, and a look of hatred and suspicion burned in his eyes. They were not smiling now, nor sleepy.

"Bradway, thet crack calls for an explanation," he muttered.

"Aw, you don't have to be told in kindergarten language. You're a bright fellow." He had rubbed

Miller the wrong way, on a raw spot. And he had gauged him correctly almost at first sight. He felt that merciless instinct, that surge of icy rage, which rose in him when he divined that he had to kill a man.

"Say, you jealous roosters!" broke in Kit Bandon. "Don't make us a scene here in the hotel. Have you no manners?" And she grasped Miller's arm and held on to it.

Bradway eased his posture and said: "Sorry, ladies; I guess your friend didn't like my remark. I'm a careless person. . . . Miller, I apologize."

"Yaass! Well, I never swallow my words. . . . You can go to hell!"

"Thanks. There's a pretty fair possibility that you will beat me there."

"Hank, cut it!" flashed Kit, as the cowboy opened his tight lips to reply. "Linc, will you join us at dinner?"

"Delighted, provided the dinner is on me," he replied.

"Lucy, take charge of him, and for heaven's sake keep him quiet," ordered Kit, leading Miller off toward the dining room. She hung on the cowboy's arm, while she obviously was delivering herself of some strong and angry language. Linc took advantage of the moment to bend toward Lucy and whisper: "Lucy, don't look like that! For God's sake, don't believe anything she told you!"

"You hypocrite!" whispered Lucy, gazing straight ahead.

"Lucy, I beg of you . . ." protested Lincoln, unhappily.

"You handsome flash gambler! Cowboy?" She let out a little scornful trill of laughter, cold as ice. "Jimmy Weston was a liar! . . . I was crazy to believe a word he said!"

"Certainly you were. And *I* ought to have my head examined for falling in love with you!" Linc's quick retort ended Lucy's defiance and the whispered colloquy, carried on behind Kit's back. She led them into a corner of the dining room, where a table had been reserved. When Kit designated where they were to sit Lincoln said apologetically: "Mis Bandon, would you mind if I sat where I could face the room?" And he moved to the chair in the corner. Kit sat down to his right and Lucy to his left. Miller laughed. "I'm not afraid to turn my back on anyone. . . . No one's lookin' for me!"

"Miller, I venture to guess you are mistaken," said Lincoln.

This exchange of words angered Kit.

"Can't you two gamecocks be gentlemen long enough for us to eat? . . . After dinner, if you must keep picking at each other go out into the street."

"Wal, thet suits me. I'm pretty hungry," rejoined Miller, and he smiled at Lucy. His presence, minus the insolent tone and look, was singularly attractive. Lincoln made the reservation that Miller might be a dangerous rival for the girl, as well as being a hard man to draw against.

"Miss Bandon, do they serve champagne in this two-bit burg?" asked the Nebraskan.

"Indeed they do," replied Kit, beaming upon him. "I have already ordered dinner for us. But you can order the champagne."

Miller spent a long moment in keen and speculative scrutiny of Bradway. Probably no man could intimidate this hombre. He belonged to the breed of cowboys who would fight upon the slightest provocation. For the moment Linc dismissed a draw with him from his mind. With the ordering of dinner and wine the situation eased. Linc Bradway found Lucy's foot touching his, but when he attempted to return the pressure, she moved it away. Twice more this happened, even while Miller talked softly to her, his eyes hungrily fixed upon her. Lincoln listened quietly to Kit's talk. She was evidently trying to shake off the apprehension or the trouble she had betrayed earlier. At last Lincoln succeeded in pressing the toe of his boot against Lucy's foot. This time she made no effort to pull away. The contact, slight as it was, heartened Lincoln and lifted the feeling of despair that had fastened itself upon him. He tried to think of some way that he could devise that would enable him to talk with her privately. He knew how she must feel about her aunt's greeting and of Kit's air of possession so clearly shown toward him. He longed to reassure her. But she seemed greatly interested in what Miller was saying to her. He turned back to Kit Bandon.

"You were expecting someone to meet you in the lobby?" he inquired in a casual tone.

"Yes. I had an appointment—about a deal for cattle," she returned, evasively.

"Your herd will be in tomorrow, I hear," continued the Nebraskan.

"How do you know that?" asked Kit, obviously surprised.

"I rode out to your ranch day before yesterday. Your Mormon riders were about ready to start the drive."

"You saw them—talked with them?"

"Surely. They interested me. Luke Mathews particularly."

"You interest yourself a good deal in other people's business?" she retorted, in a tone she had never before used with him. This information, his apparently casual speech, his inscrutability, and perhaps something that she felt lay behind his words seemed to perturb her a good deal. Quickly she tried to conceal her perturbation behind a gay laugh. But even so, Lincoln felt a chill. It was not dissimilar to one he had felt many times at the thought of death—at the imminence of death. How strange that this beautiful willful woman, all glamour and fire, should arouse such a feeling of foreboding in him.

The serving of dinner interrupted conversation. It was an excellent meal for a hotel in a border town. Bradway did not know good wine from bad, but he partook scantily of the champagne. Miller and Kit were not so chary. Lincoln watched Lucy as she hesi-

tatingly touched her lips to her glass. It was evident
that she was not accustomed to much drinking. Their
eyes met over their glasses, and she made a slight move
of distaste. Linc swore anew to himself that if his life
were spared during this hard task imposed upon him
he would devote the remainder of it to this sweet girl's
happiness, if she would let him.

The champagne, apparently, had cheered Kit out of
her distraught mood. She reached forward to pat Linc's
hand where it rested on the table just as a bellboy
brought her a note. He watched her read it, and saw
her brow become clouded.

"Hank, our—my party is waiting outside," she said.
Then she spoke to Bradway. "Linc, we must leave you
for a little while. I'm sorry, but it's important. Where
will you wait?"

"There's some champagne left," drawled Linc. "Perhaps I can persuade Lucy to have another glass."

"No, not here," Kit replied, hastily. She seemed to
be thinking swiftly. Lincoln grasped that she did not
want him or Lucy to see the person she and Miller were
to meet. "Come, Hank, we must go. . . . I'll tell you,
Linc. There's a parlor at the head of the stairs. Wait
there for us. We shouldn't be long."

"Don't hurry on our account," rejoined Lincoln,
meeting Miller's dark and speculative eyes. "I'm sure
I shall be pleasantly engaged."

"Ahuh. I get you, Bradway," retorted the cowboy,
sullenly. And he turned to Kit, who had arisen from
the table. "You go meet thet feller. I'll stay here."

"You fool!" snapped Kit. The look she gave Miller
was freighted with hate and menace. "You come with
me." She seized his arm and almost dragged him away,
turning once to beckon Lucy and Lincoln. They followed, with Lincoln a little behind the girl. This was
his chance and he could hardly contain himself. He
was afraid Kit Bandon might see his obvious exulta-
tion, but she did not look back again.

Lincoln led Lucy up the wide stairway. Her eyes
were averted, her chin up, her slender form erect and

stiff. His heavy gun bumped against her as they reached the landing. He turned to look down into the lobby; Kit and Miller were talking with a tall man who possessed the weather-beaten complexion and the cut of a cattleman. Miller was gazing up at Lincoln and Lucy with baleful and frustrated eyes; he was still gazing when Kit drew him out of Bradway's line of vision.

Chapter VII

∽∾⊚∾∽

Linc turned to the curtained doorway and peered inside. The parlor was illuminated by a lamp with a red shade. He flung the curtains aside and turned to Lucy. "Come," he said. It was an invitation, not a command.

She was reluctant to enter but finally brushed past him without looking up and walked across the room to one of the open windows. Lincoln slowly followed, going to the opposite window and looking out into the night. What seemed to be a small park with grass and trees lay between the street and the railroad yards. Beyond the tracks a sharp bluff loomed above the town. Far beyond, he knew, were the Wasatch Mountains, dark and somber against the moonlit sky.

Lincoln stepped back from the window and said: "Lucy, we have only a few minutes to talk, and I for one don't want to take all this valuable time quarreling with you about what someone has told you about me."

"What someone told me!" she retorted. The suppressed anger in her low voice startled Lincoln.

"That's what I said," he replied. "Kit Bandon has told you something about me. Will you tell me what it was?"

"It was too sickening for me to repeat."

"Well, it isn't true, whatever she might have said. Possibly it was something in reference to the fact that

131

I found her to be just as fascinating as did the other cowboys. . . . Well, I did find her fascinating. She is an incredibly glamorous and alluring woman. I don't suppose it's entirely honorable of me to tell on a woman who—who has gone out of her way to be agreeable to me, but I'm bound to let you know that I think she was sincere. Nevertheless I still believe there *must* have been some other reason prompting her besides merely wanting to collect another cowboy's scalp."

"Please stop," whispered Lucy. "It's unbearable."

"That's only because you are thinking wrong."

"How could I be thinking wrong—*you* admit it."

"I admit nothing that is shameful. Whatever she may have told you, Lucy, this is God's truth. She called me up to her parlor in the *Leave It* to warn me. . . . She put her arms around—my neck—and—and kissed me. . . . Honestly, Lucy, I thought I was struck by lightning. You see I haven't been kissed often—never by such as her. She seemed to take it for granted that I had succumbed to her charm—I suppose she is used to that. But I hadn't—not with my mind. I should have repulsed her, I know, but I doubt if the man lives who could resist her when taken by surprise that way. I don't know what she thought—but no matter what she thought, I did *not* fall for her blandishment. That's all that happened, Lucy, I swear it."

"Evidently you can lie as well as you can shoot people in cold blood."

"I'm not lying," flashed Linc, cut to the quick by the girl's accusation.

"Oh, you're just another slick-tongued cowboy trying to make game of me—like they all do."

"Don't insult me, Lucy," he said bitterly, attempting to control himself. "You'll say something before long that you'll be sorry for all the rest of your life. I know this looks bad to you, but for God's sake try to trust me. It's tremendously important for both of us!"

He took hold of her arm and tried to draw her from the window. She repulsed him, turning her face away. Angered, he reached around to grasp her shoulders and twist her about to face him. She was pale and her eyes were full of scorn. Futilely she tried to avert them from his searching gaze.

"Look at me!" he cried.

She wrenched one hand free and slapped him soundly on the cheek. Suddenly enraged despite himself, Lincoln slapped her back.

"You damned little spitfire! Haven't you any sense whatsoever?"

The red leaped to her cheek, contrasting with her paleness. He saw that he must have hurt her. Her hand flew to her face, and the tears flooded her eyes.

"I'm sorry. I shouldn't have done that, but you've been so bullheaded and unreasonable." He grasped her arms powerfully again and held her despite her weak efforts to free herself.

"Oh, you are such a liar," she cried.

"I'm not a liar, Lucy."

"You're just like all the rest of them. I hate cowboys. I've liked a lot of them and I—I—could have loved Jimmy . . . and what did I get for it? Deceit—treachery! All of them lost their heads over my aunt. That wouldn't have been so bad but they . . ."

She bit her lip, evidently realizing what she was about to betray, and for a moment she was pale and silent. Lincoln quickly lost his anger with the realization that he must convince her—that he had right and love on his side.

"Please believe me—trust me, Lucy," he said, simply.

"Oh, if I only could," she cried. "But it would be so weak, so foolish of me. You're just like the others—only you're more clever, more convincing. . . ."

"The honest truth, Lucy, is that I fell in love with you at first sight and every moment since I've loved you more."

"I—I don't believe you," she murmured, on the verge of tears.

Instead of shaking her again he pulled her into his arms and held her close.

"Let me go!" she cried, furiously, yet he could feel that she was weakening.

"Not until you come to your senses."

She struggled but was powerless to break his hold. Straining from him she bent her face backward, her lips parted, her eyes dark, her color mounting. It was almost impossible for Lincoln to restrain himself from kissing her.

"You not only are a liar but a brute! Suppose my aunt should come and see you now?"

"Lucy, I give you my word, I'm not afraid of it."

"She—she would kill you!"

"Oh, she would?" he queried, sharply. "That confirms other things I've heard. . . . But I'm not so easy to kill, even for a man. . . . I am mightily interested in this aunt of yours. And my interest has nothing to do with her charm or magnetic personality. Lucy, you will have to take me on trust just as I seem to have to take a great deal on trust. I wish that you would take back what you called me—liar and brute."

"I won't do it."

"All right. Then take this from a liar and a brute. . . ." He crushed her in his arms and pulled her face close to his. She gasped and uttered a little indistinct cry. Then he released her and she stood facing him silently, her cheeks flaming, her eyes blazing, her lips trembling. With a quick movement she turned her back toward him and with nervous fingers began fumbling with her disheveled hair.

"I wouldn't kiss a girl who could think me as low-down as you do, even when I'm mad about her. . . . So forget that for the time being. I went to our meeting place on the rim that morning. I waited hours for you. I never saw anything as lovely as your valley in the morning light. As I waited by my signal fire I had wonderful plans and thoughts about you and me when the job that brought me here was finished. It dawned on me after those long hours of waiting that you were not going to come. Since you had promised to come, I began to worry that something had happened to you.

I rode down into the valley to hunt you up. When I came to the belt of timber I turned off the road and took the trail through the willows. I wanted to have a look at the ranch before I rode in. Well, I stayed in the willows until I could hear the river. Then I smelled smoke. I knew there was a camp near, so I slipped along cautiously until I came into a clearing on the banks of the river. There was a little camp with a smoldering fire. In a tall willow I saw a man with a telescope looking over the Bandon ranch . . ."

"Oh," she replied, hurriedly, evidently perturbed. "Then what did you do?"

"I called him down out of the tree pronto. Since you are so firmly convinced that I'm a liar and a cheat, I won't supply you with any material for additional accusations, but I will tell you that interrupting this little piece of spy work made things look bad for Kit Bandon."

"It could look bad for your man, too," retorted Lucy. "What you saw could be misunderstood. I'm afraid—Lincoln, you must tell me what he said."

"Perhaps," replied the Nebraskan. Then he continued: "I rode out of the willows, crossed the river and went to the ranch house. You know, of course, there wasn't anybody home nor any message from you explaining why you hadn't met me. I decided to ride out to the roundup which the spy had been watching with his telescope. The roundup was a mile or so from the corrals and when I rode up to those Mormon cowpokes I thought I was in for a fight. I guess they were more scared than I was but certainly not as curious. I learned a good deal more from them than they learned from me."

"But what did you find out?" she whispered, nervously.

"Lucy, I know honest cattlemen when I see them. Those Mormons were good boys—and they do not know anything about Kit Bandon. Except that she pays them big money!"

"What *could* they know about my aunt?"

"What do you think?" he said watching her closely. "I can see, Lucy, that you know a good deal more than you're going to tell me now," he replied in a tone of resignation. "I can be patient. As soon as you realize I'm honest—that I love you—that I'm going to fight *your* battle, as well as Jim's and mine, you will confide in me."

"If you are against my aunt, you also will be against me," she cried.

"I'm not her enemy yet and I never will be yours."

"But *I* would be your enemy if you were hers," she said, so quietly that he could scarcely hear what she had said.

"Just a few moments ago you accused me of being her lover. You're unreasonable, girl. I know this is a hard situation for you. But try to realize how difficult it is for *me*. . . . Well, after talking with the Mormons I rode back to South Pass and took the stage early next morning and here I am."

"Did you follow us?"

"Yes, but what mainly brought me here was to meet Hank Miller."

A look of dread came into the girl's blue eyes.

"You must be seeking him—because you've heard of something—something—concerning Jimmy?"

"Yes, that is true, Lucy. However, I didn't expect to find him such a tough hombre. He would have been a bad customer to meet anyhow but he seems to have some claim on you and that's going to make it worse."

"But he hasn't any claim on me," she denied vehemently, her cheeks blazing. "It's only that Aunt Kit—" Then again she closed her lips tightly.

"Lucy, it was easy to see he was in love with you—and almighty jealous."

"Yes," admitted Lucy, "but I am not in love with him."

"No? Then who are you in love with?"

"Not with any cowboy! No cowboy will ever hurt me again!"

"You don't imagine you're hurt," said Lincoln,

gently. "But one word more about this Miller. I'm afraid I'm not avoiding tangling with him. But if he tells me what I want to know and unless he's particularly ornery and mean, I'll try to for your sake. Only if he's the kind of hombre I think he is, he'll pull a gun at the drop of a hat, and I'm simply warning you that I don't want to take any chances."

"You will be in danger, Lincoln?" she asked falteringly.

She turned away to the window again and pressed her face and hands against the pane. He saw the constriction in her throat. Suddenly he had an inspiration.

"Wait a minute, Lucy," he whispered, huskily.

He went to the door and out on the landing. Descending a few steps of the stairway he bent down to look into the lobby below. There was no sign of Kit Bandon and her companions. Then he hurried back to Lucy.

"Don't you *want* to believe in me, Lucy?" he implored.

"More than anything in the world," she answered, softly.

"All right, I can prove to you that what I said is true."

"Words are cheap. You could make black look white," she said wearily.

"Yes, but actions are truer than words."

"What do you mean by action?" she asked.

"I will marry you right this hour—if you'll have me?"

She turned to him, incredulous, as if she had not heard aright.

"Lucy," he went on, "up there on the Pass you led me to think that you respected me—that perhaps you could love me. I think you even were willing to forget that I have led a rough life in a rough country. I'm no different now than I was that day I met you. Won't you believe that?"

"I—I can conceive of such a thing . . . but the idea

of marrying you is preposterous—mad. You—we—it isn't possible."

"It might be," he pleaded. "This town is big enough to have a parson. Let me go out and see?"

"No, no. You're mad."

"I may be mad, but I love you. And I think that's the way to save us both."

"It wouldn't save us," she cried, wildly. "She'd kill us both! I didn't tell you before because I was afraid to, but Kit is truly and sincerely in love with you. She says you are the man she's been waiting for. She regrets the love affairs she's had with other men. She is counting upon marrying you. And when she makes up her mind to something, nothing can stand in her way. . . . That is why it would mean ruin for us."

That was Lincoln's moment. He seized her hands and drew her to him. "Lucy, that sweet and beautiful love you had for me couldn't have died in a moment, could it?"

"Oh, no, no, it hasn't—I tried to destroy it but I couldn't. It has tortured me—"

His lips closing on hers halted the sentence. He felt her trembling.

"Let me go," she pleaded.

"No, Lucy darling, I'll never let you go now." He kissed her again.

"Please, Lincoln—this is madness."

"My darling, say you will marry me?" he whispered and without giving her time to answer he crushed her in his arms. She struggled, but it was only a half-hearted effort. Her eyes were opened wide now and staring up into his. And as he looked down into those eyes which could never dissemble or conceal the truth, he *knew*. His heart leaped joyously.

"Don't hold—me—so tight," she whispered. "I can't breathe . . . Lincoln, please—let—me—go."

Her strength had gone and she was clinging to him, trembling.

"My dearest," he whispered.

Her head fell forward then on his breast. She had

yielded. He could feel it in her fingers clutching his coat, in her little inarticulate cry of surrender.

"Bless you, Lucy," he whispered, taking her two hands in one of his and holding them against his breast. "I swear to you, my darling, that never as long as you live, will you regret this moment."

"Oh, Lincoln, hurry before I lose my courage," she cried.

He rushed out of the room and halfway down the stairway. Then reason and caution returned to him and he made his way down the rest of the stairs and through the lobby. Kit Bandon and her companions were nowhere in sight. Lincoln went out. It was quite dark. Only a few yellow lights glimmered weakly here and there, when he turned down the street. He seemed to be treading on air. At the next corner he crossed the street, and entering a store he inquired if there were a parson in Rock Springs. He was informed that there was a Reverend Smith who was on his way to Oregon and who temporarily was holding meetings at the church right next to the depot. He found himself running the block and a half to the frame, steepleless building which served all denominations in Rock Springs. The church door was open, a small oil lantern flickering over the entrance. Lincoln caught the strains of an organ: evidently it was nearing time for some kind of service. His knock was answered by a boy who informed the hard-breathing cowboy that the preacher lived in the small frame house next door. A little round-faced, smiling man wearing the black garb of a churchman greeted Lincoln with a smile.

"Are you the minister?" Lincoln managed to blurt out.

"I am, my good sir. What can I do for you?"

"I want to get married," panted Lincoln.

"Well, where's the bride?" inquired the minister, looking behind the eager bridegroom.

"I can get her here in five minutes. What will I have to have?"

"A ring and the lady's consent. I can supply everything else."

"I'll be back in five minutes."

Lincoln rushed back the way he had come. Happening to pass a shop with a tray of jewelry in the window Lincoln dashed in breathlessly and purchased a diamond ring and a wedding ring that would go on his little finger. He did not wait for the change, but left the amazed clerk staring at him wide-eyed.

"So far, so good," he whispered. Then, for the first time, as he neared the hotel he slowed down. A quick glance showed that the Maverick Queen and her visitors still were absent from the lobby. He bounded up the stairway three steps at a time and burst into the parlor, half-fearing Lucy might have lost heart and run away. But she was still there. He was so out of breath that he could not speak clearly; in the dim light the girl looked up at him with eloquent and frightened eyes. He kissed her and pressed her hand reassuringly. Then he led her out of the room and down the stairs. By the time they had reached the street the pounding of his heart had subsided enough so that he was able to say, "Lucy—I found—a parson. I have the—it's really true—it's going—to happen."

The darkness enveloped them like a cloak. Never had Lincoln known night to be so sweet and welcome.

"Oh, I'm so terribly afraid."

"I'm not afraid now of being stopped. And I'm not even thinking about what they can do to us—afterward."

He hurried her along the street.

"Don't look back, Lucy. . . . Thank God I had the courage to ask you. And that you found the trust to come with me."

He strode so swiftly that she was almost forced to run to keep up with him. When they reached the little house beside the church the door was open and a bright light shone cheerfully through the front window. At Lincoln's knock the minister appeared and quietly asked them in. As the preacher closed the door behind them Bradway's relief was so great that he felt his legs weakening under him.

"Well, you made it in less than five minutes," said the parson, beaming upon them. "This is my wife," he continued, indicating the comely, placid-faced woman standing near.

She replied, "I am very happy to meet you."

"What is your name?" asked the parson.

"Lincoln—Bradway."

"And the lady's name?"

"Lucy—Bandon," faltered Lucy.

"Oh indeed, are you related to the famous Kit Bandon I've heard so much about?"

"Yes. I'm her niece."

"What is your business?" The minister asked somewhat doubtfully, looking Lincoln over from head to foot.

"Don't mind this rig, parson. I'm not a gambler. I bought this outfit because I wanted to surprise Lucy. I am a cowboy."

"Well, if you're in such a great hurry, we might as well get it over," said the parson producing his worn Bible.

As if in a trance Lincoln listened and made answers that he could scarcely hear. Lucy's voice likewise was almost inaudible. The cowboy's hands trembled so he could hardly slip the little ring on her finger. Then, in a moment it was all over and they were signing their names.

The parson handed the paper to Lincoln and said, "Well, Bradway, you have been married quickly but nonetheless surely."

Linc turned to Lucy. "Lucy, it's done. We're married," he whispered.

"It doesn't seem possible," she answered. "We—we are almost—strangers. I never thought it would be like this."

The cowboy's heart was full to overflowing as he kissed her. The minister's wife congratulated them and also kissed Lucy.

Linc pulled himself together. The miraculous had happened. He brought out his wallet and presented a hundred dollar bill to the parson: "You have made me the happiest and most fortunate man in the world," he said earnestly.

The minister's eyes grew round when he saw the greenback.

"Young man, it looks as if you'll be as happy as you are generous."

"Would it be asking you too much to keep this secret a little while?"

"Oh, please do," implored Lucy. "I—we—it would be best for us that it should not be known at once."

"Why, not at all," replied the minister heartily. "I've been out west long enough to know that the main thing when you marry young folks is not to worry about the particulars."

The Nebraskan put his fingers in his vest pocket.

"I forgot something, Lucy," he said, smiling, as he produced a diamond ring which burned white and gold in the lamp light. He put it on Lucy's finger alongside her wedding ring. She stared at it, mute and rapt.

"Now you're not only married, Mrs. Bradway, but consider yourself engaged, as well," he said. "But we must hurry back, I will never forget you good folks. Someday I will see you again. Good-by."

The parson opened the door and let them out.

"Good luck. God be with you."

They hurried out of the light into the darkness again and crossed the street. This time it was Lucy who was almost running as she clutched her husband's arm.

"Darling," he remonstrated. "What's the big rush? We're married. No one can stop us now!"

"Oh, Lincoln, I'm so glad that you took the bit in your teeth, and made me marry you. I'm terribly happy and frightened, too. But we can't let them know yet!"

"Not at this time!" agreed Lincoln. "But it won't do for me to run into your admirer Hank Miller while I'm in such a wild-eyed state as this. . . . Lucy, you mustn't forget to take off those rings and hide them."

"Yes, yes. But, where will I keep them?"

"Put them on a string around your neck."

"No, that wouldn't be safe. Wait," she said, clutching his arm.

In the dim light from a store window she removed the rings and folding them in a little handkerchief she tucked them inside the bodice of her dress.

"When I get a chance I'll pin them in safely."

They hurried on, and quickly reached the hotel.

"I wonder if we ought to go in separately?" Lucy said.

"No, that will hardly do," replied Lincoln, thoughtfully. "That would look sort of funny—if they happened to be in the lobby. We can say we got tired waiting and went out for a little walk. . . . It's too late for them to get the best of us now."

They went up the steps and into the lobby. It was aglow with light, and filled with noise and cigar smoke. The Nebraskan's keen eyes swiftly covered the men inside focusing finally upon Hank Miller.

"Aha! there's Miller," whispered Lincoln. "He sees us, he's coming. . . . Lucy, keep up your courage."

She showed surprising coolness, he thought; and she replied to his warning in a perfectly controlled voice by asking him if he had seen her aunt anywhere.

Bradway said, "No, she doesn't seem to be back yet."

Then Miller stood before them. His face was dark with anger and suspicion, and he showed signs of having been drinking steadily since dinner. He reached for one of Lucy's arms and jerked her rudely away from Linc's side.

"Where the hell have you been?" he snarled.

Lucy drew back from him, but there was no fear in the manner with which she confronted him.

"Hank, please let go of my arm. You're hurting me."

"Where have you been?" he repeated.

"If it's any of your business we've been out for a walk. We got tired waiting. I asked Mr. Bradway to go."

"Oh, you did, huh? I wouldn't put that beyond you and more besides."

Then Miller's sullen gaze drifted toward Lucy's escort. As he met Miller's hot red-rimmed eyes, a curious little cold stillness came over Lincoln. He knew then, beyond any further doubt, that he was going to have to kill this man.

"Where is Miss Bandon?" he asked, coolly.

"She's in there driving a hard bargain with thet cattleman. . . . So, Bradway, you got away with it."

"With what?"

"Making a play for my girl. I saw it in your eyes."

"Yes. Well, all's fair in love and war, Miller," retorted Lincoln.

He derived some pleasure out of the baffled fury in the good-looking cowboy's eye. But he saw that Miller was determined to force a showdown.

"Lucy, you go upstairs," he said.

Miller added to that: "Yes, you damn little fickle she-cat, get out of here, now. But I'll see you later."

"Miller, that isn't a very gentlemanly way to address a lady," drawled Lincoln in a slow, cool, tantalizing tone. "Much less the one you claim to honor with your regard."

Lucy gave them both a quick look and turning, she hurriedly mounted the stairway without a backward look.

"I don't like you, Bradway."

"The feeling is mutual, I assure you," Lincoln replied.

"I think you're a liar. I suspect there's something shady about *you* too."

"I return the compliment as to who's a liar," said Lincoln, "and I know *you're* shady."

"The hell you say!" exploded Miller. Again that questioning look came into his face. He wondered what this tall stranger knew. "You talk big, gambler. You flash a couple of holster guns besides that outfit you're wearing. Somebody is liable to take your stake away from you here in Rock Springs."

Despite Miller's surly temper Linc could see that he was mightily curious about the man in the store clothes. He led the way toward a quieter and less brightly lighted section of the room.

"Miller, it might interest you to know that I came to Rock Springs to find you."

"Is that so? Now, you've found me, what are you going to do about it?"

"First off I'm going to take up that little matter of you calling Lucy names. I should have done it then," said Linc with a disarming casualness.

"You'll find it a bigger bite than maybe you can chew."

"Oh, I don't know," replied the Nebraskan, smilingly.

"All right, Mister Bradway. What do you propose to do?"

"This!"

With action as swift as the word, Lincoln swung his right arm in a haymaker that landed on Miller's mouth with terrific force, knocking him over backward. For an instant he strove to recover his balance, then fell over some vacant chairs and slipped to the floor where he lay still.

Chapter VIII

The crash of falling chairs and the sodden thud of Miller's body landing on the floor brought from those nearby in the lobby excited exclamations followed by silence. Lincoln waited to see if Miller was going to rise, but evidently he was stunned. He lay sprawled on the floor, his head and shoulders up against the wainscoting. Blood had begun to trickle from his mouth. Lincoln relaxed his tense posture. He massaged his right hand with his left as he watched the man on the floor. He realized that there would be little if any reaction from Miller for some time to come.

A tall, sallow man with a drooping mustache and sharp eyes stepped forward from the crowd and said to Bradway, "Wal, young man, you hit him pretty hard."

Linc turned. Prominent on the newcomer's vest was a silver badge.

"Yes, Sheriff, I hit him all right," he replied, grimly.

"What was it for?"

"He insulted a young lady who just came in with me."

"I saw her, the young Bandon girl. In thet case I reckon I won't do anything but offer you some advice."

"I'd like that pretty pronto," replied the Nebraskan.

"Do you know the man you've hit?"

"Saw him and met him tonight at dinner, but I don't know anything about him except that he's mean. I'm afraid I'm in for it."

"You sure are," drawled the sheriff. "Miller hails from Calispel. I met cattlemen who knew him in Montana where he had a hard name. Hot-headed and quick on the draw."

The crowd of bystanders began to open up a passage to let Kit Bandon come hurriedly through. Her mysterious black eyes took in Lincoln with the sheriff, then the prostrate Miller as she approached. But there was no expression of surprise, concern or fear in her glance.

"Sheriff," he whispered, swiftly, turning to the officer, "arrest me or take me in charge."

"Wal, I reckon I savvy," muttered the law man, and he laid a hand on Lincoln's arm.

Kit Bandon now stood before them, her dark eyes smoldering.

"Linc Bradway, how come you are down here? Where's Lucy? What have you and Hank been up to?"

"Lucy grew tired of waiting and asked me to take her for a little walk," replied Lincoln. "We went about two blocks. When we came in again Miller was here and he tried to take the girl's arm. He was sore and suspicious. Lucy jerked away from him. They had a few words, then Miller turned to me. I told Lucy to go upstairs, then Miller insulted her. We exchanged a few words after that and then I hit him."

"Insulted Lucy?" she exclaimed. "Why the dirty pup! He hasn't any claim on Lucy. Why did you want to dirty your hands with him? Why didn't you throw your gun on him?"

"I did think of it but here in the crowded lobby—"

"You'll have to do it anyhow now," flashed Kit. "Miller told me he was going to badger you into a fight."

"Wal, Miss Bandon," interposed the sheriff, "I reckon you're right, but we ought to appreciate this young man's consideration for others."

"Sheriff Haught, that's funny talk for a Texan," retorted Kit, scornfully.

At that moment it was easy for Linc to read her thoughts. She had a reason for wanting him to kill Miller. Since it now seemed important to the Maverick Queen to have the young man dead and out of the way, Linc was certainly glad the meeting with Miller had not come to a fatal issue. There was something he wanted to ask the cowboy when he met him again face to face.

"Wal, we won't argue about thet now. Come with me, young feller. What did you say your name was?"

"I didn't say," replied Linc. "But it's Lincoln Bradway."

"Sheriff, are you going to run him in?" Kit queried, sharply.

"No, I reckon I won't do thet, but I'll get him out of here. There's likely to be a rumpus when Miller comes to."

"Sheriff, that is ridiculous. I'll take care of him."

"Sorry, Miss Bandon, but I reckon I'll take him along."

He led Bradway toward the door. Miller had begun to show signs of recovering consciousness. One of the men approached and knelt beside him. Kit Bandon went over to stare angrily down at the recumbent cowboy. As Linc backed out the door, he could see over the heads of the crowd Lucy standing white-faced and anxious-eyed on the stairway.

Outside the sheriff led the Nebraskan down the lighted street.

"Reckon you'd like a drink?" suggested the sheriff.

"I would, but I've sworn off."

"Thet's never a bad idea. Bradway, I don't take you for an out-and-out gambler. You haven't the look."

"No, I'm not," said Lincoln. "My cowboy clothes are old and soiled and I wanted to buy something fancier, and this rig was all I could find here in town."

"Wanted to impress the ladies?" drawled the Texan.

"Well, yes, one of them."

"Bradway, I know this Bandon woman pretty well, and I met the niece several times. She's a mighty sweet little filly. Excuse me for being curious, but is it Kit or Lucy that you are sweet on?"

"Sheriff, I don't suppose you'll believe it but it is only Lucy."

"It's hard to savvy at that, which ain't saying that Lucy Bandon is not a sweet and pretty girl. But that aunt of hers makes every girl pale in front of her. I'd like to ask you some more about them ladies, Bradway, and what they're doin' here in Rock Springs, but thet's enough for the present."

"Please hold it confidential, Sheriff," replied Lincoln.

"Young feller, I don't suppose it will do the least bit of good but I advise you to get out of Rock Springs tonight."

"Sheriff, I can't run away from any man, let alone a hombre like Miller."

"Then you'll have to meet him tomorrow. And if I know hard customers you'll have to shoot mighty quick and mighty straight. I thought perhaps you wouldn't want to mess up things while the ladies are in town."

"I'll have to overlook that. You heard Kit Bandon. She'd like to see me throw a gun on Miller."

"You bet your life I didn't miss thet," quickly replied the Texan. "Wal, my advice is this: I'll take you to a little hotel down this street. You go to your room and tomorrow stay inside until I come down and tip you off how the land lies."

"You will do that, Sheriff?" asked Lincoln.

"Glad to. It wouldn't do any good much to arrest Miller tonight. I couldn't hold him and so long as you intend to stay in town I think a meeting can't be avoided. I hope it will be *you* I'll have to arrest afterward."

"You can bet on that, Sheriff."

He halted Bradway in the middle of the next block. They entered a quiet little hotel where the sheriff made arrangements for Lincoln's lodgings and bade him good night. The Nebraskan was shown to his room on the first floor, and after bolting the door and pulling down the blind he sat down on the bed to think over all the things that had happened during this most eventful evening of his life. It seemed impossible to believe Lucy really was his wife! By what miracle had this wonderful thing happened to him? Out loud he repeated several times "Lucy Bradway, Lucy Bradway." It was the sweetest name in all the world.

His thoughts drifted to the dark, surly cowboy whom he would have to meet; he must plan what he was going to say to the cowboy—if he had a chance before the shooting began. But suppose they met, and he had a chance to find out what the cowboy knew? Suppose he came through unscathed. What about Kit Bandon? Now that he was Lucy's husband, must he keep off Kit's trail which every day was growing more tangled? And what would be Kit's own reaction when she found out he had married Lucy? She would be a desperate woman to cross, but the hope persisted that he or Lucy would not betray their secret until he had cleared up the mystery surrounding Jimmy Weston's murder. Then, perhaps he and Lucy might ride away before Kit could discover the truth about them. Fate was drawing tight lines about her, and it was possible that she had come to realize this also. Why did she want to have Miller killed? There was only one answer to that! Miller must be aware of that *something* which Kit wanted so desperately to be kept secret. Did it concern Jimmy Weston, and the manner in which he had been killed? That was the dark truth to which Lincoln had committed himself to uncover. It was a strange and tragic mystery, all the more baffling and poignant because of the probable implication of both of the Bandons. Even Lucy, his own wife, knew more than she would tell.

Presently Lincoln stood up and began to undress. He wanted sleep and rest in order to have a clear brain and steady nerve for tomorrow's crucial problems. Before he went to sleep, however, he worked out in his mind the needed details: he must *see* Miller first, try to force him to disclose his guilty knowledge if there was time, then if he was satisfied in his mind that the cowboy was implicated in Jim Weston's murder, it was just a question of beating Miller to his gun. That was the last resolve Bradway kept in his consciousness before he lost himself in slumber.

He slept rather late, remaining in bed until the sun was high. He dressed slowly and went out for his breakfast in the small dining room connected with the hotel. The slowness of the service suited Lincoln's plans. During the meal he occupied himself with a newspaper from behind which he occasionally peered when he heard a footstep. He made a leisurely meal of it. Several other customers came in but paid no attention to him. At ten o'clock sharp Sheriff Haught entered and immediately approached the lounging Nebraskan.

"Mawnin', cowboy," said the Texan cheerfully, as he seated himself.

"Howdy, Sheriff. I was afraid you weren't going to show up."

"Wal, the stage is all set."

"Yes? Then you've seen Miller."

"Thet's the truth."

"Is he rarin' around town looking for me?"

"Thet's how I figured, but it didn't turn out thet way. Miller is at the hotel, clean-shaven, sober as ice, and none the worse for wear. I had the luck to see him with Kit Bandon just a little while ago. They were havin' a hot argument. My hunch is thet Bandon was not persuadin' him to avoid you. It might have been the other way around. I stopped on the stairway to light a cigar and stayed there as long as I dared hopin' to hear somethin' interestin'. Later I passed Miller in the lobby. He was as het up as a wild stallion at the sight of his first rope. I saw him pace up and down the lobby and every little bit go out into the street. He's lookin' for you, or my name ain't Haught."

"Then he won't have to wait long," replied Lincoln, curtly rising from the table. "Sheriff, I'm mightily obliged to you."

"Not at all. All I want is for you to have an even break. Now you walk up on the other side of the street and keep your eyes peeled. I'll be hangin' around thet hotel corner and if there's any need to give you a tip I'll do it. Wait a few minutes after I've gone and then you follow. I don't have to tell you what you're up against."

The sheriff turned on his heel and left the dining room. Lincoln ordered another cup of coffee but did not drink it. Presently he arose, gave the waiter a bill and went out. It was a beautiful sunny morning, clear and crisp; many people already were about; several wagons creaked down the street between groups of mounted horsemen. The Nebraskan crossed to the other side and headed east toward the principal hotel. This was the main thoroughfare. It was a long block up to the hotel. He kept close to the buildings; the presence of the pedestrians, he concluded, being enough of a screen to prevent his being seen before he reached the corner. Here he halted and removed his long frock coat, draping it over his left arm. Passers-by stopped, turned to stare at him in mild amazement. There were several loungers standing outside of the hotel and Lincoln could see that the lobby was filled with people. Something drew his gaze up to an open window in the second story of the hotel. Standing back from the opening he could see Kit Bandon, tense and expectant, her dark eyes fixed on the street below. Quickly Bradway lowered his eyes to the sidewalk. At that moment Miller emerged from the hotel. His advent was a signal for several men to bolt from the building by a side entrance. Evidently Miller had spied Lincoln from inside the hotel.

Holding his hands low and away from his hips, the cowboy slowly descended the steps and continued even more deliberately across the street. With a slight movement with his right hand he motioned Linc off the sidewalk. This slight action and the way Miller wore his gun convinced the Nebraskan that he was left-handed. Dropping his coat over a railing Lincoln edged sideways into the street facing the cowboy. Miller was cautious, yet bold: evidently he was not going to make a hasty issue of this meeting. He appeared to be as curious about the situation as Lincoln.

They were still the width of the side street apart. Warily they crossed the dusty street almost as far as the railroad park. Miller was the first to stop. Lincoln immediately halted in his tracks. The two men were about twenty steps apart. Linc welcomed the chance for a close scrutiny of his antagonist's face.

"The deal's on, cowboy," said Miller in a voice that sounded strained and high-pitched, "but I'm sure curious. Where are you from?"

"Nebraska. Does that mean anything to you?"

"Not a damn thing," flashed Miller. . . . "You another one of this woman's maverick hunters?"

"Not on your life," retorted Lincoln.

"She told me you were."

"She lied."

"She said she was going to marry you."

"I can't help what she thinks. Maybe she doesn't know that I've got a wife."

"Makin' up to Kit—playin' with Lucy—and all the time you're married?"

"It might look like that but you're wrong. That all you want to say to me?"

"I don't savvy your game."

"You will pronto."

Miller betrayed an intense anger that could have been inspired and inflamed only by the Bandon woman.

But despite the anger and violent emotion that blazed in the cowboy's face, Linc could see that Miller was consumed with an intense curiosity. And he recognized that this was the moment: the advantage was his. He could break this hard cowboy's nerve. Quickly he said, "Kit couldn't have meant what she doesn't know—*that Lucy is my wife!*"

For an instant Miller seemed incapable of speech. Then he roared hoarsely, "I don't believe it!" He forgot completely that he had challenged a man to a gun duel. He shook his head bewilderedly. He turned back to look at the hotel. Then he muttered:

"That accounts for it. Lucy didn't act like herself. But, hell, stranger, Kit Bandon said—"

"Wrong, Miller," interrupted Linc. "That is not what Kit Bandon meant."

"Hell's fire, man, what else?"

"I'm Jimmy Weston's friend. That's what brought me to Wyoming."

"Wha—at! The hell you say!"

"I know, Miller, that you hauled him away from Kit Bandon's ranch alive or dead."

"Not alive—*dead!*" burst out Miller as he jerked for his gun.

Lincoln saw over the spouting flame of his own weapon the belching red of Miller's, but the Nebraskan's bullet reached its mark a fraction of a second before Miller's. Then a stunning blow high up on his body staggered Lincoln; a searing pain ran through his shoulder.

Miller's gun dropped and his lax arm fell to his side. A blank look slowly spread over the face which a moment before had worn a grimace of bitter hatred, and he fell face forward to lay still on the hard-packed dirt of the street.

Lincoln took several steps toward the fallen man waiting for some sign of movement. There was none. He heard loud voices and the footsteps of running men; then suddenly dizzy and blind he wavered to his knees, but he did not fall or lose consciousness. He heard a woman's piercing scream; then someone laid hands upon him and helped him to his feet. As his mind cleared momentarily he saw that Sheriff Haught was supporting him.

"Are you bad hurt, Bradway?" asked the sheriff.

"I don't—know. I guess not," replied Lincoln, haltingly.

The sheriff took his gun. There were men bending over Miller who manifestly was stone dead.

"Where did he hit you?" asked the sheriff.

"Somewhere—high up."

"Do you taste any blood?"

"No, I don't."

"Here, let's see," said Haught, tearing at Lincoln's shirt. Blood was running down Lincoln's left breast. Haught felt the bullet hole, from which blood was slowly seeping.

"Not bad. Too high to catch the lung," he said with relief.

The sheriff folded a scarf and placed it on Lincoln's shoulder.

"It was a narrow shave, Bradway. . . . Here, somebody help me with him," he said to the bystanders.

A citizen came to the other side of Linc and supported him. A third followed with the wounded man's coat. They walked, half carrying him across the street. At that instant Kit Bandon came running down the steps, lips parted, her eyes wide and dark, her face expressing fear and concern. She stopped before the trio and looked searchingly into Bradway's drawn face.

"Is—is it bad, Lincoln?" she whispered huskily.

"It's—it's—nothing," he replied faintly.

"Miss Bandon, he's all right," said the sheriff. "I'll take him down to my place and call the doctor."

She moved along with him and the crowd followed. In some way she had been able to get hold of one of his hands. By the time they had gone half a block or more Lincoln began to feel that consciousness was slipping away from him. Before everything went completely black, he felt himself being lifted and carried.

When he recovered consciousness he found himself on a couch in a stone-walled room with barred windows. Someone was working over him. He smelled strong antiseptics. Someone he recognized to be Kit sat on the other side of the bed watching him anxiously. Sheriff Haught, with his coat off and sleeves rolled up, evidently was helping the doctor.

"How is it, Doc?" he heard Haught ask.

"Clean as a whistle," replied the doctor. "Went clear through. Never touched the collar bone."

Kit stood up and laid her cool hand on the wounded man's forehead. "Are you in much pain?" she asked.

Linc shook his head. His eyes seemed to be searching the room for someone.

"Where's Lucy?" he whispered.

Kit Bandon did not reply.

"Doc, how about giving him a slug of whisky?" asked Haught.

"It might be a good idea. Got any handy?"

They lifted Bradway's head and helped him to drink. He felt liquor surging through his numb body. He tried to sit up. Kit sprang to place a pillow under his injured shoulder.

"Now, Kit," said the sheriff. "He's all right. . . . Mustn't be excited. I think you had better leave him with me. My housekeeper and I will take turns keeping watch over him."

"Of course I will go," said the Bandon woman, "but you must keep me posted on how he is."

She bent over the Nebraskan and kissed him on the forehead. "You're all right, Linc. Lie still and bear it." Then she hurried out.

Haught began carefully to remove the injured man's boots. They had cut away the bloody top of his shirt. In a few moments the doctor had finished his bandaging.

"Did it hurt?" he asked the cowboy.

"When you stuck that thing through—it sure did."

The doctor rose and went into a little anteroom where Linc could hear him washing his hands in a sink.

"Sheriff," he called, "I'll look in tonight unless you send for me before that. I don't anticipate any aftereffects. He'll be up in three days walking around. This younster could stand half a dozen bullet holes like that. Keep him quiet. I'll leave something for you to give him if he gets restless."

He returned to pick up his coat and put it on, then

packed his instruments and medicines. Sheriff Haught stood looking down upon the cowboy with a smile.

"I sure was scared, Bradway. Must be gettin' chicken-hearted about gunfire. I've seen a deal of fightin', but there was somethin' different about this—must have been the women. . . . Miller was one mean hombre. If I'd known how fast you were with a gun I wouldn't have been as concerned. Curious about him, Bradway?"

Lincoln shook his head faintly. He fastened somber eyes upon the sheriff.

"You beat him to it, but not very much. Your bullet took him right in the center of the left vest pocket and it was a right good job. All the same I had to arrest you."

"Then I'm—in jail?" asked Lincoln.

"Sure are, but we'll call it a hospital."

"Could—could I send a message to my—to Miss Bandon at the hotel?" he asked.

His eyes fell shut and he could not distinguish what the sheriff was saying. Presently he slipped into a stupor. When he awakened after a while, he became aware of a throbbing pain. He heard footsteps now and then and low voices. Evidently the afternoon was waning, for the room slowly darkened. He became aware that a comely Mexican woman was watching over him. When he asked in a whisper for water, she gave him a drink from a tin dipper. Then she lighted a lamp on the table back of his bed. Soon afterward he was visited by the doctor and Haught. After a cursory examination the doctor said, "I reckon you'll have some pain tonight, Bradway, but I'm not going to give you anything to put you to sleep."

"How about anything to eat or drink?" asked Haught.

"He can have water, of course. The only thing to watch is restlessness or possibly a delirious spell in which case we wouldn't want him to wrestle about."

The doctor bade them good night and Haught dismissed the woman.

"Bradway, go to sleep if you can. I'll read and take catnaps until Marie calls me."

The Nebraskan had been wounded more than once and a good deal more seriously than this. The pain and the feverishness were not unbearable, but what he dreaded was that grim black reaction that inevitably followed taking a man's life in anger. He forced his thoughts from the realization that he had killed a man. How would Lucy feel? Once she had called him a killer. Why did Lucy not come to see him? Kit had come. Was Kit keeping his wife from coming? He fell into a fitful sleep, but was awake near midnight, when the woman came in to relieve Haught. Those wakeful hours of pain, which grew longer and longer until they seemed unbearable, slowly passed. At last, toward dawn, he fell asleep and when he awoke the sun was shining through the barred window. He felt much better, except for the throbbing in his shoulder. He did not have a fever. When Haught returned he said, "Good morning."

The sheriff replied cheerfully telling him that he had made a good night of it and that there was little to worry about.

"Sheriff, don't let anybody see me today, not even— not even Miss Bandon. I can get up and move around if I have to. I don't want anything but cold water."

"I know how you feel, Bradway. I've shot some bad hombres myself in my day. It isn't pleasant the morning after, but from what I hear and from what Kit Bandon tells me you ought to have a medal."

"You're a peculiar sheriff," whispered Lincoln with a wan smile.

"Thet is kind of funny considerin' I've run you in and have to keep you here for a while."

"I'd rather be here than anywhere else, just now. But why do you have to keep me? It was an even draw."

"I'll tell you in good time. I don't want to get you excited."

"That woman!"

"Which one?" said the sheriff quizzically.

"Kit Bandon, of course. I've a hunch she wants me kept in here. Well, I'm glad. . . . Sheriff, will you go to the hotel and bring back my bag and clothes?"

"What'll I tell the women?" asked the sheriff.

"Tell Kit I'm terribly bad, but when you see Lucy tell her the truth."

"Oho!" said the sheriff, laughing. "I'll be doggoned! This is goin' to turn out to be the most interestin' shootin'-bee I've had in a long time. You were asking for Miss Bandon, last night, when you were a bit delirious, but I never dreamed it was the filly you wanted."

He stamped out noisily and in an hour or so returned with the cowboy's belongings. This time he moved quietly and left without speaking. Linc heard the key grate in the lock.

Bradway pulled himself upright to attempt walking around the room. A throbbing pain seared his shoulder and left him dizzy. But if necessary, he could have mounted a horse and ridden away. He paced the room, lay down again only to come to his feet restlessly and move around once more. There was blinds over the windows which he pulled down to keep out the glare of daylight. Then he made no further effort to avoid the ghastly reaction. He settled down to a grim and dark fight. The day passed with the spell hard upon him; when night had fallen he was gradually recovering from its somber grip and eventually he was able to sleep again.

Next morning Lincoln was himself again. The bullet would still made him twinge, but his mind was at peace once more. He shaved himself and donned a clean white shirt, but since he could not leave the prison he went back to bed. Marie stolidly brought him breakfast from the hotel, the meal being accompanied by flowers. Lincoln had a fair idea who sent them.

The prisoner had scarcely finished his breakfast when Sheriff Haught entered with the doctor and Kit Bandon. She was dressed in white and appeared as gay as the flowers she admitted having sent him. The doctor's examination was brief. At its conclusion he said, "Sheriff, you can let him out of here today."

"Oh no, I cain't. He's under arrest."

"Well," said the doctor, "my work is done. Young man, when they release you come and see me."

"Thank you, doctor. I'll be coming pronto."

Kit sat down on the bed beside him, and began stroking his forehead with a soft hand.

"You look fine, Lincoln. All clean-shaven and white-shirted! You must have expected—someone. . . . Are you in any pain?"

"Not to speak of—physically," he replied, regarding her steadily.

As he looked up into those tender dark eyes and felt the soothing administrations of the annoying woman's almost hypnotic hands, he recalled that Lucy had told him about Kit's being madly infatuated with him. Soon she must learn the truth about Lucy and him. There would be hell pronto. He knew that Lucy would keep their secret, but he, himself, would have to tell her if she—didn't leave him alone.

"Where's Lucy?" asked Lincoln, with an effort at casualness.

"She wouldn't come. She's been very nervous since yesterday. Poor kid, she seems to think all this was on her account."

"So it was, wasn't it?"

"Not on your life, darling."

"Did Lucy see me—the meeting?"

"No, I'm glad to say she didn't. But I did. . . . I got the thrill of my life until I saw you were hit and staggered and almost fell. I almost died then, Linc! You see, I knew that Miller was quick as lightning and a dead shot and I thought he had outdrawn you in spite of the fury I aroused in him before he went out to meet you. Oh, it was terrible! I never suffered like that before, Lincoln, though I'm afraid you must think me hard and unfeeling."

"Well, Kit, seein' three's a crowd and thet Bradway doesn't need me now, I'll take myself off," Haught broke in, gazing down upon his prisoner, and as he looked, he winked one of his shrewd gray Texas eyes, in a message of understanding and warning. Then he went out, his heavy foot treads ringing on the board floor.

To Linc's amazement and dismay, he suddenly felt his companion pressing against him. Her arms slipped about his neck, and her warm fragrant lips were pressed to his own. Lincoln felt her full breast throb against his. She was quivering slightly.

"Kit, this—is—very sweet and sympathetic of you," labored Lincoln awkwardly, "but you're rather heavy—leaning on me."

"Oh, I'm sorry, Linc," she cried. "That was a moment when I seemed fully to lose that awful fear that nailed me yesterday and which I could not get rid of. . . . But sympathetic! You've got me wrong, cowboy. What I feel is ten million times more wonderful than sympathy. When you get a little better—well, never mind."

"How long is this sheriff going to keep me here?"

"I don't know," replied Kit hesitatingly. "A week perhaps."

"But why?" asked Lincoln.

"He said something about the magistrate having gone to Salt Lake. He has to make *some* pretense of enforcing the law."

"Well, I'd just as soon be here as anywhere so long as I have to take it easy. I suppose you and Lucy will be going back to the ranch?"

"No. My cattle deal has missed fire. Besides I wouldn't think of going until you are out. . . . Linc, hasn't it occurred to you yet that I might have some very serious ideas in my head?"

"I daresay," replied Lincoln constrainedly.

"What do you think is behind all this—this interest I've taken in you?"

"I hadn't thought very much about it. You have the reputation of showing interest in—cowboys, especially new ones to the country."

"That ought to prove to you how really sincere I am now," replied Kit broodingly. "Did—did you hear some talk about me in South Pass?"

"It would be rather hard to avoid hearing things about you. . . . You're the main topic of conversation on that range."

The woman's face flared red and her eyes blazed, but she kept control of her temper.

"A good deal of it is true, Lincoln," she finally said soberly. "How much depends on what has been said! When I get hold of myself I will confess more than I ever have to anyone in my whole life before. . . . Lincoln, this is my confession—there's something in you I'm not used to finding in men. I never realized it about any other man that I took a liking to . . . perhaps I'm letting my heart run away with my head."

"Kit, you couldn't expect me to believe your— well—feeling for me is any different from—well, from what you felt for all the others?"

She bowed her head for a moment. Then she whispered:

"Linc, with all my heart I want you to believe that."

"Well, I don't," replied Lincoln bluntly. "I don't want to brag, Kit, but you may find me a little different than the others."

"That's just it, I'm afraid. You do have more education than most men I've known—certainly you must come from a good family. But above all, you're clean and fine—I sensed that in you when I first met you. Cowboys live hard lives, and when off duty many of them get drunk, bat around, go for dance-hall girls and all the slatterns that infest these towns. But you're not that kind of a cowboy, Lincoln. Perhaps that has something to do with my sudden—liking for you. I don't know. But I'm inclined to think that if you *had* been the toughest cowboy on the range, I would have fallen for you just the same."

Lincoln laughed shortly. "Well, I hope, my dear, that you get over it pronto. As a matter of fact, Kit, you'll *have* to!"

She fastened dark unfathomable eyes upon him. She seemed suddenly to sense that here was a will as strong or even stronger than her own. The flush left her cheek and she grew pale; her eyes burned darker by contrast. She bit her lip.

"Lincoln, I shall have to convince you of many things. I am willing to make many sacrifices. I am willing, too, to fight for the man I love," she cried with a proud look.

"Kit, you surprise me each time we meet. I don't know what's in your mind—I don't suppose anyone could ever divine that, but there are reasons why such confidences as you are making should not go any further."

"Lincoln! Why—?" she exclaimed.

The wounded man silently shook his head.

"You don't care *anything* about me—?" she cried in amazement.

"I couldn't say that," replied Lincoln gravely. "Any man you interest yourself in would be bound to care in some way. You are a beautiful, dangerous, mysterious woman. Does than mean anything to you?"

"I take it as a compliment," she replied, smiling. "If I'm mysterious, dangerous, beautiful already, I don't see that I have much to worry about. All that I have to do is turn my back on the past."

"Kit, either I'm loco or you are," he retorted, trying to keep his tone light. "I think we've said enough about it today."

"I still want to talk to you—about your meeting with Miller."

"I'd rather not say anything about that either," replied Lincoln coldly.

"I'm sorry, but you'll have to," she said, simply. "You have something on your mind. I want it cleared away. Do you realize that but for me—for my upsetting Miller, it would have been one of those even breaks in which both men die?"

"That has crossed my mind," said Lincoln. "You riled him, unnerved him, made him meet me without that cold nerve which he surely would have had. But I said something to him that upset him even more. Wouldn't you like to know what it was?"

Kit look startled for a moment. Then she went on: "I tried to persuade him to avoid meeting you. Of course, that was a pretense. I told him you would beat him to a gun. I lied to him about you and Lucy. And I sent him out there to ask you something that he *had* to ask before he killed you."

"You wanted Miller killed, didn't you?" he queried.

"Yes, I did. He was a bad hombre. He was driving Lucy crazy. He wanted money out of me. But these things weren't important, Lincoln. I wanted you to kill him so that he couldn't kill *you*." She was earnest and persuasive, but he divined that she was not telling the whole truth. Something dark and furtive hid behind her show of tremendous sincerity.

"Was he trying to blackmail you?"

"Yes, but it was a bluff. Bad as Hank was, he wouldn't say anything against me—even if he knew it." An incredible egotism and faith in her own powers were manifest in her tone and in her words.

"Miller asked where I was from, down there in the street."

"Yes, he wanted to know who the hell you were and I didn't tell him. But did *you* tell him?"

"I wracked my brain for something that would give me the edge. . . . I told him—that I was Lucy Bandon's husband!"

Kit Bandon's icy little laugh rang out, but there was no amusement in the laugh. "Well, if you aren't an inventive cuss. So that was it! . . . I know just when you said that. What did he say?"

"Well," replied Linc, "he seemed to take it rather hard."

"Then what did you say?" burst out Kit, in a voice that was husky with eagerness.

"Kit, my gun did the rest of the talking," he answered, simply.

She arose and paced the floor, fighting for command of her feelings yet for some reason apparently immeasurably relieved. Lincoln was relieved also. He had deliberately exaggerated Miller's reaction to his revelation about Lucy because he did not want Kit to know what that last terrible exchange of words between him and Miller had been about.

Presently Kit turned away from the window, once more composed although her dark eyes still revealed her deep emotion.

"Lincoln, I'm glad it's all over now and that I understand. I must say you are as clever with your wits as you are swift with a gun. . . . I have troubled you, Lincoln. Forgive me. I'll go now and come back sometime later."

She bent to kiss him, but there was no ardor now. A moment later Sheriff Haught was letting her out of the door, and locking it behind her.

Long after Kit had left the sheriff's jailhouse Linc Bradway lay on his bed deep in thought. He had wanted to put this tragic problem out of his mind a little while longer but it was no use. What was the truth? Kit Bandon knew something about Jimmy Weston's death, but had she anything to do with it? The possibility haunted him. If Jimmy had met his death at the Bandon ranch, that would be damning proof of her complicity. Guilt he had seen in Miller's eyes but it was guilt without fear: no murderer could have watched the cowboy's expression on the brink of dealing death and perhaps meeting it himself. Despite his guilt, those last furious words of Miller's seemed to ring with inherent truth. Miller might have killed Jimmy but Lincoln doubted it. Miller was not the man to kill cold-bloodedly without having betrayed his duplicity to Lincoln during their encounter. At that dark moment Lincoln felt as far from the solution of the mystery as ever.

Chapter IX

Lincoln was left alone until noon, when the waiter brought his lunch from the hotel. It was a lavish spread for a cowboy, and included wine. Noticing the wine, Haught, who had just entered, remarked dryly, "You're putting on a lot of style, young feller. The daintiest of grub and wine on the side!—Of course, you're not payin' for this?"

"No, I'm not. I suppose, of course, it must be Kit Bandon."

"Yes, she told me she'd take care of your meals," replied Haught.

"Well, if you hang around you can share some of this wine with me."

"I sure will hang around all right," said the sheriff amiably, seating himself comfortably on the bed.

"Sheriff, how long are you going to keep me in the calaboose?"

"I thought you wanted me to keep you locked up for a while?"

While Lincoln busily applied himself to the food Haught studied him shrewdly.

"Yes, I did say that," replied Lincoln. "But I'm O.K. now and the little embarrassment that I expected to meet is passed. Frankly, I'd like to get out." This was not strictly truthful, for he was very well pleased where he was. However, he really wanted to find out why he was being detained.

"Well, son, I spread it around about thet it was a matter of law—but it isn't thet."

"All right. I'm glad of that. But I want to know what's behind it."

"This is strictly confidential, Bradway. The Bandon woman is behind it. She wants you kept here for a while."

"That was plain to see. But why? Are there any pards of Miller's around town that she's afraid I'd clash with?"

"No. Thet hombre was a lone wolf. She swore out a warrant, and I didn't have no choice in the matter at all."

"Thunderation then!" exclaimed Lincoln. "Why does she want to keep me locked up? Is she afraid I'll interfere with some shady deal of hers?"

"It's beyond me. I figured hard on it. Either there's someone here that she don't want you to meet or she wants to keep you away from her niece or she just wants to keep you for herself."

"Have you seen her with anyone?"

"Cattleman I don't know," replied Haught. "He's from Utah. Didn't strike me as bein' a Mormon. I made friendly advances to him which he certainly didn't meet. I know thet she is sellin' a big bunch of mavericks and some other stuff which is bein' driven to Rock Springs. The stock arrived yesterday and I went down and had a look at it."

"How many head?" asked Lincoln.

"Not a big herd. Something short of three hundred. But there was a remarkable lot of yearlings in the bunch."

They exchanged penetrating glances, each attempting to read the other's hidden thoughts. The prisoner had divined that the sheriff was very curious, but that he really knew very little about Kit Bandon. He had been markedly friendly to Lincoln and it did not seem that he could be unduly influenced in her favor.

"Sheriff, let me rest your mind on one thing. I am not in love with Kit Bandon nor mixed up with her in any way."

"Well, I wondered about that. I'm glad you came clean because I didn't want to step on your toes. I reckon if you were a little sweet on the girl thet would explain how the wind blows. Son, you're skating on thin ice."

"What do you mean by that?"

"If this Kit isn't loco about you, I've lost my way of figurin'. She's chain lightnin', that woman is! I wouldn't want her daid set on me unless I shared her feelin's."

The sheriff left the room with the tray but either intentionally or accidentally did not lock the door this time. Bradway was left alone but the hours now moved more slowly as his wound had ceased to bother him; also there was much to keep his mind occupied. Late in the afternoon Kit Bandon visited him again, and brought flowers and candy.

"Kit, are you bent on spoiling me?" he asked with a smile.

"I sure am," responded Kit soberly. "I never yet met the man who couldn't be spoiled."

"But what's the idea?"

"Lincoln, you're not as dense as you make out to be." She sat beside him but refrained from making any other demonstration. There was a look of hunger in her dark eyes and a suggestion of a sad droop in her red lips. She regretted that her stay would have to be short—that she was laboring through an irritating business deal with a cattleman—that there were other petty difficulties bothering her. The cowboy ventured to say, "Why didn't you fetch Lucy over? Sometimes I get pretty lonesome."

"I asked her to come," replied Kit a trifle evasively, it seemed to Linc, "but she wouldn't do it."

"Well, perhaps seeing me might be rather dismaying."

"No, it isn't that at all," said Kit. "It's her vanity.

Lucy is buying a new gown and hat and for some reason or other she just can't be satisfied. I never saw her so contrary. As a matter of fact, I gave her a hundred dollars and told her to spend it on clothes. The girl lost her head. I suspect I've been pretty selfish. I always wore the best clothes that money could buy without any thought of Lucy. She really is a pretty girl and ought to wear clothes that become her. Sometimes I think I've been jealous of her good looks and sweetness."

"Jealous?" he questioned, as if surprised.

"It's one of my many faults. I always was jealous of anyone young and attractive."

"But you needn't be."

"I needn't have been a lot of things, Lincoln. But I must leave you now. Good-by until tomorrow."

He lay there revolving in his mind the many puzzling and disquieting facts he knew about Kit. Again he wondered if the strong unrest she manifested could really be due to an awakening of conscience. Somehow, he did not think so. He believed that up to this time in her life Kit Bandon never had bothered with such a thing as conscience. Perhaps this recent perturbation was due more to the wounding of her inordinate vanity—because, in effect, he had not succumbed to her charm and power to dominate men. She would brook no opposition to her will, and his resistance would only make her more dangerous to deal with.

Presently Lincoln heard voices outside in the sheriff's office, and those sometimes drawling, sometimes curt, familiar tones brought him up with a start. It was undoubtedly Vince. An argument appeared to be taking place. It grew louder and more heated. "What do you want for two bits? Shall I go out an' get pinched to be put in yore old jail? I tell you Bradway will see me if you tell him his pard is here. The name is Vince."

"It's O.K., Sheriff," shouted his prisoner. "Bring him in, will you?"

At length Haught grumblingly consented; his footsteps were accompanied by the slow tinkling footfalls that Lincoln recognized. The door opened to admit Haught escorting in a most disreputable little figure. Vince was ragged, dirty, haggard and unshaven. His face was hollow-eyed and gaunt. "Hello, pard. Say, what in hell's the matter with this law man? He wasn't goin' to let me in."

"Bradway, I wasn't taking any chances, for he certainly was a tough-lookin' little hombre—inclined to be too cocky for his own good. Is he a friend of yours as he claims to be?"

"I should say he is. He must have gotten into some kind of a mess to look this way. . . . Vince, shake hands with Sheriff Haught."

"Sorry, I am sure, cowboy," replied the sheriff, as he complied with the request. "I reckon I'd be glad to meet any of Bradway's friends." He left the two together.

Linc called out: "Lock the door, Sheriff, and don't let anybody in, especially Miss Bandon if she should happen to return."

Vince strode over to the cot and sat down upon it to grasp Lincoln's hand in both his.

"Vince, you look like a scarecrow," said the Nebraskan, grinning. "No wonder the sheriff didn't want to let you in. You've been riding hard, hanging out in brush, going hungry and sleepless. What has happened to you? How did you know where to find me, pard?"

"Hell! Plenty's happened. But never mind about me. What has happened to you?"

"More than plenty, Vince. I think I've got you topped. Didn't you hear anything down the street?"

"We heard a lot of stories—all different."

"Who's we?" asked Lincoln.

"Mel Thatcher an' me. He come over with me."

"How come?" queried Lincoln in surprise.

"Wal, me and Thatcher got pretty thick. He's true blue, an' I shore think he's had a rotten deal. He was broke and couldn't get any kind of a job. Wuss fix than me. Lee tried to drive him out of South Pass and out

of the country fer thet matter. I reckon I kept Mel
from mixin' in a bad fight. He shore was seein' red.
I dragged him up to my place at the livery stable an'
kept him there till he cooled down. We got to be pards.
Always did think a heap of Thatcher anyhow. He was
at his wit's end an' I think he'd hev gone to smash
if I hadn't taken him in hand. I questioned him about
you an' I found he's fer you all the way. Sooner or
later, pard, you'll be wantin' riders to ride fer you and
fight fer you too, an' I recommend Mel Thatcher."

"Well, I'll be damned!" exclaimed Lincoln. "Well,
Thatcher made a good impression on me, too. Will he
talk?"

"Close-lipped as an Injun dummy. Same as me. But
thet don't say thet he'll always be thet way. . . . I'll
tell you afterwards what happened to me an' Mel, but
when we got here we heerd in the furst saloon we went
in about yore run-in with Miller. We was plumb upset.
After thet everywhere we asked questions the story
grew wuss. We run plumb into Kit Bandon an' if looks
could kill, Mel an' me shore would hev been daid long
ago, but we ducked out of her way an' hunted up the
jail. When this Texas sheriff told us you was all right
I never was so glad of anythin' in my life."

"How do you think I look?" asked Linc.

"Hell! You look to me like a geezer who was on his
honeymoon."

Lincoln laughed. "Well, it takes two to make a
proper honeymoon, but I'm feeling pretty fine, thanks."

"Where did you get plugged?" asked Vince, feeling
gently around Lincoln's bandage.

"Under the collar bone. Clean as a whistle. I'm
rarin' to go right now."

"Wal, what's keepin' you here? It was an even
break. This sheriff hasn't got no case against you."

"That's true. Haught admitted it. But it seems Kit
swore out a warrant and wants me kept here for a
while for some mysterious reason. I thought I'd not
make a break just yet. I have several good reasons."

Vince looked around at the vase of flowers, the box

of candy on the table, the plate of cake and then met Lincoln's gaze with a quizzical look. "Pard, I'm not shore yit whether you are the onluckiest cuss in the world or not. Comin' back to Miller, he gave you a run fer yore money, eh?"

"I'll say he did. I made a couple of cracks that upset him and that gave me the edge on the draw."

"Ahuh. What was the cracks, pard?"

"Vince, they had to do with Jimmy Weston."

Vince whistled under his breath. "You nagged Miller into tellin' you somethin' jest at the moment of meetin' him?"

"I'll tell you later," responded Linc. "But I've got some news, Vince, that I can't keep any longer."

"Yea? Wal, you kinda look like you was bustin' with somethin'."

"The first day I got here," began Lincoln swiftly, "I ran into Kit and Lucy with this fellow Miller." The Nebraskan went on to relate the events leading up to his marriage to Lucy.

"Wha—a—t!" stuttered Vince incredulously, *"You,* married to Lucy?"

"I did that, pard," said Lincoln. "It sounds like a dream but it happened."

Vince stared at his friend. "An' all the time Kit Bandon has lost her haid over you—the fust time in her life!"

"I don't know about that, Vince, but she comes in here and acts and talks like it."

Vince threw up his hands and began to pace the floor. He was the picture of consternation and dismay. He actually wrung his hands. His distress was too genuine to be laughed at.

"Lord amighty, pard. Yore as good as daid right now," he finally burst out, stopping before Lincoln. "You've signed yore own death warrant. You might as well cash in right now. Haven't you got no sense? Couldn't you wait? Didn't you hev any hunch about what kind of a woman this she-cat is? . . . She'll *kill* you, man, as shore as yore the onluckiest cuss who ever breathed. An' like as not, she'll kill pore Lucy too."

"But, Vince, she doesn't know it yet! Besides, you don't think I'm going to sit idly by if Lucy is in danger!"

"But she'll find it out," expostulated Vince. "The longer she's fooled the wuss she'll be. . . . Pard, didn't you know Kit Bandon had personally killed two or three men? More, for all I know."

"I heard that but I hardly believed it."

"Wal, I believe it. She certainly come awful damn close to givin' it to me."

"That's a confession, Vince. You'll have to tell me about that."

"Did you fix the parson so he won't tell?" queried Vince.

"I'm sure it won't leak out there."

"Who else knows?"

"Only Lucy—and I told Miller that last second before he died."

"Lordy! Yore a cold-blooded hombre. . . . Lucy ought to know Kit well enough to keep her mouth shet but it won't hurt none to scare her half to death. And how about you, Mr. Bridegroom? Can you keep from shootin' off yore chin?"

"I don't know, Vince. Sometimes I'm afraid I can't. If she drives me too far——"

"Nuff said," interposed Vince. "I can guess the rest. Now fer Lord Amighty's sake, listen to me. Explain this to Lucy no matter what risk you run and let Kit make all the fuss she wants over you even if it kills you. It'd be better to stand fer that, wouldn't it, than to be daid?"

"Vince, I can't let Kit make a fool of herself," protested Lincoln.

"Why cain't you?" queried Vince angrily.

"I can't—because, well, I just don't trust myself where that woman is concerned," retorted Lincoln desperately. "I know she's playing a deep game, and may be implicated in Jimmy's murder. But in spite of all that I can't hate her for it. I *couldn't* love her, but—neither can I hate her. . . ."

"She's got hell's fire in her veins," interrupted Vince. "Take my hunch, pard, keep thet secret until you an' Lucy can run away or till somethin' happens, an' you can bet yore life somethin' is goin' to happen."

"What do you mean, Vince?" demanded the Nebraskan.

"I don't know. I don't know any more than you. But, man, in the very nature of things out here on this Wyomin' border where there ain't no law or morality, where the times is hard an' men are desprit, I jest cain't believe thet even a woman, beautiful as she is, can go on forever makin' fools of men an' bein' a law onto herself."

"All right, Vince. I'll keep the secret if I can prevail upon Lucy to trust me."

"It'll be tough, but yore married to her an' Kit cain't take thet away. . . . Now, listen to what I've got to tell you. There's been some high old goin's on in South Pass since you left. The cowboys is upset because of the rumor thet the cattlemen in the Sweetwater Valley are goin' to fire them in a bunch an' go to Caspar an' Cheyenne to hire other hands. I reckon thet's only a rumor. It's too farfetched to be true. There's more'n 80,000 head of stock in the valley an' you know thet takes aplenty of outfits to run. The cattlemen cain't afford to do thet. But the upset among the cattlemen is shore a real fact. Lee is the ringleader of the ranchers. He's a Texan an' powerful full of spunk. Some say he's crazy about Kit Bandon and others say he hates her. I reckon he does both, because Kit made a fool out of him same's the rest. Hargrove, Burton, Nesbit, Seymour, MacNeil, all the cattlemen down the river were in town fer two days. They had a secrut meetin'. Mel an' I sneaked round back of the hall an' got chased away fer our pains. Nobody knows what went on at thet meetin'. It had to do with these cattlemen bandin' themselves together to put a united front against any and all kinds of rustlin'. These cattlemen hev been slow to wrath. There's a reason fer thet which you might guess. But it's settled now—they're as mad as hornets an' it's goin' to go hard with any-one they ketch stealin' cattle."

"Well, Vince, that was in the air when I was in South Pass."

"Yes, but it hadn't come to a haid yet. The day after thet meetin' Thatcher heerd from Bill Haines thet a cowboy had been caught red-handed an' was bein' held down in the river bottom by the riders who had caught him. Later me and Mel got ahold of Haines and scared him into the middle of next week. He's a good friend of Thatcher's an' we finally forced him to con-fess where the cowboy was being' held. Thet night after dark Thatcher an' me rode out of South Pass packin' some grub an' blankets an' we made a beeline fer the river bottom. When we got to Hargrove's ranch about midnight we scouted all around lookin' fer a campfire. Couldn't find nothin' so we made camp ourselves.

"Next day we kept out of sight but we watched the trails. Thatcher went one way an' I went another. Long in the afternoon late Thatcher came back an' said he had spotted buckboards an' saddle hosses on the Hargrove road. We sneaked out along the edge of the willows until we caught sight of them an' then we hid an' let them pass. Then we followed them. They stopped at Hargrove's ranch. This was along about sunset. A little later we saw a man come out of the willows below us, look all around as if he didn't want to be seen, an' then run across the road into the ranch yard. We figgered thet he was goin' to inform these cattlemen where the prisoner that had been reported caught was bein' held. We figgered we were gettin' pretty hot. We found a trail enterin' in the brush jest below us an' we hid close to it.

"Wal, to make a long story short, as soon as it was dark a bunch of men took thet trail single-file behind their guides and went into the brush. Me an' Thatcher followed but not too close. Half a mile in we saw a light in a clearin' an' we planned to sneak off the trail one on each side an' get as close as possible. An' we arranged to meet at our campin' place later. I didn't hev to go very far on my side before I came up to the edge of the thicket an' saw the campfire a hundred steps or more away. I lay low an' watched an' listened. Someone threw brush on the campfire an' it blazed up bright.

"There was thirteen men in thet bunch not countin' a young feller they had tied to a saplin'. I couldn't see his face well but it was familiar. I recognized Lee, Hargrove, Burton, Nesbit, and Summers in the fire-light. There wasn't any doubt about who they was. They meant business. It was jest like a hangin' party. Lee and Hargrove did the talkin' but I couldn't ketch what they said. But I distinctly heerd the cowboy say no. He said it several times an' shook his head vio-lently. Then they ripped off his coat an' shirt and beat him over the bare back. Lee was the fust to use the whip. Purty soon he stopped and asked the cowboy again some question. He cursed somethin' awful. It was plain to me then thet Lee wanted him to confess somethin'. I heerd Hargrove say, 'But they caught you rustlin' calves.' An' the cowboy yelled: "Hang me and be damned!'

"They tried beatin' him again in which several of the cattlemen took a hand. They were a pretty hard bunch, at their rope's end. They had been drinkin' too in South Pass. But they didn't hang him. Mebbe they thought they could make him give up later. Anyway they untied him and led him away. I waited until they was gone and then slipped out in the open and made my way to our camp. Thatcher did not come back fer two hours. I told him what I'd seen and waited fer him to spill what he had seen. But he didn't do it. All he said was: 'Wait!' He seemed kind of dazed. Long after I rolled in my blanket I saw him sittin' by the camp-fire. In the mornin' early we rode back to South Pass in time to get the stage."

Lincoln maintained a long silence. "Vince, as if I

didn't have enough to think about without worrying about you! ... Suppose you shave yourself and put on one of my clean shirts. By the way, is Thatcher as tough looking a hombre as you are?"

"No, he ain't, pard. But he's pretty seedy at thet."

"And of course you're both broke."

"Wal, I had jest enough money left of thet you gave me to get here."

"Well, I'll dig up some more. Now clean yourself up and rustle out of here."

While Vince made haste to wash and render himself more presentable, Linc lay back on the bed and thought over what the cowpoke had told him. What significance had this story of Vince with all that had preceded it? Common sense would indicate that any drastic movement in Sweetwater Valley had significance for Bradway and his problem. He went over Vince's story again. The Nebraskan had experienced many an uprising of the cattlemen, but this was the first time he had ever known it to be a war to be waged upon cowboys. Vince discharged; Thatcher, a valuable and trusted cowhand, disgraced and threatened; some unknown cowboy made prisoner and beaten—these were indeed events that hinted of even worse to come. The next thing these irate cattlemen would do would be to kill a cowboy or worse, hang him. But what for? The answer was too easy. Rustling! But Lincoln could not persuade himself to believe that was all. Why did they beat the unknown cowboy? He had been caught red-handed stealing calves—but they would not beat him for that. Obviously they wanted him to talk, to betray someone else, to reveal to them what he was going to do with the stolen calves. The cowboy had refused to talk. Stripped and beaten, yet he resolutely clung to his secret, whatever it was. "Hang me and be damned!" Certainly such defiance as that must be in protection of a mighty important cause. A cowboy would have to possess great nerve and incentive to taunt a bunch of angry cattlemen in such circumstances. Lincoln cudgeled his brain over possible motives. From whatever angle he approached the mystery, every trail led in the same direction— toward the Maverick Queen—Kit Bandon.

The deduction was inevitable. It pointed to a grave and complex situation in the valley; it involved Kit Bandon's machinations, whatever they were; a good many of the cowboys, perhaps all of them; and probably more than one rancher. What was this vigilante band of cattlemen really aiming to accomplish? To stop the rustling? Or was it something else? He must hurry back to South Pass in order to find out. Hanging the unknown cowboy would precipitate a most unusual and dangerous situation. Unquestionably it would be followed by further bloodshed. Lincoln had never quite liked that little cold deadly glint in Vince's eyes. If the other cowboys, whether they were guilty of anything crooked or not, were treated in such a manner, they would rise in a body for vengeance, organize into a full-scale rustler band or start a war. They would not betray Kit Bandon. It was the code of most cowboys, gallant and sentimental, perhaps, but one to which they all adhered, never by word or deed to say or do anything that could be detrimental to a woman.

"Wal, boss, how do I look?" spoke up Vince, approaching his partner.

"Very much better, cowboy. Now you take this money and join Thatcher, get him to make himself look decent, catch yourselves something to eat. Then keep your eyes peeled and your wits about you. No more red liquor, no bucking the tiger, and avoid the Bandons. Savvy that?"

"O.K., boss. I'm shore Mel will be glad yore takin' him on."

"All right. That's fine. Bring him to see me early in the morning."

Vince met Sheriff Haught in the corridor. "Wal, cowboy, you don't look quite so disreputable. Stick that gun you're packin' round under your coat so it don't show so plain."

"Much obliged, Sheriff. I kinda think you might be

a regular feller after all. But when are you goin' to let my pard out of jail?"

"Well, I reckon it'll be a few days yet," returned the sheriff. Leaving the door open he approached Lincoln. "Bradway, I went out and had a talk with thet other cowboy and I'm bound to say that I liked him. Fine upstandin' cowpuncher, and plenty intelligent. He's pretty close-lipped. I know the rancher Lee that he worked for. There's hell brewin' over there in that valley. Now I want to know if you're on the right side."

"I think so, Sheriff. I'm sure of it," replied the Nebraskan thoughtfully.

"Well, that's good. Both of these cowboys who came here to see you are on the dividing line between goin' to hell and goin' straight. Not thet I think they haven't gone straight but somethin' has rubbed them the wrong way. Somethin' mighty dangerous. I've seen Texas cowboys like thet and I know 'em like a book. Are those boys goin' to work for you?"

"Yes they are, Sheriff, and I'm pretty sure I can control them."

"I'll feel better about thet when you leave here."

"When will that be?"

"Well, I reckon you're at liberty to go most anytime now."

"Fine. But I'll hang around a few days longer, Sheriff. There're reasons."

"I should smile there's reasons!" replied the sheriff. "Today when I was down street a stunnin' lookin' girl came up to me. It took me a little bit to recognize Lucy Bandon. She was all dressed up in blue, happy, excited, and she asked me about my prisoner—meaning you, of course. I told her that you were a little weak from the loss of blood but you would be all right soon. I asked her to come down and call on you. She said, 'Oh, I wish I dared. Maybe in a day or two if my aunt goes to Salt Lake. Will you give—a— Mr.—a—Bradway my—my best wishes?' Told her I shore would. Now, Bradway, I haven't known you a great while but I've taken a likin' to you. But even if

I hadn't, the fact that a purty girl like Lucy Bandon's sweet on you, would be bound to influence me."

A melodious voice could be heard outside in the corridor. "Ahuh," continued the sheriff, "speaking of angels or would you say the opposite—I think you have callers, Linc." After he had stamped noisily out, Lincoln recognized the two feminine voices in reply to the sheriff's greeting. Kit Bandon entered, followed by Lucy and Haught. Haught stopped in the doorway to speak to someone else outside. The Nebraskan forgot all caution. His glance passed by Kit, and for a moment his eyes met the blue eyes of Lucy Bradway. Almost imperceptibly she shook her head. He turned quickly to face Kit Bandon, who evidently had missed the exchange between the two.

"Hello, Linc," said Kit. "I thought I would run up a few minutes, and I finally prevailed on Lucy to come with me."

"How do you do, Lucy?" said Lincoln.

"Good evening," replied Lucy composedly. She walked up to the couch and gazed down upon him. She was quite pale in the dim light and her eyes shone darkly. "And how are you?"

"Just fine—for a cripple," replied Lincoln. "It is very good of you to come and see me."

At that juncture a waiter appeared bearing a white-covered tray which he deposited upon a little table by Bradway's couch.

"Bring it in, boy," called Kit to someone outside. A boy entered, carrying a large lamp. "Lincoln, I brought something to light up this dismal place." In a moment the place changed from a dingy cell to a warm and comfortable room. "There, isn't that cheerful? And here are newspapers, and a couple of books."

"Thanks," replied Lincoln. "You're awfully good to me—but I'm not going to stay in here forever."

"No, of course not," said Kit. "But you had better start in on your supper before it gets cold. Sheriff, will you take Lucy into your office while I talk over some business with Mr. Bradway?"

Sitting up, Linc caught Lucy's eyes again and he made a slight motion with his head, which he hoped she would interpret correctly. Then he said: "You talk, Kit, while I eat."

She waited until the sheriff had ushered Lucy out of the room and into his office across the corridor. Lincoln noticed that the girl was not as radiant as she had been when she came in a few moments before. She was quiet and tense, and her eyes were dark and sad.

"You'll have to do most of the talking, cowboy. I want to know some mighty important things."

"What about?" he asked. He was not perturbed: he held the advantage over Kit Bandon in every way, except in regard to Lucy. Kit pulled a chair close to where Linc now was sitting at the table.

"Lincoln, I just ran plumb into Mel Thatcher and that excowboy Vince," she announced. "Do you know them?"

"I met Thatcher in South Pass and I'm quite well acquainted with Vince."

"Could they by any chance be here to see you?"

"They could, and they are," replied the Nebraskan coolly.

"I guessed it then," retorted Kit with a snap of her fingers. "What is their relation to you?"

"Well, I'd say Vince had the makings of a real pard. According to him, Thatcher will stack up about the same way."

"How did this come about?" queried Kit.

"I ran into Vince in South Pass. He was down on his luck, broke and hungry, and I cottoned to him, that's all. According to Vince, this cowboy, Thatcher, is pretty bad off too. Lee fired him. He can't get anybody to give him a job on the range, and naturally he was pretty desperate. Vince brought him over here to see if I wouldn't have him throw in with us."

"Kind of a Good Samaritan, eh?" inquired Kit with a touch of sarcasm in her voice.

"Kit, maybe it's a weakness, but I am pretty liable to take the part of the underdog, especially when he happens to be somebody I'm fond of. I like Thatcher and I think a heap of Vince."

"What do you aim to do with them?"

"Well, I've got plenty of money, as you know, and I'll let them trail around with me for a while."

Kit half rose from her chair. "You can't do that," she said, her voice rising.

"Beg pardon?" inquired Bradway, politely.

"I said you can't do that," repeated Kit.

"And why not?"

"Because I won't stand for it."

Linc laughed. "Excuse me, lady, but what I do, what friends I choose to make, and what cowboys I put on my payroll have nothing at all to do with you."

"Lincoln!" she cried incredulously. He quickly perceived that she had completely overestimated her power over him.

"Kit, you have been flattering enough to express your interest in me and you've certainly been very kind to me since I got shot up. I'm grateful, of course, but you must know that I can't take orders from you."

She turned perfectly white, her eyes turned like glittering daggers upon him. The cowboy could see that it was with great difficulty that she was retaining her composure. Quick as a panther she arose and the sound she uttered was like a hiss. For a moment she stood looking down at Linc, her dark eyes mere slits. Then she walked to the window, her face twisted and tense.

He calmly went on eating his supper, but inwardly he was completely alert. In a few moments she came back to him again, her venomous mood gone as suddenly as it had seized her.

"Linc, listen. Both Thatcher and Vince are bitter enemies of mine. Doesn't that mean anything to you?" There was a note of appeal in her voice.

"I don't believe that," he retorted. "At least they haven't confided in me. But if it's true—why should two cowpokes be Kit Bandon's enemies?"

"I liked them. I felt sentimental about them as I

have about so many cowboys, but when they began getting jealous and insistent I soon tired of them."

"Reason enough," said Lincoln shortly.

"Reason?" she queried. "For what?"

"Why, it's a woman's privilege to shed herself of a man when she is tired of him. Are you sure that you didn't overdo your—let's say sentimental interest in them?"

It was evident that she was unused to this kind of indifference from any man. She controlled her anger with an effort.

"Lincoln, I have made some great plans—which involve you."

"You are very good, but don't you think you should consult me before making plans which involve me?"

"I want to sell out my cattle and my ranch and move down the Sweetwater into new country. . . . I'm going to Salt Lake tomorrow to see my banker and make a deal for my property. I will have a pretty big stake when the deal is settled. Will you leave this part of Wyoming with me?"

"In what capacity?" asked Lincoln curiously.

"Partner."

"Kit, I couldn't make a deal like that with you."

"Why not?" she flashed quickly.

"Well, there are several good reasons. I still have some unfinished business to settle around South Pass, and I would not let down Thatcher and Vince. I don't like the way things are shaping up in the Sweetwater Valley, and I would not want to share in any way with your other partner, Emery."

"I'll get rid of Emery," she said shortly.

"Well, that's something—but still . . ."

"What do you mean by things shaping up in the valley?" she interrupted, sharply.

"Thatcher and Vince brought me some very disquieting news. Looks like a cowboy and cattleman war is brewing over along the Sweetwater."

"I've seen that coming for a long while," she replied, without losing her composure. "That's one reason why

I want to get out before it comes to a head. But those cattlemen are slow to act. . . . Too many of them distrust each other. I question if they would hold together if it came to a showdown."

"I don't share that opinion, Kit," replied Lincoln, coldly. "I am anxious to go back to South Pass and find out for myself. I think there have been some developments in the last few days. It might be of more interest to you than you think."

"What might be?" asked Kit.

"Why, just what these cattlemen are up to over there. From what I gather, they don't like you. Some of them wanted to marry you and got scorned for their pains. And there are some other reasons which you probably know better than I do. Lee, Hargrove, and for all I know, others might share a good deal of animosity toward you."

"That might well be," replied Kit, thoughtfully. "In fact I know it's true. But what can they do to me?" Her voice expressed pride, arrogance, and conviction. "We'll go back home the day after I return from Salt Lake. I'll say good-by."

Linc arose from the table. "Kit, I don't promise that I'll be here when you return." He did not mean this remark, but he was curious to see what her reaction to it would be. She appeared startled; her restraint broke and she came close to him manifestly agitated, and at that moment more appealing to him than she ever had been. Suddenly she threw her arms about him and kissed him passionately.

"Lincoln, I'm crushed by your indifference. Perhaps I've been too rash in revealing to you how I feel. I've always had my way. But surely . . . well, never mind about that, now. Just kiss me good-by."

The Nebraskan forgot his promise to Vince; it was as if he were being carried along by an irresistible current. Kit's face took on a rosy flush. She laughed happily and broke from him and ran toward the door. Linc heard her gaily call to the sheriff and Lucy. Gloomily he wondered if they could leave without the girl saying good-by. When they had gone without a word of farewell, he returned to his supper minus his appetite. From the window he watched the sheriff and Kit quit the hotel, with Lucy behind them. His heart sank: would not Lucy even turn back to wave her hand to him? But yes, she had turned to look for him through the bars of the window. Warily, even timidly, she stopped to touch her hand to her lips in a token kiss. Her action brought comfort to the prisoner. But it also brought shame for his weakness of a few moments before.

Chapter X

∽◦∽

Lucy Bandon's shy but eloquent gesture held Lincoln at the window for some time. Finally he returned to his big chair, happiness for the first time crowding out the somberness of his former mood. Perhaps it was not too much for him to hope for a happy culmination of their love.

Next morning he awoke at dawn. While dressing he noticed the sunrise flush upon the snow of the Utah peaks. From the other window in the distance he could see the familiar features of the Wyoming foothills, glorious in the clear morning light. The morning was fresh and cold. Through the rarefied atmosphere the slopes and swales and hills and ranges appeared magnified. Beyond Rock Springs the purple slopes of sage spread for miles and miles, gently rising, spotted with clumps of aspen and pine with here and there an outcropping of gray rocks. They led up to where thickets and patches of timber showed dark against the rangeland. Beyond began the open country of capes and rounded escarpments growing steeper and higher and dimmer as distance augmented the effect of loneliness and solitude so characteristic of the Wyoming foothills. Valleys cut through these foothills, but they were in deep shadow. At an angle a little north of east, like a great backdrop, reared the Wind River Mountains, magnificently high and clear, peaks and notches burning with a snow-fired glory. This was the southerly end of the range. Somewhere down under that mighty upheaval of the earth's crust lay the little mining hamlet of South Pass; over to the left, the unseen valley led up to the source of the Sweetwater in the uplands. He could well understand Lucy's fondness for her favorite wilderness at the head of the little river. At this hour of the morning the brilliant light and varied color were almost unbelievably beautiful.

With a rush Linc felt his love and appreciation of this cleansing wilderness returning. He had come to avenge a crime and had found his true mate here in these hills. He knew that this love of Wyoming was permanent and ineradicable and that somewhere under the shadows of these peaks he would make his home.

Haught came bustling in, cheery and friendly.

"Sheriff, I wouldn't be surprised if I was giving up your hospitable quarters in a day or two," Lincoln said. "Your jailhouse wasn't a jail at all. Most of the jails I've been locked up in were dirty and lousy, and the jailer often didn't bother to feed his prisoners. In fact, it's really worthwhile getting arrested over here in Rock Springs. . . . Perhaps when I come back I'll do something that will set you after me again."

"Don't make such rash boasts, son. I'm glad you liked it here. As long as I'm sheriff this is goin' to be the cosiest little jail in the West. But as a matter of fact I have another cabin where I lock up hombres thet are really tough."

After a brief conversation Lincoln's breakfast arrived, followed soon after by Vince and Thatcher. The two cowboys were clad in clean jeans and showed the good effects of sleep and rest. Sheriff Haught stood by the door as they came in.

"Good mawnin', boys. I hope durin' your sojourn in Rock Springs I won't have to escort you here officially." He went out, his little eyes twinkling merrily, and closed the door.

"You're just in time for a cup of coffee and maybe

something else besides. The hotel waiter usually brings me a good deal more than I can eat."

"We had our breakfast," said Vince, "but I reckon another cup of coffee wouldn't go so bad."

"Vince, I think I want you to go back to South Pass today."

"O.K. by me," replied Vince. "Any orders, boss?"

"Wait," returned Lincoln. "Thatcher, how would you like to throw in with us?"

"I'd sure be glad and powerful lucky. Things have broke out bad for me in the valley."

"So Vince told me. Just now I don't know what we will be up against but we may have some serious work to do. I'm on the trail of something big here in Wyoming. You may have guessed what, or Vince may already have told you. Later, if we're lucky I'll get me a bunch of cattle and a ranch and we'll go partners. I still have the money, and all we need is the luck. Now, Thatcher, I appreciate that you were in some mess similar to Vince's. But I assure you I'm not going to be curious. Tell me what you like or nothing at all, as you see fit—the important thing is, are you willing to throw in with us?"

"Here's my hand, Bradway," said the cowboy, thrusting out a lean brown paw. "I think you're a square shooter. I've been on the ragged edge for a few days but this offer of yours gives me a new start."

The Nebraskan returned the strong handclasp and watched the warm light that shone in Thatcher's eyes. He knew cowboys, and these two would be fit partners to tie to. "Good," he responded heartily, "that settles that."

"Bradway, I'll get this off my chest pronto. Did you come here to meet Hank Miller?" queried Thatcher.

"Partly. But really I reckon I was following Lucy Bandon. Has Vince told you how it is with her and me?"

"No, Vince didn't say much—but I guessed it."

"Lucy agreed to meet me at the Pass and when she failed to show up I became worried and thought it best to follow her. I was afraid that Kit was trying to make Lucy think her aunt had me roped and tied."

Thatcher let out a short laugh. "Ha! Kit could do that little thing, pronto—Now about Miller. He forced you to draw on him?"

"He sure did."

"Bradway, it strikes me you fellows wouldn't draw without a word with each other."

"No, we had quite a few words," replied Lincoln grimly.

"Were you aiming to find out anything?"

"Yes," replied Lincoln.

"He didn't know you—never had heard of you?"

"No, I was a stranger to him. Hadn't the slightest suspicion that I was Jimmy Weston's friend."

"Then you asked him—something about Jimmy?" queried Thatcher, a little huskily.

"Yes, I told him plenty. I said: 'I know that you hauled him away from Kit Bandon's ranch dead or alive.' . . . And Miller replied, 'Not alive—*dead!*' "

"Pard, Miller would seem to have insinuated there that he had killed your friend. But as a matter of fact he didn't kill Jimmy."

Vince emitted a prolonged low whistle. Linc stared. He wondered about Thatcher's agitation.

"As a matter of fact I really didn't suspect Miller of killing Jimmy," Lincoln continued. "In the last moment he showed guilt of some kind but not that kind of guilt."

"Never mind how I come to know, but that's the truth," concluded Mel hurriedly, snatching up his cup and gulping its contents.

The Nebraskan dropped his eyes to his plate. He did not want to reveal more just then. Mel had added another thought-provoking angle to this mystery. It was conceivable, Bradway thought, that he might know who actually had killed Jimmy, but the fact that Thatcher, through his own choice, did not go further in untangling the plot seemed to be a proof that somehow Kit Bandon was involved in it.

"Thanks, Mel," he said thoughtfully. "That's something. Let's not talk about it any more now."

Suddenly Vince spoke up. "Boss, excuse me, but I think this is the time to ask you somethin'. Not fer my sake, or fer Mel's, but fer Lucy's! Now thet she is a part of this thing, you jest cain't handle the deal as you were goin' to before."

"All right, Vince, come out with it."

"Don't hold this agin me pard, but wouldn't it— jest wouldn't it be a good idee fer Lucy's sake to fergit about this Jimmy Weston deal?"

"What are you talking about, Vince? How can I overlook it—even for Lucy's sake?" expostulated Lincoln.

"Wal, I see it thet way, thet's all. Is it fair to Lucy fer you to go on diggin' up this lousy deal? Yore pretty shore to hev more gunplay and you cain't be so damn shore thet yore goin' to go on bein' lucky."

"Vince, I appreciate how you feel, old timer, but I can't give up this deal. I suppose I am bull-headed enough—conceited enough perhaps—to believe I can avenge Jimmy's murder and still get out of it with a whole skin."

"Thet's fair talk, pard. One way or another Mel and I are bound to trail with you."

"All right. Let's get back to business. Here's some money. You and Mel take the morning stage back to South Pass. I'll be there in two or three days—maybe sooner. I want to know more about the activity of the cattlemen there. Use your own heads and smoke out all you can. If you go down in the valley leave word at the livery stable with Bill Headly where you're going and where I can find you. I'll trail you pronto. I don't need to remind you any more to lay off the drink— We've got to have clear heads."

"Bradway, I must tell you," interposed Thatcher, "something that I've kept from Vince. I wanted to think more about it. I recognized the cowboy who was beaten that night. His name is Bud Harkness. I knew him pretty well. Just as fine a cowpuncher as ever forked a horse. Now, I'll tell you something else. If they don't hang him, Harkness will kill Hargrove because while Lee is evidently the leader of these vigilantes, Hargrove and his hired men are responsible for tripping Harkness up."

"That only makes things worse," said Lincoln. "There'll be a cowboy-cattleman war over there as sure as I'm sitting here."

"That's exactly what'll happen if the cattlemen don't lay off the cowboys," broke in Vince.

"But beating a cowboy over his bare back for stealing calves! There's more to it than that," exclaimed the Nebraskan.

"Maybe they didn't beat him for stealing calves!" said Thatcher, darkly.

"They wanted to make him talk," declared Linc.

"Sure," admitted Thatcher. "And Harkness won't ever talk."

Vince spoke up. "Boss, we'll hev to rustle if we ketch thet stage. We'll hev more to tell you when you get to South Pass. I reckon you better try to get set to come along pronto."

"I think so," replied Lincoln soberly. "Look for me day after tomorrow. Good-by and good luck."

After their departure Lincoln sat for a few moments in deep thought. And out of his conjectures he was able to reach one definite decision—that he would leave for South Pass on tomorrow, whether the Bandons returned or not.

He had not dared to hope that Lucy would come to see him today. Still, there was a possibility. Quite probably Kit would not wish to take Lucy with her to Salt Lake.

At that very moment Lincoln heard the sheriff's deep voice greeting someone in the outer room. It was followed by an excited little laugh, quickly recognizable as Lucy's. He leaped to his feet, upsetting the chair in his haste. The door swung open and Haught stuck his head in, his gray eyes twinkling.

"Bradway, can you spare time to see a young lady

who says she wants to pass the time of day?" he drawled.

"Haught, bring her in or I'll—I'll—"

The sheriff shoved open the door to reveal Lucy, clad in a new becoming blue costume with a small bunch of flowers adorning her coat. To Lincoln it seemed that he had never seen anything so beautiful as the blue of her eyes or the flush that tinged her cheek.

"Go on in, lady," said the sheriff. "He looks kinda like he might want to see you after all. . . . Wal, young folks, I'll lock this gate and stand guard." He closed the door, chuckling to himself. For an instant they stood looking into each other's eyes; then she literally ran into his arms. . . .

"Lincoln, oh my poor darling!" she whispered.

Lincoln strained her to him, kissing her flushed cheeks and closed eyes and at last her parted lips. For a moment her ardor equaled his own; then she drew back, protesting, "Oh, Lincoln—I can't breathe." When he loosened his embrace she whispered, "But Lincoln—is there anybody—who could see us?"

"No, my darling wife, no one can see us. It has been so hard to be so near yet so far away from you. Yesterday—"

"Oh, Linc, it has been terrible! Especially after I knew about you and Hank, when I knew you were wounded."

"It's really true, then?" he queried, tenderly.

"Is what true?" she asked, tremulously.

"That you really love me?"

"Do I? Oh, wonderfully, terribly, Lincoln. But since that night—not so despairingly."

"Oh, Lucy," cried Linc, "when your aunt said she was leaving for Salt Lake City, I hoped that you might come—"

"Kit was undecided whether to take me or not, but when I said I'd rather wait for her here she decided not to. She won't be back till night, and then in the morning we take the stage for home."

"Lucy, I'll be on that stage."

"Oh, wonderful. But will the sheriff let you go?"

"He can't keep me any longer. There really was no case against me. And my shoulder is fit as a fiddle. Put your head against it and see for yourself," he urged.

Lucy followed instructions and found it very fit indeed.

"I can't stay as long as you want me," murmured Lucy. "You see, my dear—husband—I have a lot of packing to do. I'm afraid I can stay only till lunch time. Will that be long enough?"

"That depends on how sweet and wifelike you can be," he said, and again he gave way to his joy and rapture to overwhelm her with his hunger for the sweet fire of her lips. For a space they wholly forgot themselves as they clung to each other in their close embrace. Then Lucy drew away from him to remove the hat he had disarranged and the flowers that he had crushed.

"Lincoln, you're almost a savage," she said, archly. "But oh, darling, I'm going to spend my whole life taming you! Not too tame, lover, but tame enough so that I won't have to go to jail to see you whenever I want to tell you that I love you."

"Where are your rings?" asked Lincoln.

"Here," she replied as with shining eyes and with unsteady fingers she turned back the collar of her dress revealing the white, graceful curve of her breast and a little folded silk handkerchief which was pinned to the cloth of her bodice. "Here they are," she whispered. "I wear them pinned inside my dress. I've acquired such a habit of putting my hand to feel if they are safe that Kit already has remarked about it. She asked me if I'd caught cold or if anything ailed me. I try to be more careful now."

"You must be, Lucy. A great deal depends on that. Never forget for a minute that our secret must not be discovered. . . . That brings me to something I must get off my chest pronto." Lincoln hesitated, then plunged on. "I don't like to admit—but I'm afraid Kit really has a case on me. Evidently she still believes that no man can resist her. And that's where I am in a predicament. She seems to have no conscience about revealing her feelings and I'm afraid modesty was completely left out of her make-up."

"But, Lincoln, it wouldn't do for you to—to show your true feelings—until—until we——" He kissed her faltering lips. She understood and he was glad.

"So I promised Vince . . . that no matter what she did I would not upset the chuck wagon. In other words, for the time being, until we know where we stand in this deal, I've got to play along her way. Are you sure this won't make you unhappy—make you jealous—make you distrust me?"

"I'll never distrust you again, Lincoln. I'm not so sure about not being jealous, but I'm your wife. What will sustain me is that before long we will get away on our own. I can stand anything as long as I am sure of that. Only, when Kit makes so—so much over you, please don't tell me."

"Lucy, you are a thoroughbred. That was the only thing that I was afraid of. I think I can handle the rest of it."

"Do you think we can get clear away from all this hateful situation soon?"

"Probably we'll have to. But not until my job here is done."

Lucy averted her face and made no comment.

"Lucy, when you and I do make our getaway, I don't want to go too far away from this part of Wyoming," he continued. "I love it here. It's a beautiful country, rich in land and water and grass and game. There are many good ranches from which a man can choose. I've got the money to make a start. Once let us get out of this mess and we can begin making a home for ourselves."

"Lincoln, there is one spot that I want you to see. It's on the headwaters of the Sweetwater—the valley I told you about, where my friend the old trapper lives.

He has homesteaded some acreage up there, and just above it is the loveliest country in the world."

"I'm afraid that's a little close to South Pass, but tell me about it."

"It is close," replied Lucy thoughtfully. "About twenty miles over the hills and a little less from our ranch. There's a good trail. I can ride it in two hours, but of course that is going at a pretty good clip."

"Are you free to ride up there whenever you choose?"

"Yes. That's one place Kit does not object to my going. You see, it's out of the way, no roads to cross, no cattle or cowboys, seldom any Indians. I never go in hunting season. I've met bears and bull moose and elk on that trail that were as tame as cows."

"All right. But tell me what it's like—"

"Well, the Sweetwater winds through a narrow valley of willows and aspens and oaks for perhaps twelve or fourteen miles . . . climbing all the time but just enough to make pretty swift water and rapids. Some day someone's going to find out that this stream has the finest trout fishing in Wyoming. After the valley opens out it is crisscrossed by a succession of canyons that lead up to the great bulk of the mountains. At the top there's a belt of black timber that stretches for miles, then beyond are the gray and white peaks reaching high into the sky. The trapper has his cabin pretty close up under the valley wall. He has never had to leave that valley to trap all the beaver and martin and fox that he could take care of. It's a paradise for game."

"Sounds pretty exciting, Lucy," responded Lincoln. "But tell me more of the spot you picked particularly."

"It's about halfway up this valley and fairly high up on a terrace from which you can see the sun rise and set. It looks down on the Sweetwater winding in and out among the willows. The white water shines and there are still pools in the bends. There are hundreds and hundreds of square miles of wonderful pasture land, and from that spot you can see a waterfall that drops half a thousand feet down the mountainside. This

bench or terrace where I dreamed that someday I
would build a home was made for someone who loved
beauty. It is one of those carved and curved benches
that you see all over this country, covered with purple
sage, and at the back rocky ground rises in short steps.
A beautiful stream comes rushing down off these rocks
onto the terrace which is surrounded by pines and aspen trees. There are perhaps ten acres of level ground
on top of my terrace, most of it good soil in which
you could grow almost anything. There is plenty of
room for barns and corrals and pastures under the lee
of the rocks protected from the northwest wind that
blows so fiercely here in winter. I was up there once
in October and I was just spellbound by the marvelous
coloring. Ben Thorpe tells me that the snow never lies
deep down in there. Perhaps the only drawback I
could find was that it would take a good deal of work
and expense to build a wagon road."

"Well!" exclaimed Linc, with a long breath. "If we
live anywhere in Wyoming, that's the spot!"

". . . But Lincoln, the most difficult thing is settled,"
she said with a smile. "The rest is only a matter of time
and work."

"And what's that?" he asked.

"Don't you remember what you and I said to the
preacher that night—?"

"Oh, you mean you've corralled me?" he drawled.
"And I thought it was the other way 'round."

"We're both in the same corral, darling," replied
Lucy, seriously. "Oh, I wish the suspense and waiting
and anxiety were over so that I could show you our
home-to-be."

The hours flew by, while the lovers dreamed and
planned, gazing out of the window toward the mountains that hid the valley of the Sweetwater, quite oblivious to the fact that they were in the town jail and that
Linc was still a prisoner. The noon hour arrived before
they were aware of it, and reluctantly Lucy told Lincoln that she must leave.

"I'll leave these poor crushed flowers with you, darling," she said.

"I'll keep a couple of these mangled buds," responded the cowboy, gallantly, taking her in his arms, "just to remember the first kiss I gave you."

"You make pretty speeches, Lincoln, and I would love to stay longer to hear you make more of them, but I must go. Is there anything we have forgotten?"

"We haven't planned to meet again."

"Well—how about one week from today?"

"But that seems so long!"

"It won't be long, dear, with all we have to do. I'll plan to ride up the river in the early morning one week from today, Wednesday. When you wish to meet me, leave South Pass early in the morning—at sunrise, ride up the stream to the head of the canyon, climb straight to the top and head west. Four or five miles across you can see down into the Sweetwater. It'll be rough going down the slope but you can grade down without any trouble and find the trail. I'll be waiting for you either at the trapper's cabin or up on our terrace."

"I'll be there, darling," he replied. He rapped upon the door to call Sheriff Haught. In another moment Lucy's heels were clicking down the corridor, bearing her away from him.

The subsequent night was long and wearying for Lincoln, owing to frequent wakeful spells, but with the dawn he arose early, glad that the time had come that he was to leave Rock Springs. He packed the black gambler's suit, thinking as he did so that its success had hardly justified its expense. That first meeting with Lucy, however, when she had scarcely recognized him, was something to remember. He shaved rather carefully. Then he donned his worn cowboy jeans, boots and spurs, and checkered blouse. For a necktie he used a red scarf. The short jacket of this suit revealed his gun hanging very much in evidence below his hip. A few minutes before he was packed and ready to go Sheriff Haught entered.

"Well, son, you're goin' to leave me, I see."

"It's about time," replied Lincoln. "I owe you a lot of good will and gratitude. How about board money?"

"What for?" asked the sheriff.

"Well, you've served me nothing but the best. Or else you may want to fine me for disturbing the peace."

"No thanks, Bradway. I cashed in plenty on your sojourn heah," he replied with a smile. "I sure have enjoyed knowin' you."

"Haught, you're the best sheriff I ever knew, and that's saying a lot. I won't forget your tipping me off about this man Miller. It could be that I owe you my life. Good-by and may we meet again."

Haught walked with him down the corridor to the door with one hand on his shoulder. "One last word, son. Watch your step with Kit Bandon. I've a hunch she'll go haywire when she finds out about you and your Lucy."

"I've lost considerable sleep over that myself, Sheriff. Good-by."

Lincoln went to a restaurant on a side street and while disposing of his breakfast had the woman put him up a lunch. As he was leaving the eating house he remembered that the doctor had expected to see him once more, but as he felt perfectly fit again, there seemed no necessity for another examination. He asked directions to the stagecoach stop and went directly there. Presently the stage rolled up and he was pleased to note that the only other passengers were the two Bandons and that Kit made no effort to conceal her surprise and chagrin over his presence. Lucy sat on the driver's seat, clad in a long gray ulster with a veil wound around her hat. Her eyes passed over Lincoln roguishly, with an air of possession, although she merely acknowledged his greeting with a nod. The driver, a stalwart man whom Lincoln did not know, helped him with his baggage and told him to climb inside. Inside Kit had recovered from her surprise and was leaning forward eagerly to greet him. She too wore a long dark coat, and appeared rather worn and tired, but her eyes were bright enough and her smile something to conjure with.

"Hello, Kit," he replied to her greeting. "Looks like we're not going to have any company."

"Yes, aren't we lucky? It will be the first time I ever rode home without being crowded."

"A little nippy this morning," observed the cowboy. "I wish I had a sheep-lined coat."

"I have a shawl there which you can use if you get cold. . . . Lincoln, did you remember to get some lunch?"

"Yes. I had the woman put up some sandwiches and chicken."

Presently the stage heaved and creaked as the driver climbed to his seat. Soon it was rolling out of town behind two fresh teams. Linc put his head out the window and raised his voice above the clatter of hoofs, the rumbling of the wheels, the clink of chains to call: "Lucy, you're going to get pretty cold up there and dusty too."

"Well, I'm no tenderfoot like some I could name," replied Lucy saucily. "I'm going to ride outside if we run into a cyclone."

"She's not very flattering," said the Nebraskan, turning to Kit. "She doesn't seem to want to ride inside with us."

"Three's a crowd," replied Kit. "But what with all these bags and boxes we won't have any too much room as it is. I did a good deal of buying this trip."

"Going home broke, then, I suppose?" queried Lincoln lightly.

"Not much. I drew out my cash at the bank and I have the check for my cattle deal, so I'm pretty well heeled, cowboy. If we get held up by any road agents mind you do some pretty quick shooting."

"We're not likely to get held up on this route."

"I'm dead tired and sleepy," said Kit. "I couldn't sleep on the train and I imagine I won't be very good company today."

She sank down against Lincoln and before they were

well out upon the prairie she was asleep. They were occupying the front seat of the stagecoach. When Lincoln stuck his long arm out the window he managed to touch Lucy and eventually take hold of her hand. The soft pressure of her fingers was comforting, but he wished he could be up there with her on the driver's seat.

The long hours passed swiftly. Traveling back in the opposite direction he found the land looked familiar; the gray sage reaches rolled by him endlessly. Looking ahead he could see the curved hills and the ravines choked with green and occasionally a stream winding away toward the south. Before they had traveled many miles Lincoln's keen eye began to locate wild game. Antelope were abundant, and in the swales he could see jack rabbits and coyotes and deer too numerous to count. In some stretches he could view far horizons but no mountains. The road was smooth with very little grade, and the horses made fast time. Several hours out, the driver halted in a grove of trees through which a brook ran.

"Here's where we rest a bit and have a snack of grub," he called out cheerily.

Lucy clambered down over the big wheel and peered in the window to see Lincoln trying to rouse Kit. "All out for refreshment, Kit," he said, gently shaking her. She awoke finally and sat up sleepy-eyed. "Where are we, driver?" she asked, looking out.

"Halfway to West Fork," he replied. "This is the only good place to stop to rest the horses and camp for a while."

"Driver, it looks as though we are going to have some weather," announced the Nebraskan.

"Yes, it's clouding up. Snow squall coming down from the hills."

"I'll eat my lunch inside," Kit decided.

"Cowboy, you build a fire," suggested the driver, "while I take care of the horses. Then I'll make some coffee."

"And I'll stretch my legs," said Lucy, swinging off

under the trees. When she returned coffee and sandwiches were being served and Lincoln observed that Lucy warmed her hands by the little fire. The wind blew chill, rustling through the trees and presently as the sun paled and then disappeared altogether, it grew quite cold.

"Lincoln, who sold you this tough chicken?" asked Kit in a petulant tone.

"Why, I was just going to say it tasted pretty good," replied Lincoln. "And I notice Lucy is doing very well with hers." Then silence fell on the little group.

"Wal, I think we might as well be movin' along," announced the driver. "And Miss, you ride inside this afternoon. It's goin' to be squally."

"How long to West Fork?" asked Lincoln.

"Oh, it won't take us long," replied the driver. "All downhill. We'll make it easy before dark. But you folks want to cover up well."

Once more in the coach, Linc found himself seated across from Lucy. Kit was not slow to make herself comfortable, appropriating Lincoln's shoulder and closing her eyes.

"Cover me up well," she ordered sleepily.

What with a blanket and a heavy robe they were reasonably well protected from the drafty stagecoach. Lucy stretched out, her feet coming in contact with those of her husband. She gave Lincoln a sly little smile before she closed her eyes. Kit was the first to drift off to sleep, and Lucy quickly followed suit. The first snow squall enveloped the stage and scurried by, the hard pellets of ice and snow rattling against the closed windows. At length Bradway was forced to let down the curtains on the windy side, but swathed by the heavy robe and with Kit heavily asleep on his side he did not feel the cold. The gray leaden sky and the intermittent snow squalls were not conducive to watchfulness and at length Lincoln too fell asleep.

When he was awakened by a sudden jar of the stage he found that the afternoon was far gone and they had reached West Fork, where they were to spend the night. The storm had passed, but the late afternoon air was cold for June. The inn was very comfortable, with a huge open fire and many oil lamps. After seeing the two women safely inside with their baggage, the cowboy went outside to stretch his cramped legs. It had cleared off crisply but in the west, dark storm clouds still loomed. The Nebraskan walked out as far as a little pine grove and back again, glad indeed that the ride was half over. Inside the post supper was ready, and with the innkeeper and his family there were several other travelers at the table. From their talk he judged that they were waiting for the westbound stage. After supper Kit and Lucy did not remain long in front of the hot fire, but the Nebraskan conquered his feeling of drowsiness in order to listen to the conversation. At length he accosted some of the westbound travelers, inquiring about affairs at South Pass. Learning little of particular interest, he finally sought the little room assigned to him and went to sleep.

When he awoke shortly after dawn he found the inn already bustling with the morning's activities. Dressing quickly, the cowboy went into the dining room to find Lucy ready and breakfast on the table. A moment later Kit came in, brisk and cheerful, evidently having completely recovered from her exhaustion of the day before. After breakfast, they stepped outside the post to find a glorious sunshiny June morning awaiting them in which to embark on the final stage of their journey.

When they pulled out of West Fork, Linc discovered that they still had the coach to themselves. Lucy rode on top with the driver; and Kit blithely informed Lincoln she would make up that day for her dullness of yesterday. She quizzed her traveling mate concerning Vince and Thatcher and also asked about Sheriff Haught and what he had told him about her, if anything. "Did he give me away?" she asked archly.

"What do you mean?" queried the cowboy.

"Did he tell you that I hired him to keep you in jail?" she went on mischievously.

"Well, he hinted it," he replied. "What was your idea in doing that?"

"Oh, I wanted you well taken care of where I could see you alone. That didn't get me very far, did it?"

"I think you went plenty far," he replied.

"Tell me," she said simply, "what seems to be the difficulty between us?"

"Between us?" he echoed. "Why should there be? There's nothing between us."

"I mean obstacles," she explained.

"Obstacles?—Obstacles to what?"

"Don't be a blockhead, Linc. You know what I mean. You know what is the matter with me. You know what I'm going to do."

"Well, I'm afraid there are a few obstacles, Kit. One in particular is that I don't seem to feel the way you are trying to make me think you feel."

"I gathered that. It's a sad blow to my vanity. Serves me right, though. But *that* is no obstacle to me, as you will discover, cowboy. Name some of the other ones."

"Excuse me, Kit. I'd rather not hurt your feelings."

"But you have already hurt me terribly," she protested. "A little more or less won't make any difference."

"No!"

"Is it my partner, Emery?" she persisted.

"Well, his relation to you is none of my business, but as a matter of fact I thought it was pretty lowdown for you to be associated with a rat of a gambler in that dive."

"Yes," she admitted frankly. "But if I realized it before, I didn't care. Now I do care. I'm not the same Kit Bandon. Just the same, this one thing you must believe, Linc. I have been mixed up with Emery in the *Leave It* but that's all. Usually I have never cared what one man thought about my relation to another man—but I want you to know that he was *not* my lover."

Lincoln did not venture any reply to her plea to be understood.

"Lincoln, you believe me, don't you?" she demanded.

"Yes, I believe you," replied Lincoln, slowly.

"Thank you. . . . Then is it the gossip you heard about me in South Pass? My name being linked with Lee and Hargrove and other cattlemen?"

"That meant nothing to me," rejoined Lincoln, truthfully.

"They all ran after me, made love to me in their clumsy ways—the old goats," she said, scornfully. "I'll admit I did play around with Lee, perhaps too much. A couple of years ago I thought I might even marry him. It might have been a good idea. . . . As a matter of fact, it would have been much better for me if I had—but I didn't know it then. Lincoln, you don't seem to be the jealous type; but just the same, men *are* alike. I want you to know that I went around with Lee off and on because I really liked him . . . is that clear to you?"

"Perfectly clear, Kit."

"You won't have any queer ideas about Lee and me now that I've set you straight?"

"Queer? Hardly that. I suppose it's a woman's privilege to lead any man on if she wants to, but it isn't very honorable."

"You really have heard a lot about me, haven't you?"

"Kit, you don't seem to realize that a colorful person like yourself is bound to be talked about. Every move you make makes gossip—good or bad."

She was silent awhile, resting her cheek against his shoulder and clinging tightly to his arm. "Then it is as I have feared," she murmured, not at all displeased, it seemed to Linc. "It's the gossip about me and all these cowboys."

Lincoln had no ready answer for that. Presently he said: "Kit, I—I never paid much attention to gossip. One lone beautiful woman out among a group of cattlemen is bound to be talked about. Naturally I was interested in you more because of the unique and attractive place you occupy out here. But the only thing I ever actually heard was that you were, well—not fair in your sentimental dealing with cowboys."

"What did Jimmy tell you?" she whispered.

"He wrote me that you took him away from Lucy— and the words he used were hardly fit to quote to you."

Her head sank a little on his shoulder. He felt her fingers tighten then relax. Mention of Jimmy Weston's name always seemed to stir her. Would he ever discover what the true relationship between those two had been? He was more than curious to hear what she would say. Yet he felt convinced that she would not tell him the truth, although why he could not quite understand. Presently she spoke, quite composedly: "Lincoln, I did come between Lucy and Jimmy. She was taken with him and I was afraid she would overdo it. I'm bound to admit that I liked him myself pretty well. He was good-looking, gay, full of mischief—the best company ever, but he was as unstable as water, absolutely unreliable, impossible for me to accept as Lucy's husband."

Lincoln at length replied somewhat huskily: "In that case probably you were justified in separating them. But not by making him care for you. I am speaking frankly, Kit, because Jimmy was my best friend."

"That has always been my weakness," she rejoined, simply. "That is my weakness now and it's ten thousand times stronger than it ever was."

"Jimmy wrote me a wild, disconnected letter probably under the influence of despair or liquor and I did not take that part of it as absolutely reliable. But I'd appreciate it if you would let the subject of Jimmy drop between us."

"That's all right with me," she replied in quick relief. "As for the other cowboys, you must remember that I am a rancher; dealing in cattle is my business. I've hired dozens of cowboys in the valley. I've befriended them—gotten them out of jail, redeemed their saddles and guns that they had pawned, lent them money—in fact, had a sort of motherly feeling for all of them. Then, you must remember again, I am a young woman—and even if *you* never seemed to be aware of it, they have told me repeatedly that I am rather attractive."

Bradway laughed at this. "Yes," he said coolly. "Even if I never let you wind me around your little finger, Kit, it wasn't because you were hard to look at."

"Please don't joke at a moment like this, Lincoln. I'm going out of my way to try to establish my true character in your mind. The fact that good-looking cowboys fell in love with me from time to time never troubled me until you came to South Pass. I'll admit, I even encouraged them to. . . . Now all I want you to understand is that this cowboy nonsense and foolishness is behind me. I'm through. You can give yourself the credit for that."

"Thanks, Kit, but I'm a cowboy, too."

"Yes, but if you must split hairs, I was speaking of those thoughtless friendships, trifling and of no consequence. . . ."

"Kit, all this confidence of yours is interesting but it's a little embarrassing. I don't know what you're driving at."

"You'll find out pretty quick. My vanity has been bleeding to death for days . . . but I know what has happened to me and I have lived with it, slept with it, dreamed of it till it has taken possession of me!" She fell silent then. Presently her left hand slipped around back of his head and touched his cheek and neck with an exquisite softness. Her mood seemed to shift again; she leaned against him, in one of her abrupt changes which he recognized and tried to steel himself against. Suddenly the woman beside him had become warm, quivering, vibrant, radiating a charm that Linc again found to be almost irresistible. Her physical beauty was only a small part of her charm, lovely as were her dusky eyes, her soft skin, her youthful body. But there was more, a great deal more. He decided then, in a moment when his perceptions were deeply sensitive, that her great power was a singularly vital and compelling zest for life, which drove her into adventure for the pure love of adventure. She had the recklessness of a man which, added to her all-too-conscious attractiveness for men, made her power completely transcendent.

"Lincoln," she said after an interval of silence, "please listen. If I ever spoke the truth I'm telling it now. If good can ever overcome selfishness and love of power in a woman then it has done that to me. I always feared this thing would happen to me. It is perhaps no different from what other women have experienced but in me it is a thousand times stronger. . . . All that life—all that has happened since I came to the Sweetwater is passed—gone forever. I can even conceive of praying to God eventually to let me forget that old life. I intend to sell my ranch and I want to move somewhere else in Wyoming far away where no one ever heard of me. I love you, Linc, as no other woman ever loved in this world. If you ask me why, I'd say it was retribution. I have held love lightly. Now it holds me in a grip which I wouldn't loosen if I could. At this moment, Lincoln, I'm so humble in my love that I would be willing to plead with you to take it. I will be happy with anything you can give. Linc, you don't realize what it means that the one proud woman whom they call the Maverick Queen is on her knees before you. With all my heart and soul I swear my change of heart. . . . Lincoln, will you go away with me?"

"Kit—I can't," he replied huskily.

"Is it because you don't care for me?"

"No."

"Is it because you don't care enough?"

"No."

"Is it because you still doubt—?"

"No, it's not that either. Kit, I don't know that it would make any difference to a man whether he had any doubts about a beautiful woman like you if he knew he wanted her to be his wife. I think the only thing that would count with a man would be what his heart told him. You are a gallant lady, Kit Bandon. Life would be an adventure with you that a million men would give their souls to undertake with you. But it is impossible to go away with you, Kit."

"Tell me why," she whispered patiently.

"You wouldn't understand the reasons I gave you," he replied hurriedly. "The main reason—is that I've already got a wife!"

Startled and amazed, she jerked up from his breast, clutched his arms with fierce hands. The eyes that blazed into his were those of a cornered puma.

"Good God! Linc, what are you saying? A wife!"

"That's—what I said—Kit," he replied haltingly.

"Are you separated from her?"

He uttered a grim little laugh. "Separated. I should smile I am."

"Could you get rid of her?"

"I'm afraid I couldn't."

"Well. That is the only thing I didn't think of," she replied, still obviously shaken. "I don't know that it makes so much difference to me at the moment. Of course I wanted to be your wife and by the high heavens, I swear I will be! . . . I will go right on making my plans. All that matters to me is that you don't despise me—that you care a little for me. The rest will all come in time. . . . But what you have told me has shocked all the plans I had made right out of my head."

"Kit, if you think that this was easy for me either you are very much mistaken." Putting his head out of the window, Lincoln called up to the driver to stop. When the stage rolled to a standstill Lincoln called: "Lucy, climb down. I want to change places with you."

Laughingly she complied. "All right with me," she said. "I'm about blown to pieces. Did you notice how fast we went down that last hill?"

"No," replied Lincoln, giving her a long significant

look, "I'm afraid I didn't know whether I was riding or walking."

"Indeed you must have been preoccupied. I drove that last ten miles myself. Look at my gloves. If the teams didn't run away with me, I'm missing my guess."

"I'd like to drive some myself," said Lincoln, as he climbed up over the wheel.

"Sure, son, go ahead. Saves me the trouble," the driver said good-naturedly.

Lucy entered the stagecoach and slammed the door. The stage lunged on again.

"Must have been making good time, driver," said the cowboy.

"Wal, where hev you been anyhow?" he chuckled. "Here's the head of Sweetwater Valley, that is, this west fork. Thirty miles more or less to the Bandon ranch. We'll be there in two hours or more."

"Doggone!" ejaculated Lincoln. "You sure have been traveling."

For an hour the Nebraskan devoted himself to piloting the spirited teams. They pulled so hard on his arms that he was forced to brace his feet powerfully on the dashboard. Now and then he had to use the brake. With this physical exertion and his attention to the horses and the condition of the road he was fully occupied, and when he relinquished the reins to the driver he was thoroughly tired, his seething and conflicting emotions quieted. He was now within sight of the Sweetwater Valley. He gazed down that purple expanse with infinite appreciation of its beauty and a perplexing wonder as to what it had in store for him. The sun, halfway down in the west, had begun to lose its brightness and mantled the lower reaches of the valley with a dark rosy haze. Lincoln tried to pick out the escarpment with a clump of pines which had been his rendezvous with Lucy, but the distance was too great. He confined himself to admiration of the southern end of the Wind River Range and to wondering what was taking place between the two women in the stage behind him. Somewhere up under those sunset-flushed peaks was the wild and fertile valley with which Lucy had intrigued him. But thought of making a home there seemed as far away from reality as it was in the purple distance.

It developed that Kit had not left any word with her foreman as to the time he could expect her return, so the driver good-naturedly turned off the main road and took the valley thoroughfare down to the Bandon ranch. Lincoln noticed the picturesque bridge and river and ranch house again with poignant feelings. Beautiful as the spot was, it was haunted for Lincoln; something had taken place there that he might never discover and which he ofttimes almost hoped would remain forever a secret. The stage rolled up to the gate with dragging brakes.

"Wal, hyar we are," the driver called down cheerily.

A lame man, old and gray, appeared from around the house. A woman, evidently the housekeeper, appeared in the kitchen door, turned back, and a moment later opened the door that led out onto the porch. Linc wondered absently where they had been the day he had called. Then he leaped down and, hoisting the baggage that the driver handed to him, carried it onto the porch.

"Here, Linc," said Kit, "is the rest of our stuff."

She dismounted from the stage, followed by Lucy. Lucy removed the long coat and veil and shook the dust from them.

"That bag and package belong to Mr. Bradway," said Kit. They were replaced in the stage.

Lucy turned toward the house, and from the porch called back at him, archly: "Adios, Mr. Bradway. I enjoyed your company very much—what little I saw of you." Then she picked up two of the bags and entered the house.

"Well, what kind of a speech was that?" queried Kit. "What's the matter with the girl? Jealous, I suppose."

"Didn't strike me that way," returned the cowboy. "I think she was poking fun at me."

"All aboard," called the driver, now a little impatiently, taking up his reins. "We've got to get to South Pass before dark."

"Lincoln, it was a sort of wonderful trip—wasn't it?"

"I should smile it was," replied Lincoln. "Good-by, Kit."

"Good-by. Will you come down to see me soon or shall I have to come to South Pass to find you?" she asked with a sharp glance which revealed that she had not yet recovered from the shock of the cowboy's revelation.

"I don't know what to say to that," replied Lincoln evasively. "I've got lots to do. Let's not be in too much of a hurry about seeing each other again."

"This is Thursday," said Kit. "I'll be over in town not later than Saturday. I've got business to settle up there in connection with the sale of the place. Don't forget what I told you about Emery."

The driver snapped his whip and once more the stagecoach rolled on. Lincoln looked back vainly to see if Lucy was visible. Kit stood in front of the ranch house, burdened by her parcels and coats, her great eyes shining darkly from her unsmiling face. They passed over the bridge and Lincoln looked no more.

It was sunset by the time they reached the slope of the escarpment. When the long zigzag slope had been surmounted, Lincoln looked back. This was his first view of the Sweetwater Valley at sunset. It was as if he had never seen it before: dusky red and orange banners reached out over the sage; the winding reaches of the river caught some of the last gleams from the dying sun; down in the valley the windows of the ranch houses reflected the level beams with a golden light; above the hills in the west the flattened orb was almost a sinister red. Lincoln suddenly discovered that in these last few hours he had subtly changed. He would never want to live in the valley of the Sweetwater now—not as long as Kit Bandon lived there.

From there on the horses made fast time over the hard road. It was dark when they reached the slope leading down into South Pass, and all over the valley lights were twinkling. The driver trotted his team down across the brawling brook, turning into the main street illuminated by oil lamps, to make his scheduled stop at the hotel. Lincoln climbed down stiffly with his bag and packages, peering about him to see if Thatcher and Vince were awaiting him. They were not in sight. It was the early evening hour but the street was already thronged, and the discordant hum of the mining camp's night activity had begun. The Nebraskan hurried away toward his lodginghouse. The landlady let him in with a welcoming word and he hurried to his little room to light the lamp.

"Glad to get back, lady," said Linc. "Seems like I've been gone for ages."

"Well, Mr. Bradway, you weren't gone so long that word didn't have time to come back to South Pass about your doings."

"Yes," Linc replied. "This place is not the only place where things can happen."

"Have you talked to anybody?" she asked.

"Not a word with anyone."

"It's been tolerable lively here today," she said crisply. "Bud Harkness rode in on the warpath."

"Oh, he did?" queried Bradway with quickened interest.

"I didn't see him, but I talked with those who did. He rode in without saddle or bridle and he didn't have a coat or a shirt to his back. And I hear that his back was a sight to see! Hargrove and Nesbit were in town with some other cattlemen. I heard they had a secret important meeting and then went out and got drunk. They were having a big gambling game at Emery's, when Harkness suddenly appeared on a new horse. He had found some clothes and he went into Emery's holding a gun in each hand. I heard the row from here.

Don't know how many shots. According to reports he ran afoul of Emery and his henchmen, one of whom he killed. I don't know which. Then he broke up that poker game, crippling Nesbit, and killing Hargrove. After that Harkness was seen to ride out of town up the hill road toward Caspar."

Chapter XI

Deep in thought, Bradway left his lodginghouse and warily walked toward the main street, keeping in the shadow of the buildings. He went around the back way and up to the livery stable. There was a light in Headly's little office but he did not seem to be in. Lincoln had taken only a few steps in that direction when Vince and Thatcher appeared out of the shadows.

"Howdy, boss," Vince greeted him. "Shore am glad to see you. I was waitin' when the stage come in, but I didn't want to show myself."

"Hello, Bradway," spoke up Mel Thatcher. "Reckon I'm just as glad as Vince to see you."

"What's all this I hear?" queried Lincoln sharply, but in a low voice. "My landlady tells me there's been hell a'poppin' today."

"There shore was," said Vince. "Boss, come back in here where we won't be seen."

They went into the hay-scented gloom of the livery stable. Vince extinguished his cigarette with his fingertips.

"I hope you fellows didn't get mixed up in it," said Lincoln.

"Not so anyone would notice it," replied Vince. "Mel an' I was downtown all day snoopin' around—an' shore it's been an important day—an' we seen

214

Harkness ride in acrost the brook. He was bareback and half-naked. You could see the red stripes all over him. He rode up the hill as far as here. Figgerin' there was hell to pay, Mel an' me split up. He stayed downtown an' I hurried up to Headly's the back way. I found Harkness up here foamin' at the mouth. He had learned from Headly about Hargrove and his rancher pards bein' in town an' whoopin' it up. 'Vince,' he said, 'I'm on my way, but I've got a little job to do before I slope. I've got to hev a gun an' a hoss an' some clothes.' I told him thet he'd come to the right guy. I gave him my shirt an' my old coat an' thet new gun you got me an' the old one you left here an' I also gave him all the money I had. He made a deal with Headly for a saddle hoss an' saddle, an' I'm bound to say Headly was a friend in need. I asked Bud what he was goin' to do. Boss, you never seen a man burn an' spit fire like that hombre did. 'Wouldn't it be a good idee to wait till after dark?' I asked him. 'Wait nothin'. I'm rarin' to go.' Then I said, 'Bud, I guess it's all right fer me to tell you thet me and Thatcher, soon as we found out about yore bein' taken prisoner, rode hell fer leather down into the valley an' were lucky enough to find thet camp near Hargrove's ranch. We saw them men lead you into the brush and we follered. We sneaked up on the campfire where they had you tied an' I hate to tell it, Bud, but we saw them beat you.' 'The hell you did!' said Harkness, amazed. 'Wal, I reckon I couldn't hev had better witnesses for thet dirty deal. But thet wasn't nothin', Vince. They tied me up in a cellar an' starved me to make me talk. About noon today I slugged a guard an' ran away, luckily freein' my hands. I caught a hoss an' hyar I am. . . . I'm goin' to slope. If I stayed hyar I'd lead a bunch of cowboys against them cattlemen an' you know, Vince, thet would drag you an' Thatcher in with me. Much obliged fer the good turn yore doin' fer me. I hope to God somebody will do the same fer you someday. Don't follow me now an' get yoreself in trouble.' He forked his hoss an' went pilin' down the street. I reckon thet I'd better take his advice an' stay out of sight."

"Are you sure, Vince, that your helping hand in this will not come to light?" asked Linc anxiously.

"Shore I am," replied Vince. "No one seen me, an' Headly won't tell."

"It'd be a bad thing for us to get mixed up in this," said Lincoln seriously. "Come on—what happened then?"

Thatcher took up the story. "I was standing in front of Emery's with some other hombres when Bud came riding down," he said. "He scattered the gravel all over us as he halted the horse. And if a cowboy ever looked dangerous Harkness sure did then. He pulled two guns and bolted into the hall. The other fellows ran but I had to see what was going to happen next. It seems that Emery and that big black-bearded man of his, Bannister, is his name, were standing right there. I figured afterward that they were keeping curious people out of the gambling den where the big game was going on. 'Get out of here, cowboy,' yelled Emery. Bud told him to move pronto. Emery used poor judgment here because evidently he took Bud for a drunken cowboy throwing a bluff and he ordered Bannister to throw him out. That cost Bannister his life and Emery, waking up a little late, ran to the door just in time to save his own life. I learned afterward that Bud's bullet took him in the rump, making a nasty but not a dangerous wound. The gun shots stopped all the noise in the place and Bud ran into the gambling alcove. I was taking a risk but I had to see that too, so I stuck my head around the door jamb. Harkness yelled at them like a mad man. There were six men in the game and the table was loaded with liquor and money. 'Hargrove, you—! I wouldn't talk for you before but I'll talk now,' cut out Harkness fiercely. 'If I did steal a few marvericks from you I shore didn't deserve the outrage you brought upon me. Ranchers like you will have all the cowboys in the valley up in arms. Bad as I was you were worse. When this thing comes out as it is bound to do you and Lee won't stand very well in this country. Now take this for your part of the dirty work!' And he shot Hargrove through the heart."

"So help me heaven, Thatcher, Bud called the turn!" exclaimed Lincoln. "It looks like war!"

"Yes, and that is nothing to what is going to happen," went on Mel huskily. "Hargrove is a heavy man and he fell over on the table, uptipping it. Glass and money and chips slid off with a crash. The other gamblers made a mad scramble to get away. But Nesbit, as he got up, pulled his gun. That was all he could do before Bud filled him full of lead. They say he hasn't got very much chance for his life. Then Harkness ran out, mounted his horse and rode out of town."

"Well, he got even, didn't he?" exclaimed Bradway, darkly. "I wouldn't be one to judge him, but you know what this will precipitate, don't you, Mel?"

"It means war unless the cattlemen lay off the cowboys."

"Come on, men. Let's go down and get supper. I'm starved," said Linc.

They went down the dark cross street, passed the infrequent yellow lights to the restaurant where they usually ate. They ordered huge beefsteaks.

"Vince," said the Nebraskan, speaking low, "we'll have to be a little careful about how we get some more hardware for you."

"I was thinkin' of thet," said Vince.

"Guns are easy to buy in this town," spoke up Thatcher. "All we need is the mazuma."

"Tomorrow is time enough," returned Lincoln.

"Boss, heven't you anything to tell us?" asked Vince.

"Nothing much. The ride over from the Springs passed without incident. At least, the passengers seemed to behave themselves," added Lincoln with a short laugh.

Conversation was interrupted then by the arrival of their supper. After they had eaten heartily Lincoln said: "I've been feeding pretty well lately, and I'm spoiled."

"What are we going to do now?" asked Thatcher.

"Split up and walk around town and keep our eyes and ears open. What was that cattleman meeting about, do you suppose?"

"I couldn't find out," replied Thatcher. "I've a hunch the cattlemen have not been having an easy time deciding what steps they are going to take. Some of them would be on the cowboys' side if they dared open their mouths. Lee is the hardest shelled one of the outfit. It's a good thing he wasn't here today or he would have got his, too. That leaves him boss of the rebel cattlemen. There are not enough of them to run the cowboys out of the country. This mess today will make them leery of mistreating any more cowboys. In my opinion a good many of the cattlemen will want to back out now if Lee will let them. It's a good bet though, that any more meetings they hold will be down in the brush."

"Well, I'll sleep on it," spoke Lincoln thoughtfully. "But I'm inclined to believe that the solution to our own problem is down there in the thick of it."

"After this row kicked up today a feller's life won't be worth two bits if they ketch him snoopin' around down there," said Vince.

"We won't make any false moves. Now you two hombres go around and hear what you can hear. I'll take a look for myself. In the morning I'll meet you and we'll have breakfast. Then I'll buy some more guns and shells. Here's some money, Vince: use your head now. This trail is getting pretty hot."

They went outside and separated. Bradway began to make his way toward the main part of the town. He walked slowly and gave attentive eye and ear to everyone he passed. When he gained the center of the town he backed up in a shadow of a wall and looked about him. The lights from the stores and saloons cast a dim yellow glare over the thoroughfare and upon the crowd surging up and down the street. From where Lincoln stood he could see at least a dozen small groups of men engaged in what appeared to be animated conversation.

There was a distinct feeling of excitement and expectation in the air along the street. Pulling his Stetson down over his face and turning up his collar, Lincoln set out to try to learn what they were talking about. A group of men lounged on the hotel steps just above where he stood. Lincoln made his way unobtrusively toward them and when close by paused and stooped to light a cigarette.

"Never been anything like it here," spoke up one man. "I, for one, think the ranchers have gone too far and gone the wrong way about it."

"But I tell you, John," replied another, "all the cattlemen are not in this by a long shot."

"You can't tell," spoke up the third. "Maybe they're all in it."

Lincoln strolled on as far as the corner where three more men stood close together talking. He halted again and lazily went through the motions of lighting another cigarette.

"Doc told me he dug a handful of lead out of Nesbit," said one. "And he said he'd be damned if he didn't think the man might live."

"I was told by a witness that Nesbit made a fool move to draw a gun. That hell-bent cowboy," replied the other, "was addressing himself to Hargrove. Everyone in town is buzzing over that cowboy's strange talk."

"Hold it," whispered the third man, "there's a cowboy now."

Bradway kept his back turned and sauntered on. He had been right in his conjecture about the subject of the whole town's conversation. If the cowboys were not actually in disfavor they certainly were being avoided. Across the street another group of five had congregated—miners and workhands—none with the cut of cattleman about him.

"But what was it all about?" asked one man.

"Didn't you hear?" spoke up another. "Cowboy run amuck. They say he rode through town without any coat and his back was all bloody where he'd been whipped."

"Never heard of the like of that. If the ranchers beat him up, what was it for?"

"There's a lot of things being whispered about town but not out loud."

The Nebraskan went on, his ears tingling. The killing of a couple of men by a wild cowboy was no unusual procedure any more than was any other shooting event. It was the unprecedented ride of the half-naked cowboy through the town where he was seen by a hundred people that had aroused the wide attention and had given rise to the excited comment.

The next group that Linc came upon stood in front of a lighted window. One of them was a cowboy, red-faced and grim.

"I can't tell you any more than that," he rasped out.

"But do you really believe these cattlemen beat that fellow Harkness with whips?"

"You can't prove it by me," replied the cowboy curtly and he disengaged himself from the group and walked away.

"That's the third cowpuncher I've heard tonight," said one of the men. "None of them know anything, but they're a sore-haided bunch."

"Wal, hyar's another," he said, espying Lincoln. "Say, cowboy, was you around when it come off?"

"No, but I heard about it," replied Lincoln coldly.

"What's caused the bad blood between the cowboys and the cowmen?"

"What do you think?" queried Lincoln, curtly.

"I'd be afeered to tell you, cowboy. So mosey along."

In the street which crossed the center block where Emery's gambling hall was situated, he listened to learn what he could from half a dozen other groups. There was an intense curiosity and eagerness manifest in the questions asked. But the replies did not confirm anything. The fact of a prominent rancher having been killed and another perhaps mortally wounded apparently did not elicit the sympathies of the town people. Life was cheap and there was a shooting scrape every day or so. The invariable speculation had to do with why that cowboy had been beaten—not with his summary revenge upon the ranchers. Dire punishment for rustling had come slowly into the Sweetwater Valley. The threat had gone abroad that the cattlemen were going to end up by hanging maverick thieves: but here was a cowboy, assertedly caught red-handed in the act of rustling, beaten with whips until the blood ran down his back. What for? What else was behind this affair seemed to be the persistent and unanswered question.

In front of Emery's place there was a crowd of two dozen or more. Lincoln backed up against the wall where the light could not strike him, and listened. There was a good deal of talk among individuals who seemed to have interests other than cattle running. One burly fellow with a white apron, evidently a barkeeper, was holding forth at a great rate.

"Bannister just croaked a few minutes ago," he said. "He was conscious till the last. He cussed Emery somethin' awful for sickin' him on that cowboy. Emery is in there cussin' just as bad 'cause the doctor hadn't had time to get to him. He's not shot up much but he bled like a stuck pig. He'll have to do his gamblin' standin' up for a while."

"Four men shot," added another speaker. "Looks as if Emery is the only one who'll pull through and he's the one that should have got it."

"That's sure right," said another. "Emery is about played out in this man's town."

"Did anybody hear what made this cowboy run hellbent for election?"

"Reckon it was just plain bad whisky."

"I've had a heap to do with cowboys in my day and this feller's work did not bear the earmarks of likker," said a bald-headed man. "Bert Adams was comin' out of the saloon when the cowboy run into him. His guns were smokin'. Bert said he never seen such eyes in any human bein'. He sure wasn't drunk. You can always tell when a feller's under the influence of drink. That cowboy was under the influence of somethin' pretty damn awful."

"I wonder what will come of it?"

They continued talking, and presently Lincoln left his post and entered the building. He peered into the saloon and discovered that business was going on as usual. Groups of drinkers were lined up at the bar; a gambling session was going full blast in the room where the shooting had taken place. In the large room the roulette and monte tables were also occupied. Linc strolled to the wide saloon door and entered. He noticed five cattlemen drinking at the far end, and simulating a man rather the worse for liquor, slid along the bar until he drew reasonably close to them. He called for a drink. One of the cattlemen looked as though he had seen the Nebraskan before but could not place him; all of them evidently were laboring under suppressed emotion. Lincoln heard one whisper hoarsely: "We've gone about it in a wrong way. Lee was right. These thieving, murdering cowboys need to be handled openly."

A second, whose back was turned toward Lincoln, said, "Another deal like Hargrove's and there'll be war!"

"Wal, why not? The cowboys on this here range are ruined forever. Let's drive them out of the country."

"Men," spoke up a tall rancher, "we're split on that from the beginning. I lean toward Lee's idea. There won't be many of us, but we'll mean business and if we carry out Lee's plan this cursed festering sore down in the Sweetwater will be cured forever."

"Impossible," whispered another cattleman with a violent gesture. "That way's unthinkable. I am from the South."

"So is Lee from the South and he says it's absolutely the only thing that can be done."

"We doubt it. I'll gamble he can't get a score of cattlemen in the whole valley to see it his way."

"If the cowboys got wise to that they'd clean us out. I tell you every cowboy in this valley is rank poison."

"Well, one way or another it's a bloody mess. Let's wait until Lee calls his secret meeting next week. This shooting of Hargrove and Nesbit has brought the pot to a boil."

The cattlemen filed out past Linc who was hunched over the bar. He left his liquor untouched and presently made his way outside. Once out of the *Leave It* he was careful to keep in the shadows and to give the cattlemen a wide berth.

Crossing the street he took the back way and then hurried up to the livery stable. There was no sign of anyone. The light in Headly's little office was out. He heard the thumping of horses in the stalls. The cowboy seated himself to think and wait. All that he had heard was interesting, but only the last conversation was of any significance. The cattlemen had worked out some drastic move against the cowboys or some other plan calculated to end the trouble in the valley. It seemed that they wished to stop the stealing cowboys but did not know how to do so unless they resorted to direct violence. Knowing cattlemen well, Lincoln concluded that was what would come to pass, yet there were other baffling angles to the situation. All the ranchers in the valley were suffering from these rustler depredations but why could not Lee get them together in one band? One rancher had said, "Impossible! Unthinkable!" and he had added, "I am from the South!" Lincoln pondered long over this. But Lee was from the South also. Yet evidently Lee had stronger feelings about the movement he had instigated than any of the others. Again Lincoln's thoughts turned to Kit Bandon. She had been the nucleus of this cowboy-cattlemen feud; it might be that Lee wanted to arrest her, disgrace her by somehow blaming this maverick stealing upon her. But how was he going to prove it? Hargrove's fiasco and tragic death proved the futility of trying to exact any proof from the cowboys.

That evening Bradway came to the decision that he

would ride to the Bandon ranch, hide in the brush and watch at night to see if he could unveil the mystery that he was sure centered about that part of the valley. Apparently the situation concerned a matter of honor with these cowboys involving principals that they would die before betraying. Yet he felt somewhat guilty at the idea of spying on Kit Bandon. If he failed to uncover any vital information then he must in some way induce Lucy to tell him all she knew, even if it necessitated his swearing to her that he would take no action, no matter whom her confession involved. He had five days before his momentous appointment with Lucy; during that time he should be able to find out a great deal. He debated the idea of bringing Vince and Thatcher with him, but concluded that it would be better if he went alone this time. If the cattlemen should happen to run across Thatcher and Vince down among the willows they would suspect something was afoot among the cowboys. He did not think he ran any great risk in attempting it by himself, even though any cowboy, local or strange, would be under suspicion if caught riding down by the river. His cogitations were interrupted by the return of Vince and Mel. They did not see him until he spoke.

"Howdy, gents. What's the good word?"

"It wasn't so good," replied Vince. "Lot of talk by different people who were in the dark about what come off. All of them speculatin' on a fight between the cowboys an' the cowmen."

"Didn't you hear a word of speculation as to *why* the cattlemen beat up Harkness?" queried Lincoln.

Vince said no, but his boss was not too sure that he was telling the truth.

"How about you, Mel? What did you run across?" asked Bradway.

"Lot of gab—no sense to it at all," replied Thatcher, shortly.

"A lot of help you hombres are," retorted the Nebraskan, and as they both fell silent he reproached himself for insinuating they were not being loyal. No doubt in the same situation he would have been quite as evasive and tight-lipped. Still his impatience was such that he vented one sarcastic protest. "You cowpokes must all have thought a hell of a lot of Kit Bandon."

Vince spat out his cigar and sat down without a word.

"Don't *you?*" queried Thatcher quietly.

Linc cracked his fist in his palm. "By God, I deserved that one! I did and I do. . . . I guess we've all got something we're keeping under our hats."

"All O.K., boss. We savvy what a tough place this is fer you. We ask you again to git Lucy and ride with us to hell out of this damn country."

"We can't do it. For one thing I'm locoed on this Wyoming country. And I don't expect to see Lucy till next Wednesday. You hombres are going with me. She wants to show me the most beautiful ranch site in the West. It's a valley up at the source of the Sweetwater."

"Boss, you don't mean to say yore goin' to settle down hyar permanently?" asked Vince.

"Yes, and by golly, you fellows are going to be here with me," retorted Bradway. Then he reported to them in detail the conversations he had heard along the street. They made no comment until he included the conversation among the cattlemen in the saloon. At that Vince leaped to his feet with an oath.

"By God, Mel! I had a hunch about thet," he said hoarsely. "I had figgered thet all along."

Thatcher's response was a quick nod of affirmation.

"I reckon I gotta go bore Lee an' do it quick," muttered Vince fiercely.

Linc jumped to his feet and confronted the two angry cowboys.

"What'n the hell has got into you fellows? What kind of talk is this? I don't care what you've got up your sleeve, but I won't let you make outlaws of yourselves like Harkness did. You promised to throw in with me—to stick with me. I like you both. I see big cattle prospects for us in this valley. No matter what your reason, you couldn't be justified in shooting Lee. Now I want a showdown from both of you."

Thatcher spoke up first. "It's not so easy to do, Bradway—but I give you my word of honor that I'll try to see this thing your way."

"Wal, me too, boss," added Vince, somewhat mollified. "I lost my temper. I see thet this man Lee is goin' to pull a low-down trick an' I saw red. Jest overlook it, pard. I will be all right."

"Much obliged, boys. You had me worried for a minute," said their boss, sitting down again. "Now let me figure a minute. I'll be gone tomorrow and maybe Saturday and Sunday. But I'll see you in the morning and we'll buy that hardware. You hombres stay in town and keep out of mischief. Kit Bandon will be in town Saturday and, between you and me, she's going to break with Emery. You might be lucky enough to hear what comes off. Well, I'm pretty tired and I think I'll hit the hay."

The cowboys bade him good night and, lighting cigarettes, they sat down on the steps, evidently for further talk. Lincoln returned to his lodgings by the back way and was soon in bed and asleep.

Next morning he found his friends waiting for him at the Chinese restaurant. They were cheerful and talkative but refrained from alluding to the topics of yesterday. After breakfast the three men went to the general store and while Lincoln stocked up on needed supplies for himself he gave the others money to buy what they needed. Vince had given his coat to Harkness and he was well satisfied to get a new and better one. They made careful selection of guns. Lincoln told them not to forget any of his instructions of the night before and then he took his leave. Returning to his lodgings, Lincoln considered his next action. He had planned to go down to the valley that night and scout around. To that end he had bought dried fruit, some sliced beef, biscuits, and a good-sized sack of oats. His plan had been to fill his saddlebags, pack his blanket and the sack of oats, to facilitate his staying there for a couple of days in reasonable comfort.

By midafternoon his plans were set. Headly was at the livery stable when he arrived, but his cowboy friends were not in evidence. For the first time in his life Linc Bradway was baffled by a feeling of indecision. Something seemed to be holding him back from this venture, yet something more powerful seemed to be urging him on. After packing and saddling his horse he was assailed by another spell of doubt as to the wisdom and the correctness of his plan. Finally in a fit of angry wonder at himself he mounted his horse and set out across the open lots toward the creek.

It was approaching dusk; sunset waved red banners across the grassy slopes of the pass and turned the snow peaks to gold. By the time Lincoln had topped the long slopes that led to the pass the road that zigzagged into the valley was in darkness. He rode more and more slowly as he approached the edge of the plateau. After a quick glance down into the black gulf below he halted, abruptly.

"Lordy, I must have the jitters or something," he muttered. "Am I losing my nerve? I'm not afraid of those cowpokes and cattlemen. What's wrong with me, then?"

Dismounting, he stood there staring down into the mysterious depths of that great valley. Here and there he perceived pinpoints of light, flickering vaguely, enhancing the silence and the loneliness, rather than relieving them. One of those faraway lights was the Bandon ranch. Bay nickered gently and rubbed his nose against the cowboy's sleeve. He seemed to feel the loneliness and the mysterious spell, too. And as Linc stood there his doubts and his indecision disappeared. Something stronger than a hunch had brought him on this errand. He no longer felt that he was pursuing a doubtful course. Some force, wiser, stronger, truer was impelling him forward. Quickly he mounted and spurred his horse down the road.

When he reached the level he put Bay into a long,

swinging lope. It was not long before he discerned the black strip of timber against the dark sage. Less than a mile from the bridge which led to the Bandon homestead he came to the willows and searched carefully for a spot to tether Bay, one which he could find quickly upon his return. Then he took off his spurs and set out toward the ranch house on foot.

He knew then that he was certain as to his motive. When he reached the open again he skirted the edge of the willows near the ranch. Every few paces he would stop to listen. Coyotes were barking in the distance. Now and then he heard an owl in the willows, and presently the rush of the swiftly running river. It would be moonlight shortly; and by that time he wanted to be safely hidden near the maverick corral. He listened for the sound of wheels or the clip-clop of horses' hoofs, but no close sound broke the cool stillness of the night. Warily he crossed the bridge and, keeping to the shadow of the trees along the river, made a wide detour that brought him up behind the corrals. He shortened his step, straining his keen faculties to hear sounds that would tell him of the activities he wanted to know. When he reached the long line of sheds, the moon topped the valley wall and shone upon the roof of the white homestead. Lincoln cautiously moved on in the shadows until he came to the shed that opened out upon the maverick corral. Waiting until his eyes could discern objects in the darkness, he entered the shed. He made sure of his location by peering out of the window. He recognized the bleached pole fence and high gate, and beyond him he searched for the neatly stacked pile of firewood. At first he could not find it, but presently he discerned it, dismayed to realize that it had shrunk to half its bulk. Part of that pile had been used; fires had been built; mavericks had been branded since he had been there!

It grew light enough in the shed for Linc to make his way about. He found a seat close to the wall in the deepest shadow where he could not be seen, yet could watch any activities that might be taking place. Then

with a sigh he settled back to wait. Lincoln tried hard
not to let his thoughts wander. He wanted all his mind
objectively riveted upon the issue at hand. He could
have gambled everything he owned that something
startling and significant would come to pass before
many hours were gone. He made no effort to explain
to himself this certainty. Ever since that moment when
he had stood looking down into the darkness of the
valley below he had known that it would happen.

The minutes passed by. Time dragged. Somewhere
near at hand horses thumped in their stalls; coyotes
ranged across the sage with their hue and cry; otherwise the dreaming silence of the night continued. Perhaps an hour passed by, though it seemed an age.
Suddenly the watcher's keen senses became conscious
of a sound. What was it that he had heard? Then again
it stopped his pulse and he recognized the sound of
horses' hoofs. Then they ceased. It might have been
an animal in the corral or over in the pasture but his
sharp perceptions told him otherwise. Presently he
heard another slight sound which he recognized to be
the faint metallic clink of a spur. Linc listened, scarcely
breathing. Then he heard the squeaking, complaining
noise of wood rubbing against wood—the opening of
the corral gate. Peering out, Lincoln espied a shadowy
figure letting a calf into the corral. Breathing heavily,
the man halted a moment in the open gate. Bradway
heard the snaky sound of a lasso being dragged along
the ground; then the calf jumped to find he was free
and gave an exhausted little bawl. The man cursed
under his breath, then went out, closed the gate behind him, and disappeared. Linc traced his faint footsteps by the tinkle of spurs. Then they, too, ceased.

The watcher relaxed from his tense strain. His sus-
picions were being confirmed; here was a cowboy with
a stolen maverick and he had gone to exact his tribute
from the Maverick Queen. What would he do when
the cowboy came back? Perhaps he could risk holding
the cowboy up, catch him red-handed, as he was, in his
guilt. But the Nebraskan reasoned that he would be

just like all other cowboys: he would fight before he would talk. Linc did not want to risk a possible killing in Kit Bandon's corral.

As the moments dragged by he broke out in a cold sweat. In spite of his self-control, he wanted that cowboy back quickly—at once—right now! To his unutterable relief, the cowboy was returning, but this time he was cursing under his breath and making no effort to walk noiselessly. He jerked open the door of the corral. Lincoln heard the slap of a coiled lasso against the fence. Then the rustler froze in his tracks.

"Well, I'll be——!" he muttered.

The hoofbeats of another horse sounded softly on the ground. Lincoln heard the tussling of a half-choked calf that was evidently being dragged toward the corral. Then came the crunch of boots pounding hard on the gravel.

"Hello, Bert," called the first cowboy in a harsh and not by any means restrained voice.

"That you, Monte?" came the sharp reply from the darkness.

"You know it's me."

"What the hell are you doin' heah? You said you'd be gone long before midnight."

"I said a lot of things that didn't happen," growled Monte.

The next moment the man called Bert loomed in the silver moonlight dragging a calf over the ground. He stopped at the gate and, loosening his lasso, kicked the calf into the corral.

"Wal, Monte, reckon we'll have to cut the cards for who goes in first."

"Nope. I've been . . . Bert, the fire's out."

"Watcha mean? You haven't started any fire heah."

"Cowboy, are you drunk or loco?"

"I ain't nothin' but plain sore. I ain't so damn sure thet I wasn't seen tonight with thet calf. All for nothin'. Kit turned me down. I'm bound to admit she was nice and kind, but she says she's through. She won't take no more mavericks."

"Wal, I'll be damned!" exclaimed Bert. "That's a sticker. What's she got agin you, Monte?"

"Nothin' at all. She was jest sweet as pie lettin' me down. She wasn't sore at me. She's jest changed her mind about takin' more dogies."

"Hang around a little bit," retorted the other. "I'll betcha two bits she won't turn me down."

"Say, Bert Rawlins, you shore do hate yorself. I'll bet you my saddle and gun and spurs she does turn you down."

"Yore on, Monte. Don't get tired waitin' for me neither." And with that he strode off into the silvery gloom.

After a moment or so Monte began to roll a cigarette. "It'd be funny if Bert was right," muttered the cowboy in tones perfectly audible to Bradway. "I always thought Kit didn't fancy me too much. And Bert is a handsome dog and has a way with women, damn him!"

He closed the gate and leaned against it smoking. The calves that had evidently been dragged around considerably were beginning to recover and be active. Lincoln lay there almost afraid to breathe. He was feeling considerable relief over developments. He had almost been ready to believe that Kit Bandon had lied to him. Now if the second rustler returned with her refusal to accept any more stolen livestock, then he would know that she had told him the truth. The moments seemed interminably long. He did not want to count on Kit Bandon's regeneration through love, if in another moment it might be dispelled. His suspense came to an end abruptly. Suddenly the other cowboy loomed up.

"Got a smoke, pard?" he asked huskily.

"Got the makin's heah. . . . Bert, you didn't stay very long."

"Ha! Why should I? She came at my first call. She told me the deal for mavericks was off. I argued with her. She was reasonable and patient with me, tried to make me think she regretted our deals in the past.

Thanked me for what I'd done for her but thet kinda talk didn't go with me. Then I got sore. 'Thet may be all right, Kit,' I said, 'but I've done my part. You give me what I want *now!*' By God, she said 'No!' and believe me, Monte, thet wassn' a slap in my face. I cussed her good and then she flashed a gun on me. I saw it shine in the moonlight. 'I owe you nothing, Bert Rawlins,' she said. 'You got what you wanted for every cow you stole until now. But no more. I'm through with this for good. Leave now or I'll shoot your leg off.' And I shore ran."

The cowboy ended out of breath and with a broken, uncertain little laugh that hinted of inexplicable defeat.

"Can you beat that? Bert, are you goin' to crawfish on your bet?"

"Hell, no. I'll throw in my hoss if you want it," returned Bert dejectedly.

"No, I don't want your hoss nor the bet either. But for Judas' sake, what's happened to Kit Bandon all of a sudden?"

"Monte, I didn't know that woman any more. She looked like an angel in the moonlight, and her voice was jest as sweet as an angel's until I made her mad. . . . But, lordy, what will become of me now? I jest lived on the hope of seein' this woman—of hearin' her voice—of—"

"Wal, pard, you ain't holdin' the sack all by yoreself. Come on, let's rustle out of heah."

"What'll we do with the calves?"

"Leave the gate open. They'll wander out into the sage."

Chapter XII

～◦～

The Nebraskan arose from his cramped position and stretched himself. Emerging from the shed, he stood in the shadow, resolving to himself to put what happened out of his mind for the time being. Now should he let well enough alone or venture further with what was the terrible suspicion that was growing in his mind, one that he was almost afraid to think about? But was it really true? While considering his next move he gazed about him. The full moon was bright. Shadows from the eastern side of the corral were beginning to lose their length. Passing along the shed, he came to the ranch fence which reached from the corrals to the house. Suddenly a wild idea flashed into his mind: Why not call Kit out himself? He dismissed the mad impulse, but it returned more insistently than ever. He remembered that one of his cowboy gifts, which had stood him in good stead many a time, was the power to disguise his voice. Why not impersonate a third cowboy and see for himself what Kit's reaction would be? If she refused him, then at least he would be certain that she had put her unscrupulous past behind her. He paused a moment to estimate the risk. If Lucy heard him, she would not know him from some other cowboy. If he could give a convincing performance, the chances were that he would not give himself away. But he realized that he must know the real truth for once and all.

He decided to stay inside the fence and go around the house on the inside. Like a skulking Indian he made sure that the coast was clear, then glided stealthily along the fence to the yard. The gate was open; he passed through and in a short moment reached the deep shadow of the ranch house. Here he paused again to listen. The night was very still; stars were sinking in the west; Lincoln heard the soft murmur of the river and the sad song of insects and the beating of his own heart. To a man as inured to excitement as he was, this incident should have seemed trivial. But it loomed tremendously in his imagination; he could not understand why. He glided along the house again, presently gaining an open window no higher than his head. He gave a start as his sharp eyes recognized Lucy's sombrero and scarf on the window sill. Acting upon sudden impulse without analyzing his reasons for it, he made up his mind to awaken Lucy, but by calling Kit's name. Putting his head over the sill, and not forgetting to disguise his voice, he called low: "Kit, wake up!"

He heard a sudden movement, then a low, angry voice. "Go away, cowboy. This is not Kit's room."

It was Lucy's voice. He whispered: "Lucy, it's Lincoln. Come here to the window."

He heard a gasp, then the flinging aside of bed covers and the soft pad of bare feet on the floor. In a moment more she appeared at the window. Dark as it was on that side he could distinguish her pale face, her eyes looking big and dark, her hair falling over the white of her gown.

"Am I dreaming or plain crazy?" she whispered. "Is it you, Lincoln?"

"Yes. Don't be frightened, Lucy. It's all right."

"Oh, but what in the world are you doing here?"

"Wait. Where's Kit's room?" he asked.

"It's on the other side of the house. The living room is between hers and mine."

"Good!" he exclaimed. "I wouldn't want her to catch me." He took hold of Lucy's trembling hands. "I tell you, don't be scared. It's all right. I came out here to do a little reconnoitering. I hid inside the shed behind that corral. I stayed there until I had found out what I wanted to know—that Kit Bandon wasn't going to take any more stolen mavericks. I decided to call Kit myself and pretend to be another cowboy bringing a stolen maverick. I want to be certain that she has had a change of heart. I want to have that proof in case I ever have to defend her against the cattlemen."

"Oh, Lincoln, I hope she has changed," murmured Lucy, her voice suddenly distraught and strained. "It's almost too good to be true. She has been sweet and lovely to me ever since we got back from the Springs. She talks of leaving the Sweetwater Valley soon. But I'm still afraid. . . ."

"Then you *know* what she really does to get those mavericks."

"I've never been sure, but . . ." Lucy's voice faltered. "She always told me she bought them and I never wanted to believe anything else. But now . . . Oh, Lincoln, I hope she's given this awful business up before it's too late. . . ."

"Perhaps I can find out," whispered Linc. "At least we will know if she really has given it up. I'll go around the other side and call her the same as those other cowboys did. I'll disguise my voice and pretend to be another cowpoke who's a stranger to her. I'll say I stole a calf and brought it to her. I'll argue and insist and demand. Then we'll see."

"Oh, Lincoln, be careful. If she learns who you are and thinks you were spying on her she'll shoot to kill."

"I will. But I'm in no hurry. It's sweet to be here with you like this," he whispered. "I'd almost forgotten that you are my sweetheart, say nothing about being my wife." And pulling her face down, he kissed her.

She was breathless but far from unresponsive in her

return of his caress. Suddenly Lincoln was seized with a mounting madness.

"Lucy," he whispered.

"Yes?" she answered.

"You're my lawful wife, you know. I have a right to come in there. Would you let me?"

"Mercy!" she gasped. "If she caught us she would kill us both."

"You darling! I was only pretending. . . . But some day, I warn you, I won't be satisfied to whisper to my wife through windows. Don't worry about me. And don't forget our date next Wednesday up on the Sweetwater."

Tearing himself away from her clinging arms, he slipped silently away among the shadows. Now he knew why Lucy had been so reluctant to allow him to awaken Kit. Probably if he had stayed longer, she might have said something or persuaded him not to go. At the end of the house under the shade of the trees he halted to compose himself. He stole soundlessly around the end of the house, halting at the corner. There was only one window on that side, half obscured by the shade of a tree a couple of steps outside the wall. It was open. Lincoln went to the edge of the window and called in: "Kit Bandon!"

He heard her stir in her bed. "What? Who?" she asked. "Is that you back again, Bert Rawlins? You've got nerve to come back here, cowboy."

"No, it ain't Rawlins," drawled Lincoln. "Come over to the winder." He stepped back into the shadow of the tree, hiding his face with his sombrero. She was slow to reach the window and lean out. He heard the thump of a gun on the window sill. He realized that a man took perilous chances in trifling with this woman.

"Who are you?" she called, peering hard at him. In the partial moonlight he could see her distinctly—a startling and beautiful apparition in night clothes.

"I'm a stranger," replied the Nebraskan, slowly nerving himself to the ordeal. "Cowpoke. Name is

Orville Stone, lately come to Sweetwater. Ridin' fer Perkins down the river."

"Yes, and what do you want?" demanded Kit. "What do you mean by coming to my home in the middle of the night and awakening me from my sleep."

"I was tipped off by a cowboy friend."

"Did you meet any other cowboys round here?"

"Yes, two of them, but they didn't see me."

"Well, hurry and state your business."

"I've brought you a maverick. . . ."

"I don't want it," replied Kit sharply.

"Why not? I was given to understand."

"I've changed my mind. I'm not taking any more mavericks from cowboys."

"But, lady, I heard diff'runt. I've took a damn big risk an' gone to a lot of trouble packin' this calf in my arms over twenty miles. I wisht you could make an exception in this case," he pleaded.

"Oh, I don't blame you. It's a rotten deal. Did I ever see you?"

"No, but I've seen you three times an I'm afraid them three times has jest about throwed me."

"What do you mean?"

"I mean—well, this here is the fourh time I've seen you an' I'd like fer you to let me come acourtin' now an' again. I've fallen purty hard fer a cowpoke, ma'am."

"That is worse and more of it," replied Kit with a note of weary regret. "I'm sorry, but whoever told you was honest enough. He thought I would take your livestock, cowboy. Won't you let me off this deal?"

"I don't see why I should. It's a deal jest as much as if you asked me to come hyah."

"Oh, I realize that's true. But you see, I'm not in this business any more. I won't make any more rustlers out of cowboys. I won't take another maverick from any cowboy."

"But *why*, Miss Bandon?" the man in the shadows whispered eagerly. "I acted in good faith. The way I see it, you *owe* it to me to take this maverick off my hands."

"Why?" she flashed angrily, and her white and black beauty blazed in the moonlight. "You don't know it, but I've prayed God to forgive me for enticing you boys to steal mavericks. Something has happened to me which has changed my heart and soul and mind. . . . Now, cowboy, that's sayin' a lot to a stranger. You talk like a gentleman. Be one and spare me—"

"Woman," interrupted the cowboy in a nasty tone. "Will you keep your word?"

"No, damn you! Not even if I have to kill another man."

Bradway stood in silence for a moment thrilled with the knowledge that the Maverick Queen had renounced her throne. What he had hoped and prayed for was true. Then speaking once more in his natural voice, he said: "Kit, be careful what you do with that gun."

"My God!—*who* are you?"

"It's Linc Bradway, Kit. Forgive me for playing this trick on you, lady."

She dropped the gun outside the window and fell forward against the sill to bow her head. Her long black hair fell around her shouders.

"Oh, Lincoln, you've—found me—out," she whispered heartbrokenly.

Lincoln stepped forward and recovered the gun. He stood up close to her.

"But not too late, Kit," he whispered.

She raised herself up and rested her chin on her bare arms. In the moonlight she seemed transcendentally beautiful. Her face was as white as her nightgown. Her great dark eyes were wide and tragic.

"Lincoln, you spied upon me?"

"Yes."

"What did you do it for?"

"I had several reasons," he replied. "The main one was to catch you in the act—"

"What—act?" she interposed.

"I wanted to catch you in the act and then *try* to persuade you to save yourself and Lucy by stopping it. But, as it happened, I didn't have to. I hid out there in the shed back of the corral. Monte came with a stolen calf, then Bert Rawlins came with another, and I lay there listening and presently when they got together I heard them talking about the amazing change in you. They couldn't undersand it. But I do. After they left I conceived the idea of seeing for myself just how you had changed. I came and I fooled you, Kit. I'm sorry, but I had to know for myself."

"I didn't want you ever—ever to find out," she cried passionately. "I wanted to get away with you before that happened. Why, oh why did you have to come here?"

Somberly he replied, "Kit I had to find out the truth, but I don't feel the way toward you that you suspect."

"My God, what *do* you feel for me—now?" she demanded brokenly.

"I feel . . . a great respect for anyone who could do what you have done, but then give it up."

"But how could you? I've done *all* the things you suspected me of, Linc."

"Because I feel you *have* changed, Kit. Somehow I can tell. I did fall for your charms. The only reason I didn't go further was that I did not love you—that I know is hard for you to believe. But now, Kit, I respect you for wanting to make things right."

"Oh, Lincoln, respect is something—but even a little love would be—" and she reached for him with her bare white arms.

Lincoln did not resist her embrace.

"Darling, if you could love me, even a little—would you leave this country with me?"

"I can't, Kit. I told you. I'm a married man."

"But you have saved my soul," she protested.

"Kit, listen," he began earnestly, releasing the white clinging arms. "That's all very well about saving your soul. I hope to God it is true, but I want to save you and your niece from disgrace—and give you hope of happiness—certainly your freedom and perhaps your life."

She was startled. She drew away from him wildly. "My—my life!" she exclaimed. "What do you mean?"

"Maybe that is an exaggeration," went on Lincoln hurriedly, "but I'm worried. A terrible flare-up between the cowboys and the cattlemen has broken out. It's on your account, Kit. The cattlemen know that your rustlers have gotten out of hand. They can't do anything to the cowboys. The ranchers have found that out. The beating of Harkness was a crazy blunder. The murder of Hargrove and desperate wounding of Nesbit have proved that. The cattlemen do not present a united front. They've split. But there's one faction that is for revenge. I don't know who they are, but Lee is at the head of it. Lee is one of your conquests, and you should know that he's dangerous when he has been crossed. You mocked him, flouted him, made his name a laughingstock in the valley. I know cattlemen of his type. Only his infatuation for you kept him from sending you to jail—or worse. Lee has enough on you to hang you. These are hard times on the range."

"But, Lincoln, it can't go on. I'm through. I will never take any mavericks again. This turndown of Monte and Rawlins will spread over the valley like wildfire."

"I hope to God it isn't true—but it may be too late," he whispered.

"Oh, no, Lincoln, I'm sure you're wrong," she said with passion. "I can handle the situation. I'll make amends in whatever way I can. I'll break with Emery. I'll find some way of placating these bitter enemies of mine."

"All that takes time, Kit," said Bradway earnestly.

"I will be in town tomorrow or Sunday," said Kit. "Oh, I can't take seriously what you say, but I'll try to think of everything. Go now, Lincoln, so that you'll get back to town before daylight. I wouldn't want it known that *you* had been here."

She kissed him good-by and pushed him away from the window. He laid her gun on the sill. He could not refrain from taking a last look at her in the moonlight: white shoulders, white arms, white face standing out against the ebony of her loosened hair. Then he wheeled and ran out under the trees to the road.

Now that he had left Lucy and Kit behind him, all that had been lonesome in the valley seemed accentuated—only the faraway howling of wolves broke the unearthly silence. As the cowboy strode through the sage he soon lost the sucking, gurgling sound of the river. He reached the edge of the willows where he had tethered his horse.

He found Bay asleep with the nosebag still hanging over one ear. The sight of his faithful horse gave Linc a lift from the painful depression that overcame him. He mounted and was soon out upon the valley bottom. The sage was thick and tall and the ground was full of burrows, which made traveling painfully slow. He had purposely turned off the trail because it was too close to the ranch house. As he rode he tried to recapture the glow that his short whispered conversation with Lucy had stirred in him—and the terribly mixed emotions that raged in him about Kit Bandon. That she had satisfied him, that the change in her way of life was to be permanent was consoling, but that she refused to leave the country without him, however, presented an almost insurmountable problem. When the time came to go away it would be Lucy, not Kit, who would ride with him. That time had not yet come. There still were some things he had to know. In that respect the night's adventure had not been completely successful. Jim Weston's murder had taken place on this very ranch. Kit had not admitted it, but meanwhile he was reluctant to leave the beautiful, fragrant, colorful, verdant Wyoming country. If the land at the headwaters of the Sweetwater was all Lucy claimed it to be, he wanted above all to make a home for her there. It was perhaps too close to South Pass and the valley where Jim had met his death, but it was far enough away so that they never would need to visit it again.

When Bradway reached the road, he urged Bay to a swift, ground-gaining lope. At the base of the escarpment he slowed Bay to a walk, and the horse easily climbed the zigzag road to the summit. Lincoln did not look back. The moon had gone; its light had dimmed to the darkness that precedes the gray of dawn. Once more the cowboy urged his mount to a lope and soon covered the distance to the mining camp. He approached by the roundabout way, reaching the livery stable before daylight and without being seen. Putting Bay away in his stall, he hurried to his lodgings and went to bed.

The next day Linc did not venture out until evening. He did not meet his friends at the restaurant nor on the street afterward. He remained clear of the stores and saloons. He avoided the vicinity of Emery's hall because he did not want to risk meeting Kit there. He walked the streets until he was tired; then again he returned to his lodgings.

It was late Sunday morning before he left his room again. It was the usual noisy, busy day, little different from any other day in this mining town. At noon he visited the Chinese restaurant, hoping to meet Vince or Thatcher there. The waiter informed him that they had been in early that morning. The Nebraskan lingered nearby for some time, hoping his partners would return, but by three in the afternoon there was still no sign of them. Then he lost no time getting back to the livery stable. Headly was in his office and told him, "They hain't been back since early mornin'. Did you notice thet the town is full of cowboys?"

"No, I didn't," replied Lincoln. "What does that mean?"

"I'll be switched if I can call the turn on that," said Headly, shaking his shaggy head. "There are too blamed many of them for a Sunday off. No doubt thet mess-up the other day in Emery's place has brought things to a head."

"Are there any more cattlemen in town than usual?" asked Lincoln, curiously.

"Wal, I should smile. Whar are yore eyes, cowboy? I've got five buckboards and two spring wagons in the backyard now, and hain't got room for no more teams."

"Did you see Kit Bandon's buckboard?"

"Nope. I reckon she hain't come along yet."

Lincoln sat down to wait. He wanted very much to go back downtown, yet he wanted to avoid tangling with Emery's crowd for the present. He would wait until the boys arrived. They strayed in at last, their faces tight-lipped and set. Bradway inquired rather impatiently where the hell they had been.

"Boss," explained Vince, "we expected to run into you downtown any minute."

Thatcher spoke up: "We didn't think you would be holed up here."

"Well, all right. Better late than never," grumbled Lincoln. "I suppose you fellows are hungry as usual?"

"Starved to death," vowed Vince. "We were too busy to think of dinner."

"Busy at what?" queried Linc.

"Wal, we was tryin' to find out what the hell was goin' on down there."

"All these cowboys and cattlemen got you kind of lathered up, eh?"

"It's pretty interestin', boss. Mel has his idee an' I hev mine. We'll let you do yore own figgerin'."

"All right. Let's go eat," replied Bradway shortly.

They went downtown. Linc had not seen so many pedestrians, so many saddle horses, or so many vehicles since he had come to South Pass. They found the restaurant with more customers than usual, but fortunately their table was vacant. Ordering dinner, they ate in silence. At length Thatcher, bending over to light a cigarette, puffed a huge cloud of smoke and spoke from behind it.

"Bradway, I've got one thing to report—"

"Don't call me Bradway," interrupted Lincoln irritably.

"All right, boss. Vince and I have been snooping around for two whole days and nights. I had the luck to find myself sitting pretty with a dance-hall girl, one of several just come to South Pass, and I was upstairs in the little parlor with her when Emery came limping along the hall with Kit Bandon. That was today about one o'clock. I could see from behind the curtain. Kit was white and steaming like she was about to erupt. . . . 'I tell you, Kit,' said Emery, 'I won't oppose your splitting with me here but I can't pay you for your share.'

" 'And why not?' snapped Kit.

" 'I haven't got the money.'

" 'You're a liar,' said Kit.

" 'To tell you the truth, Kit, I'm in bad here in South Pass. I only found it out since these cattlemen have been in town. I've been forced to pay debts. Some of the men I owed money to living right here in town talked damn queer. One of them said he might show up the irregularities of my gambling hall. Another said I had to be careful or I'd be run out of town. That's honest, Kit. These men have all been heavy losers at my game and they're sore.'

" 'I'm sore too,' Kit replied. 'Dig up part of the money anyhow to pay me for what I invested in your gambling deal!'

"Emery looked much surprised and worried. "You putting on the pressure too, Kit Bandon!' he exclaimed. 'I'll do my best to oblige you. But does that mean you want to split on our cattle business down in the valley also?'

" 'That's exactly what I mean,' Kit said. 'But never mind that until later.'

" 'Well, you'll find me tough on that proposition,' he retorted angrily. 'You've been treating me mean enough lately and now you make up your mind in five minutes to quit me cold. You act as though I was contaminated. Well, I won't do it! You're bright enough,

Kit Bandon, to know that I have a pretty good hold on you!'

" 'Yes, I'm bright enough to know that you've always been a double-crosser. Furthermore, you have no hold on me!'

" 'Listen, Kit. This place is getting hot for you as well as for me. Suppose I talked?'

" 'I've shot men for less than that. There's a saying that dead men tell no tales, Emery. Think it over. We split right here.' "

Thatcher paused for breath. Then he said:

"Boys, you should have seen her look at him. If eyes could kill he would have been done for right then. Then she left him and ran downstairs. Emery limped back to his room and I wouldn't be surprised if sooner or later they find Emery very neatly bored through the middle."

"Well!" exclaimed the Nebraskan under his breath. "That *is* news. Particularly about Emery being forced to pay his bad debts. There sure is something doing in this mining camp."

"Aha!" ejaculated Vince. "You only said the half."

"Boys, I'm glad to know about this Emery business," said Linc earnestly, leaning toward them, "for I know that Kit Bandon is going straight. Never mind how I know she's turning her back on the old life and her old crowd. This break with Emery is the fourth proof I have of it. . . . She will never take any more stolen mavericks from rustling cowboys."

Vince stared up at him with questioning eyes. His cigarette dropped from his lips, but Thatcher, hardly less impressed than his comrade, replied in a breathless whisper:

"By God! You know, I'm not surprised. Kit could do that! Boss, I'll gamble that you had something to do with the Bandon woman's change of heart!"

Vince shook his head. "Pard, I'll believe thet when I see it. I'm not sayin' anythin' about Kit Bandon's spots but if she's changed them it's a miracle, 'cause some of them go purty deep."

"Boys, I'll have more to tell you by and by," went on Lincoln. "What I want to do now is find out what all these cowboys are doing in town."

"Boss, they're just talking among themselves," said Thatcher.

"About what?" asked Lincoln.

"I don't know. But I can guess."

Vince leaned over and whispered: "Pard, the cowboys are talkin' about what the cattlemen are up to."

"Will these cowboys talk to me?" the Nebraskan asked.

"Not likely, but you can try," replied Mel.

"I'll tell you, boss, if they don't ride out tonight it means they've quit their jobs and that's jest one hell of a thing. Cowpokes on the loose are jest so much dynamite."

"We'll have to have a try," said Linc. "I suggest we split up. We'll approach every cowboy that we can get to. If we can fill one full of liquor he may talk."

"Sure, boss," replied Thatcher, "but the queer deal is that these cowboys are not drinking a single damn drop."

Vince suggested, "Pard, we might find one cowboy who's goin' to slope who'd give the deal away if we paid him enough. Thet is if he really knows what they're goin' to do. I don't believe anyone knows."

"Vince, you ought to know if anybody knows," said Lincoln, looking at him sternly.

"Shore, I ought. But I'm afeerd to believe what I think."

"Afraid!" exclaimed Lincoln, unbelievingly. "What are you afraid of?"

"Figger thet one out for yoreself," declared Vince truculently. "Come on, let's mosey along. We're wastin' time."

The two cowboys started in one direction, while Linc set out by himself. He spent three or four hours that night approaching one cowboy group after another. He found them in the main civil, good-natured, and reserved. They recognized him to be one of their own kind, but when he tried to get them to talk they showed an impassive and stony aloofness in regard to their presence in town. The Nebraskan stayed out of Emery's gambling hall. He was more than satisfied with Thatcher's report of Kit Bandon's ultimatum to Emery. About midnight he went back to his lodgings, baffled and not a little worried. He was annoyed with himself to find that he was becoming more interested in what would happen to Kit in the event of a range war than in the mystery which he had come West to solve. Then, too, there was the attitude of his two partners. They knew what was going on, but told him only as much as they wanted him to know. He was convinced that however they were bound by their own peculiar cowboy creed, if there were any real danger for Kit they would acquaint him with it. It was a long time before he fell asleep.

Next morning he found his friends at the restaurant waiting for him

"Anything to tell me, boys?" he inquired.

"Yep. We got a good deal as far as it goes," replied Vince.

"Leastways, Mel has, 'cause I wasn't with him last night."

"Boss, this is what come off: Last night the cattlemen, at least some of them, held a secret meeting in the bank in the dark. They must have gone up there by ones and twos and around about, and after they got off the street they wore masks."

"Ahuh. How the devil did you find all this out?" queried Bradway.

"No more about that for the present," replied Thatcher with an odd curtness. "It's my hunch, boys, that the cattlemen will be slipping out of town today and that sure will be interestin' to the cowboys."

Later in the morning Linc ran into two clean-cut young riders whose looks he liked.

"Howdy, boys. Will you have a drink this morning?" he asked cheerily.

"Well, we don't care if we do," one of them replied, surprisingly.

The Nebraskan took them into a saloon and bought a round of drinks.

"You boys want to talk turkey to me this morning about business?"

"About what business?" asked one, glancing quickly at his partner.

"I'm going to start raising cattle," replied Lincoln, "and I want some good riders. I've located a range about twenty miles out of town, not down in the valley, and I want to put two or three men to work at once. My name is Bradway. Just getting started in this part of Wyoming."

"Sounds good to me 'cause I quit my job on the Sweetwater," replied the one with the tawny hair. "Have you got the money, and what will the job pay?"

"Yes, I'm pretty well heeled and I'll pay you ten dollars a month more than you've been getting."

"I'm on, mister. Name is Slim Morris. Been ridin' for Higgins in the valley. Gimme a couple of days or so to ride down to the ranch and get my other horse and what stuff I've got."

"Fine, Slim," responded Lincoln heartily. "Be at Headly's livery stable some time Thursday."

"Tom, don't you want to ring in on this, too?" asked Morris turning to his companion.

"I can't, gosh dern it," replied the other. "I've overdrawn a couple of months' wages and I cain't quit Sam Blake till I've worked it out."

"Will it square you with Blake if you pay him?" asked Lincoln.

"Well, I reckon it would," rejoined Tom with a smile. "None of Blake's riders have quit on account of this mess-up in this end of the valley."

When he found out from the cowboy what he owed the rancher, Linc handed the amount over to Tom and told him to come back Thursday with Morris.

"Boys, I feel I've made myself a good deal in getting

you to ride for me. And I think you will find that you've done likewise. Now tell me one thing. Haven't most of the cowboys in this locality quit their jobs?"

"That's correct, Bradway. *All* the cowboys north of the forks on the river have quit their jobs. You can hire as many riders as you want."

"Thanks. That is good news. I'll look around and see if I can find any I like as well as I do you boys."

Their new employer bade them good-by and went on up the street. He made the rounds of the stores and the saloons and approached perhaps half a dozen more cowboys. He really did not want to hire any more hands, but he used the pretext as an excuse for making himself acquainted. All this took time and kept him indoors a good deal of the time. In the afternoon, however, when he headed up the street toward the livery stable he noted for the first time that there were no buckboards in sight or any other kind of vehicle. At Headly's livery stable all the conveyances that the ranchers had left there were gone. Headly said curiously: "They sure sloped out of town mighty sudden."

As soon as Vince and Thatcher arrived they talked at length about this sudden departure.

"Suits me just as well," said Mel enigmatically.

Linc spoke up quickly. "You mean they've split—couldn't agree—don't know what they're going to do—perhaps weakening on whatever they had in mind?"

"Reckon thet applies to most of 'em," said Vince, but Thatcher made no comment.

Linc told them about the two cowboys whom he had hired to ride for him and named them.

"I know Slim Morris," said Mel. "Comes from way down the river. Salt of the earth. Blake's riders are still farther south. They're really out of this mess. I don't know the one you called Tom."

Vince said, "Wal, let's go hunt them up and get acquainted."

Linc felt the constraint in them and was agreeable about letting them go off by themselves. He had supper alone that night and went to his room early. Having ascertained that Kit Bandon had gone home, he could have gone into Emery's place or anywhere else feeling perfectly free, but he decided against it. He was about tired of this endless spying that seemed to get him nowhere. The only bright spot in the picture was his meeting with Lucy day after tomorrow. Reverting to thoughts of finding her in her mountain paradise, he found the hours passing swiftly with the pleasure of dreams and hopes and plans.

The following day he did not find his comrades until late.

"Boss, hev you noticed anythin' in particular?" asked Vince.

"Not this morning. I've been too busy thinking about tomorrow," replied the Nebraskan, smiling.

"Wal, we're the only cowboys left in this whole damn town."

"You don't say!" exclaimed Lincoln. "I'll be dog-goned. You Wyoming critters are the queerest I ever knew. Well, you boys are leaving town, too. I'm going to take you with me over to the head of the Sweet-water. You needn't pack anything except a little grub, for we will be coming back tomorrow night. I want to leave about sunrise. We'll head up Rock Creek and go through the miners' diggings to the slope just before the canyon boxes and climb out there. What I particularly aim at is laying out a grade where we can build a road."

"Wal, you can see from hyar," said Vince. "I could drive a wagon up thet slope without any road."

"It does look pretty good going," replied Linc squinting up the sage slope. "But it may be pretty rough over the hill."

"What do you aim to do?" asked Thatcher.

"Find the easiest way we can to get in and out of that valley over there."

"How far is it?"

"It's eighteen miles or so from the Bandon ranch up the river, but I calculate it's farther than that from here. Anyway we want to cut across the pass and work along the western rim just far enough so we see that we can cut a road down to the valley."

"That sure will be fine," declared Thatcher. "New job all by ourselves, a lot of pioneer work, plenty of game to hunt, log cabins to run up—I sure like the prospect."

"I'll be glad to quit this loafing spell, myself," replied Bradway.

Chapter XIII

〜ᕦ〜

At sunrise the next morning Lincoln and his two comrades climbed the slope from South Pass to the summit of the hill. The day promised to be fair. The early morning air was cold and fresh, and there was just a touch of white frost on the sage. Once on top the eagle-eyed Vince pointed to a buckboard pulled by four horses winding up the road out of town toward the west.

"Wonder who that is?" queried Lincoln. "Hitting it up pretty fast on the grade."

"I've seen thet buckboard before," said Vince thoughtfully.

They rode on, finding the going fairly easy on top, with a slight upgrade, and straggling bits of brush and pine scattered over the terrain. Clumps of aspen and oak could be seen in the distance. The frosty sage took on a tinge of red, and the black stands of timber and the walls of gray rock and the long white slopes leading to the distant peaks all played a varicolored tribute to the sunrise. Lincoln found to his satisfaction that to make a road across the pass would require comparatively little labor. They kept to a course quartering away from a direct route across the pass. The thickets and the little groves of aspens and oaks increased with the altitude. A ride of perhaps five or six miles brought them to the narrow valley of the Sweetwater, which here was merely a wide ravine with shallow slopes choked with green timber so thick that the noisy river could be heard but not seen.

"Well, it's easy enough to grade a road down here," said Bradway. "I'll tell you what, boys, I'll go down and take the trail so as to save time. You work along this slope till you come to the valley, then look over the lay of the land and pick out the most suitable place westward to cut the road up to the level."

"Pretty far, I'd say," replied Vince. "I cain't see the valley from hyah."

"Well, you can figure on me riding up out of the valley some time this afternoon. You can keep your eyes peeled for me and I'll do the same for you."

The Nebraskan bade them good-by and urged his horse down the slope and into the brush. It was easy going underfoot but he had to twist and lay low in the saddle to keep from being brushed off by the low branches. As he descended, the thickets grew more and more open; presently he reached the level that he had calculated was several hundred yards across to the other slope. Groves of willows lined the bank of the sparkling and swift-flowing river. He rode out into a well-defined trail, in which he espied fresh pony tracks made no longer ago than that morning. They gave Lincoln an exuberant feeling of happiness. Assuredly these tracks had been made by Lucy's pony swinging along at a good fast lope. He put Bay to a like gait and soon was flying along the cool, shady trail. The ravine grew more picturesque as he rode along, the trail twisting along a serpentine course, fording the river often over gravelly bars. There appeared to be a scarcity of birds, but deer, rabbits, and other small game were constantly springing across the clearings into the brush as he went by. On the rim of the slopes he saw antelope silhouetted against the blue sky and occasionally coyotes standing boldly watching him.

Presently the trail rounded a higher eminence on the valley slope, from which Linc was suddenly confronted by a breathtaking view of the length and breadth of Lucy's wonderful valley. He stopped his horse, gazing spellbound out over the most beautiful valley he had ever seen in his life. He was eager to find Lucy, yet the scenic wonder of the vista before him compelled him to linger. He looked this way and that up the length of the long valley and across its wide breadth, along the precipitous walls. His quick eye saw slopes along which a road could be dug up to the top. The valley slopes on each side were gray and purple with sage with a fringe of golden willow at the base. Here and there were outcroppings of craggy rocks and vine-covered cliffs crowned with patches of green pine. A belt of bright green aspens with their white stems alternating with a rough border of oaks ran along the top of the farther wall. The sheltered valley under the looming mountains was of a deceptive size and dimension which Linc tried to estimate. He felt sure that it was at least four or five miles wide in the center and perhaps twice that long. Its floor was a level area of gold and green, along which meandered a stream shining like a ribbon bordered by willows and low bushes. As far as he could see the valley's steep western slope consisted of gray sage and glistening rock forming cape after cape and scallop after scallop until they emerged in one magnificent escarpment which seemed to run up under the brow of the mountain. Now and again he caught glimpses of waterfalls, like white plumes against the blue and gray of the distant palisade.

With one last lingering look Linc set off up the trail again. As he rode along this lonely and beautiful valley he kept a sharp lookout for Lucy. It was several miles, however, before he caught a glimpse of her. The trail had borne somewhat to the left along a long bench leading down from the great escarpment. There was something familiar about this plateau above the river, and then it came to him that this was the homesite Lucy had described to him so enthusiastically. As he gazed upward at the bench his quick eye sighted something red glinting in the sunlight. In another instant he made out Lucy standing out on a rocky eminence waving her red scarf at him. As he spurred Bay along the trail at a reckless pace he seized his Stetson and waved it with boyish exhilaration. He found a fairly steep trail with two long zigzags leading up to the level bench. Reaching the level ground he halted Bay there, and as he leaped off he saw Lucy running toward him, her bare fair head shining in the sunlight, the red scarf streaming out behind. She was wearing her riding garb and looked like a slender graceful boy bounding forward to meet him. Her face was rosy, laughing, inexpressively sweet.

"Oh, Lincoln," she screamed. "Here you are! In my valley! I saw you—all the way—from the entrance."

He took her in his arms and held her, murmuring over and over again, "My wife, my darling Lucy."

"Tell me quick," she pleaded paintingly. "What do you think—of my—of our valley?"

"I haven't had a good look yet," replied Lincoln, "but from what little I saw it tops any place I ever saw."

"Hurry then and take a hundred looks," she commanded laughingly. "Stop looking at *me*. I want to know—if this is to be our home."

"Lucy, I don't have to see any more to decide that. Thatcher and Vince are on the other side somewhere, farther down from here, looking for a place to build a road."

"Oh, we've got all that settled!" she exclaimed.

"We? Who's we?"

"My old trapper friend, Ben Thorpe. His cabin is up here a ways. We'll ride up to see him presently. He has trapped twenty-two hundred beaver skins this winter."

"That's something!" exclaimed her husband, though he hadn't heard a word, so entranced was he looking at Lucy's happy countenance. "I saw beaver dams down below."

"The valley and the streams that run into it are thick with them."

"Perhaps we'd do better trapping than ranching."

"I don't approve of trapping," said Lucy. "Come, let me show you where we can build our homestead. If you ever saw a more beautiful location I won't believe you. See, this bench is level and has about ten or a dozen acres. It's steep in front and on the side you enter, but the other slope has a gradual slant where we can grade a wagon road. It will run straight across the valley from here and up through the only outlet except the gateway through which you entered. Ben says if we fence that gateway, not a head of stock can ever climb out. What do you think of that?"

"I think it grows more wonderful all the time," responded Lincoln.

"Now come this way," she said, eagerly dragging him by one arm. "Did anyone ever have such a backyard as we are going to have? Look! There's where our brook comes tumbling out over the rocks and runs around in a circle. Back here it forms a beautiful pool that's actually so cram-jammed with big trout that there's barely room for us to swim in it, even if the water were warm enough, and then it runs across the bench to cascade off the rocks just where you see the pines out there." She finished out of breath, and Linc seized his advantage and kissed her again.

She led him several hundred yards back over the green sage and flower-dotted plateau. The rocky wall extended up rather high from that point in successive ledges and low vine-covered cliffs, over which an amber stream came tumbling down, skirted by tiny aspen thickets and clumps of oak, to enter the circle and pool Lucy had described. Then it emerged, plunged over a little waterfall, and took its merry and melodious way as a narrow stream that murmured gently out across the bench.

"Look!" exclaimed Lucy, clapping her hands and pointing like a little girl. "Look at that big trout! The pool is full of them. Ben says there are even more in this stream up above and down below the falls than in any other branch of the Sweetwater."

"Say!" ejaculated Linc. "This just ain't so. This is a dream."

"Yes, it's a dream come true, Lincoln. If only we can have the luck—Never mind, I just know everything's going to turn out happily. Now look over here. Do you see those clouds of white steam? No, this way. About five hundred yards back and a little higher than we're standing."

"Oh, yes, I see it now," replied Lincoln. "What's that from? A geyser?"

"No, but it's a spring of hot water, boiling water in fact, clean and pure without alkali or sulphur that can be piped right down to the house."

"Well!" exclaimed Lincoln. "All made to order for us."

"Think what boiling hot water will mean to a pioneer wife in the winter time."

"Great!" agreed Lincoln.

"And Ben Thorpe says this valley is protected in winter," continued Lucy. "It never gets terribly cold as it does out on the pass. We can put in a big garden here, irrigate it with cold or warm water, and grow more things to eat than anywhere else in this country."

"You've had that all figured out a long time, haven't you, Lucy?" queried her husband, with a gentle smile.

"Yes, I have. Oh, Lincoln, it's been such great happiness to dream and plan."

"Did you figure on any special kind of a pioneer to share this paradise with you?" he asked.

Lucy blushed. "I used to have visions of a husband," she admitted, "but they sort of faded until—quite miraculously, I just stumbled onto one. . . . I think you know him! Oh, Lincoln, when do you think we can come up here and start making a home?"

"Lord, I don't know. But soon—I hope soon. We might run off and leave an explanation for Kit, put some men to work here, and then come back. What could she do then, what can she do now?—We're married and we have the certificate to prove it. Lucy, I think the time has come—not to run away, but to face your aunt with the truth and get it over with. After all, *you're* my job now, not solving a mystery which had better remain unsolved."

"Don't ask me. When I think of what she'll do when she finds out—Oh, Lincoln, let's not think about it now. Kit is selling the ranch and the stock she has on hand and she's determined to leave Wyoming. She still thinks you are going with her."

"Not any longer does she think so! I told her I was a married man, Lucy."

"Oh, you didn't!" she cried, terrified.

"I didn't tell her to whom I was married," he reassured her with a grin.

"Lincoln, if we have a honeymoon, I want it to be up here."

"That suits me fine! We could live in a tent while we were building a cabin. By the way, that cabin is going to be no pioneer shack, but big, with living room and open fireplace, bedroom, storeroom, kitchen and a wide porch running all along the southern and western exposures. . . ." And so they talked for hours, arms about each other, as they walked to and fro over the bench, blissfully oblivious of everything save their cherished hopes and plans for the future.

Finally Lucy said, "Lincoln, I have one more sight to show you: the one I've reserved for the last. But first we must ride up to see Ben Thorpe."

Linc secured Bay, and mounting, met her at the upper end of the bench. Once off the level they turned a corner of the bulging stone rampart and there before them the upper part of the valley lay spread out before their view. The valley rounded to an apex which was formed by a sheer black mass of rock, split in the middle, and through the cleft between the sheer slopes fringed with timber tumbled a magnificent waterfall between five hundred and a thousand feet high. Sliding out of a V-shaped notch to fall downward, the water was feathered by the wind into white lace and iridescent spray, later striking a great ledge of rock, sheering outward and down like a colossal snowy mushroom. Below, the stream spread in many little rivulets to foam down the stony slopes beyond the timber and converge with the source of the Sweetwater.

"Glorious!" exclaimed Lincoln, his voice filled with awe. "Lucy, I took you at your word, but I was not prepared for this."

He was so struck through and through with the grandeur of this unspoiled wonderland that he had no fitting words for another and smaller waterfall across the valley, for the numerous beaver dams at the head of the stream, the enormous herd of elk that he saw down the slope, or the natural amphitheater which circled the head of the valley and sent its perpendicular walls aloft almost to the sky. Snowy canyons and black ridges led up to the far peaks where all was pure glistening white.

In a sheltered place now close at hand Lucy pointed out the trapper's little cabin. They rode up to it and dismounted, at the open door. It was a crude but comfortable little habitation, the front of which was adorned with the bleached antlers of elk. At one side a roofed structure housed bundles of beaver hides. A column of blue smoke rose from the stone chimney; at Lucy's gay call a black dog came bounding toward her and the spare form of the buckskin-clad trapper emerged from the doorway. His shaggy head bore a great shock of silver and tawny hair, but unlike most trappers, he wore no beard. His visage was lined and weather-beaten, with the clear gray eyes of the wilderness man.

"Ben, you did not really think I was serious, yesterday," Lucy said laughingly. "But he did come. This is my husband, Lincoln Bradway . . . Lincoln, my friend, Ben Thorpe."

They shook hands with each other and exchanged greetings. The Nebraskan was impressed by the trapper's striking appearance. He was not a young man by any means, but he did not seem old. It was easy to discern the affection he held for Lucy. Before they seated themselves on the rude bench, Linc peered into the comfortable cabin and the shed full of beaver hides.

"Wal, young man, is it true you are goin' to throw up a cabin an' homestead this valley?"

Lincoln laughed happily. "Ha! My mind was made up before I ever saw this valley and now I'm ten thousand times more set on it. Will you be glad to have company?"

"I shore will be," replied the trapper puffing at his pipe. "It didn't used to be so lonesome but I guess I'm growin' old an' have a hankerin' for human voices an' faces. This is only a day's long ride from South Pass but from one year's end to another I never see any but a few Shoshone Injuns. You see, there's so much game in this country that in the fall hunters don't have to go a mile from South Pass to kill all the deer an' elk they could pack."

"Well," said Lincoln, "let's get down to business. How about a road into this valley? Lucy tells me you have it all figured out."

"Right across there," replied the trapper, rising and pointing. "See that break? We can grade out a road there in a few days. Not so easy out on top but a roundabout road through the rocks and trees would not be more than thirty miles from South Pass."

"How about your working for me?" asked Lincoln. "I've got four cowboys hired. We can build the road, then two of you can haul in supplies while the others cut and snake down timber for the cabins and corrals. It will take until the snow flies for me to build what I want. I will pay good wages."

"Never mind the wages, son. I've got four good horses that I've packed for years, but they're broke to a wagon."

"Have you got a wagon and tools?" asked Lincoln.

"No wagon and I'm about out of tools," said Thorpe apologetically. "Son, it'll take a good deal of money to do this thing the way I reckon you would want to."

"I have plenty of money," replied Lincoln cheerfully. "When can you begin?"

"Right away," said the trapper. "Can't start too soon for me, I'll wrangle my horses, pack my beaver skins to town, ship them to Cheyenne and be ready to haul anything back you want."

"That's fine," responded Lincoln giving Lucy's arm a squeeze. "I'll look for you in town in two or three days. We'll buy two wagons and all the tools they'll hold. Also camp outfits and supplies. We'll work in from the other direction. My four men under your directions can cut the road down the hill and across the valley while I pack in tents, grub, and whatever Lucy and I will need to start our homesteading, because we certainly are going to be here to boss this job."

"That's a big order, son," said Thorpe thoughtfully, "But I reckon we'll be up to it."

"Then it's settled!" exclaimed Lincoln. He stood up and shook hands heartily with the trapper. "Sorry we can't make a longer visit, Ben. There's too much to see and talk over, besides I want Lucy to get home before dark."

"Wal, I reckon so. I haven't anything to offer you to eat except elk meat, and I'm out of flour and coffee."

"We've got a bit of lunch with us," said Lucy rising. "But just think, I will be up here next week for good! Good-by till then, Ben."

Mounting their horses, they rode back toward the bench. Lucy appeared to be in a seventh heaven. But now that the plans were made, Lincoln suffered a sinking sensation in his breast. It now seemed possible that their beautiful plan would work out, but he could no longer put off the inevitable showdown with Lucy's aunt. Why should he want to? He knew his own mind and his own heart. And now that he no longer felt the paramount importance of avenging his friend's murder, there was no longer any need to propitiate that beautiful woman. It galled him to think of how he had kept Kit Bandon dangling. It made his and Lucy's love seem almost stealthy and ashamed. He would—

"Dearest," complained Lucy suddenly, "you aren't listening to me."

"No, I wasn't. I'm sorry. What were you saying?"

"I was talking about the furniture and fixings for our cabin. They will have to be ordered."

"That's easy, darling. I'll get a catalogue at the store in town first thing, and then you'll be busy."

"But I still want to show you that wonderful place I was telling you about—*my* place, where I used to hope and dream about the future . . . and lately my dreams there all have been about you, dearest. It's a perfect spot to have our lunch. And I'm hungry—even though I am in love!"

They rode along the bench until they came to a grassy promontory overlooking the valley. Lincoln made a seat for Lucy with his coat and while she spread the lunch, still talking excitedly like a happy child, he took his first look at the valley from that point.

From the great waterfall leaping through the cleft down to the narrow green-choked gateway below their valley lay spread before them. Never had Linc seen in one place such a panorama of natural scenery, such a variety of color, in which green and gold and purple were predominant, and with the pool and stream mirroring the azure sky and white fleecy clouds. He became aware that Lucy was tugging at his leg.

"Sit down and eat," she begged. "I made this lunch especially for you."

He, too, discovered that he had an appetite after all and while he relished the tasty meal his wife had prepared he could not help gazing speechlessly from time to time upon the beauty of this valley of paradise. Lucy watched him, happy that he was so thrilled by her beloved spot. The towering mountain range loomed sublime and awe-inspiring in the distance; but the canyons and belts of timber, the waterfalls and stained, weather-beaten cliffs did not seem so aloof; near at hand there were more pastoral scenes: green meadows dotted by elk and moose where he envisioned one day his herd of cattle would be grazing. Following the line he had made with his eye across the valley, the Nebraskan made out a narrow rocky ledge where the stream took its final white plunge into the valley floor below. At this point the gully could be bridged and thus a dry road made across the valley directly from the one outlet to the bench on this side, where the range house was to stand. To a prospective cattleman such as Bradway felt himself to be, the valley below him offered many square miles of magnificent pasturage where thousands of cattle could be raised and fattened and cared for at a minimum of expense.

Lucy, reveling in Lincoln's rapture over her chosen homestead, ceased to talk and watched him with her heart in her eyes. After a time he became aware of other familiar pleasant sensations that began to register their impression in his consciousness. It was easy to locate the musical rhythm of softly falling water but that was not the only sound which brought exquisite memories back to him. Golden pine needles drifting down from above reminded him that a forest of pines was near. The wind in the pines! It was a soft, sad sound which he had been used to during all his years in the West. How many times had he been lulled to sleep on the high lonely ranges by this wilderness murmur. There would probably never be a moment when the wind would not be working in those pine tops; it would range from this gentle sweet summer zephyr he now was hearing to the fierce winter gales when the legions of the storm kings were crashing through those branches. Still, this was not all that intrigued him: there was no sound in nature like the fluttering of the quaking asps. Softly, almost silently, every leaf was quivering on its stem and the millions of leaves in that little grove united into a song that was gay on a day like this one, but sad on a day that was cloudy and cold. The sun had moved around to the west; flecks of gold touched Lucy's hair and the gray rock and the mats of pine needles. The poet has said that "The thoughts of youth are long, long thoughts." Lincoln Bradway's thoughts, inspired by the beauty that surrounded him, ranged far and wide—from the days of his boyhood in

Missouri down through the rough and lonely years to the sweet security of this moment. A warm tide of thankfulness swept over him.

A little hand crept into his, and suddenly he descended from the clouds. With a start he turned to look at Lucy's sweet face. A warm flush was added to its tan; her gold-flecked short curly hair tumbled rebelliously about her forehead and temples. Having appeased her hunger she was wiping the crumbs from her lips, and her laughter rang out as she saw the expression on Linc's face. This man beside her was her husband, a stranger no longer. She was unutterably happy. She could not have asked for more in this world. The days of her unhappiness, of her insecurity, were past. This man, whose hand she held, was her happiness and her security now. For a little space she met his embraces and caresses with an unrestrained fervor and joy, but her ardor and strength were nothing compared to his. Holding her close in his arms he was taking his last toll of those warm lips and cheeks when he heard a tinkle of a spur. For a moment he thought it might be one of his or Lucy's, but suddenly his sharp ears caught another sound. He drew back from Lucy's lips, suddenly freezing as immobile as stone. He sensed something that was not explained by the switching of an aspen branch. He sat bolt upright, and with his hand on his gun turned his eyes toward the aspens. At the same instant he heard what sounded as though it might be the sharp intake of someone's breath. There before him he saw Kit Bandon, standing not twenty steps away, holding herself rigid between two aspen saplings.

Chapter XIV

～～ふ～～

Lucy must have felt her companion's violent shock and sudden immobility, for she cried quickly, "What is it, Linc?"

Lincoln stared. His scattered wits began to function. "Ah—*Kit,*" he said hoarsely.

Kit Bandon's face was that of a rattlesnake about to strike. Linc could see that the two little saplings to which she clung were trembling in her grasp. When she let go of them they came together with a violent swish that set the leaves to quaking and dancing. It was as if they were alive.

Kit moved forward slowly as if some great weight were holding her back. She was garbed in a black riding habit which made her look slim and somber. There was a gun in her belt sheath. She was bare-headed, her face white as paste, and her eyes resembled black banked furnaces. He scarcely knew her. It was as though she were wearing a mask.

"Why—Kit," began Lincoln haltingly, "where did you—come from?"

"I knew you were here," she replied in a cold, even tone. "Emery came out this morning. He saw you climbing the ridge out of South Pass. Then later he saw Lucy riding up the Sweetwater trail. But I never thought to find this—this."

Lucy uttered a little strangled cry and scrambled to her knees. A burning scarlet wave swept over her face from neck to brow. Her eyes shone with terror.

Lincoln hastily got up, spurs clinking, boots scraping. He noticed then that Kit wore gauntlets and carried a whip in her hand. She was peering past the cowboy at the kneeling girl.

"You double-crossing little cat," she snarled, her lips writhing.

"Oh," cried Lucy, as if stunned.

"Look here, Kit," expostulated Lincoln. "No more of that talk, please. Don't blame Lucy. This is my doing!"

Kit stepped aside from Lincoln to confront Lucy. "So you're the fine decent little girl who wouldn't kiss the cowboys," taunted Kit, her cold, even voice rising. "Look at your face! Look at your hair! Look at your blouse! *You*—who were so—so damned prudish and proper and horrified when Jimmy Weston—"

"You—you—are mistaken, Aunt Kit," faltered Lucy, her hands going to her open blouse.

"I should smile. I was mistaken about you, you little alleycat, you—" spat out the raging woman. "Is this the thanks I get for bringing you up, for giving you a home, for—" Suddenly she raised her arm and lashed Lucy across the face with the whip.

Then Lincoln, emerging from his paralysis, reached forward and snatched the whip so violently from Kit that her glove came away with it.

"Have you gone completely mad?" cried Lincoln.

Kit paid no heed to him. She still faced the cowering girl. She was trembling as if suffering from an attack of ague.

"You wouldn't take a lover from your cowboy friends," snarled Kit, her voice gathering passion. "You always threw yourself at mine . . . now you've made a fool out of the only man I ever cared for."

"It's a lie," cried Lucy rising, white and furious, from her knees. "Everything you said is a lie. I never— Linc and I—"

"You know what I mean, Lucy Bandon. Your innocence! I wonder that I could be so blind. No woman can blame a man, but *you*—"

Lucy stepped forward to confront her aunt, one hand on the red welt across her cheek. "Kit, I didn't betray you. Lincoln Bradway doesn't care anything for you. He never did! Tell her the truth, Lincoln."

"You brazen little bitch!" burst out Kit, all control now gone.

"Enough of this, Kit," interrupted Lincoln harshly. "I won't have you abusing my, my—I think it's my turn to talk now."

"Listen, you double-crossing sneaking spy! I'll talk to you when I get through with her."

"That's right, take it out on me if you want, but leave Lucy alone." He put his arm protectingly around his wife, who now was weeping bitterly.

"Leave her alone!" shrilled Kit, beside herself. "Why the dirty little—"

Lincoln slapped her so hard across the lips that it brought blood. The blow staggered her. He took care to keep close to her. His quick action had liberated him from the strange inhibition that had bound him during the powerful scene. Now he was cool and capable of coping with the situation.

"You struck me—for *her?*"

"Yes, and I'm liable to hurt you worse if you keep on screaming like a madwoman. Lucy is honest. She's done nothing wrong. If there's any blame it's mine."

"Hear the loyal champion. You're as rotten as she is."

"I did come to feel great respect for you, Kit, but I never loved you. I couldn't help it if you imagined things."

"You talk just like every cowboy caught in the act."

"I tell you I had no love for you such as I feel for Lucy."

"You fling it in my teeth?" shrieked Kit.

Bradway realized that there was no further possibility of keeping the truth from her. The time had come to end this wretched secrecy and dissemblance. He took Lucy's hand and together they faced the hate-contorted Maverick Queen.

"I'm sorry, Kit," he said, "that you have to learn the news in this wise. Lucy and I are married. Lucy is my wife!"

She regarded him as if she had not heard aright or as if he were crazy. "What?" she demanded, utterly incredulous.

"Yes, Kit Bandon," interposed Lucy, passionately, "ever since that first day in Rock Springs—when you were so busy with Hank Miller that you left us alone."

"You're both liars," shrieked Kit.

"No, Kit, it's the truth. Look here," cried Lincoln hurriedly. And producing their marriage certificate, which he had always carried, he thrust it before Kit's eyes, which looked suddenly old and beaten.

She saw it, read it, then gasped. "How? When?"

"Kit, it was early in the evening just about dark while you were so busy with that cattleman," replied Lincoln.

"Was that—the first time—you met?"

"No. I bumped into Lucy in the street the first day I was in South Pass and fell in love with her at first sight."

"And you—Lucy Bandon?"

"It was the same with me."

"Oh, I see," returned Kit trembling in every muscle. "But you never told me."

"I asked Lucy to keep it quiet for my sake. It would have been easy to pick up our feet and leave for Nebraska without saying a word to anyone. But I had a job to finish before I could go—"

Kit still faced her niece. "You let me fall in love with this man knowing he was yours. You might have saved me from letting me make a shameless fool of myself. I can never forgive you for that. You have both wronged me."

"We did not," cried Lucy. "It was your monstrous

vanity. It was the same vanity that made you take Jimmy Weston away from me."

"Don't be ridiculous, Kit," interposed Lincoln giving way to anger. He was afraid of what was forming in her mind. "It is you who have made the blunders. And the worst blunder you made was what you did to Weston."

"Don't throw that lovesick simpleton in my face."

"If he was lovesick you made him so," retorted Lucy. "He *did* care for me. And you, Kit Bandon, are the one who knows what it cost him."

"All right, girl. You know there's no turning back on this trail."

"Yes, I know," responded Lucy. "But I'm no longer afraid of you, Kit Bandon. I can tell you right in front of Lincoln—that Jimmy was bad—that he was faithless—that he deserved punishment—but not a disgraceful cowardly death while he was drunk and asleep."

Kit uttered an inarticulate cry and with face distorted by fear and rage she drew her gun with lightning swiftness. But quick as she was she was not quick enough for the tall Nebraskan. With a sudden lunge he seized the hand that held the gleaming gun and wrenched it upward so that the belching discharge passed harmlessly over Lucy's head. Lincoln, with both hands on her wrist and the gun, held her arm above her head. She was as strong as a panther. She fought like one. She struck with her free hand. She kicked. She writhed and twisted in his grasp. She bit him on the back of the hand.

"I'll kill you, Lucy Bandon, for that," she screamed. "And you, Linc Bradway—I'll blow your guts out!"

"For God's sake, Kit, come to your senses," implored Linc. "Drop that gun. Let me have it. Would you murder your own flesh and blood? . . . Kit!"

"I'll kill you! You two can't live on the earth with me!" She reached for the gun with her other hand and was straining, panting, writhing with extraordinary and insane strength to tear it way from Linc. He could feel her muscular body strain and swell and thrash against him. In that moment, Kit Bandon revealed her true self. He gave her gun hand a quick backward twist. She screamed with agony and helpless rage. The gun went spinning beyond over the rock. She fell away from him against the tree and then slid to the ground. She did not move.

"God!" whispered Lincoln. "I guess it was the wrong time to tell her. . . . Lucy, she would have murdered us both."

"I told you, Lincoln. I *know* Kit Bandon," replied Lucy, her face white and drawn. Is—is she breathing?"

"If she's dead it was done when her head hit the tree. . . ." Lucy knelt beside the still form and slipped her hand inside Kit's blouse. "Oh, she's alive. Thank God, Lincoln. I wouldn't want you to be the cause of her death. Get some water in your sombrero."

He snatched up his sombrero and strode to the brook. As he filled the sombrero he noticed how his hands were shaking. No wonder! If he had not suspected her and kept close to her, he and Lucy would at that moment be lying dead on the promontory. What kind of a story would Kit have sent abroad about such a tragedy? Probably it would have been made to look like murder and suicide. He hurried back with the water. Lucy began to bathe her aunt's face with the icy water while Lincoln, at Lucy's instigation, began to chafe her wrists. Their joint activities brought Kit to. At first her great dark eyes stared blankly up at Lucy and Linc; then, as she recognized them, her color came flooding back into her cheeks.

"What happened?" she asked faintly, as her eyes went from one to the other.

"We had a fight, Kit, and I had to disarm you," returned Lincoln. "You struck your head when you fell and lost your senses."

"What was I—going to do?"

"Never mind. We want to forget it."

Kit gave a long, heart-rending sigh. "I remember . . . you and Lucy—love at first sight—never told me—

married at Rock Springs. . . . Now what is to become of me?" and she broke into an uncontrollable fit of weeping.

Her hysteria was so prolonged and her sobbing so violent that Linc thought she would do herself some injury, but she could not be comforted. Lucy put Kit's head in her lap and held her and spoke soothingly to the distracted woman. It seemed to Linc that the Maverick Queen had aged ten years in the past half hour. Her secret was out. Her hope of finding love was forever gone. She had come within one frantic instant of murdering in the heat of passion the only two people she ever had loved. As Linc looked down at her he scarcely recognized the woman that was Kit Bandon. She looked old, and sick, and beaten. She sat up presently, and Lucy helped her to her feet.

"It's getting late," said Lincoln, taking one of her arms. "Kit, do you think you can ride?"

"Yes, I guess I'm all right now," she replied, quietly.

"I'll get your horse. And yours, too, Lucy," said Lincoln. And he hurried away to find them.

Kit's horse had wandered off the bench and required a few moments to locate. Upon returning to the grove with the two horses he found both women composed.

"Lincoln—Lucy," Kit Bandon spoke in a flat, dead tone of voice, "it could have been worse. But that was not to be. I'm glad—I don't know just what you said and what I admitted, but I ask you to forget it. Would that be too much?"

"There, there, Kit," replied Bradway earnestly. "Whatever was spoken, or whatever was done here today, shall be forgotten by Lucy and by me."

"Oh, yes," replied Lucy in a low voice. "It is all forgotten—and forgiven. It was an hour of madness."

"Are you sure you can ride?" asked Lincoln.

"I think so. Where's my horse? Let me try." She did not mount so readily, but she appeared to be steady in the saddle and Lincoln calculated that she would be all right.

"Take her home, Lucy," said the Nebraskan. "As

long as she's all right I'd rather not go. I'll ride across
the valley and climb out on top where I expect to meet
the cowboys. I'll be seeing you in a day or two. . . .
Good-by, Lucy—Don't take it so hard, Kit. After all
it was a bad place for you. Good-by."

He watched them ride across the bench and down
the trail. Soon they broke from a trot to a lope, assur-
ing Lincoln that they would reach home safely.

"Well!" he soliloquized. "I thought that was my finish . . . but somehow I just can't feel as happy as I
want to feel."

He climbed down over the rocks and securing Kit's
gun put it in his pocket and returned to the level. The
day was far spent. The sun had gone down behind the
peaks in the west. Hurrying to his horse, he mounted
and rode down off the bench. He found a trail there
that led straight across the valley. Crossing the valley in
a lope, he reached the summit of the slope and found
Thatcher and Vince waiting for him.

"Wal, boss," drawled Vince with a grin, "you didn't
'pear to be a hombre thet would punish hoss flesh thet
way. I reckon Mel and I figgered the devil was after
you."

"By George, you're right. I didn't realize I was push-
ing the horse." Linc found that Bay was wet with lather
and breathing heavily. "Slip his saddle, Vince. We'll
rest a little."

Bradway sat down with his back to a tree and wiped
his hot face. Then he espied a lean-to made of pine
boughs, several blankets thrown over the bushes, a
little campfire burning with a coffeepot boiling, and a
skillet heating up. A parcel of food was spread on the
ground.

"So you've made camp?" queried Lincoln.

"Shore," replied Vince. "It wasn't no trouble to pack
this little stuff an' you never can tell."

"Good idea!" exclaimed the Nebraskan. "We'll stay
here all night."

"That'll be best, Linc," put in Thatcher. "It'll be
dark pretty pronto and we want to map out your road

from this point. You'll be surprised to learn this is the only place along this eastern side of the valley where we can build a road."

"Shore is the greatest corral for stock I ever seen," added Vince. "All you hev to do is to fence the opening where you come in and build a little fence and gate down heah where you see it so narrow an' you'll be jake."

"Linc, if you can throw a few cattle in there you'll get rich," said Thatcher, thoughtfully.

"You're wrong, boys," responded Linc. "I can throw a big herd of cattle in here and we'll all get rich."

"Doggone! Darned if I don't believe you, pard!" ejaculated Vince. "Now you talk to Mel while I toss together some grub."

Thatcher seated himself cross-legged beside Bradway. "Most wonderful place, boss. Of course all this western part of Wyoming is wonderful, but this has any country I ever saw beat. We moseyed along slow, getting off our horses now and then to take a look. That field glass we bought the other day is a great help. We couldn't begin to count the head of game we saw. There are several score of cattle down there that might be as wild as the elk."

"The elk aren't wild, Mel," returned the Nebraskan. "Only the big bulls showed any disposition to get out of my way. Only the moose down there are wild."

"It'll be many a long year before this country will lack game to any extent." Mel leaned over and began to scratch up a little pile of pine needles. "I reckon we've got to tell you. . . . Several hours after you left us we spotted Kit Bandon riding hell for leather up the trail. It was a sure bet she was trailing Lucy. . . . Vince and I knew that she must have caught up with you long before you got up the hill yonder."

Vince, kneeling at the campfire with his back turned, moved his head slightly and stiffened.

"Ha!" Lincoln expelled a deep breath. "Did she catch us? She almost caught us for good!"

There was an eloquent little silence, which presently

Vince broke. "Wal, you seem to hev got back to us without bein' full of holes."

"Yes, by luck or the grace of God!" muttered Lincoln. "Fellows, Kit knew nothing whatever about Lucy and me. We had forgotten the world and Kit slipped up on us and caught Lucy in my arms."

"Whoops!" yelled Vince. He loud exclamation was not expressive of his feelings.

"How in hell did you ever get out of *that?*" asked Thatcher, bursting with excitement.

"I was lucky, I tell you. I wouldn't be surprised if she had it in her mind to kill us—she was plenty mad. But you know how women are. . . . Afterward she broke down and then came to her senses when she found that she had a new good-looking nephew-in-law like me. You boys must know that there is a good side of Kit Bandon."

"Yes, I know," said Thatcher. "But, Linc, we thought we heard a shot."

The Nebraskan laughed. "Kit shot at a gopher and then she felt better. She lets off steam that way, I reckon."

Vince turned around from the fire, his face red, his eyes piercing. "Pard, you mean to stand there and say thet you got away with it? Thet Kit let you off?"

"Yes, that is what I mean," replied Bradway thoughtfully. "What is more, she seemed to be resigned to the fact of my marriage to Lucy—and, in short, although it seems a miracle, I believe she'll be our friend."

"Shore she will," returned Vince. "An' it'll behoove you to be a friend of hers in the bad time thet is comin' pronto."

"I will be," returned the Nebraskan. "But let's don't talk any more about Kit now. I want to talk about homesteading this valley, and get your advice and angle on what's to be done."

"Wal, we'll be darned glad to give thet," said Vince heartily.

" 'Nother thing I ought to tell you, Linc," spoke

up Thatcher with evident embarrassment. "I have a sweetheart back in Cheyenne. Haven't heard from her for a long time, but if she has stuck to me, I'll want to settle down for keeps. Would that be all right with you?"

"Right? It's perfect!" responded Lincoln enthusiastically. "That will please Lucy. Vince, couldn't you dig up a girl?"

"Wal, I could dig up one of them dance-hall girls I met the other night," replied Vince seriously.

"I've known cowboys who married dance-hall girls who turned out to make fine wives," said Linc, "so that wouldn't be so bad either."

"It'd be kinda fine at thet," returned Vince, and then once more applied himself to the preparation of supper.

Presently Lincoln was sitting cowboy fashion with his two comrades to enjoy their frugal meal. The setting was one he had never seen equaled. While they were eating, the afterglow of sunset turned from gold to red, burnishing the whole valley in shades of flame color. As dusk came on, they made plans concerning their future ranch in the valley until the fire burned low and the stars came out and it was time to turn in.

When the three cowboys awoke, the early sun had colored the peaks a soft rose, the pine needles were drifting down on the breeze, and the valley and the lake and the streams below them were shining with the glory of the dawn. To the tall Nebraskan the tragic events of the day before seemed already to have faded into the past. Yet as he lay there for a moment watching Vince and Mel stretch, pull on their boots, rub their eyes and fold their blankets, he wondered how it was with Lucy in the Bandon ranch house. Had he been wise to let the girl accompany her aunt home after Kit's attempt to kill her?

They broke camp early and set off eastward, searching out the best route for a road among the rocks and the thickets which grew along the hillside toward the Pass. They slowly made their way, leading their horses, blazing the trees to indicate their route, cutting brush, and marking thickets through which the road would pass. It took them all morning to work down from the rim of the valley to the point where the timber thinned out and failed. From then on the going was less rough down a gradual slope over fairly even ground. Toward the middle of the afternoon they reached the bluff overlooking South Pass. The town, bustling as usual, appeared hazy with the smoke from the smelter. The last miles, leading down the long slope across the brook, they rode; and from their unaccustomed footwork, they were thoroughly tired when they reached Headly's stables.

"Wal," suggested Vince, "let's wash up an' mosey down to set an' see what's come off since we've been gone."

"O.K., boys," agreed Lincoln, "but it's early yet. So let's head for the big store and buy 'em out. I forgot to tell you about Ben Thorpe, the trapper over in Lucy's valley. He's got two teams of horses and he's going to work for us. We'll leave the harness for him to pick out. I'll buy a couple of big wagons and you hombres select all the ranch tools that we'll need. It's good that this is a big store with a full line of hardware. And, Mel, don't forget plenty of carpenter's tools."

"Huh. Talks like he had a gold mine," said Vince. "Thet stuff is goin' to cost a heap of money."

"We've got plenty, pards, and maybe I'm not glad I saved it! Pile in now and let's do the best trading we can!"

At the restaurant two hours later, Bradway spread out the checked lists and read the items aloud. "Not bad for so short a time," he said with satisfaction. "Tomorrow we'll finish and order what Dockery Brothers did not have in stock. We'll have those two wagons packed before Thorpe gets here."

"Boss, we're forgettin' tents, beddin', stoves, stove-pipes and a lot of things beside the grubstake we'll need to start the work on."

"I haven't forgotten anything, boys," responded Linc. "We'll hire somebody with a small wagon to go along with Thorpe and we'll build our road, camping as we go, right down into the valley."

"It's a right pert job and strikes me where I live," said Vince with a faraway look in his eyes. "I wonder—" The arrival of their supper prevented him from uttering what he had been about to say.

After supper they emerged from the restaurant to find it dark and the lights lit in all the windows. They sauntered down the crowded street, looking—as was their habit—for cowboys and cattlemen; but only miners, and the typical disreputable town hangers-on seemed to be in evidence.

"Hey, look there," said Vince, pointing down the street. "Somethin's come off. Biggest crowd I ever seen in front of Emery's."

"That reminds me," returned the Nebraskan. "Emery left South Pass yesterday morning. He saw us climb the hill a little after sunrise. You remember pointing out the buckboard going at a pretty good clip? Well, he saw Lucy riding up the Sweetwater trail and putting two and two together he tipped Kit off to where we were going."

"Emery leavin' to go down the valley must mean a whole lot," said Vince, thoughtfully. "Let's find out."

"All right," agreed Lincoln. "Let's split up and ask a few questions; we'll meet later and compare notes."

The South Pass gentry seemed to be distinctly cold to cowboys that evening. One of the men, a mining foreman at the mill, recognized Bradway and made a significant remark: "You ought to know more than we do about what's come off. You belong to that outfit."

"I only asked a civil question," returned the Nebraskan sharply. "What outfit do you mean?"

"That Emery-Bandon outfit, cowboy. That's what I mean."

"I won't call you a liar, because you're probably only peddling gossip, but if you mention again that the Emery-Bandon outfit is *my* outfit, then I'll have to call you, pronto."

The miner, catching the glint in the cowboy's eyes

and his low-swinging guns, subsided quickly, and Linc pushed his way inside the saloon. It was more crowded and noisy than he had ever seen it; gamblers occupied every table, with others awaiting their turn. In the other room a line crowded the bar three deep, drinking and waiting to be served. Bradway noticed that none of the employees of the *Leave It* seemed familiar to him. Finally he found two miners inclined to be somewhat loose-tongued and mellow from drink, who appeared to be willing to talk. According to the gossip that was going the rounds, they said, Emery's creditors, big cattlemen from down the valley, one of whom was Kit Bandon, had taken the gambling hall away from him and run him out of town. In a rage at being dispossessed, according to what they had heard, Emery had sworn vengence on somebody whose name they didn't know. The rumor persisted that on account of certain shady cattle deals in which he was implicated it might be wise for Emery to quit the valley while the going was good.

After gleaning from his tipsy informants all that was possible, Lincoln went outside to wait for his two partners. He did not have to linger long for Thatcher. The Nebraskan lost no time informing the cowboy of all he had learned.

"I got just about the same story," said Mel. "Emery always was a crooked gambler and it was well known that he ran a crooked house, but he couldn't be held for that because in this territory gambling isn't legal. It's a wonder he had not been shot long ago. But he stood in with the other gamblers and shared his profits with them. It just happened that no cowboy had been cheated and riled enough to draw on him. But, boss, the people now feel pretty sure that Emery has been in crooked cattle deals with Kit Bandon. That's a horse of another color. I don't like it. These cattlemen who are seein' red might get a hold on Kit through her known association with Emery."

"I don't like it either," responded Linc, gravely. "Kit has been careless about her reputation. Why did she

ever tie in with a crook like Emery? He must have had
some hold on her. What can we do?"

"I reckon we ought to think about our own hides,"
returned Thatcher, tersely.

"Lordy, we ought to be able to do something to help
Kit and still save our hides. That is, if she will accept
our help."

"There isn't a cowboy in the valley who would not
help Kit Bandon. But I question the wisdom of our
mixing any deeper in this mess. You're married to a
fine girl and you are ready to settle down homesteading
and ranching it. And there's nothing you can do about
it anyway. And I'll tell you, pard, I'd like to get out
from under, make up with my girl, and start straight
with you in the cattle business."

"You're sure talking sense, Mel," admitted Lincoln.
"But—but I just can't help it. I *want* to save Kit Bandon from her own mistakes."

"That's the way Vince feels. That's the way with all
the cowboys who have fallen under her ill-starred influence, but I've finally got some sense and I think you
have, too. I'm telling you to let well enough alone.
You were damn lucky that Kit Bandon let you off
yesterday, when sure as hell I thought she was out to
kill you."

"That's one reason why I'd risk a lot to save her."

"All right. I'm with you," returned Thatcher soberly.
"Said I'd stick and I meant it. What do you aim to do?"

"That's where I'm stumped. I don't know. We'll have
to wait until we find out what is threatening Kit."

"No! Wait nothing. You'd better want to help her
before anything threatens."

"But if I don't find out what's threatening her I can't
persuade her to leave the valley while there's still time."

"Bradway, *I* can find out what might happen to Kit
Bandon," rejoined Mel, his voice low.

"Mel, if you can find out and will help me I will—"

"O.K., I'm off," said Thatcher quietly. "I wouldn't
tell Vince if I were you because he'll trail me, and I'll
tell you that hombre is bad medicine." With that Mel

gave Lincoln's arm a squeeze and strode off down the street to disappear among the pedestrians.

"Well, I'll be damned," muttered the Nebraskan, just as Vince came shuffling up.

"Hello, boss," he said. "Where's Mel?"

Linc felt that no matter what the risk, he would have to be honest with Vince. "I told Thatcher that I wanted to know exactly what was threatening Kit Bandon. He said he could find out and he went off almost on the run."

"Hell's fire!" ejaculated Vince in an injured tone. "I knew Mel was double-crossin' me. He hasn't told me everythin'."

"Well, there's nothing for us to do, Vince, but wait till he comes back. . . . Did you get any angles on Emery being driven out of town?"

"There's plenty of talk," replied Vince. "An' I suppose you got about the same as me. But don't you savvy, boss, thet these miners an' townspeople hevn't any idee what's behind all this."

"I think I begin to savvy," replied the Nebraskan.

They walked up and down the street with Bradway doing most of the talking and Vince growing more somber and noncommittal as the time went by. When the hour grew late he tried to get Vince to share his lodgings that night.

"Nope. Thanks, pard, I want to wait up for Thatcher," and bidding his partner good night Vince went his way. Linc went to his room and to bed.

The next morning to his dismay the two cowboys did not meet him for breakfast. He went up to Headly's stables to find that sometime during the night they had saddled their horses and left town. Headly did not know whether or not they had left together. He now was becoming greatly perturbed. He had no idea what direction they had taken or on what errand they were bound. He wished he had not allowed Mel to become implicated in this deal with Kit, and he reluctantly compelled himself to wait. The hours passed slowly. Occasionally he stalked the streets, looking for his friends, but they did not come. Having omitted his lunch, he spent the afternoon with the merchant with whom he had placed his order the day before, and finally rounded out his necessary orders for supplies to his complete satisfaction, obtaining a generous discount on his bill of goods. He had supper alone, afterward walking the streets again from one gambling hall to another, hoping to meet Thatcher or Vince, but in vain. At midnight he returned to his lodgings. His range instinct prompted him to be ready for an emergency. He removed only his gun belt, boots and coat. Despite his worry, somehow he soon went to sleep. He seemed only to have closed his eyes when a loud pounding on the door roused him. He leaped off the bed. "Who is it?" he called, seizing the bar.

"It's Thatcher," came the swift, hoarse whisper. "Let me in. There's hell to pay."

Linc removed the bar and opened the door.

"Hello, Mel," he said. "Strike a match and make a light. You'll find a candle on the stand there."

"Couldn't get here sooner," replied Thatcher. The candlelight flared up, revealing his pale, set face.

The Nebraskan sat down upon the bed to pull on his boots. "Where's Vince?" he asked.

"I didn't run into him but I have an idea that he was looking for me."

"What time is it?" asked Linc.

"It's an hour or two before dawn. We've got to do some fast riding, pard—and even then I'm afraid we'll be too late."

"I felt that same way lately somehow," replied Bradway. He got up and buckled on his gun belt. Then he got into his coat. "Where did I leave my sombrero? Hold up the candle, Mel." He found it on the floor.

"It's good you didn't undress," said Thatcher. "We've got to rustle. I had to change horses so I saddled Bay while I was at the stables."

They went out together in the chill gloom. A few lamps were still burning along the main street; the resort that had been Emery's was still blazing with light. Two horses were standing in the street, tossing their heads and champing their bits. Lincoln tried the cinch on Bay, then he turned to whisper hoarsely to Mel.

"If we've got to ride, we won't be able to talk. Gimme a hunch quick what you found out."

"Never mind how I found out, boss, I still have friends down there. . . . There's an outfit of cattle-men—not many—hard and brutal men, sick with how they've been imposed upon and mad as hell at the cow-boys, and those ranchers are out to get Emery and Kit."

"What are they going to do?" asked Linc.

"Lord only knows, but I reckon they are prepared to take the law into their own hands."

"Do the cowboys know?"

"Not many. They've been thrown off the scent. Vince knew all the time. It's a sure bet he will turn up with some of them."

"I can guess the rest," returned the Nebraskan grimly. "Let's ride."

They mounted and headed down the street toward the creek, splashed across, then urged their mounts up the long slope that led to the pass. Thatcher led the way. Once on the road, they broke into a swinging lope. They crossed the pass in perhaps a quarter of an hour and were heading down the winding road on the valley side.

"Look there!" cried Thatcher excited, reining in. "A bonfire!"

"I see it," replied Linc, reining in beside him. "That may mean we're too late. Let's rustle. Once we're off this hill we've got straight clear road for ten or twelve miles."

Down the zigzag slope they saved their horses, and reaching the level they dismounted to tighten their cinches. Mounting again, they were off riding at a ground-eating lope. Lincoln allowed Thatcher to set the pace, and the way he handled his horse indicated the tenseness of the occasion. A long swinging lope led to a gallop, then to a dead run. The horses were fresh and fast. The night was cold, and the wind nipped Lincoln's nose and ears. The road could be seen dimly, a pale streak leading off into the gloom. After covering several miles Thatcher reduced their gait to a trot but he did not give the horses a long stretch of rest. Soon the horses were going full speed through the night which was at that darkest hour which precedes the dawn. Three times Mel changed gaits and at the end of the last run the big bonfire seemed less than a mile away. He brought his horse sharply to a standstill, with Lincoln following suit.

"Reckon this is—far enough," panted Thatcher. "We sure made fast time. Now take a good look, Linc, and see what you can see."

Bradway already was peering through the darkness. "I can see the bonfire. Believe it's located near some big trees at the edge of the timber. . . . There! I can make out some dark forms passing in front of the fire."

"Same here," replied Thatcher. "That must be the outfit. It's a sure bet the cowboys wouldn't make any fire. Do you think we ought to get a closer look?"

"Let's cut off the road, keep out of sight and hearing, tie our horses in the willows, and sneak up on that outfit."

"Wouldn't it be better to ride down on them?" queried Thatcher. "If they mean business we haven't got a lot of time."

"If it's too late it's too late," said the Nebraskan somberly, "but I've been on some of these vigilante rides. They keep moving after dark and aim to do their work at daylight. We'll take a chance."

"O.K. We're probably outnumbered ten to one. So let's keep our eyes peeled," concluded Mel.

They turned their heaving horses into the sage. Dawn was close at hand. Already there were gray streaks in the east and the stars had dimmed. It was not long before the riders saw the low, dark line of timber encroaching upon the valley floor. When they had reached to within a couple of hundred yards of the fire they dismounted, both with the same thought, and stole forward, eyes and ears keen to detect any movement of horse or man. Reaching the willows, they led their horses some distance before tying them to convenient branches. They stepped into the open again. Thatcher suddenly gripped Bradway's arm.

"Hold it!" he whispered in Lincoln's ear. "Listen."

They heard horses moving, then low voices. Mel glided ahead noiselessly, a couple of steps ahead of Linc. There were openings in the thicket and lanes spreading between the trees. Into one of these open places vanished Mel. Lincoln crept forward more cautiously until he caught up with Thatcher again. As they paused there in the shadow they heard the hoofbeats of several horses and low voices passing by.

"Bunch of cowboys," whispered Thatcher excitedly. "Let's follow along. Don't make any noise, Linc."

They reached the edge of the timber just as half a dozen horsemen were vanishing into the gray gloom. Apparently the bonfire had died down somewhat or else the brightening sky seemed to have dimmed its light. Keeping under cover of the trees Thatcher led his companion in swift pursuit. Linc did not look up. He watched where he was going so that he would not break a stick or step in a hole. Presently Mel stopped him and drew him into the shelter of some underbrush; they waited a while seeing and hearing nothing. After a tense moment of silence they heard the thud of hoofs moving forward again. Once more Thatcher glided forward with the Nebraskan at his heels. And again the two silent men came to a sudden halt. A group of riderless horses could be distinguished blackly etched between them and the dull glow of the firelight. The moving figures beyond appeared to be men pacing in front of the fire.

"What's become of those cowboys who passed us?" whispered Thatcher, worriedly. "I can't hear them. Maybe they worked their way inside the willows. Let's go."

Another tense interval of cautious advance brought

them to a point where they could make out the dim shapes of moving horsemen.

"Look," whispered Mel. "There's more of them than when we saw them first. Nine or ten."

"Not enough if they mean to ambush the cattlemen," whispered Linc.

"I don't know. They might be crazy enough to do anything. But they'll wait to see how many are in the vigilante bunch. What do you figure, Linc?"

"I'm figuring hard but haven't got anywhere," replied Lincoln tensely. "It's getting light. See that red in the sky up there?"

"Pard, I reckon it's a very appropriate color," replied Thatcher ominously.

"Meaning this bunch of cowboys are going to spill blood?"

"It's a safe bet. Don't overlook the fact that Vince is in that bunch and it's a hundred to one he's leading them."

"Then we'll go on following them. We can keep inside the willows all the way."

"All right. Let's mosey on a little while longer, then have ourselves another look."

They confined themselves now to a slow, stealthy advance through the willows. They walked silently, carefully parting the brush and branches to be sure that they did not break any dead snags and constantly peering ahead cautiously, as they drew closer to the blazing fire. Linc recognized the spot: the big trees standing out in the open he had passed under so very recently. He tugged Mel's sleeve and whispered to him that they were not more than a mile from the Bandon ranch.

"One more spell like this last one and we'll be getting somewhere," returned Thatcher. "Take it easy now. I reckon we don't want to be caught by these cowboys. When the fireworks start they won't pay any attention to us, but we want to make damn sure we don't get caught between their lines of fire."

According to the way Linc figured it they would

soon be passing the spot where the cowboys ought to be, and it behooved them to be exceedingly cautious. When again they approached the edge of the thicket, the sky was light, though it still was dusky in the willow grove. The fire still glowed but not one of the men grouped about it made a move to throw on any more fuel. Linc looked back across the valley and noted that the sun had not yet risen above the farther wall.

"Let's get a little closer," whispered Mel.

They crossed a projecting neck of the timbered bottom to come out almost at the spot where the group of cattlemen waited. They were a little too close for comfort. One of the group was pointing in the direction of the Bandon ranch. All of the men showed sudden animation, as another of the men started for the place where the horses were tethered.

Suddenly Thatcher seized Linc's arm in a grasp so tight that he winced with pain. "Godamighty!" he gasped. "Look, pard—*look!*"

A group of horsemen in a half-circle were bringing two bareheaded riders, with hands bound behind them, across the flat toward the three big trees and the waiting men. "By Judas priest," Linc whispered hoarsely. "That's Kit—and Emery."

"Yes, and it looks bad, Linc."

The Nebraskan had seen many a posse of riders move along in that sinister, businesslike manner half surrounding their prisoners. He knew what it meant—the law of the range once more was being fulfilled.

"Pard, it wouldn't have done any good if we'd gotten here sooner," whispered Mel. "This outfit of cowmen are hell bent on execution."

Linc knew that Mel was right. It was hard to believe that these desperate men could drive themselves to execute a woman. Emery, yes, but a woman—! His heart sank.

But the practical Thatcher was less moved. "We can get closer presently. Pretty soon these cowmen will be so intent on their dirty job that they won't hear us. . . . I'm just wondering what Vince and those hombres back yonder in the willows will do. If I know him and them they'll ride right up on this bunch."

Lincoln had no heart to reply. There were ten men in the party approaching. That made twenty-three of the vigilantes in all. Each of them wore a wide-brimmed hat pulled down over his eyes. Blue handkerchiefs masked the lower part of their faces. Lincoln's keen sight did not miss the fact that they were all heavily armed. They moved forward silently with almost mechanical precison, and halted under the biggest trees just beyond the pile of embers that had been the fire, where they were met by the cowmen, now mounted, who had been waiting for them. The two watchers were conscious of sounds off to their left in the willows. Mel pointed over his shoulder. "Those fool cowboys are going to rush the cowmen's party. They're going to get themselves killed for their pains," he muttered.

Now the two groups of cattlemen had come together, and under cover of the confusion Linc and Mel crawled closer to a point where they were only fifty paces from this sinister company and easily within hearing. Some of the vigilantes were already on foot and several of the men dismounted to meet them. A tall man with the shape and movement of the rancher Lee appeared to be the leader.

"Are we all here?" he asked sharply.

"All here, Captain, but there's a few riders prowling around."

"We can't let them hold us up now," returned the leader. "Now Emery, it's time for you to talk." He turned away from the two mounted prisoners and said, "Men, I promised the gambler freedom if he'd tell us what we want to know. We want the proofs."

"Let's rustle, boss, and get it over with," spoke up another gruffer voice.

The Nebraskan did not want to look but he was forced to against his will. The two prisoners were in plain sight. The sun had risen and gold and red light bathed the valley in its mellow glow. The sage rippled with the morning breeze. Lincoln saw Emery astride his horse, his hands bound behind him, his dark face haggard and drawn. The other rider was Kit Bandon. She wore a long black coat, evidently hastily thrown over her sleeping gown. Her white bare feet dangled above the stirrups which she could not reach. Her white face and black hair made a striking contrast in the morning light. Her eyes appeared like great black wells that emphasized her pallor. Lincoln's gaze could not discern any terror, nor cringing in her appearance. Her white face with its scornful eyes was averted from the terrified man beside her.

"Emery, come out with your evidence," rasped the leader stridently.

"I was her partner in plenty of cattle deals," replied the gambler, his voice a little louder than a hoarse whisper.

"He's a low-down liar," cried Kit scornfully. "I had no partner in my cattle deals."

"She corrupted the cowboys—ruined them. She got them to steal for her. She's nothing but a low-down whore. And her price was *one maverick steer per . . .*"

"Kit Bandon, what have you to say to that?" growled the leader.

"I have given you my answer. You can believe what you wish," was her cold rejoinder, uttered between clenched teeth.

"Men, you've heard. We have the proofs. We're justified. Somebody cut Emery's arms loose and let him go."

Two stalwart men approached Emery and freed him from his bonds. One of them gave the horse a resounding smack on the flank.

"Rustle, you skunk, before we change our minds," called one of the men.

Emery, with convulsed visage and trembling jaw, reined his horse from the group confronting him, and had just gotten beyond the farthest of the three trees when he was met there by the charging cowboys. They barred his escape. Then things began to happen.

Linc caught a look of surprise on several of the

faces of the cattlemen. Then he heard the whistle of a
rope and a dull crack as the noose pulled tight about
Emery's neck. His sudden scream of terror was cut
short. His body jerked backward off his horse and fell
to the earth. At the same instant the cowboy with the
lasso flicked the other end over the spreading branch of
a willow. As he did so he shouted some command to
his companions. Linc recognized that voice. It was the
voice of his partner Vince. Three cowboys were out of
their saddles in a twinkling. They grasped the dangling
rope and with a violent tug jerked the body of the
gambler five feet off the ground. Just as quickly and
silently they made the end of the lasso fast to a sapling
and then leaped into their saddles again.

The vigilantes, as though paralyzed by the speed of
the action that had taken place before their eyes, gaped
at the grotesque figure of the gambler. They made no
move to interfere with what was going on. Perhaps they
thought, as did Linc and Mel, that only justice was
being meted out under that willow tree.

The cowboys were strangely silent. They watched
Emery jerk spasmodically, shrugging off the black over-
coat he had been wearing. The convulsive movements
must have lasted several moments. Then the body was
still, stretched limp, moving to and fro with the swaying branch. The slanting beams of the early sunlight
touched the dark face of the dead man, adding a touch
of horror to the stark scene. Bradway turned his eyes
away from the dead man to the calm figure of the other
prisoner. If she had witnessed Emery's brutal hanging,
there was no evidence of it on her countenance. Her
eyes blazed straight ahead in that white mask that was
her face.

At that moment the harsh voice of the leader of the
cattlemen rang out.

*"Kit Bandon, we condemn you to hang for your
proven crimes!"*

The words of doom seemed still to be trembling in
the still morning air when there was a sudden movement behind the group of cattlemen. Linc had torn

himself free from Thatcher's restraining grasp and was stumbling forward in the direction of the half-circle of vigilantes.

"Wait, men! Wait! You can't do this!" he cried as he ran forward, his empty hands held high.

There was a stir among the men and several exclamations and muttered threats. Now Linc was facing the leader.

"You men don't know what you are doing," he said in a clear, steady voice which all could hear. "You represent law and order in this country. You can't hang a woman in cold blood. Some of you have wives and daughters. If this woman has plotted with these reckless, simple-minded cowpokes to steal your stock, then she deserves to be punished. But you don't have to turn yourselves into beasts to exact your punishment. You can't hang a woman—a neighbor—like a . . . like a dog," he pleaded earnestly.

Some of the men were beginning to nod their heads as they listened to the stranger's plea. One of them spoke out: "Boss, this hombre is right. I say we turn her over to the law. I don't feel right about stringing up a woman."

Linc took advantage of the interruption. "Men, you'll regret such a deed of violence all the rest of your lives," he urged. "I don't know whether she's guilty or innocent. It's none of my business. I'm not interceding—but even if you are satisfied how she has got your mavericks, hanging her is not the answer. . . ."

Another voice growled: "Me, too, chief. Count me out on this deal. If my wife knew I had my hand in hangin' a woman—"

The leader spat into the dust as though to rid himself of some burning poison. "You yellow-bellied fools," he rasped. "Don't you men realize that if we turn her over to the law, she'll wriggle herself out of it—and then come back and do the same thing all over again."

The Nebraskan moved closer to the man he now

definitely recognized to be the Texan, Lee. He started to renew his appeal.

"No use, Linc," cried Kit Bandon, her voice deep and full. "God bless you for trying to save me from this man's jealous hatred." She turned and faced the leader defiantly, her eyes blazing. "I know you, Lee, even behind your mask. Damn your rotten hide. You knew about me from the beginning—but you kept it quiet because you wanted me all for yourself. And then when I refused you, you wanted your vengeance. What you do to me will be on *your* conscience and that of every man here—"

"Silence, whore," the leader spat out and raised his hand as if to strike her.

"Now, hold on a minute, Lee." One of the other men grabbed his arm. "Let her have her say—it's only fair."

"I have nothing more to say, except to you, Linc." She turned back to him, her eyes shining strangely in the dim light. "Whatever will happen to me—*you* saved my soul. And I have to tell you one more thing— about your pal, Jimmy Weston. It was Emery who killed him. Weston was in love with me—wanted me to give it all up and go away with him. When I refused, he threatened to expose Emery and me. I could have— God have mercy on me—I could have stopped Emery, but I didn't. . . . If I had only known you sooner." Her voice broke. "But it's all over now—everything is too late—except for you and Lucy. . . . And I thank God for that."

"That will be enough," snarled Lee. "Get back there, Bradway, or I'll bore you. . . . This woman hangs!" He dismounted, stepped forward, and tossed a noose around Kit Bandon's neck. Then he pulled the rope tight about the slender white throat and threw the end of the lariat over the branch of the tree just above her head.

As he stepped back a terrible cry rang out, a hoarse bellow of hatred and defiance. A horseman dashed into the circle about the Texan and his prisoner, dismounted and confronted the cowmen's leader. It was Vince, and now for the first time Linc heard him raise his voice above his accustomed drawl.

"She's called the turn on you, cowman!" he shouted. "It's yore hate—wuss than thet, yore jealousy—thet makes you pull this lowdown deal."

"Keep your mouth shut, cowboy," Lee snarled.

"I'm sayin' all I'm goin' to say, Lee," he spoke more quietly. "An' by God, I say you'll hev no share in this hangin'." As Vince spoke his gun exploded twice, and Lee stopped, looked surprised, swayed and fell face downward under his horse.

Bradway had time only to cry "Vince" when a volley rang out. The cowpoke whirled and fell. The next moment Linc saw his partner lying on his back in the dust, one arm beneath him, one arm outstretched. A dozen bullets had entered his body.

Linc felt himself pushed aside. He heard a hoarse shout from one of the vigilantes. "Hyar, men! Lay hold hyar an' swing this devil-woman before some more of us stop lead. No one of us is safe as long as she's breathin'."

The Nebraskan turned away. He felt suddenly sick. He saw Thatcher beside him. He heard the trampling sound made by many boots, the sound of many strong bodies in concerted action, the sound of a tree branch violently shaken, the sound of a strangled cry. As he stood there supporting himself against a tree he waited for the sound he knew must follow, a volley from the six-guns of the cowboys. But it was not forthcoming. The sudden silence was unbearable. Slowly he opened his eyes. The sight he expected to see met his eyes. Kit Bandon's slender body, clad only in her nightdress, was slowly turning under the swaying branch. Her dark hair had loosened and covered her features. Then a gunshot rang out. Lincoln heard the dull thud of a bullet striking flesh. A cowboy's merciful bullet had put an end to the hanging and the suffering of the Maverick Queen.

There followed the sound of many voices, of tinkling spurs, of the creak of saddle leather, of clattering hoofbeats. Two men ran forward with a riderless horse. They lifted the body of Lee and hung it over the saddle. Then mounting their own horses, they rode away across the sunlit sage, leading the dead man's horse by its reins. As the sound of their horses' hoofs died away in the distance, Linc became conscious that the cowboys had come for Vince's body. The range war was over. Vince was dead. Lee was dead. Kit Bandon was dead. Emery was dead. And Jimmy Weston was dead. They were all dead and nothing was settled.

Mel Thatcher was shaking him gently.

"Don't look, pard. It's all over. Leave the rest to us. Rustle for your horse and ride like hell to tell Lucy. But don't tell her how Kit died, Linc. You'll know what to say. Take Lucy away with you. Stay out of South Pass until all this blows over. Leave the rest to me."

Linc heard his partner's words as though they were spoken in a dream. He was conscious of the other cowboys gathering about the body of Vince. As they passed him where he stood by the tree he could see that they were staring at him curiously. He shook himself and broke the strange spell that had bound him since the moment of his tragic failure to save Kit Bandon. The feeling of lassitude and futility was passing. There was work to be done. He walked over to the group of cowpokes gathered around his dead friend whose body seemed poignantly lonely and forsaken there on the valley floor.

"Boys, Mel here will tell you that Vince was our partner, his and mine," he said. "I wish you would take him to a spot Mel will show you, and bury him there. And if there's any expense I'll pay it."

Then he walked over to the willow where Kit's pathetic figure swayed in the unnatural radiance of the June morning, looking more like a slim girl than a mature, hardened woman who had died with a sneer of defiance for her executors upon her lovely face. Taking out his clasp knife he cut the dead woman down. Covering her body with her cloak, Linc stood there for a moment, remembering all of the vitality and animation and passion and love that once had been present in that one tiny body.

The cowboys were watching him as he returned. Mel Thatcher spoke up: "We'll take care of that, too, pard. No cowpoke in this valley will every say we didn't give Kit Bandon a decent burial. She used some of us a little rough, and Vince isn't the only one who stopped lead because of her, but nobody in this part of Wyoming, long after we boys are gone, will forget the Maverick Queen. I guess the Lord busted His mold when he made Kit Bandon. There will never be another like her in Wyoming."

"Thank you, Mel," said Linc, "for those words. Nobody, saint or sinner, could have a better send-off than you gave her."

Then silently the Nebraskan shook hands with Thatcher and with the other cowboys, took one last look at Vince and walked slowly with clinking spurs in the direction of the place where long years ago, as it seemed to him now, he had tethered his horse.

Mounting Bay, he rode through the dew-dampened sage to the road. Then he urged the eager horse to a sharp gallop toward the Bandon ranch house. As he crossed the bridge he saw movement under the trees before the house. The lame hired man was limping through the gate looking down the road. As Bay brought him rapidly nearer, Linc caught a glimpse of someone in the shadow of the porch. The tumult in his breast told him who it was. At the gate he pulled Bay to his haunches, scattering the gravel as he leaped off.

"Simpson," he said to the hired man, "you've probably guessed it—your mistress is dead. Hitch up the buckboard pronto. I'm taking Miss Lucy away. You stay here until you get further orders. My partner is taking care of the—of Kit Bandon."

Then he turned toward the porch. A white-faced girl with her bright golden hair streaming over her shoulders was running to meet him.

"Linc—Linc, please tell me," she cried, "what have they done with Aunt Kit?"

Tenderly the tall Nebraskan took the stricken girl in his arms. Her tear-stained face was tight against his breast. One of his hands were stroking her hair.

"Listen, my dear," he was saying, in a voice that was husky with tenderness and love. "It's all over. Kit and Emery—have paid—the penalty. . . . I'm taking you away for a little while. . . . Just pack up some clothes and some few things you will need. Thatcher will take care of Kit's—things, and will close up the house. I don't think either of us will ever want to come back to this ranch again."

Lucy's head made a movement of negation against his breast.

"When we come back," Linc continued, "we will start all over again—up there in our valley." As he finished speaking Lucy raised her head from her husband's shoulder, and as one, they turned to face the dark patch against the distant hills which marked the valley that one day would be their home.

WESTERNS THAT NEVER DIE

They pack excitement that lasts a lifetime.
It's no wonder Zane Grey is the bestselling
Western writer of all time.
Get these Zane Grey Western adventures
from Pocket Books:

- _____83102 BORDER LEGION $1.75
- _____82896 BOULDER DAM $1.75
- _____83422 RIDERS OF THE PURPLE SAGE $1.95
- _____82692 DEER STALKER $1.75
- _____82883 KNIGHTS OF THE RANGE $1.75
- _____82878 ROBBERS ROOST $1.75
- _____82076 TO THE LAST MAN $1.75
- _____83534 UNDER THE TONTO RIM $1.95
- _____82880 U.P. TRAIL $1.75
- _____83022 ARIZONA CLAN $1.75
- _____83105 BLACK MESA $1.75
- _____83309 CALL OF THE CANYON $1.75